Death Whispers
Book One of the Death Series

by Tamara Rose Blodgett

Death Whispers

Copyright © 2010-2011 Tamara Rose Blodgett
http://tamararoseblodgett.blogspot.com/
ISBN 978-1461058663

For Joshua

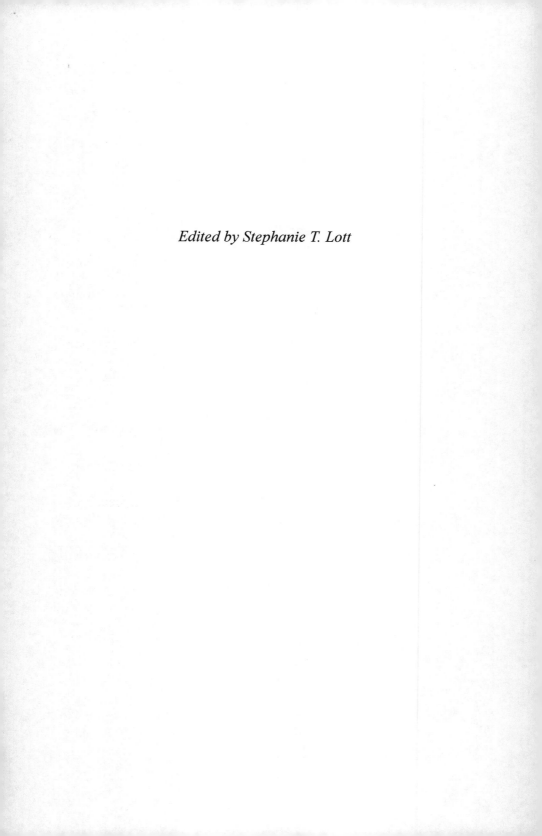

Edited by Stephanie T. Lott

PROLOGUE

I am Caleb Hart, son of the first scientist to map the human genome back in 2010. Now, fifteen years later, all us kids (during puberty because we're so lucky) get to draw what's equivalent to a winning lottery ticket. What paranormal power would we have, would I have? It could be anything as benign as Empath, Telepathy, Pyrokenesis, Astral-Projection, and the real creeper, Affinity for the Dead, AFTD. New abilities kept cropping up, like an untended garden. The paranormal ball had begun to roll and it was all downhill from here. As long as I didn't get anyone's attention, I was down with that. I should think Science is the bomb, but it's not, it's a bomb alright, right on my head.

In eighth grade, we're required to take pre-Biology. My teacher is enthusiastic, so there's never a dull moment.

Especially with me fainting all the time.

That's how it happened the first time. The frogs came in and I went out... like a light.

At least that was the first time I hadn't been able to ignore it anymore.

Xavier Collins had reined in his ranting about bees becoming extinct and other huge rage-topics on the environment, to delight in telling us our next experiment would be dissection.

I didn't have Mark "Jonesy" Jones in this class but my other best friend, John, was here, so not a total loss. Jonesy kept school in balance, making jokes at the expense of the teachers (very wise). John countered with keeping Jonesy from getting us in trouble (not always happening). The drag of it was the two kids that hated my guts in a steaming pile were in Biology.

Carson Hamilton and Brett Mason sat next to each other, never giving me a moment's peace about anything. Carson had everything anyone could want, money, looks (he's a mirror-lover) and parents that didn't care about anything he did. My parents had not caught the disease of indifference yet. Brett didn't have it so hot, but he was as miserable as Carson.

John sat down next to me with two pencils up his nose while Collins was at the whiteboard, discussing how to pin the frogs down.

Nice.

"Did ya make sure the erasers were in there first?" I asked him.

"Yeah, duh." The pencils bounced as he spoke. For a smart guy, he had some weird ideas about self-entertainment. It was very "Jonesy" of him.

"You still buzzing?" he asked.

I looked at John. "Yeah, it's on and off." I felt kinda defensive about this part, I was avoiding thinking about it myself, and didn't really want to talk about it.

"I've been thinking about that," he said.

How he could think with pencils up his nose? A mystery, "Yeah?"

"I think you have the undead creeper, like that Parker dude," John said.

That would be bad.

"He's the one that could corpse-raise, right?" I asked.

John nodded.

Hadn't I just been thinking about how much that ability sucked? However, the rareness of corpse-raising might come in handy. Not likely to happen though.

"It would suck for you."

Nice, John restating the obvious. Yeah, it would suck. I mean, what's so great about communicating with the dead, locating the dead? Any of that... ah, *no*. Nothing in it for me but weirdness.

"Government took him. Bye-bye... gone." John made a fluttering motion with his hand like a bird flying away. The pencils kept bouncing in a distracting way.

I'd heard about that. Corpse-Manipulation, rare-much. Jeffrey Parker was the only recorded case.

"Why do you think?" I was interested for once, sometimes John would lose me on a tech-rant and it was all over.

"Are you shitting me? Dead people... come on." I got an image of zombies with M-60s, interesting.

"No, think about it. They could get people raised and force them to do stuff. From a distance, they could look like they were alive, important people." He raised his eyebrows.

"Presidents?"

"Rulers or whoever," John said. "He was a five-point. He could do the whole tamale. I think the government exploits whatever they can; using whoever they can."

I laughed.

"What?" he asked.

"I can't take you seriously. You look like a dumb-ass." The pencils dangled indignantly inside each nostril, humiliated.

John pulled them out, checking the ends for gold.

Huh.

I'd been wondering why my head was buzzing. Now memories surfaced. When had the buzzing started exactly? What triggered it? Could John be right?

"Okay people, zip up here and pick up your trays. Your sterilized utensils should already be at your desks," Collins said.

John went for our trays, minus the attractive pencils. I stared out the window, the splatters of rain causing rivulets that looked like gray streamers marring the glass.

I shook my head, clearing fuzziness. I couldn't shake the buzzing, a dull noise that ebbed and flowed. I felt it today the strongest. As soon as I entered class, the buzzing increased, like whispers.

"Here you are. One frog for the both of us." John plunked down a frog that had once been green but was a bone-gray now, staking pins gleaming under the LEDs.

That's when the screaming started.

The whole earth felt like it was swiveling on its axis, and I was on top. The whispering grew in volume until images flooded my head. There were marshes and swamps. A frog, in the bloom of its life, shiny with amphibian iridescence, leaped to a log, hoping to fool a small water moccasin close enough to take it.

(NO!)

Right behind you I shouted in warning. But I couldn't be heard, these were images... memories.

A motor boat was closing in on the frog, getting ready to take it with a metal pole and loose net on its end. Caleb heard the frog's thoughts, *strange predator must seek cover... noise... hurts...*

(NO! *NO!!!*)

It wasn't the only frog with memories. Every cut my classmates made, a new flood of memories came. I realized through some dim sense that I was on my back on the Biology floor. Carson and Brett in the background wheezed with laughter.

"He fainted over a frog? Seriously?" Carson ranted.

Brett, not to be outdone caterwauled, "He's a woman!"

Collins was moving his hand in front of my face, holding up fingers, but I was caught in the grip of the death memories, absorbing my consciousness. The last thing I remember was John's anxious face taking turns between telling the dumb-ass duo to shut up and seeing if I was gonna live. My vision became gray at the edges, a pinpoint of black expanding to clear my mind of everything and I knew no more.

CHAPTER 1

Trees surrounding the cemetery danced in the languid breeze of the mild spring night. I looked behind me at the pair of eighth grade boys who'd come to egg me on. They had discovered my secret: that I knew the dead, heard the dead.

Headstones glimmered as loose teeth in the moonlight, the whispering there like white noise, a steady thrumming in my head. My hands grew clammy thinking about what may happen.

"Caleb, show them you're not a frickin' poser," said Jonesy.

"I don't pose." My thoughts raged against each other in contrary purpose. Proving to Carson and Brett that I had AFTD wouldn't keep them off my back completely, but it'd notch down their stupidity to something me and my posse could manage. That's where it was, managing their shit behavior.

I took a step through the high, Victorian-style gate, my foot touching its reluctant toe on hallowed ground.

The feeling of being forced pressed uncomfortably against my mind.

Crossing the threshold of sanctified ground, the whispering turned into voices. One voice whispered to me the strongest. I stopped feeling tentative and like an invisible string pulled, was drawn toward one of the gravestones, standing sentinel near the middle of the cemetery, glowing softly in the moonlight. I came to stand in front of the headstone which read: *"Clyde Thomas, born 1900, died 1929."*

"Wake me..." it said.

"What?" I whispered.

It speaks.

"Wake me..." it repeated.

"Caleb, who are you talking to?" John asked, lack of understanding clear on his face.

My head swung in slow-motion as if through quicksand, moving in his direction, blood rushing in my ears and my heart beating thick and heavy in my chest. Everything became crystallized in that moment. John's frizzy hair and freckles stood

1

out like measles. A microscopic chip on the headstone shone in stark contrast to the white marble.

Something... something... was building, rising up as if underwater, rushing to the surface. I was supposed to finalize something, but what? The whispering of the corpse in the earth so loud it drowned out John's words. John's mouth was moving but no sound was coming out.

What-the-hell? He was arguing with Jonesy, his teeth a pale slash against his dark face.

Flailing, Jonesy's hand suddenly connected with my face. My teeth slammed into my tongue and the taste of copper pennies filled my mouth. I leaned over and a drop of blood hung tremulously on my bottom lip, falling to the grave like a black gem.

Everything clicked into place, vertigo spinning the graveyard on its axis as if it had been waiting for this moment. The ground rushed toward my face and I threw my hands out to brace my fall, fingers biting into damp earth. A clawed hand broke through the ground like a spear through flesh. Searching, it grasped my wrist, the bones pressing in a vise like grip that captured my breath, the intense coldness of the grave lingering on its dead flesh.

The head of the corpse broke free of the ground, its shadowed gaze meeting mine, the hand releasing me. I scuttled backward, standing up, swaying, overcome with, excitement? Fear? I had done this thing and now, didn't know how to undo it. The corpse moved with purpose, pacing me as it used the undisturbed ground to leverage itself as another drop of my blood fell and landed with a dull plop on the corpse's forehead.

The zombie's gaze fixated on mine, it put a hand on its knee and began to push itself upright. Dull, lank strands of hair hung loosely from a scalp strung together by a tight mask of rotten sinew.

Jonesy had long since run out of the cemetery and was at a "safe" range from what the ground had disgorged.

He better get his ass back here. He couldn't get away with whacking me *and* not helping me with corpse-boy.

"Why have you awoken me?" The words sounded garbled, (maybe there was *some* tongue in there).

It asked me to wake it.

Must not be rude, not my strongest point.

Out loud I said, "You asked me to."

John was standing at my right, trying to mask a fine, all-over tremble. His freckles stood out on a pale face like beacons of fright.

"What the hell is this?" John asked.

He didn't really just ask that? John... duh.

The zombie looked at me with eyes that clung from threads of sinew; moving wetly in its sockets, sucking like a vacuum.

"Why have you woken me?" it repeated, shambling a step closer. The smell... wow. It rose like a torrent of rotting garbage and *other things.* John clapped his hand over his nose, taking a step backward.

The corpse took another step... figuring this out would be good.

"Got any brilliant suggestions?" I asked John, my eyes steady on the zombie, hoping like hell John would lend an intellectual hand.

"Do *not* have the Zombie Handbook handy," John said, his eyes a tad wide.

Not helpful.

The corpse looked at me, head tilted, "You're just a boy...how could you know for what purpose you have disturbed my slumber?"

Uh-oh, coming up with an excuse, *so* not my thing.

"I didn't... mean to wake you up..." I fumbled out. I wasn't usually this tongue-tied but meeting a corpse in the flesh (ha-ha) stole my speech.

"You do not know what you would have of me? You use your life-force to waken me and yet... without purpose? Put me back," he said thickly. His clothes hung in tatters and the smell was definitely old, dark coffin, not that I knew what *that* smelled like.

John's look clearly said, *do something!* I guess what I hadn't told my friends was that I had never thought that I could actually raise the dead. But here he was, standing before me in all his rotting glory.

Looking out amongst the teenagers collected outside the cemetery, "To whom much is given, much is expected. Put me back," he said.

Adults were all the same, even dead, lecture, lecture.

"How?" I asked.

"You are the necromancer, boy, not I." Again that quizzical brow over rotting facial countenance.

Interpretation challenge... but I was managing.

"A what?" I asked, surprisingly calm, for the first time, there were no whispers. Perfect, blessed silence filled my head. It was the most natural thing in the world; talking to the dead. Looking at the corpse, its eyeballs, like inky marbles stared back at me with uncanny devotion.

"A diviner of the black arts, magic..." he replied.

All that time with the star in my basement, huh, *right*.

I could still taste distressingly metallic blood in my mouth. I was connecting dots here, but I had an epiphany, I could put it back with blood! Things had only gotten über-weird when I had my lip busted open by Jonesy. I looked back at the corpse (*Clyde,* a person once), no longer feeling that sense of swimming power just underneath the surface. Now was not the time to get queasy with the dead. I needed to regain that essence, fast.

"Ah... hang on a minute," I said to the corpse, who stared blankly back... ah-huh.

"John, give me your blade."

"What the heck Caleb? What are you planning to do with this..." John said pointing his finger at the patient corpse, "...thing?" who was as immobile out of his grave as in.

"I figure my blood made it jump out of its grave, now I need some to put him back and you're going to help me," I said in a one sentence rush.

John's face got paler, if possible. "Ah, we're good friends and all but no, not a good plan! We don't know that for sure anyway." The logic-master was not feelin' it. Couldn't say I blamed him, me holding a knife and all.

"... here's the deal, let's do a little 'friendship blood bank' just for the sake of putting the dead guy back in his grave, eh?" I began tapping my foot on the disturbed mess of the grave. John would ante up the blood or this was gonna be a long damn night.

"What?" strained trust crowded his eyes.

"Just here, give me your forearm." I placed the side of the blade on his forearm where it shone black in the pale moonlight. My left hand wrapped tight, steadying his flesh for puncture.

John took a deep breath,"Okay, but you're going to owe me, big time," the whites of his eyes bulging.

I pressed the point of the blade against his arm until the pressure broke the skin. John sucked in a lungful, blood welled and I let up the pressure. The zombie's head jerked at the sight of the blood, causing the disturbing sound of neck bones popping.

Would I ever get used to that noise? I repeated the process with my own arm. Our identical wounds pressed together, I offered it to my zombie. I could feel somehow that he was mine, I knew it.

A vibrating tuning fork of trembling power welled up inside me. A strange mixture of fear, dread and excitement paralyzed me. My teeth throbbed with the intensity of it. The zombie's hand snaked out, taking hold of the offered forearm. It felt cold against my warm flesh, like iced tentacles. I swabbed a blot of blood, inking it with my index and middle fingers on the zombies forehead, like warpaint. It rolled those empty eyes up at me, its dead bones clinging to my fingertips.

We shared a suspended moment in time, a terrible beauty of control balanced precariously. "Go back and rest," I said, feeling that balance reached, that *I* was choosing for both of us.

The zombie reluctantly let go of my arm, sand through a sieve, lying down on the disturbed ground while his grave encased him in a shroud of earth.

I was a corpse-raiser, one of two, and it was not a safe thing to be.

John and I stared at each other over the grave for a swollen minute, his face showing a mixture of sympathy and dread. He knew what this distinction would mean for me in the world we lived in.

I was shaking from the intensity of it all, there was no controlling it. This was not the same as Biology experiments and roadkill, this was real, this was huge. Looking outside the cemetery perimeter at two enemies and one friend, I knew it was time to swear the group to secrecy. A trickle of sweat slithered down my back, pooling at the waistband of my jeans, instantly chilling against my fevered flesh. I didn't want the same future as Parker, that loss of freedom was so *not* a part of The Plan, my plan.

John and I headed out of the cemetery in a wave of uncertain promise.

CHAPTER 2

I smacked my alarm, just five more minutes I thought, dozing off.

"Caleb!" Mom yelled up the stairs.

"Yeah?" I yelled back.

"School!"

I stumbled out of my bed and looked on the floor for today's clothes... Hmm, what to wear that wasn't too wrinkled. I picked up a pair of jeans and a shirt and took an experimental whiff. Good enough! I jerked the jeans on with a hop and a zip. Opened the underwear and sock drawer, nothing. I ripped open every drawer for socks, ah-huh! Finally, a couple of socks, not matched but clean... happy day.

I trudged over to the kitchen table, scarred from a thousand meals.

"You cookin' today?" I asked, hopeful.

"No, but you're eating."

Eating in the morning blows. I was that lazy. I'd open the fridge, nothing. Then the freezer, repeat. I usually ended up cramming a yogurt down.

Mom looked in the fridge. "What flavor?"

"Do we have blueberry?" It was the only non-barf fruit I could think about eating this early.

"Last one."

"Where's Dad?"

Mom and Dad were on the opposite end of the spectrum. She was free-spirited (read: hippie) and thought the mystery of life and choice was taken when the scientific puzzle of the genome mapping was solved.

It made for an interesting family life.

"He is working on that new project."

Great, hopefully not anything new for kids to rant about. I'd gone through enough being hassled when I was growing up.

"Does that mean he'll be home for supper tonight? I've got something to talk to him about." I wisely didn't want to mention the whole corpse-raising episode. Dad was logic and fairness mixed. He'd know what to do. This... I might need some help on.

"Yes, he will, you know how important meal time is," Mom said.

Maybe, maybe not. Science was important to Dad.

After I wolfed down the yogurt, knowing the beast would awaken again at 10 a.m. in class (perfect), I made a 2-point shot at the trash can. Swish! No mess, but that didn't stop the frown forming on Mom's face.

I moved quickly to grab my backpack but she blocked me and I was forced to look up at her. Every girl in the world was taller than me... wonderful.

She brushed the hair out of my eyes and it shot back down. "You need a haircut."

"No, mom." A time-sucker was all a haircut was and I had more important things to do.

Slamming the door behind me I took the stairs two at a time, cruising at a jog. I wanted to reconnoiter with the dudes, get things straight in my head from last night.

I slowed to a walk. I'd still be there early and I was feeling lazy. Looking up, I noticed the canopy of trees allowing filtered morning light to break through, speckling the ground with sunspots. My head began the familiar thrumming, a buzz seeping into the crevices of my mind as I walked toward the school.

I stopped where I stood, the buzzing had become whispering, my heart speeding, my breath quickening in response. My hands grew damp.

The whispering of the dead.

I looked around me, noticing the paved street, the pebbling of the asphalt worn away by a million cars, the shoulder giving way into the ditch.

Nothing.

I started walking again but the whispering grew louder. I followed the dull roar of the insidious voice like a magnet and was rewarded with volume.

There, on the border of the forest and the soft dirt of the ditch lay a crumpled body, torn and broken, its head at an awkward angle. My hands trembled as the whispering broke through to voices and images flooded my head like a pulse-screen.

I heard the thoughts:

headlights bursting like twin spots before its eyes as it tried to escape those lights... rushing forward... it sprinted across the street, not timing the advance properly and the twin orbs bore down on it.

Pain. Intense pain and blinding light.

The cat thought of its litter, its people... then, was no more.

My breath returned in a paralyzing rush, my feet planted at the base of her body. A small body that had shared the last moments of its life with me. A life that was now gone.

I stood for a moment, taking it in, realizing that life as I knew it was never going to be the same. I wasn't going to breeze through being a teenager.

Snapping back to reality I realized I was the pied piper of road

Definitely my life-goal.

s just the kinda thing that had been happening. The
ogy, there had been so many. I hadn't been able to
hat. People would be suspicious. Why couldn't I be
mething righteous like Pyrokenesis? Now that would
ast only Brett and Carson knew the corpse-raising
hem to cooperate with silence, that was another

Never judge a book by itʃ movie.

n, my limbs heavy, my head swimming with the
undead-moment. I lifted my hands, the fine
gone. Beaded sweat decorated my upper lip and I
the back of my hand. I needed to get a hold of
on it. That's what I told myself but my gut

doors to our daily prison came into view. I went
spotting the "cemetery group," as I was not-so-
f a few of them.

sy stood apart from the others in stark contrast
ost 5'10" with a shock of frizzy, carrot-colored
eyes, John looked a little freakish but he was my
o guy when things went sideways. I gave
y look, touching my face. He had short, nappy
tood out like white Chiclets in a dark face. He

8

was taller than me too, but built stocky. They'd been with me since Kindergarten.

The rest of the group was a mixed bag, didn't feel solid here. It would take some clever conniving to get promises of secrecy from the rest. Brett Mason and Carson Hamilton stood side-by-side with identical white-blond hair and height, hard to tell apart unless you looked at them full-on. They'd been with me since Kindergarten too, but not in a good way. We had about five minutes before first bell.

Edging through the throng of kids I made my way to John and Jonesy first. Jonesy leaned against the locker, arms crossed. John looked ready to explode, not typical.

Jonesy said, "Sorry about the bludgeoning."

"Yeah... what the hell?" I asked.

"Your face sorta got in the way."

"Oh... *really*?" Gee, hadn't noticed that.

"It was an accident, John and I were discussing..." Jonesy began.

"... arguing..." John interrupted.

Jonesy gave him a look. "I changed my mind is all."

I raised my eyebrows, Jonesy never switched gears.

"About the merit of them *knowing*," John finished.

We looked at Bret and Carson. Too late now, spilled milk on the table and dripping on the floor.

Later, I thought. "I wasn't pulling a hypo in Biology," giving a hard look at Brett and Carson, the used-to-be-non-believers, "and now APs are coming up."

"Yeah, you have your dad to thank for that," Brett smirked.

I knew that was coming.

My eyes caught sight of a grape sized bruise the color of pale chartreuse, the edges fanning to green then finally purple. Brett's smirk faded under my gaze as he shifted his shoulder, his shirt falling over the mark that lingered on his throat. Someone's hand had left that, not my problem, but...

"Shut up, it's Caleb's ass on the line," Jonesy said, jamming a thumb at my chest. "You know what happens when you hit the radar as a corpse-raiser. He'd be a government squirrel, like that Parker dude."

"Nobody wants to have their life planned by somebody else," John said.

9

"My dad didn't have anything to do with that," I said.

"But thanks to him, everyone's tested now because of the mapping. All the do-gooders want to 'realize our full potential'," Brett made quote signs in the air, "what an ass-load of crap that was."

Carson chimed in, "So even if we don't *want* to be mathematicians or scientists we're on that freight train until it reaches the depot."

Carson's murky-green eyes burrowed into mine. This was an old argument. Kinda like being the preacher's kid, you got blamed for everything your parent did, or didn't do.

"You dickface... yeah you," Jonesy looked at Carson, whose eyes narrowed. "It isn't Caleb's fault that his dad started that ball rolling with the mapping. If it hadn't been him, it would've been someone else..."

Carson's fists clenched and flexed, he didn't like being told the obvious. Probably shouldn't have opened his mouth and crammed a foot in there until he choked. Kinda brain dead, kinda consistent.

"Listen guys, this isn't helping. It's the *now* we need to figure out. I don't want to pop a five-point AFTD on the APs. They're what, a week away? My dad," Carson rolled his eyes and I ignored him, plowing forward, "says that puberty is the *exact* time they test because scientists have proven that abilities come online then, sometimes for the first time." Not for me, I added silently.

The first bell gave its shrill beckon exactly then. I looked at Brett and Carson. "I need you guys to cover for me. At least until the tests are finished."

I was appealing to their good side.

You can't force us to, Hart," Brett said.

"Yeah, just because daddy's famous doesn't give you clout," Carson echoed.

So much for that.

"How about doing it because it's the right thing to do?" asked Jonesy, out of the blue.

"The human thing to do," interjected John.

"He's not human." Carson said, stabbing a finger toward my chest.

Prejudice at its finest. But what did I expect from these two? They'd never been my friends.

"You got that right," Brett agreed, walking off with Carson.

We watched them move away into the multicolor sea of kids.

"Did ya see that bruise necklace Brett was wearing?" Jonesy asked.

Yeah, some people had more than corpse-raising to worry about.

"It's the dad," John said.

Jonesy turned those liquid eyes to me, "Feel sorry for him Caleb? Don't go soft on me bro. You're always giving jackasses the benefit of the doubt."

Not yet, I thought, saying nothing.

Seeing my expression he said, "Yeah, my cup of care is empty too."

My conscious teetered on the balance of right and wrong. Brett had it bad, but he chose to act bad. It didn't make things easier, it made it more complicated.

Jonesy clapped me on the back and John gave me the nod. My friends had my back.

It was gonna be a hurricane of crap and I was in the eye of it. The Js and I walked off to Shop class. Time to make my mom a heart-shaped box, when my heart was definitely not into it.

CHAPTER 3

The Js and I had Shop first period and it was a good thing because we needed to figure out A Plan.

After talking to the ass-monkeys I couldn't get the genome out of my head, cramming into the tight space of my skull like a song that wouldn't stop playing.

The mapping of 2010 happened under pressure from President Obama. Desperate for health care reform, mapping offered incentive to activate "markers" for the population. It was the key to identifying genetic potential for: cancer, heart disease, stroke, even alcoholism and drug addictions. If the People wanted universal health care, they would be mapped, with a microchip put underneath the skin. Every marker identified genetic codes and a percentage of the person's wage taken for the "privilege." Now, if someone didn't want the microchip, no health care. There was a helluva lot more than just disease markers now. Teens were the proof.

We sat around the table together and our Shop teacher, Mr Morginstern, approached us with a cheery, "Good morning fellas!"

It was criminal he was happy. Doesn't he know the Monday-is-hateful-rule?

"Hey," I mumbled.

Jonesy and John gave Morginstern the nod. Morginstern was excited about teaching and we were excited about school ending for the day.

"So, how was your guys' weekend? Do anything interesting?" he asked, eyebrows raised.

Yeah, I think.

I imagined a conversation like: *Ah no problem, Mr. Morginstern, just creeping around illegally in a graveyard, raising a corpse, enemies seeing the blow-by-blow...real interesting.*

Instead I said, "It was okay."

Jonesy was choking up on it. I gave him a look that said clearly, *don't blow it.* "Yeah."

John was unflappably silent as usual, controlling a sly grin with effort, the anchor to our madness.

Morginstern seemed to accept our weird responses and went over the whole process of our boxes again; adults, painfully redundant. We got to decide what kind of "box" to make. Heart-shaped was the hardest shape of all (masochist). I got out my sandpaper, one-twenty grit, extra fine.

John kept his voice low, "So what's the plan?"

A fine dust fell from the interior arc of the heart onto the work table. The sanding from the three of us served as an excellent conversation concealer.

"I don't know yet, I gotta think about it more. I'm not ending up like Parker. 'Affinity for the Dead,' wasn't that cool for *him*," I said.

"Ask your dad, he's the genius," Jonesy said.

"Quiet, smack attack."

Jonesy ducked his head, half-apology, half-embarrassment.

"I'm sorry bro, it was an accident," he said.

"Gotcha, just wanted to see what you'd say," I joked.

"Oh man! Don't do that dude!" Jonesy threw his sand paper at me and I deflected, the paper landing on John, embedding in his hair.

Morginstern glanced over at us and gave us the "warning" voice, "Caleb Hart! Jonesy and John, no throwing supplies."

"Come on you guys, stop screwing around. This is serious," John said.

As serious as a heart attack, I thought, struggling not to laugh. "I'll talk with my dad tonight, he'll have ideas."

"He's got resources, right?" Jonesy asked.

"Using your big boy words Jonesy?" I smiled.

We all laughed and agreed to meet up at my place late. Maybe I'd con mom into making extra hamburger helper for the Js.

The rest of the day was not as insane as the morning. I had every class with John except PE, Jonesy was in PE (I was never without a J). That was the class where we got to check out the girls. One in particular I liked a lot.

"I want to play dodge ball today," Jonesy said.

"Yeah, that'll happen. 'No head shots, no body shots above the waist, no leg shots'..." I imitated Miss Griswold's annoying voice.

The girls are playing and that means we have to be super careful. I sighed. Dodge ball rocked but Griswold was a joy-sucker. I mean, what part of the body could we hit if everything was a no-hit zone?

Retarded.

Just then Jade LeClerc walked by, my eyes tracking her. She wasn't popular, but she had something special. Jet black hair gleamed like a curtain of silk waiting to be touched. She had the greatest eyes, green like a cat's. A memory shimmered just out of reach...a red shirt, concrete and dirt... Ow! Jonesy gave me a strategic elbow to the side, the memory slipping away in a vapor.

I turned to him. "What was that for?"

"Stop staring, she'll notice," Jonesy said. "Why do you like her anyway, she's kinda emo."

"No she's not, she just wants people to think she is. Keeps them away," I said, trying to recapture that fleeting shard of the past.

"Oh and you're such a girl expert... *right,*" Jonesy laughed.

He got the scowl he deserved. "I've watched her. She doesn't make a move to be anyone's friend, but there's something cool about her..."

Something I wanted to protect.

"She's too weird. Pick someone else. Look at them all." Jonesy spread out his hands to include the bounty of girls.

Huh, they all looked kinda average to me. My eyes strayed back to Jade. She just looked different, unique. I'd build up the courage to say something to her. I told Jonesy that.

"You've had Science with her what, almost two semesters? We're in fourth quarter and you still haven't said anything?" Jonesy stated, disgusted. "Besides, what's she gonna think when she finds out about what you can do? She saw you pass out, right?"

I couldn't deny his reasoning there. Who hadn't seen me bite the floor? Maybe, once I had a plan on how to hide what I was, I could say hey.

"Maybe she doesn't need to ever know," I said.

Jonesy arched a brow, the whites of his eyes wider in his brown face, "You can't cover forever bro." he shrugged.

I figured, but I liked to fantasize.

Miss Griswold blew her whistle and we lined up for warm-ups. We were in alphabetical order so Jonesy and I weren't close, neither was Jade. But I was close to Carson Hamilton. Real Close.

"Hey Hart, thinking about any ghosts?"

Carson-the-Clever, yeah right.

We did jumping jacks.

"Switch drill!" Griswold shrieked.

We went down to our knees and started the push-ups.

"Don't be a retard Carson, you and Brett said that I was faking shit, I wasn't. I proved I'm AFTD," I huffed out, five more.

"Switch drill!" Griswold's irritating voice rallied for the final insult.

We stood up, time for jumping power lunges. I hated these. I put one foot out and lunged so my knee didn't pass my toe then, up, jump, other side. Talking was almost impossible.

Carson managed, he had a lot of hot air.

"AFTD is so rare only freaks have it. That's why they took Parker away, the military wanted to quarantine his ass, to protect everyone."

Carson dropping another pearl of wisdom, wonderful. Like I care.

I wasn't gonna win with him. He was like a dog with a bone. He had something in his mind about me and it was made up.

Hop! Switch legs.

"Stop!" Griswold yelled.

Finally, I turned to Carson, breathless.

"Nobody'll believe you. You didn't believe until the cemetery." He would look like a dumb ass if he ran around school telling people I was a corpse-raiser (like we were running around in droves). Carson was all about what people thought of him.

He looked thoughtful, huh. Carson was a rock-with-lips.

"Maybe I won't tell anybody, but we may want something, me and Brett, I mean."

He looked down at me from his slightly taller stance and smirked. I'd love to deck him in the face. We glared at each other and Griswold approached in a stout waddle. Why do teachers always seem to know just when something is going down?

"Problem here boys?" hands on considerable hips.

"No problem, Miss Griswold." Carson said in the aren't-I-wonderful voice.

I could never contain my expression so I didn't bother.

She turned to me. "Is there a problem, Mr. Hart?"

"Nah, we're just talking," I said, she was just so... *her* and it wasn't good, being her.

"Hmm, just talking. Why don't the two of you 'just talk' when you're on your time, not our mutual time, eh?" she enunciated like we were stupid. That'd be one of us.

"Okay, Miss Griswold," Carson said.

She turned to me and I said the obligatory, "Yes, Miss Griswold."

Just as she moved out of hearing range Carson said, "Hag."

Nice, I thought. Those kids never get caught being themselves.

Griswold turned around and yelled, "Time for dodge ball, pick your teams."

The guys gave a collective groan and the girls didn't look any happier. Today was a class to survive. At least I got to look at Jade, the highlight of PE.

Jonesy gave me a questioning look from across the gym, Carson and Brett were fast moving from irritating to becoming a problem. One that I planned to contain, creatively.

Jonesy would scheme, John would deliberate and I would definitely do.

CHAPTER 4

"How was school today?" Mom asked, the chatty one in the family. I looked at Dad, who set his trade publication on the table.

Reluctantly I set down my fork even thought the hamburger helper was waiting to be engulfed, I said, "Ah... these two guys and I talked and it didn't go so hot."

I had their full attention.

"Which kids Caleb?" Dad asked in his reasonable way.

"Carson and Brett." Mom would remember them, they'd been flippin' me crap since fourth grade.

"Oh those two," Mom waved a dismissive hand. "They're not in your league, don't let them make you feel diminished sweet-pea."

Sweet pea!

"Alicia, let's not get elitist on him here..." Dad said.

"You might have a small point." Mom held her index finger and thumb together in illustration of just how "small."

His eyes narrowed. Uh-oh, here we go, just when I though we'd get something accomplished.

Mom held up a finger to ward off Dad's comment that hovered on his lips.

"Kyle, those two," she struggled for the right word, "buffoons, have been a nuisance for the last three years that I know of," she looked for confirmation. I held up five fingers, she was going to *by God*, Make Her Point, "*Five* and it's always the same thing."

Dad opened his mouth, but before he could say something she went on, "They don't like Caleb because of what you do honey. They feel threatened."

Quick dad!

Dad turned to me. "What was the problem?"

Dropping the Zombie Bomb didn't top my list of casual conversation but...

"Remember the Biology thing?"

"You passing out?" Mom asked. "Several times?"

Yeah that. The frog thing.

"Yes, we've never gotten to the bottom of those episodes," Dad leaned back in his chair.

I flipped my fork back-and-forth, back-and-forth. "I sorta got to the bottom of it. I have AFTD."

They stared at me like I'd just sprouted a giant second head. Huh, this could be going better.

I told them about the cemetery, the corpse and the growing tide of problems with Carson and Brett. This was a lit match to the C and B fire. They'd been itchin' to get something on me since middle school started almost three years ago, before even.

The silence went on for a few moments, then, "Caleb, let me recap this. You," he cleared his throat, "have caused a dead body to rise from its grave?"

"Yes Dad, that's what I just said."

And he was the smart one of the family.

Mom asked, "Is this what you were doing last night running around with the Js?"

Yeah, running around with the Js, doin' some corpse-raising. Average night on the town, *right*.

Out loud I said, "Well, yeah, but I didn't mean for it to go like it did."

"How did you mean for it 'to go'?" Dad asked.

The whole thing went down when Brett and Carson wouldn't get off my back about fainting. AFTD was the cherry on top of their cake. They'd been up my ass forever cuz they could. But they couldn't quite nail their bullshit to anything. I'd been a moving target until now. John had defended me by telling them I had AFTD. I was unconscious so he improvised. I wasn't looking stupid on purpose, there was something real going on. Should've just let them think whatever. I mean, it was Carson and Brett; they're morons.

To my parents I said, "I thought if I proved I was AFTD, that it was an ability, they'd lay off."

"There were precursors to this episode?"

He had to know the why.

"Yeah, it started before Science class. But, there was other stuff before, small stuff."

Dad's eyebrows shot up, him being a scientist and all.

"We were dissecting frogs for the class project and I started having trouble from the beginning," I said.

Now that I think about it, I'd had trouble with the *Understanding Insects* section too. Images of wings speared arose in my mind's eye.

"What kind of trouble son?" Dad asked.

"The kinda trouble that other kids notice and think you're sick or retarded."

"Caleb Sebastian Hart! That is *not* appropriate." Mom's hands were glued to her hips. I wasn't too concerned about being politically correct.

"Just a second Ali." Dad was okay with it. "So you didn't mention these," he hesitated, "fugues?"

"I guess I should've told you but everything was getting weird and their voices were buzzing all the time."

"Whose voices?" asked Dad.

"The frogs," I replied logically, shrugging. But frogs weren't *all* I heard.

"Ah, what were the frogs... saying, exactly?" Dad's eyes burning twin holes through me.

"Well, they're not saying words exactly but they feel things, miss things, they," I swallowed hard because this part bothered me. "They have memories of their life before they died." It made me sad, but crying was for losers so I opened my eyes really wide. That helped.

Mom gave me the "I'm worried about you stare". I was worried about me too.

"These dead creatures are communicating with you?" Dad asked.

"Yeah, that's what AFTD is about, Dad. Before we started the dissecting, I would have a blackout, but they were short." I thought about the roadkill, the insect dissections, shuddering.

"Like bursts or movies playing in your head or what?" Dad asked.

"It's like *I* am *them.*"

Mom's hand covered her mouth.

"... and I can see what they did. When they were taken from the rivers and marshes, they felt," I thought about the murky memories and their simple minds, "... lost. There was one frog that remembered eating a snake. They screamed when we cut them Dad," I said in a low voice. God, this was sorta awful. "That's when things got really bad with Carson and Brett. They thought I was trying to suck up attention or something gay like that."

"Caleb..." Mom's voice filled with warning, "homosexual reference."

"Mom, come on!" I said loudly. "We don't use it that way." This was important and she was worried about my words! Annoying!

"Ali, let's stay on task here." Dad was the champion of that (snark-snark).

"Okay, so how long have you been experiencing these... episodes?" Dad asked.

"Probably..." I thought about it. Easter was over and I knew when. It was around Valentine's because we have that lame winter break that's not long enough to do jack, "... a couple of months."

"That's a long time for symptoms you chose not to address with us Caleb."

I had a stab of guilt, looking down at my half-eaten food. I was used to being open with the Parental Unit, but this had a huge confusion factor.

Mom leaned over and gave me a hug. I let myself be hugged in the good mom-smell then pulled away. I gave her a weak smile. She smiled back. "It'll be okay."

Adults always say that, even when it's crap, my smile evaporating.

Dad said, "This doesn't have to be a death sentence Caleb." No pun intended.

"You know that if they find out that I can corpse-raise I'll be rammed right into one of those spook jobs." Goosebumps rose on my arms like boiling water. I looked from one to the other. "You remember that other kid, the corpse-raiser, Parker?"

Mom and Dad looked at each other.

He nodded.

"He tested as a five-point on the APs. That was big news," Mom said.

Dad said wearily, "Jeffrey Parker, that's his name. It wasn't just AFTD, there were other classifications that he had aptitude for." Dad raked a hand through his hair, it needed cutting too, standing in errant spikes. I looked at him in surprise, I thought AFTD was it for him, that he couldn't have other abilities.

"And where is he now?" I asked softly.

Mom looked at her hands while Dad looked me in the eye. "He works for the government."

Of course he would. The government was thrilled to make us all into little robots just as early as possible, with everyone in the job they were "meant" to be. Instinctively I understood I didn't want the job they'd want for me.

"So what does this mean for him Kyle?" Mom asked.

"It means we keep it quiet for now. For how long, I don't know. The APs are quite soon," he looked at me and I nodded. "We have a short amount of time to manufacture a contingency."

"I told you that 'playing God' was going to come back and bite us all in the butt. Just because the potential for paranormal ability was discovered didn't mean that it gave our government the right to experiment on our children," she huffed.

"It's water under the bridge Ali. We signed Caleb up for kindergarten and he was inoculated along with everyone," Dad stated.

When the government saw my dad's and the other scientists' findings on proof of gene markers for paranormal abilities, all mixed up there with you're-gonna-get-cancer someday they went insane. Suddenly, everyone wanted to know if they could read minds or some crazy crap like that.

Memories of the microchip implantation still felt fresh, the needle piercing flesh the same day we learned our ABCs. The needle glinted as it swung in an arc, bound for our vulnerable necks. I shook the memory loose like the teeth I'd lost in that not too distant childhood.

I looked at Dad, "So what's the plan? Do I have to be like, scared here?" I was pretty damn anxious.

"I need to find out a little more about how they administer the test. I'm familiar with the Science portion as I was a part of the revision."

"English, Dad," I said.

"I helped build the model."

"So, you can, what, manipulate the results?" I asked.

Mom's heart was in her gaze. This was her worst fears realized. Here I was, the kid of a liberal, freedom-seeker and a groundbreaking scientist. Who would think I'd be a Cadaver-Manipulator? Seriously?

"No, I can't do anything as profound as that. But, I can find something that may cause some latent dormancy," he said rubbing his chin rhythmically. "There's a drug I can acquire, which will counteract the inoculation that you were given almost ten years ago and your most recent booster. It won't last, but it may help you test weaker. However," he stared at me, "this won't go away. It's here forever. You were born with this potential. And because of scientific advancement, it's a permanent manifestation. And to answer your question, yes, we should respond with extreme caution. The government uses certain 'loopholes' for nefarious purposes. We are American, Caleb. That means something. Our freedom is precious. No one," and his brow furrowed, "should be forced into a life-long position, job or be exploited. There is no liberty in that."

My palms began sweating with just the thought of losing my independence that way. I didn't know what I was gonna be. But I sure as hell wasn't going to be some government slave! I rubbed my hands on my jeans, leaving the wetness there.

"Do you know what the component was that the pharmaceutics used in the inoculation?" Mom asked Dad.

"No, but it's a cerebral-based stimulant so a mild depressant should counteract." Dad's chin rested on his fist in I'm-formulating-a-plan mode.

"So, you're gonna give me a drug and I'm not going to be a smart scientist's kid?"

Dad smiled, Mom didn't. "It's not that funny Caleb," she continued, "we never hear what really became of the Parker boy but there have been mutterings..." she gave Dad a significant look.

He glanced her way then said, "Again, it means that discretion is the greater part of valor here. *Extreme* discretion."

Why couldn't I have just been one of the people that talk to the dead? Or, better yet, see ghosts? That's pretty safe. The government doesn't care much about those guys.

Dad wanted to see my abilities in a "controlled environment."

Didn't want a cemetery-repeat right now, thanks. I told mom she had narrowly escaped the Js for supper and she rolled her eyes.

"Now this is why I had only one son," she said dramatically. "So I could have two more children later on." She smiled, she'd always liked the Js.

Mom made noises about homework before the guys came.

No Call of Duty tonight, there was other stuff to discuss. As I was thinking that, the doorbell rang. A bright orange flare appeared through the window, an obscure flame through the glass. It had to be John.

"Come in!" I yelled.

John lurched in with Jonesy blundering behind like usual, shouting his greeting, "Hi Ali, Hi Kyle!"

The Parents smiled. John looked at the three of us, scoping reactions. I gave him the chillax expression.

The stairs reverberated like a herd of elephants as we jogged up to my room to discuss our evil plan.

John began, "So what happened with your parents?"

"It was cool," I replied.

As cool as it could be when you let someone in on your reanimation-skills. "My dad thinks that he can get some kind of cerebral downer, or..." I thought about it for a second, "inhibitor for during the test, so I won't respond like a five-point."

Jonesy piped in, "What about the rest of the test? Are you going to be all high and test stupid in everything else?"

Fair question I guess. "Nah, my dad didn't think it would affect the other subjects."

John whipped out a crumpled mess of papers from his backpack, futility trying to straighten them.

"What's this?" I asked, eying it with suspicion. I wasn't excited about reading anything informative.

"It's something I found on the Internet. It might give us some clues about what you can do."

I glanced at the first page which read:

'Affinity for the Dead' or, AFTD, is not just a genetic marker, but a new reality.

Huh, I read on about the boy that had made headlines only a few years ago.

A boy like me.

Jeffrey Parker, eighth grade student, is the first to hit the radar with full-blown, "Affinity for the Dead." As everyone understands, in 2010 Geneticist Kyle Hart and his scientific team mapped the Human Genome, thereby giving us every genetic marker that we hold as humans. This invaluable information would eventually lead to a pharmaceutical breakthrough that has now unlocked those previously unknown codes.

Flashes of psychic ability have been witnessed for centuries but now that the "key" to unlock this "door" has been discovered we will continue to have teenagers manifest different abilities that begin to awaken during puberty.

Parker is (unbelievably) able to raise the dead from their graves. He claims that he, "hears voices" that ask him for, "different things."

I looked at the Js, Jonesy was quiet for once, a miracle.

John said, "I read the whole thing. It talks about all the different abilities we *all* may have."

*"*Whoa, hold on!*"* Jonesy said. "I want something cool."

I raised my eyebrows, like *I* wanted AFTD? I'd struggled to appear average, no special attention was good.

His cheeks flamed even with his dark skin. "Listen Caleb, dude, no offense but I don't want what you got."

John glared at Jonesy. "I'm tellin' the truth!" his eyes anxious. "What happened in the cemetery made me want to piss my pants. That dead guy... *damn!*" he slapped his knee.

We laughed... *so* Jonesy.

The cerebral-downer was a temporary solution. One mess at a time.

"What about after the test?" John asked.

There he was diggin' around at the crap I had just decided not to think about. He was like that. I gave him a less-than-friendly look.

"I don't know... I thought I'd wait and see," I said.

"*Not* good Caleb." John said. "You know that ass-hat Carson and definitely Brett, are thinking about ways to make your life miserable."

I had actually thought of that. I wanted to get through the testing, then tackle the terrible twins. Didn't know if I'd be able to before they ratted me out to some adult that would make trouble.

"I heard Jade LeClerc saying something to Brett," John said. My head whipped in his direction, I so wasn't interested in Jade being near that asswipe.

Why was she talking to Brett Mason? The girls walk on the far side of the hall to avoid him, the perv. I asked John.

"She told him to 'go to hell'."

"What?" I yelled.

"Chill out. I overheard them before sixth hour PE."

That would have been before PE today? I noticed Jade didn't turn and say "hi" to me like she usually did.

My hands clenched into fists. "Was he doing something to her?" Just the thought of that butt-munch saying one thing to her made me want to punch him in the face.

"Calm down," John shrugged. "I heard your name mentioned, then she told him where to go."

Jonesy gave the thumbs up, "They saw me come around the corner and she took off. Brett asked where all my 'queer-bait' friends were."

Jonesy started pacing in tight circles around the room, excited. He's kind of a violence lover.

I could relate.

"Did you let him have it?" Jonesy mimed a fist punching his open palm, making a satisfying thwack.

John just looked at him. "Would you stop? You understand the bully laws, right?"

Those finer details were lost on Jonesy as a huge grin overtook his dark face.

I knew that look.

"What?" John asked. He thought Jonesy was gonna get us in trouble (usually true).

"I'm thinkin' about a bit o' payback," Jonesy said.

Uh-oh, we knew what *that* meant. Jonesy had rigged payback schemes, some not so successful, with Brett and Carson in the past.

You'd think they'd catch on.

"Jonesy..." I started. He held up his hand to silence me.

"Just listen. Brett and Carson are dumber than rocks, right?" John and I looked at him, ya think?

"How about I have them try a cool experiment before the APs and get 'em all distracted from their plan to sabotage your life?" For Jonesy, this was bordering on brilliant. I turned my finger in a circle, keep talking.

"How about the tube and Aqua Net trick?" he asked.

We groaned. That had gone really bad.

John scowled. "No way Jonesy. You remember what happened when we tried it!"

"Exactly! It's the perfect thing! It'll take one of them out and distract them around AP time. Then, after testing, if the cerebral-whatever-it-is works, they can flap all they want but if you're not popping the big AFTD guns, there's no proof." Jonesy spread his hands wide, *bow to my invincible logic.*

Of course, sometimes his logic could bite us all in the ass.

I ran my hand through my hair, thinking furiously. Today was Monday... so almost a week for strategy.

I said, "Okay, but you're going to what, steal your mom's hairspray?"

"It's *Aqua Net,* there is no substitute," he said, mildly insulted. "We've got spiders entombed in the corners of my parents' bathroom from my mom using it forever. Pretty damn effective."

I told him it was effective but disgusting.

Jonesy got defensive, "My mom swears by the stuff. She never has to redo her hair."

Well... good for her. Jonesy's mom's hair was stiff. I could throw a pencil and it'd stay. There was no moving it. Jonesy called his mom's bathroom time, The Ritual. Aqua Net sure worked when we tried fun-with-fire. It was worth singeing Carson's nose hairs.

John didn't like it. Out of the three of us, John was the most cautious. Of course, he'd gotten his eyebrows burnt off. They took about three months to grow back and his parents had been super-pissed.

"Come on John, just restating the obvious here. Wouldn't it be cool to get those turds back and off our backs at the same time?" Jonesy asked.

"Yeah, but if they really get hurt..."

"They won't," he said.

Dismissing John's worries I turned to Jonesy, thinking of a possible problem, "what if they tell us to stick it?"

"I'll tell 'em the same stuff I told you; we already did it and it's fun." He said with a sly wink because it had certainly *not* been fun: singed eyebrows. I could almost taste the foul perfume even after a whole year. "Then, if they smell a trap, I'll say they're sissy-sucking-titty-babies."

John gave a satisfied nod. "That'll work."

Jonesy could handle it with his boatload-of-charm.

The cemetery was the best place because Carson and Brett wouldn't want us to think they were scared after the raising-the-dead-guy episode. Jonesy said he'd talk to them tomorrow and see if they swallowed the hook. Meanwhile, Dad would get the cerebral-blocking drug and I'd be set. Now I just needed to find out what was happening with Jade, maybe start with a conversation, geez, *so original*.

CHAPTER 5

John and I always sit together in our classes. We have Miss Rodriguez for English. She's a first year teacher so she's not bored and raging at us yet. Her back was to us while I sly-pulsed to John about Sunday. We had a satisfying view of Miss Rodriguez (she's pretty hot), when she suddenly turned, burning holes into me.

I jerked like I'd been slapped, so busted, I didn't know what she'd said! I looked at John and he was wide-eyed, *don't look at me!*

"Caleb Hart," Miss Rodriguez said, my whole name, not good. "What tense is this here?" She pointed with the dry eraser pen to what I had, until just now, not noticed.

My cheeks grew hot and I wanted to sink underneath the desk. I stared numbly at the question: My family has been making plans for a snowboarding trip.

Well, definitely future tense but perfect or progressive perfect, I wasn't sure.

I sneaked a glance Jade's way and she'd written PROGRESSIVE in block letters on the back of her notebook. I slid my eyes back to Miss Rodriguez, who was looking less hot all the time.

"Future Progressive, Miss Rodriguez."

She smiled brilliantly at me, her gaze wandering over the thirty of us.

"It's nice someone is paying attention to the correct tense. Now remember class," she turned back to the white board, "at this age, it is assumed that you speak correctly, now it's time to know the 'why'. Grammar achieves this by teaching how our language supports speech."

My heartbeat slowed to a trot, that was close.

I looked at Jade again and she gave me a shy smile. I smiled back. She'd saved my ass! It was the first outward sign she liked me more than just a "hey" in the hall when we jostled through the crowd. Brett's eyes narrowed, noticing our interchange, smirking. Jade saw where I was looking and I watched the smile wash away.

English ended and we swarmed into the hall like bees, weaving our way to our lockers. PE was next period and looking at my watch, a retro thing from my dad, and realized I had maybe four minutes to talk to Jade. My eyes surveyed the long hallway, looking for the sweep of black hair. I'd overheard her say she was part Cherokee Indian, that's where the black hair came in.

Score! I scoped the hair like a black flag in the crowd. Shiny, spilling around her shoulders with movement as she talked to Sophie. I waved.

Sophie saw me and leaned forward, saying something to Jade. Jade turned and my heart paused in my chest, her effect on me was that powerful. No guy wants a girl to know that they're enthralled, so I blanked my expression.

She smiled wider as I made my way to where she stood by her locker, my backpack a solid weight, swinging as I moved.

"Hey," I began with my best casual smile.

"Hi Caleb," Sophie said then looked at Jade. "Gotta go!" she winked and a brilliant bit of color spread over Jade's cheekbones.

I'd have to get things warmed up.

"Thanks for your help in Rodriguez' class," safe intro.

"It looked like you could use it," she smiled.

"Hey! I knew it was future, I just didn't know the other."

"Riiigghht..." her eyes glittering with humor.

I huffed at her comment but it was for show, it wasn't that hard talking to her after all.

Her cat-green eyes looked up at me, smokey rimmed with soft, Kohl-colored make-up, not too much. She was hot, just looking at her made my chest tight, my heart a stutter-rhythm.

I had to warn her about Brett, "Here's the thing, Brett and Carson have me in their cross hairs and maybe who I hang out with."

She gave me a steady look, a puzzled expression furrowing between her brows.

"*Do* we hang out?" she asked.

Truth now. "I want to."

I'd rather die than say how I feel but I needed the guts to own it. I waited for her response.

"Me too," she said, looking up from under the black lace of her eyelashes; wow.

Relief flowed through me. Even with all the scary shit I was dealing with, for starters, the whispering of the dead a background symphony, Jade made me feel invincible. I could do *anything.*

The bell shrilled... *crap*! We had like thirty seconds before PE.

Laughing, we sprinted down the hall, Jade's hair streaming behind her like black water. We'd just make it through the door. Griswold would make us pay.

There's creative discipline for kids that aren't ready for PE.

Our bodies slid through the door and I watched the school clock click to 1:46, shrilling the final bell.

Griswold raised an eyebrow, "Glad you two could join us. Suit up, you both have extra calisthenics today, obviously."

Carson and Brett watched this development with interest. That's swell, just what we needed.

Jonesy was in line, giving me a look of restrained horror. He was so easy to read. You decided to make a move on Jade...now?

I looked back at Jonesy, *so sue me.*

After PE, I kept my fragile connection with Jade, I said I'd see her tomorrow. I had seventh hour band, we had a fifteen minute break. I whipped out my slim, credit-card sized pulse cell I'd gotten for my birthday.

Depressing the touch pad with my thumb the screen came alive:

Activated and I *thought, Jonesy,* then belatedly, *John.*

I almost lost my three-way, I was so distracted by thoughts of Jade. Their response lit up my screen with the familiar luminescent green characters:

*Hey, What the **profanity-block!** is with you and Jade being late for PE?* MJ

I depressed my thumb again, *Chillax... I finally told her I want to hang out*-CH

*What? You actually **talked** to Jade? This is the worst time in the world Caleb; and I hear she's a hater.-* John Terran.

Swiping my thumb, *She doesn't 'hate', she's just quiet.*-CH

*Are you going to tell her? About...-*John Terran.

*No **profanity-block!** way Caleb, it's bad enough that Carson and Brett know, we can't have this Jade-complication!*-MJ.

I have a feeling about her. Just trust me and stop being ass-clowns about it.-CH

The screen went dark for a moment:

K, but she needs to see your skills, you feel me? Oh yeah, I almost forgot, I talked to the real *ass-clowns, (*must be Brett and Carson I thought...*) it is* them, *do you have your thumb on the touch pad Caleb? I'm getting feed back.*-MJ

I jerked my thumb off. That was stupid, sometimes I forgot to lift.

Okay, now I can see just myself, LMAO. They're idiots, I told them they're too chicken **profanity-block!** *to try it. It worked* **shrugs.** *They'll meet us at the cemetery, same day and time.*-MJ
You gonna get the hairspray from your mom?-CH
Aqua Net, my man. And yeah, she never uses every squirt. I scoped a can in the reprocesser, I'll snag it.-MJ
Isn't she gonna notice? If she's like my mom, she's a total freak for the reprocessing credit on the garbage bill.-CH
Nah, I'll offer to take the separator out for once and she'll be so happy I volunteered for a chore she won't care, LOL-MJ
I think we're going to be sorry.-John Terran
Cork it pal, don't be a fun-sucker.-MJ
sighs, *we gotta get to band. I'll bring your pick, you left it at my house.*- John Terran.

That was John, all-business and worrying.

Thanks. K, talk to ya later Jonesy.-CH
Later.-John Terran.
See ya.-MJ

I swept my thumb over the touch pad setting my pulse to hibernate.

****

Band was a righteous seventh hour class, a subject I actually liked, alien concept. John's parents believed in music, they were zealots (old zealots, they were my grandpa's age). John could play everything but he really jammed at the piano. He could read music and play a piece he listened to only a few times. I struggled through learning the notes. Oh well, it was the only time during the school day that I could drown out the whispering.

John and I jammed together on a new piece Mr. Pierce had given us. We were working out the kinks, the volume on the amp turned up three quarters to full volume making my teeth rattle in my head. John flashed me a grin. He was a pretty serious dude most of the time. I was lucky to have the Js, which made me think of Carson and Brett and the cemetery.

John heard me hit a flat in my chord and winced. My concentration was sucking big time.

We wrapped up the session, hanging our guitars on the rack with about fifteen others. I made a basket with my pick in the box marked *Caleb S. Hart* (swish).

I followed John out of class. Fresh, late-afternoon spring air hit my lungs and I sucked it up. I could taste summer on my tongue and that meant Gramp's house at Lake Tapps. No school and screw off time with the Js.

John and I walked in companionable silence for a few blocks. "Why start something with Jade, Caleb?"

I took some time to answer John, he was way-different than Jonesy. He wouldn't press me for an answer.

"You don't see that she's special?" I asked with a *duh* in my voice.

"Well, she's good-looking but complicated. And that we don't need right now. And you heard about her family, right?" John asked.

I stopped walking and looked at him. "Yeah, I know her dad's a psycho, so?"

"Hey, don't get defensive on me. But you do like a project."

I was back to walking, with a scowl.

"Jade's not a project."

He sighed. "It's more than that. She lives at her aunt's and she's not much better than the dad." John said, as if by sheer force of logic I could control who I liked. Attraction doesn't work like that.

"So how's that her fault?" I stopped again on the side of the road, hands hanging loose at my sides. Cars drove past, breaking the sweet smell of spring with their passing. I felt that pressure building in my head. Getting pissed seemed to make it harder to block out. And the odd road kill hanging around didn't help, I thought sourly.

John saw my expression. "I shouldn't rant on Jade. I don't feel great about including her in this mess."

"Like I pulsed ya, I trust how I feel about Jade. And besides, you guys are stressing about my AFTD but have you thought about what you'll test-out for?"

"I have thought about it," John conceded.

"Have you noticed something?"

"No... there won't be anything for me. I'm already halfway through puberty and nothing. The tests will confirm that. Not everyone manifests."

I looked up at John, way up. He was a pretty tall dude for fourteen. He'd be fifteen soon, in September. His dad was taller, like NBA-tall. His hair stood about four inches away from his head like he had stuck his finger in a pulse socket, a fro-and-go (I smiled thinking of Jonesy's names). He let it riot, that was John. He was him all the time, the most real person I knew.

"Hey dude, you don't want this," pointing at myself.

He grinned with a wistful expression "No way. But I'd have something cool like psychokinesis."

I rolled my eyes... whatever. "John, you know that's pretty rare."

"Yeah, but look at you? AFTD is the rarest." He looked uncomfortable because we both knew it wasn't the ability to have. I bet Jeffrey Parker wished he didn't, all it got him was a one-way ticket as a government puppet.

"True." I turned and we walked again toward my house. More cars rushed past as we walked single file on the shoulder.

Grinding metal pierced my ears and fingers lassoed my arm hauling me into the ditch, our butts landing in water which instantly leeched into our pants.

A car that had been behind us was sliding on the street, careening sideways where a lone, black dog was standing in its path. It was obvious the driver had swerved to avoid the dog and almost clipped us on the side of the road.

A surreal moment ensued, the car ramming into the dog and it sailing at least ten feet to land about two car lengths from where John and I sat in the ditch. We looked at the crumpled heap of the dog on the ground and in that moment time seemed to pause.

The driver, an older balding guy, got out of his car, kinda dazed looking, and approached the dog. But not before he gave a nervous glance our way.

"You kids okay?" Baldy asked, moving on before we could answer.

Oh he gave a shit, right.

"Yeah." John mumbled anyway.

I looked away, not saying anything because... because, the dog was sending things to me, images. It knew it was dying and was sending out some kind of distress signal, that only I heard, my body humming in response.

I got to my feet without ever noticing I stood, as one compelled.

John startled, then followed me. He wasn't one to ask stupid questions. We walked across the pebbled pavement, oily from last night's rain. As I drew closer, that unique pressure built in my head, straining for release.

The dog lay before us, just a mutt. There was not a breath of life. Wait... *yes there was.*

I knelt down and reached my hand out, John at my back, when Baldy said, "Don't touch it!"

Without hesitation, I placed a gentle hand on its fur, and felt that small spark of life ignite. Unbidden, that part of me that heard the dead released and poured, no fell over the dog.

I grasped that spark and thought... *live.* Warmth welled up under my hand like liquid heat and I watched the dog's ribs expand for a shaky inhale. Its eyes opened and it looked at me. In that moment I knew he was mine.

Baldy stepped away from John and me, giving us a look that I never wanted to see on an adult's face, revulsion mixed with fear. I hadn't noticed before but now I saw a semi-circle of wary faces. What *had* they seen?

I glanced at John who said in a low voice, "We're screwed."

Ya think? Just the kind of proof I was avoiding.

The dog was sitting up but still looked injured. Its eyes followed me like I was all that mattered. My creepy new reality.

Wonderful.

A cop moved through the small crowd with a notebook in hand.

"You boys there," we looked up, his name tag read Garcia. "Step away from the dog."

We did, the dog dragging behind me with a limp.

Garcia-the-cop approached the dog reaching his hand out, the dog growled low in the back of his throat, showing teeth. Garcia backed away, his eyes remaining on the dog, he brought out his pulse.

After he depressed his touch pad he looked up again, "I've pulsed animal control. They'll be here soon."

My heart sped, I didn't like the dog being taken away.

"Okay," Garcia said. "Somebody start talking."

Baldy stepped up, wringing his plump hands, "I was driving along, doing the speed limit, when this dog just appeared out of nowhere," he spread his hands wide to show how it was just one of those things. "And these two boys," he gave us an accusing glance, (wasn't this turning out special), "were on the other side of the road and I had to avoid *them*." He gave that last word special emphasis, as if us walking on the side of the road was a crime.

Garcia opened his hand, "Identification, please?"

Baldy gave us an unfriendly look and handed over his driver's license. I felt the pressure building and tried to rein it in. When I was upset it was way worse to manage.

John looked down at me. "What's the matter?"

"That guy's a turd. I wanna get out of here."

"Yeah he's a dick." John gave a chuckle, "But we have to see this thing through and act like the dog thing wasn't talent, just coincidence. You got me?"

I nodded, I got it alright. I didn't know if AFTD was talent, but it was annoying.

Garcia and Baldy had their heads together, one a cue ball, the other an eight ball.

Finally, the cop turned to John and me. "Mr. Smith here," he motioned with his notepad to Baldy, "said that you did something to the dog?" He raised his eyebrows.

How to answer without getting my butt in a sling?

John spoke before I had a chance, "Caleb's a major animal lover," he said.

I kept the shock off my face. That wasn't exactly accurate, but...

"That's not what Mr. Smith said: 'he was'," he looked down at his notepad for the exact quote, "...'sure the dog was dead.' Then you touched it and everything 'got funny' and the dog was suddenly alive again."

"Can you explain that?" he asked.

Actually no.

John looked down at me with an "I tried" expression. Lying sucked, let's see how creative I could be.

"John's right." Garcia turned to John, seemingly taking him in for the first time. "I couldn't seem to help myself, seeing it lying there," I looked down at my shoes, hiding my expression, giving myself time to continue, "I don't know how it got better."

That was mainly the truth. Before today, I didn't know dying things could also "call" to me, image me. Everything, every being was unique: an insect was not a dog, a dog was NOT a human being. I held Garcia's stare and he seemed to decide something, "You boys live around here?"

John answered, "Yeah, Caleb lives right there," John pointed over the top of the rise, "and I live about half a mile from here."

Garcia held his pen poised over the notepad, "Names?"

"Caleb Hart."

Garcia's head jerked up and he looked at me more closely, "The scientist's kid?"

"Yeah," I answered with a marked lack of enthusiasm. "Now that's a cool relative to have," he commented with a smile.

"I guess." Whatever, he was just my dad to me.

"John Terran." John said, effectively getting me off the hook of dealing with the awkward, your-parent-is-kinda-famous moment.

"Okay, you kids get in the police car and I'll give you a ride home."

"What about the dog?" I asked. The dog looked up at me and whined softly. As if on cue, animal control arrived. A ginormous gal poured into an unflattering light tan uniform barreled through the crowd accompanied by a skinny partner. Two more opposite people you'd never see. The dog's posture immediately changed, he was alert.

I was bothered by the dog's suffering so I reached out and several things happened at once, Garcia tried to pull me away, the huge animal control gal cleared her evil-looking baton from her utility belt and John pulled me back. I missed purchase on the dog as Garcia did on me. The dog eluded the baton with an attached noose, parking himself behind John and I.

Garcia said to me directly, "I don't want any trouble and I already told you boys not to touch that dog."

"I thought I could help, he seems to like me," I said.

"Let animal control do their job, son," Garcia said.

Ignoring him, I put my hand on the dog thinking... *sleep.*

"That's it!" Garcia said. He strode the two feet over to where John and I stood and took us each by the arm to his patrol car. I chanced a look behind me and saw the dog knocked out cold. Garcia was tallish, my feet skimmed the ground as he hauled me and John to the car where we were unceremoniously dumped inside.

He pointed his finger at us. "Stay put."

We watched him walk away. He lingered with Baldy for a short time who nodded his head vigorously, casting dirty looks at us whenever Garcia turned away. Then he spoke with animal control who were collecting the dog. Skinny was the "collector," and Humongous was "supervising" this process while standing importantly with Garcia.

Garcia jogged back to the patrol car. John and I were surveying the inside of the patrol car and I deemed it pretty gross. I could see remnants of goop all over the back of the seat, floor and handles on the door. The black upholstery didn't hide it either. There were dried patches of "mystery fluid" in strategic locations. The contents of lunch began to rise in my stomach. John reacted similarly, hunching in on himself so less of him touched his surroundings.

Good luck with that one.

Garcia slid into the front seat and turned around to look at us. "I am required to take your statements with your parent or guardian present," Garcia said, in a matter-of-fact voice.

Sounded like he had said that a few times. My parents were gonna have a turtle when a police car pulled up in front of the house!

Thoughts swirled in my head like: how did I stop that dog from dying? Why didn't I need blood to do it? Was that a coincidence at the cemetery? Or, because it was a person (before) and it was "fully dead," I needed something extra? I didn't have those answers. As I put my head between my knees to quell the dizziness that threatened I knew tonight I'd read some more about paranormal abilities and Jeffrey Parker. It was time to get up close and personal with AFTD, I needed to rule it, not the other way around.

CHAPTER 6

Garcia surveyed my house briefly. "That's unique."

It was a ranch style with cream-colored arches across the facade, covered in stucco, really different for rainy Washington.

We followed Garcia and Mom came through the door and under the open archway before we had a chance to get to it.

Garcia seemed to "get it," putting his hand out in an inoffensive way like, *everything's okay.*

"The kids aren't in any trouble Mrs. Hart." Garcia began, but my mom cut him off with a dismissive wave of her hand. "Ali's fine."

"Okay... *Ali*," he paused, "they witnessed a vehicular accident in which a dog was hit and I need to take down their statements with an adult present."

Mom's face looked relieved that some catastrophe (she was always ranting about my safety, which got to be annoying) had not befallen us. She stepped backwards, to let Garcia pass. While she waited for us to trudge through, I watched Garcia look around our house. It smelled like cookies and bread, those were good smells. John gave the air an experimental whiff too.

The Appetite Beast was alive and well.

Garcia sat down on the psychedelically colorful couch.

"Do you care for anything to drink, Sergeant Garcia?" she asked, checking out Garcia's name tag.

"Ah, sure, thanks."

Mom usually made cookies once a week. Jonesy liked to show up just as they came out of the oven.

As if I had just conjured him up, he walked through the door.

"Hey Caleb, what's with the cop car outside?" he asked loudly so there was zero chance to deflect it. The words landed like a bomb in the middle of the room, John cringed.

Garcia turned to Jonesy. "Caleb witnessed an accident so I am taking his and John's statements."

"No kidding? Well, I'm going to stay for this!" Unfazed by the cop in our living room, he proceeded to ask mom what she'd made today.

"Peanut butter, chocolate chip cookies."

"Yes!" Jonesy pumped his arm up and down. Garcia sorta looked down, smiling.

For Jonesy, Garcia just happened to be in my house where Mom made cookies and there may be a cool story as a bonus. John just looked at me and shrugged, *what do we do with him?*

Garcia took a long gulp of water, then turned to John and I, Mom perching on the armrest of the couch.

"Okay Caleb, tell me what happened," he glanced down at his notepad briefly, then looked up, "you heard a 'screeching,' then, you saw Mr...." he tapped the notepad, "Smith's 2023 champagne-colored Ford Grun strike a dog." He looked at me, then John.

"Is this accurate boys?"

I was opening my mouth when Jonesy busted in with. "Did the dog die?"

I gave an inward grown, my peripheral vision telling me John was trying to alert Jonesy to shut up. That never worked. Getting Garcia away from thinking about the strangeness of the dog was epic-fail with Jonesy bringing attention to it. I looked over at Jonesy happily stuffing cookies and slurping milk.

"Yeah, that's accurate," I replied.

Garcia gave me the "cop stare." Adults want kids to fill those awkward silences. That's where I'd get tripped up. Mom was giving me a puzzled look. She knew something was going on.

"Now, it's interesting that you mention the dog." Garcia began, (actually, Jonesy had) "because Mr..." he rolled his eyes up, "... Smith, " he remembered, "said that he was certain the dog had been killed."

My heart sped, my hands immediately dampening. "No... no, he was still alive, barely."

"Okay... Caleb," he paused, giving a small smile, "there were some witnesses who said that you," he glanced down at his notepad (man, was I beginning to hate that thing), " 'laid hands' on the dog and it began breathing again." Looking directly at me with a piercing stare out of eyes which blended with the pupil, I was suddenly reminded of Brett. He had those eyes.

"Maybe he was dead for a minute..." I began, choosing my words slowly, "but he must have revived or something."

Garcia didn't even pause, "One witness said that the dog's breath had gone out of it before you reached it. That when you touched it, there was an 'energy' around you."

My head snapped back up. What? Was that possible?

"The witness is an Aura Reader, Caleb."

I was screwed! They identify paranormals. I am sure I had my panic-face on. John was as pale as a ghost (hardy har-har).

"You know, Sergeant Garcia," Mom's voice was all sweet, but dude, I knew that tone!

"Caleb is a minor (that word came out sounding vaguely like lawsuit, I noted with grim satisfaction), and hasn't perpetuated any crime, so I'm not sure that this line of questioning is justified."

I heard: stop bugging my kid or I'll make you sorry.

Garcia looked at Mom thoughtfully. She tilted her head to the side and a large, gold hoop swung forward, peeking out of her thick hair, twinkling in the late sunlight streaming through the window. I had a sudden stab of love for Mom, standing up for me. I decided to man-up, I wasn't little anymore.

I broke the silence. "I have Affinity for the Dead."

It sounded like a disease, ya know: I have cancer, I have two weeks to live. I wasn't going to die. I was going to start living *now* and stop being scared. The Js looked at me like I was insane.

Garcia startled.

"Caleb!" Mom said sharply, her mouth in a thin line.

"It's okay Mom, I know that he won't tell anyone."

He needed to feel the burden of my trust, roll it around and taste it like candy in his mouth. I was hoping that Garcia believed in what he was, a policeman: to serve and protect.

"Caleb's right," looking at me with kinder eyes, "I don't have to tell this part. You're right too, Mrs. Hart. He *is* a minor, and hasn't committed a crime."

I felt a *but* coming.

"But," he said and I smiled, "there were witnesses. A young woman noticed what Caleb did. She is under no such restrictions. There is no law that will keep her from sharing what she saw."

Garcia leaned back and crossed his legs, his ankle resting on his opposite knee. His black uniform looked crisp, the sharp creases in his pant legs bisecting the center. His tie tack glinted in the sun as he shifted.

"I cannot protect Caleb's information." He turned to me, "Why do you want to hide it, Caleb? There are other AFTDs."

Because it threatened my freedom. I thought of Gramps, who always told me freedom was more precious than money. I was beginning to believe him.

"I don't want to end up like Jeffrey Parker," I said.

Mom looked at me with her mouth in an "O" of surprise. I didn't want to work for the government and have no choices, duh! John nodded, *he* knew what had happened to Parker.

Jonesy gave a nod because his mouth was full.

Garcia was thoughtful, the whole room held its collective breath.

Finally, Garcia said, "Yes, that would be enough to give anyone pause." A silent consent passed between him and Mom. My identity stripped away, a possible slave for a government that would use me under the guise of protecting the nation or some crap like that, ah... *no*.

Dad walked through the garage door with his hair in disarray, briefcase in hand.

"What's going on here?" he asked, fingers balanced on the doorknob, tossing his coat on the hook by the door.

I sighed, it was gonna be a long night.

Mom and Garcia started to speak at the same time, laughing nervously. Jonesy looked from my mom to my dad then back to Garcia like a tennis match gone wrong, shrugged, and grabbed another cookie. John had his arms folded across his skinny chest silently watching the drama unfold.

"You go ahead," Mom said.

Garcia gave her a brief nod. "Mr. Hart," he stood and held out his hand, "I'm Sergeant Garcia with the King County Police." Dad took the hand Garcia offered and gave it a few hard pumps.

I looked at dad, such a huge contrast to the very Hispanic-looking Garcia. Dad loomed a little over Garcia, standing six foot-one to Garcia's shy six foot. Garcia stepped away and folded his lankiness back onto the couch, Dad balancing on the piano bench.

They faced each other. "Kyle Hart." Dad smiled.

Garcia was braced for some hostility, but my parents didn't automatically think someone was out to get them (well Mom did, some).

Garcia went over the whole story, beginning with how the dog had been in the road, and Baldy (Smith) had hit him. He ended with, "... and now you see, Mr. Hart, we are at an impasse."

I deliberated... a standstill! Gotcha.

Dad's face had been thoughtful during this retelling, becoming somber at its end.

Finally, he nodded, "We thought that we could allow ourselves some time to devise a plan that would garner Caleb some options, to come to terms with his new skills. But his 'skill set' is accelerating on course with other puberty manifestations," Dad finished, his expression expectant.

Jonesy was near drooling at a speech of complicated proportions, his eyes vacant and glassy, John looked mildly confused and Mom was irritated. Garcia was valiantly figuring it out.

"Dad... English!" I berated.

Dad smiled sheepishly. "Sorry folks, thinking aloud. His face fell into stern lines. "In other words, he is gaining abilities that I cannot predict and they are popping up at extremely inconvenient and public locations."

Understatement of the year!

I did a mental face-palm when Jonesy piped in, "I still wanna know what happened to the dog." This said mid-chew on a cookie.

John looked at Jonesy.

"What?" Gulp, slurp with the milk. Mom wrinkled her nose.

"I mean, this is good news because, my bro here," brandishing his empty glass in my direction, "saved a dog and everyone is freaked over it," he said, shrugging. For the Jones-man this was a simple affair of right and wrong. Jonesy didn't do shades of gray.

John spoke up, "Yeah, it's cool about the dog but not everyone is going to think it's cool Jonesy. In fact, I bet some may notice that we don't want noticing. The same ones that noticed Jeffrey Parker."

John's speech struck everyone mute.

Mom spoke next, "I was cleaning out your room Caleb."

Great, as I visualized all the crap strewn over the floor.

"And I found some papers that talked about the Parker boy. Once he was identified with AFTD and the government became involved and enacted an amendment against some of his rights as a person; his freedoms were stripped."

Mom was gonna rage, I felt it coming as sure as I was sitting here.

Garcia must have been more astute than I gave him credit for because he gestured with his hand, *wait a sec*. Mom popped her mouth shut. Huh, she hadn't even Made-Her-Point.

"Mrs. Hart, let's not panic yet. That was a decade ago. Parker was the first, extreme case that had been seen. You remember the headlines."

As I had only been five in 2015 when that first inoculation round had been given, I didn't remember.

"He was not typical."

Garcia turned to Dad, seeking confirmation.

Dad, no intellectual slouch. "You're right. This wasn't a teen that just talked to the dead, divined ghosts, or gleaned how someone had died. He was a Cadaver-Manipulator."

My parents and the Js all looked at me.

I opened my mouth to spill my guts when Garcia said, "Well, isn't it fortunate that Caleb doesn't have to worry about that. Controlling the dead is a whole other ball of wax."

"Very fortunate," Dad agreed, giving me his best, I-will-throw-lab-beakers-at-you-if-you-talk stare. I snapped my mouth shut. The Js were as silent as the tomb. I mercilessly repressed a wild urge to laugh.

Garcia braced his palms on his knees and stood, smoothing his uniform as he straightened. Dad stood too, running a nervous hand through his hair and making it messier than before.

Garcia fished something out of his perfectly ironed shirt pocket. I leaned forward to look.

He handed me a card that read: Sergeant Raul Garcia, Pulse: 206.968.8640.

I told him I'd never seen that area code.

"Yeah, it was my dad's, he was a cop too." Rolling his shoulders in a shrug, "I got it when he retired."

Dad did the humph sound. "I haven't seen one of those in thirty years."

Garcia smiled, shaking my parents' hands and with his other hand resting on the oversized bronze handle, he gave me good eye contact.

"You call me if you need anything. Just thumb my number in your pulse," he raised his eyebrows. "Yeah, I've got a pulse."

Brain Impulse phones were newer but who wanted to text the old way?

He nodded. "... anytime, for whatever."

His gaze traveled to the parents and I was sure he knew there was something more but he let it go. Stepping back into the threshold of the doorway, the twilight edged around him like a halo as he slipped out the door.

Mom leaned against the closed door, locking the dead bolt backwards as she stepped away.

"Wasn't that close!" she said.

"It's safe to say we're fast running out of time before there will be a contingent of people with a clearer understanding of just what Caleb is capable," Dad said.

"I think he's a good man. But, he may not be ready to know that last part," mom hesitated, "Cadaver-Manipulator might be a bit much."

Jonesy burst in with, "Corpse-raiser, corpse-raiser, it rocks!" air-pumping with his fist.

John corrected, "You didn't think it 'rocked' when you sprinted out of the cemetery," John paused for effect, "or when Caleb and I had to do the little blood ritual."

Mom's mouth unhinged itself from her jaw and Dad looked astounded.

"Blood ritual?" they asked in unison.

I wiped my hands off on my jeans. Geez, this sucked.

"Well, I didn't know if it was gonna eat me or what, I knew you guys could handle it." Jonesy grinned at us both, extolling his faith in our bravery... riggghhtt.

"You didn't tell us that detail," Dad said, thoughtful.

Mom said, "Is that how you think you did it?" She was frowning now, thinking about all the ways my safety could have been in jeopardy (it was), or some other thing that could have befallen me (it did).

"Well, kinda," I began.

Dad was measured. He waited for me to spit it out. Mom was biting her tongue on about nine different levels.

"Caleb, just barf it out," Jonesy said.

Huh, so much for time to gather any thoughts.

I fought not to tap my fingers on a surface. "I felt like a tingling... an energy."

Dad made the circle gesture with his hand to go on, "... as soon as I stepped through the gate of that cemetery I knew there was one voice above the others that was calling me." I put my hands over my ears in reaction to the memory.

They all waited for me to continue, even Jonesy.

"When I got there I felt like I was in the middle of a whirlpool, that something was just under the surface, waiting to rise. It was like all the energy in the world was waiting for me to take that next step," I said.

"And then I hit him a good one!" Jonesy interrupted with a loud thwack of his right fist smacking into the palm of his left.

Mom jumped, giving a nervous laugh.

I glanced at Jonesy. "Yeah, thanks for that."

He gave the *what?* expression. John shook his head, hopeless.

"Do you think, after Jonesy hit you the catalyst was the violence or the blood? Because blood is organic, but so is violence, if one thinks on that," Dad said.

Now that was interesting. I hadn't thought violence was any part of it. I'd assumed that the blood was somehow an integral part of why the corpse rose to begin with.

"That would explain the dog," John said quietly.

We looked at him while he shifted his weight, arms still locked over his chest. "I mean, the car hitting the dog was an act of violence, right? If Baldy..." John continued.

"Smith," I corrected.

"Whatever," he shrugged. "If Smith," he gave me The Look, "hit that dog, then he wasn't being careful. There are protections about obstacles now in all cars, it's standard," he stated. John was kinda stiff, but he was making some good points. "Really, if you think about it, he shouldn't have hit the dog at all."

Dad was nodding. "John's right."

John sat on a stool, speech finished.

"Which brings me to wonder: why that wasn't the first thing Garcia was after, not your possible ability," the look he gave me spoke volumes. "Do you boys remember this witness? This young woman that Sergeant Garcia mentioned, the Aura Reader."

I shook my head, with all the action happening, the crowd was the last thing I remembered.

Jonesy brightened. "I saw that hot girl from PE in the crowd on the way here."

John just looked at him.

"What? He asked."

Dad laughed. "That's okay. I think there's more than just professional interest. I'm thankful we didn't blindly tell him the extent of your abilities. Not before I've had a chance to see them. And finalize the use of the cerebral inhibitor."

"Kyle, that worries me," Mom said.

"This is the lesser of two evils, Ali. If he shows his hand, they may do a 'Parker' on him."

"Even now?" Mom asked.

"Especially now."

"Your mom and I have been reading up on Parker, how our government responded to him. It looks like Parker took the Aptitude Test and was the first student, nation-wide, to hit that high of a score on AFTD, five-points." Dad said, holding up all five fingers. I knew this part, "There hasn't been another."

Until me, was the unspoken ending.

The Fam-pulse chimed, as Mom walked over to the wall pocket and pressed her thumb to the pad.

Dad asked, "Who is it?"

Mom held up her index finger.

She turned to Jonesy. "It's your mom, apparently you didn't tell her you'd be over today."

Jonesy sighed and went to the Fam-pulse, thumbing the pad. He sat there silently for a minute, then lifted and read the screen. He depressed one more time then turned...

"I gotta go, mom's on a rage."

Mom frowned. "Maybe knowing where you are is sort of important Jonesy." Doing the I'm-going-to-stick-up-for-the-other-parent thing.

"Yeah Ali, I know." He brightened. "Thanks for those cookies..." Mom was already getting a little ecobag for the road, Jonesy grinned. Delayed gratification.

He gave me a finger salute, turning for the door. "See you dudes tomorrow. Let me know what's going on Caleb."

John lifted his chin in goodbye, then we heard his pounding footsteps and the front door slamming.

Dad got back on topic. "Being prepared is the most important defense."

"True, as long as we're on the same page with this cerebral," Mom searched for the word, "depressant."

Dad corrected her, "Inhibitor."

Dad continued, "Caleb, tell me what happened at the accident, especially about this mystery dog."

I started with how we had been walking home like usual and ended with how I was sure the dog had been alive, at least a little, because I had felt that "spark." Dad latched on to the word.

"Okay, let's go over the cause and effect one more time, Caleb."

John and I groaned out loud. I actually face-palmed.

"Dad..." I started.

"No Caleb, let's look at this with some applied logic. The dog was hit and flew," Dad paused, "you said ten or twelve feet in the air?" I nodded acquiescence. He pressed on, "... and it lay there for how long?"

John interceded, "We went to the dog right away. I mean, Caleb went to it and I followed."

"Yeah. It was like he was calling back to me, it was faint. I could feel its will, or whatever. It wanted to be alive, he didn't want to die."

Dad put his elbow on his knee and cupped his chin. "It hasn't been mentioned that Parker has this ability. As a point of fact, I hadn't heard that this was a part of AFTD."

Mom asked, "Would Caleb's ability to bring something back from the brink of death still be the same thing, categorized similarly?"

"Perhaps..." I heard Dad's whiskers as he rubbed his chin. "We'll have to put some things to the test and see exactly where his abilities reside."

A thrill of fear shot through me. I wanted to use the AFTD, it made the whispering almost disappear. It felt good, *right*. So far, all AFTD got me was two enemies at school and a dog's reclaimed life that brought me notice from an observant cop.

"What are you thinking, Kyle? That we give him what, a pre-aptitude test?" Mom asked.

He nodded. "Exactly. If we can nail down his skill set, know *how* to defend ourselves, defend him, and decide his future."

"Maybe Caleb doesn't want to be some government puppet." John said.

Exactly what I'd been thinking.

"It's a terrifying proposition, the loss of one's freedom," Dad said and Mom nodded.

"I think I want the dog," I said suddenly.

My parents looked at me with identical expressions of shock.

"Why, Caleb?" Mom asked.

"Because I feel responsible for it now."

"We can't just go and take in everything you," Dad stumbled over this next turn-o'-phrase, "raise or save son."

John smirked, this was kinda funny in a perverse way.

"I know, but when I think about him..."

"It's a he?" Mom asked.

"Yeah."

"Well, how do you know?" she asked.

"I just do mom, it's all part of it." Unimportant random details! Dad said, "Go on."

"Anyway, I can hear him if I listen and he's lonely for me."

John looked at me with a puzzled look, *he is?*

I answered his unspoken question, "Yeah and he doesn't like wherever he is."

Dad held up his hand. "Let's just say, hypothetically, that we were to agree to letting this dog become your pet. What would that mean for you?" he finished.

Okay, more chores, dogs have to have food and water, and they gotta make a mess in the yard (and guess who'd clean that up... oh joy).

Out loud I said, "Responsibility, I guess."

"And?" his expression unhelpfully neutral.

My mind went blank, I couldn't think of a thing.

"You're fourteen now Caleb. You have four years left until graduation and then the dog would have to become our pet."

"We're not sure we want that, Caleb," Mom said.

"Oh." I hadn't really thought about them. "Can you think about it at least?"

"I see that you're anxious son, but we can't make a snap decision."

"It's important to me, Dad."

Dad stood up and clapped me on the shoulder, squeezing it. He nodded once. He understood.

Mom came to stand behind him, her gaze steady on mine. They'd think about it.

John had to go and told me to read the rest of the papers.

"Yeah, okay." I'd been planning to anyway.

Dad sat down heavily in his usual seat for supper, steepled his hands, looking at me. I popped a large piece of lasagna into my mouth and did the tongue dance, realizing too late that it was hot-as-hell.

"I know you've been through a lot today Caleb," Dad began. Ah-duh.

"But, I am fascinated with how this connection with the dog unfolded." he waited expectantly.

Mom rescued me. "Why don't you let him finish eating and we can get the gory details afterward, hmm?"

Mom knew about The Hunger. In fact, I would use the phrase, I Hunger. Which loosely translated meant something like: what is there to eat in this house in the next five seconds? My friends also had The Hunger and we'd fall upon the kitchen table like locusts and The Hunger would be abated, temporarily.

"So Caleb, what's going on beside dead stuff?"

She turned, carefully setting a glass in front of Dad, hand on hip. She just missed putting her hand on one of the tiny bells of her skirt. I was fascinated by my mom's fashion sense. I don't truly think she had one, but she was a believer.

"Nothing much besides Carson and Brett still being jerks." I hesitated over the next thing; it was hard to keep this kind of news to yourself.

Mom sat next to me, skirt bells tinkling slightly as she adjusted her position.

I really had their attention because I wasn't just blurting stuff out like usual. I wasn't in Jonesy's league, but I wasn't super-quiet like John.

"I like this girl named Jade, Jade LeClerc." I said. Just saying her name made my heart beat faster.

"LeClerc," Dad tilted his head, thinking. Mom looked stumped too.

"Ya know, her dad is a mechanic for the car shop in the valley."

He did his best not to scowl when he realized who Jade's dad was.

Mom didn't bother to hide her expression. "Terrible news, that."

My body tensed, I wasn't going to let Jade get lumped in with her crap family.

"Wasn't she..." Mom began.

I finished for her, "... yeah, she was and it's not her fault."

"Removed from a domestic situation," Dad said, adding, "of course it wasn't."

A contemplative silence fell on the table. Sunlight streamed through the kitchen window, dust motes circling lazily in the air.

"I know the father, and he is not welcome but Jade is. After all, with a family like that..." Dad trailed off.

Mom finished for him, "... she could use some positive affirmation."

"Is she a cute girl?" Mom asked slyly.

I wasn't falling for that! "She's cute to me."

Mom mock-huffed and crossed her arms, "Caleb Sebastian Hart!" she said, teasing. I didn't know if talking about a girl I liked was easier.

Raising the dead, or girls... let me think.

Dad joined in, "Now we have to know what your lady-love looks like just in case we pass her on the street and rudely not give salutations," he winked.

"Lady-love, Dad? So retarded!"

"Caleb!" Mom said, mouth unhinged. A theme today.

"Sorry," I mumbled. But it *was* retarded, who said that? They couldn't help it, being old and all. Hard to believe that mom was Gramps' daughter.

"You have to be more sensitive with your language."

" 'Lady-love'?" eyebrows raised to my hairline.

"I guess that was a little out-of-date," Dad agreed.

"Ya think?"

"So tell us more about Jade," Mom said.

"Well, she is really interesting."

"That's not what I thought about your mother when I first saw her," he said with a smile aimed at mom.

Over share-much..."I mean, she is different than the other girls. She doesn't do that stuff girls do that's super-annoying."

Mom crossed her arms again. Uh-oh, I'd stepped in it.

"What do girls do that's so annoying?" she asked in that innocent tone (translation: I will eviscerate you).

I looked at Dad for help but he looked back, *clearly, you couldn't have just said that.*

I was on my own.

Girls make us nervous, they act like they like us then treat us crappy the next day. In a word, confusing.

What I said was, "She treats me the same all the time, not just when she's in the mood. She pays attention to what I'm saying, she actually listens."

A slow smile spread across dad's face while mom sat speechless at my words, a rare thing, "She sounds great. I like a woman that is self-possessed."

"And she's cute too, right?" Dad winked.

"Yeah," I said. "There is that," grinning back.

"Oh you two, annoying guys." Mom smiled.

Dad said, "Tomorrow we flesh out your abilities."

"What are you doing tonight?" Dad asked. Mom looked up from wiping down the kitchen table.

"Ah... John brought over some papers about the Parker kid."

"Don't you have a textbook from school that addresses these abilities?" He looked a question at Mom.

"Yes, he does. He must. First semester in eighth grade they're required to have one quarter health and one quarter paranormal development. They're linked you know," Mom stated.

Yeah, they were linked alright. That Health class had been the *dumbest* on the planet. I can never get their lame-ass music out of my head. It was some stupid thing like, "Body changes, everyone goes through... body changes."

No shit, Sherlock.

"Were you listening Caleb?" Mom asked.

I stared blankly at Dad.

"Hey pal, I asked if you still had the textbook here in the house from last semester?"

I looked at mom. "Try under your bed, that would be my first guess."

I turned back to Dad. "I don't know, I'll take a look."

"Okay, good. Now that these events are coming to pass, a refresher would be an excellent pursuit of your time. The sooner the better," he said with gravity.

I jogged over to the stairs taking them two at a time. Tearing open my door, I launched myself on my bed, scooping the papers up as I fell.

I bent my head over them and began to read.

CHAPTER 7

Chocolate-brown eyes stared through the mist, luminous, shining. I blinked and they were gone. My eyes flicked down at my feet that were bare, my boxers my only clothing. I looked at my surroundings and realized with dawning horror that I was in the cemetery again.

I glanced to where the eyes had been and the dog stepped forward, an inky silhouette in the midst of an ethereal fog. The mist was wet, swirling around my face, drenching my hair like fingers attached to my skull. With a start I realized that it was The Dog, from the accident.

He spoke, whispered, thought: *Rescue me.*

The eyes bored into mine with an eerie intensity, that connection I'd felt since the accident still tied.

Images flooded my head from the dog, like a movie running frame by frame:

A boy, close to my age, throwing the ball. The Dog's pure joy at the chase, the return, and the reward of the boy's laughing acknowledgment of him.

Then, a stranger that coaxes me/us with food and a terrible trip in a thing of metal that moves. Alarming smells wafting in through glass that is sometimes a hole, too many to identify. Terrible loneliness for The Boy.

Suddenly, an opportunity to escape the confines of the frightening and noisy box that moves. the Dog leaps out of the hole that is sometimes glass and runs until he finds a road, where he scents two boys. He knows they are close to his Boy in Life and he will find his Boy again. He pursues them.

His last memory is a metal machine hitting him and his life ebbing. Then one of the boys is there, calling to him. He struggles, deciding he wants to play ball again and be a dog for this boy. He Lives.

I snap out of the reverie of the dog's emotions, our glances lock, his eyes imploring, and I know, that somehow I am responsible for this life, this dog. The midnight-black tail wags like a friendly exclamation mark, moving the mist slightly. Wait, what was that horrible sound; beep, beep, beep, *BEEP!*

I opened one blurry eye, slamming my palm down on the alarm. All a dream! I flopped over on my back. Well, that was freaky. The dog was communicating with me while I slept.

I sighed, sitting up and swinging my feet around to slap the floor, the warmth of my bed like clinging fingers begging me to stay.

Ignoring that, I walked over to the window noticing the field shrouded in mist. Tall, Western Red Cedar and Douglas fir trees were scattered like soldiers in battle, leading down to Clark Lake.

I turned away, feeling uneasy from the dream and went for the bathroom. A shower would chase the lethargy away. I was definitely going to find clean clothes, thinking of Jade.

But my thoughts strayed back to the dog. He was a part of my life now, whether I wanted him to be or not.

After showering, great smells made their way upstairs; fried egg sandwiches. Yup, that was it.

I plopped down in my seat and Dad looked up from his reading. "How did that reading go last night?"

"Kinda scary."

Dad raised a brow.

"This Parker kid," I hesitated, "was a lot like me."

Mom's hand paused, then landed the egg on the buttered toast. She turned and gave me a look, *go on.*

Mom placed the glass plate in front of me with a perfectly centered, two-egg, cheese-laden breakfast. Steam rose from the eggs, the cheese melting at the edges. Ah... bliss.

I waded in without preamble. "He also 'heard' things from animals. He was off the charts on his aptitude for the AFTD."

Dad said, "We know that."

He seemed annoyed. That I didn't need. I just found out I had this ability and was trying to hide it. Get the dog, get the girl; no pressure!

Mom shot Dad a look. "What Dad means, is we'd like to hear anything that you felt could help you with this." She gave me an encouraging look. I relaxed.

I used my fork like a knife to shear off a corner of the egg sandwich and popped a satisfying hunk in my mouth. I chewed and watched The Parental Unit.

"Looks like he could see ghosts too." Dad shrugged his acknowledgment. That was a typical aspect of AFTD.

This is where I landed the bomb. "He could control them too,"

Dad stilled, his whole body stiff. Mom glanced at him and they had a look that passed, one of those annoying ones that said a lot but not to others.

"That's not good," Dad finally replied.

I knew why I thought it wasn't a potentially good thing for me to have but I wanted to hear Dad's thoughts.

Mom echoed my feelings with. "What are your thoughts, Kyle?"

"If he can control ghosts... hauntings, rather," looking at us in that quietly intense way of his, "then that is another useful tool. Dad continued in the well of silence, "Him being a Cadaver-Manipulator is certainly rare, but controlling hauntings?" he threw up his hands to emphasize just how big that "little" skill would be.

"I guess a little terror would go a long way," I said.

"Let me get this straight," Mom queried. "Caleb is what? A domestic terrorist now?" She looked incredulously at Dad.

"In a word... yes."

We were quiet, letting that potential future sink in. My egg began to cool. Well, nothing was going to get in the way of my appetite. I shifted my gaze to the clock, ten after eight. I stuffed down the remains of breakfast.

"Have you seen ghosts, Caleb?" Dad said breaking the silence.

"Nope." I said, using the last bit of bread to wipe up egg yolk.

Mom let out a sigh of relief. "I guess we don't have to worry about that."

I hated to burst her bubble but....

"That was the last skill he gained before the government took him."

"What year did your reading say that he was transferred to the 'government school'?" Dad made airquotes.

We weren't dumb enough to think the school was anything more than a farce so they could exploit kids.

I thought about that. The first year that they could push through their FDA approval for the drug that made us all "reach our genetic potential" was 2015, or 2016? Didn't matter, it was in those years that the first group of teens, nationwide, had been inoculated for a hell of a lot more than Hepatitis B. It had all been in those papers. The more I read, the scarier the connections became. It was starting to stink like conspiracy.

I said, "I think 2016...?"

Dad nodded. "Yes, that rings a bell."

Mom looked at the clock. "You better skedaddle there."

"I have a plan, we'll talk after school," Dad said.

I stopped my jog and turned slowly. "You're gonna be here, Dad?"

"Yes, I'm taking the day off." Since Dad never took a weekday off unless it he had the barf-o-ma-tic it must mean this was top priority.

"We'll experiment with your skills."

"Don't forget we need to talk about the dog," I reminded.

Forget jogging, I shifted right to sprinting until my lungs burned, singing their resistance. That's all I needed: possible detention. Carson was a regular feature in detention hall.

I burst through the main entrance, the bell shrilled behind me as the two-way door swung back and forth on its hinges, slapping empty air.

CHAPTER 8

I plopped down next to John, Jonesy was across from me with his head in his palm.

"What's your problem?"

He was absolutely *never* quiet.

"Can't wait for Sunday, I'm itching for payback."

John rolled his eyes.

"What is it today, Wednesday?" I asked.

John nodded.

"Well, get over that. Let's talk while we work on this." I looked down, studying my heart-shaped box. Mr. Morginstern sauntered up, hands thrust into his pockets.

"Good morning gentlemen," he said in his I-love-mornings voice.

We all said hi.

Morginstern studied my box and pointed out some rough spots, emphasizing that if those weren't perfectly smooth, they'd hang up the lid.

"You see this here." He pointed to an almost invisible bump on the interior arc. I squinted and there it was, huh. I nodded.

"That is the kind of thing that can make a project frustrating."

Geez, really? The whole project had been pretty hard. I wished now that I had chosen a square, like Jonesy, or a rectangle, like John. Mother's Day was coming up. Mom always said she didn't care but if I knew girls and I was getting the hang of that, she would say that but feel bad if I didn't.

It was a ruthless minefield.

Morginstern studied Jonesy's box and had a similar lecture for him but pronounced John's as ready for the lid. Jonesy and I both looked at each other in perfect understanding, John just got stuff.

Morginstern wandered off to bug the other kids and we put our heads together like a football huddle.

"I'm in deep crap. I read the Parker kid's stuff last night." Nodding in John's direction, "He had some things that I haven't done yet, but, if I play out like him, I will too. It's even more important that I not spike their radar on the tests this Monday."

"Did your dad get the cerebral inhibitor?" John asked.

I nodded. "Yeah, he's got it and he took the day off because he wants to go over The Plan."

Jonesy stuck out his jaw, leaning back. "What 'Plan'?"

I leaned forward, motioning to get closer. Jonesy's eyes were so brown the pupils were lost in the darkness, John tilting his head, worried.

"I don't know. The minute we talk I will pulse you and let you know."

"Kyle thought it was okay that we knew?" Jonesy stuck a thumb in his chest.

I laughed. "Yeah, you were there, there's no hiding any of it; the black outs, the fugues..."

"The cemetery," John stated the obvious.

That reminded me. "Have Carson and Brett said anything?"

We both looked at Jonesy, he talked to everyone.

"Not yet," rubbing his hands together with undisguised glee.

As John leaned forward, his frizzy hair covered an eye. "Don't take this too far. We don't want to hurt them."

"*Too* much," I said, winking at Jonesy.

John smacked my shoulder. "Don't give him any ammunition Caleb!"

Morginstern looked our way. "Get back to work boys."

We picked up our sand paper, Jonesy and I hitting the bumps with the eighty grit we thought we wouldn't have to use anymore.

John got up with a self-satisfied smile spreading over his face.

"I guess I'll go over and use the jig saw for my lid now," John smirked.

"Don't be an ass," Jonesy said.

"Yeah, what he said," I echoed.

John walked off, his fro of hair flopping as he moved between the tables.

CHAPTER 9

It was between bells and I was trying to glimpse Jade. Crap, I didn't see her by the locker. Bending down, I tore open the zipper on my backpack without any of my usual finesse and threw my crap in my locker. I wasn't hauling all that to Math.

I straightened up and there she was, close enough to touch. I gulped. She'd come to me.

"Hi," I croaked out. She flashed me a smile, the kind that reached her eyes. "Do you want to hang out at lunch?" my voice steady, yay for me.

She turned her head to the side and that long curtain of hair swung forward, hiding her expression. Then she looked back up at me through the veil of her black eyelashes bordering eyes that shone like emeralds.

God she was beautiful.

"I'd like that," she said. Those gorgeous eyes studied me. She wasn't a girl to fill silences with a lot of chatter, another great thing about her. I was making a list.

The other kids would notice us being together. That's all that kids talked about, how much school sucked and who was going out with whom. Maybe I could tell her about my problem. The Js were cool but you don't show your friends your fear. Girls were better that way.

As we turned away from each other it slid through my mind that it sucked, only having her in two classes.

Carson and Brett walked by then, wasting a glare on me. Brett made a pistol hand, taking a "shot" at me as I walked by. Dick. Carson threw his head back and laughed, delighted by his friend's cleverness.

Jonesy's hairspray idea was sounding sweeter by the second.

Math dragged by, I couldn't wait to see Jade. John saw me look at the clock and raised an eyebrow. *Later*, I looked back. He shrugged, his shoulder blades poking out like weapons and went back to studying, his hair a wall in front of his eyes. How he read anything was a mystery.

Math over, I raced to my locker to get my backpack, slapping my beanie on and took out my pulse. Depressing my thumb on the pad I selected music. Let me see, who to play? I chose the oldies shuffle: Seether, Hinder and Underwhelmed.

Thinking into my touch pad: *volume 15*. The screen illuminated in phosphorescent green the correct volume and I *thought: accurate.*

Music filled my ears and I hummed a little, sliding through the throng, my mind already with Jade. Jonesy slid beside me, narrowly missing a posse of girls, who giggled as he walked by. He took the time to salute them with a fingertip, winking, which caused another rush of laughter.

I don't know how he did it, but the girls were nuts over Jonesy. He called it his Undeniable Attraction. Whatever. He was cool, but I didn't see him as manly.

John came late from Science not even bothering to put his backpack away, heading straight for us and falling into step by me.

I ran my thumb over the touch pad and *thought: volume five...* then: *accurate.*

"Jade and I are hanging at lunch today guys."

Jonesy stopped dead in my path and I missed running into him by a hair's breadth.

"You're kidding. I mean, are you guys, like, going out?" John waited.

"*No*, but I don't want the first time that we can actually talk to be around you dorks."

Jonesy threw up his hands. "I know you're hot for her, but Bros before 'hos man, bros before 'hos."

He looked at John for agreement. John nodded then turned to me.

Jonesy... so classy.

"Come on guys! If you had a girl you liked, you'd want to be with her." I looked from one to the other, they had to see reason. Jonesy sulked. Kids swirled around us on a tide that moved like the ocean.

John said, "See where it goes today, but don't let a girl interfere with important stuff." He looked at me in his steady way, his eyes tight and angry. I wasn't going to let my friends' lack of excitement screw my lunch with Jade.

"Okay," I said.

Jonesy looked around once. *Traitor,* that look said.

There was nothing but a sea of faces and talking. My Pulse was on the lowest volume. Soothing, retro music wafted through the ear discs that were permanently embedded behind my ears, where the skull is most prominent. Technology rocked.

There she was! A small hand rose, a lone flag of welcome in the cafeteria.

I didn't hear the music as I walked toward her, instead I saw the soft triangle of her face, full, deep pink lips, silver hoops catching the light as she laughed with Sophie. Huh... Sophie. I ditched the Js only to have to share time with her?

Sophie looked up at me, her clear, blue-green eyes full of laughter, turning to Jade she said, "Catch ya later." She jumped up and away, hurrying to another table.

I sat down awkwardly next to Jade. She turned to me, small hands neatly on the table. Then she did the unexpected, reaching one of those small hands to cover mine. Instinctively, I closed my hand around hers, grinning like an idiot. Every struggle had been worth it to be in this moment with her.

"So," she said, still hanging on to my hand, "what did you want to talk about?"

I looked down at our clasped hands and my mouth got dry. Okay, Hart, you got this. She obviously likes you, so start with that.

"Well, I know we don't know each other very well but, do you want to go out?" I stumbled over that last part, simultaneously hoping my hands didn't choose then to sweat.

She smiled, a little shyly and answered, "I thought you'd never ask."

No one in the history of the universe could have possibly been happier.

"Let's go somewhere and talk," I said.

"Okay," she stood up and stuffed her pulse in her pocket. We made our way into the open hallway. I didn't want to let go of her hand, ever.

She leaned against the wall and I took her other hand and looked down at her. There were *some* girls that were actually shorter than me.

"I'm so glad you finally asked me," she said.

It's not like she hit me over the head with clues or anything.

Jade grinned at my expression. "You're the guy, you have to ask."

"That's not true, you could have given me a hint," I said, miffed, but not really.

She smiled and lifted my hand up with hers, tilting her head and laying the top of my hand against her cheek. My heart paused in my chest. Her skin felt like silk under my hand. Letting go of her hand I cupped the side of her face, noticing how small it really was. I leaned down and whispered in her ear, "Meet me after band today."

She turned her head into mine, smelling like a ripe peach and whispered, "Okay."

My stomach rumbled and I laughed. "I guess we better eat,"

I looked at her lunch tray, girls sure ate weird.

She saw my expression. "What?" All innocent like.

I shrugged. "No wonder you're so small, you don't eat anything real."

She looked down at her tray and pointed a finger at the biggest offender, the salad. "This is real."

I made a grunting noise and she pursed her lips. She gave my tray the look she thought it deserved. Pizza was definitely the food of the gods, I thought with satisfaction.

The Js were at our regular lunch table and just finishing their pizza. Smart food choice.

Jade followed me over to our table and we plunked down.

Jonesy looked up and with a lingering glance at Jade's tray. "Are you kidding with that?" he pointed his fork at her tray with Jonesy-disdain leaking from every pore.

Jade put her hands on her hips and said, "You boys need to clean up your eating habits."

John looked down at his three crusts, fourth piece in hand and shrugged his skinny shoulders, taking a bite that polished off half the slice. Jonesy laughed and used his crust to wipe up the last vestiges of his ranch dressing.

Jade stared with fascination at Jonesy's ritual. His pears and green beans lay lonely and untouched in a forgotten corner of his tray. This was an introduction to Eating Habits of Boys. Jonesy mowed through his dessert cup of sherbet while expertly eying whatever food John had been dumb enough not to finish.

I didn't have my normal appetite. After all, it wasn't every day that you got yourself a girlfriend.

Jonesy was licking the spoon that was shaped like a small paddle when he blurted out, "So you two going out now?"

John sorta choked on that last hunk of pizza, some of it escaping his mouth.

Jade stopped the fork midway to her mouth, fruit balanced on the tines.

I answered, "Yeah Jonesy, we are." My tone said it all. Could you just... not.

Jonesy smiled evilly. I knew he was sticking it to me because I had ditched them at lunch. Fine, payback's a bitch and Gramps would add: and then you die.

"Sorry about your lunch," I mumbled.

"It's okay." she curled her small hand around my forearm, where a tiny pulse beat, captured in the delicate skin of her wrist. She fascinated me.

I recovered, "Tomorrow we'll actually eat and talk." The Js stood and we followed. Carson and Brett sauntered over, Brett eying Jade.

I didn't like it.

"Hi Jade," Brett said, nodding to the Js and me. Carson didn't bother.

"Hi," she said, sensing major awkwardness.

"Hey Hart, gonna see ya at the cemetery on Sunday," Carson said, looking hard at Jonesy but talking to me.

Jonesy stepped forward and Jade stepped a little behind me, Jonesy and I were side by side.

Jonesy said, "We'll all be there, I told ya."

Brett looked at Jade. "Even your little girlfriend is coming?" And before anyone knew what was happening he reached out, his hand passing through the end of her hair.

"Don't touch me!" she yelped, startled. Some other kids turned to stare and she backed away.

"Leave her alone, dickhead," I said, facing Brett, my hands balled into tight fists. I was ready for a hammer session.

Brett moved up until our noses almost touched, our chests a millimeter from contact. Singing tension filled the moment.

"Caleb, we have eyes," John said in a low voice.

I didn't take mine off Brett.

Carson stopped things from getting out-of-control. "Leave it, he can't do anything and the girl's not worth it," he sneered.

We stood back and the tension dissipated. Carson pulled Brett along with him, who kept walking backwards, looking at me the whole time. A moment before he vacated the double doors his gaze shifted to the left and became thoughtful. I followed his gaze to see what he was looking at and Jade filled my vision. Her anxious face was pinched and nervous. Rage filled me that someone would threaten her. I put my arm around her and scooped her up against me while my other hand stroked her hair. She shivered under my touch while I looked over at the Js, their grim expressions matching mine.

Jonesy broke the silence first, "Sunday can't come soon enough."

He and John walked off, Jade and I in tow, my arm still around her shoulders, where it felt like it had always belonged.

CHAPTER 10

John was listening raptly to Xavier Collins, aka, Biology teacher extraordinaire. He ran around the room, boiling with energy, making his point. Unfortunately, I had worn out my welcome when we had dissected the frogs and I kept passing out and getting hauled off to the nurse's office.

Collins was jogging back and forth in front of the board, smacking his fist into his open palm, doing a rant about the bees. That again, I thought a little glumly. Between Dad, big time scientist in his pants and Mom, environmental activist. I knew what was wrong. I put my head in both my palms. John nodded with marked enthusiasm at what Collins was saying.

"This alarming trend of the decimation of honeybees is appalling. The origins of which precedes 2010. It was in that year that nearly one million honeybee colonies were wiped out," Collins said.

Having a swarm of anything die would be a fresh hell for me.

"Caleb Hart," Collins paused, "what say you on this subject?"

Oh great. Like this day couldn't get any more stressed. "Ah... what do you want me to say?"

"What are your thoughts on the continual decline of this critical species which impacts our habitat at every turn?"

"Well, my mom had me help her plant flowers in the garden that attract bees," I said.

Carson covered a laugh by coughing. He was such a jerk. I blushed. It was lame that I admitted helping Mom. But, my choices were cleaning the bathroom or gardening. Gee, let me think about it.

Collins turned sharply to Carson. "Do you have something to add, Mr. Hamilton?" his gaze steady on Carson's face.

Carson squirmed under the scrutiny.

"No," Carson finally said.

"Good, very good," he said and turned his attention back to me.

"Well, go on then, Caleb."

"That's it. I mean, I hear my parents talk about the environment a lot." My voice conveyed how obvious that would be in my household.

Collins was trapping me. I wasn't his favorite so why question me? I looked over at John, he was as confused as I.

"What plants did she select?" Collins asked.

Wow, easy question. "We plant flowers in blue and violet, mainly. But my mom has rhododendrons in a bunch of different colors. She says it's important to plant different types and try to use native plants."

A speech for me. I actually knew something about this because of my role as The Gardening Slave.

"Very good, Caleb. Caleb's family is doing exactly what we all need to be doing. This 'pocket gardening' technique emphasizes that if all of us were doing our small part to propagate the environment, that cumulative effort would have tremendous impact. These insects need all of us to resurrect their dying numbers."

Suddenly, Collins spun around and pointed a finger at me. "What's your favorite plant for bee attraction, Caleb?"

"Sunflower," I flung back.

Collins smiled and jogged back to the whiteboard. John gave me the thumbs up and Carson gave me the finger. I turned back to the teacher with a smile on my face. Some days were okay.

During English and PE I was distracted by Jade. Jade using her pulse-pad, Jade doing jumping jacks to the tune of Ms. Griswold's sandpaper voice.

I couldn't believe the school gave us credit for playing music and in between sets we discussed Jade. It was easier without Jonesy around, who was sorta anti-girlfriends right now.

"Are you gonna tell her?" John asked during Band.

"Don't really have a choice. Carson and Brett said something in front of her."

"Yeah, what was with Brett doing that to Jade?" he asked.

"I don't know but it pissed me off."

"Maybe he likes her. You know, *likes* her," John said.

Brett was always a little mean to her. I guess a guy as lame as Brett can't think of a better way to act so they just fall back on what they know... lameness.

"He lives kinda by her, ya know."

Yeah, I knew that.

But now that she lived with her aunt was he still close? I asked John. He thought she still lived pretty close to her old house.

"Is her aunt like her dad?" my voice trailed off. John looked thoughtful.

"You know her dad's a big-time drunk, right?" I nodded, everyone knew. "Well, I don't hear the same stuff about her. It was some kind of protective custody thing," he said

I knew some of the history. She was getting beaten (my heart sped with adrenaline). I heard the aunt had called Child Protective Services and they still kept tabs on her. Her creeper dad would be a problem.

"Yeah, she's never said anything about her dad to me," I said.

John gave me a look. "Before today, did you talk to her much?"

He had me there. "No, I was kinda freaked."

"She's just a girl, Caleb." his blue eyes were serious, sunlight glinting through the window made his hair into a flaming halo.

Just a girl.

"Coming from you that means a lot, Terran! With your harem-o-chicks!" John blushed a fine, blazing red that only true redheads can. I was just the first guy in the group to have a girlfriend and it was new, to all of us. It's not like we were big "players."

"I plan to get to 'know her' a little better after band..." the sentence trailing off suggestively.

"Huh? You're gonna take her home to meet the Parents?" he smirked.

"We're not *that* serious!" I exclaimed.

"Not yet." John looked down and strummed a chord, making my teeth vibrate this close to the amp. It being Thursday, we had lost our beginning of the week warm up problems. Tomorrow would see us playing really well.

As we headed for the door, John and I hung our guitars on their respective wood pegs. The sun blazed light through the huge windows, dust motes swirling lazily in the air, suspended in an invisible web.

Stepping outside my eyes locked on Jade.

I took in the sight of her like a cool drink: shining black hair, tight pink cami, covered by a soft, chocolate-colored T-shirt, jeans so blue they were almost black and little strappy sandals. I loved a girl that dressed like one. She smiled when she saw me and it was all I could do to not pick her up and spin her around. Must keep feelings in check!

John cleared his throat, we turned and I waved at him in a, *you caught me* way. We started walking toward my house. John gave me the thumb sign for me to use my pulse later, I nodded and kept walking. Finally, a chance to talk,.. but not my house, not yet. I wasn't ready for the whole meet-the-parents thing. I was a little shaky on having told them about Jade anyway, with all the other stuff that was closing in on my life like a noose.

****

Dappled sunlight struggled through the canopy of trees in the small park that stood at the opening of my neighborhood. Little more than a drainage area when the development was first built in the 1970s, it has become over time, a small oasis with structures all around, except for the back, where the city park borders it, separated by an ugly, cyclone fence. Huge indigenous evergreens tower in the park, broken here and there by a lone Alder tree. These too, cast pools of shade in the late afternoon light. Jade and I sat on a well worn bench which stood just inside the entrance to the woods, little more than a dirt path where a patch of sun slanted across her forehead.

Our hands were still entwined when she asked, "What's going on Sunday, Caleb?"

"Maybe you should pulse your aunt and let her know when you'll be home?"

Jade pulled out her (slathered in iridescent lavender hearts) pulse. "Good idea," she said, sliding it back in her pocket and leaning back against me.

"What did ya say?" I asked.

"I told her I was hanging out with a friend."

It occurred to me that maybe not all kids would just blurt out their romantic processes to their parents. I couldn't imagine Jonesy doing it and not at all John. Huh.

"Did you tell her about us?" I asked.

"Well, I didn't tell her a name. I just said I liked a boy at school."

"What's your aunt's name?"

"Oh...Andrea," she responded absently, as if her mind was already a million miles away.

I whipped my pulse out of my pocket (it was all-black because it's cool like that), and pulsed Mom:

*Mom, it's me-*CH
Hey honey, whatcha doin'? AH
*I'm here in the woods with Jade-*CH
You are, are ya? **laughs***-*AH
We're talking; when's supper? CH
*Usual time-*AH
*Okay, I'll be on time-*CH
*Jade is welcome anytime, Caleb-*AH
*Gotcha, see ya-*CH
*Love you-*AH

I passed my thumb over the pad and the luminescent characters faded to black. I looked up.

"Your mom." A statement.

I nodded. "She says you're welcome to come over anytime."

Jade looked down, her long hair falling like ink spilling.

She twisted in my embrace to look at me. "You told your parents about me?"

I put my hand up, palm open. "Yeah, I mean, it's not different than you telling your aunt Andrea, that you like a boy. But," I looked directly at her this time, "I gave them your name."

Jade squirmed, wringing her hands.

"What?"

"Do they know about..." she trailed off a little, then resumed, "my dad and our family and all?"

"Yeah, I didn't tell them but they already knew."

We sat in silence for a few moments, not awkward but like people that fit together like puzzle pieces.

"I love my aunt," she said suddenly.

What could I do to make this better?

I knew. "My parents don't care and neither do I."

"Really?" she asked shyly, her hands unclasping.

"Really."

A huge grin appeared like sunlight breaking through storm clouds. I grinned back. The moment held, grew and became a perfect memory.

She did a little shiver as I gave her a side hug. I was diggin' on that response.

"Sunday," she said.

Oh yeah, *that.* Mood-killer.

"Okay so, the APs are coming up on Monday?" She looked at me like, yeah... duh.

"Well, I found out that I have AFTD."

I expected shock, surprise or something. But Jade just looked back at me calmly.

"I already knew."

What the hell? "How?"

What she said next took my breath away: "Because I'm an Empath."

It was like the biggest puzzle piece falling into place! I understood her behavior! She already knew about my "problem" because she had one of her own!

I became instantly self-conscious. She knew stuff about me that maybe I hadn't wanted her to know, like how much I liked her. Couldn't a guy have a few secrets?

She sensed my tension. "This is why I haven't said anything."

I tried to relax.

"You haven't told anyone but me?" I asked.

"And Sophie. I was thinking about telling Andrea but she may tell my dad."

I was surprised. "Why would she do that?"

"I don't know. She knows he's crappy, has been crappy, but she thinks he has a right to know important stuff. She'd think this was."

"Well, she's gonna find out after Monday."

She nodded, she knew.

"My dad's got a cerebral inhibitor that I'm gonna take so I won't hit the radar as a corpse raiser."

"Caleb, they're gonna know that you're AFTD."

"I know, but I can be a lesser AFTD and I won't be that important. Ya know, a two-point or something."

"How do you know you can raise dead things?" she asked.

I explained the cemetery, then the dog. Jade showed a lot of sympathy for the dog. Just thinking about him was bringing his "emotions" like a flood to me.

"Where is he now?"

"I don't know for sure but the impressions..."

She cut me off. "Impressions?" Jade asked with a raised eyebrow.

"Yeah, if I think about him, he's like, *there* with me." I tried to clarify.

"Like when I touch people..." she mused.

"I don't know if it's like what you have, but all I know is that I *thought* he needed to live, then he did." It was hard to make somebody understand when they couldn't do it, "...and afterward I could sense his emotions."

Do dogs really feel? Well yeah. Frogs do, I shuddered, remembering pre-Biology.

"So, what do you know about people?" I asked.

"Ah-uh, you're not getting off that fast!" She laughed. "No off-topic, tell me about Sunday."

"Well... Jonesy thought we needed to teach Carson and Brett a lesson."

Jade's brow furrowed into two, neat lines, kinda like a number eleven.

I rushed forward, "He thought it may divert them enough during the Aptitude Tests that they wouldn't be paying attention to me or think to let a teacher in on what I can really do."

Jade's face knitted together in concentration, her head tilting. Finally, she said, "I think it will work for that but later, they're going to retaliate."

Huh, I knew what that meant: they're gonna open a can of whoop-ass all over you.

"I guess that's a chance we'll have to take."

Jade rolled her eyes.

"Boys," she said.

As if that explained all reason in the world.

"Listen, you remember what I told you about the cemetery?" I threw out a little impatiently.

She nodded.

"Well, they won't respect me until I dominate them. They're just that type. You see that, don't ya?"

"Yeah, I guess so. Brett lives by me. He has always been," she looked up, "difficult."

I looked at her dumbfounded. She couldn't be sympathetic to that loser?

She whispered, "His dad's worse than mine." She looked away and I didn't really know what to say.

The silence rolled out and I let it. Guys are good at that. Girls, and Jonesy, who was sometimes classified as something entirely new... a sub-species maybe, seem to want to fill silences with talking. Guys didn't feel that obligation.

"When we were little and met at the bus stop, his dad would sometimes meet him in the afternoon and right there, in front of all the kids, he'd be shit-faced drunk. Of course, he'd wait until the driver pulled away before he started hitting on Brett." She looked down, her hands tightly clenched together, twisting, "... then he would drag him off to the car. The next day at the bus stop Brett would be all beat up."

Jade looked up, standing tears shimmering, her eyes very wide so they wouldn't fall. "He had it worse than me. At least dad didn't yell and beat me in front of people."

I gulped, hell, this was horrible. And she thought that was better?

My life, even with the stupid AFTD was better than a lot of people. I didn't want to feel bad for Brett. He was such a raging dickhead. But, I could see the why of his behavior. Carson was still a mystery though, he had everything going for him. It came down to choice. And Jade had a similar background to Brett and she wasn't acting like a jerk.

Jade seemed to understand my thought process and answered almost as if I had spoken out loud (duh... empath), "His mom is the same and never did anything to stop it. At least my mom is dead. I just had the one parent. When things became really bad," she shuddered, "I would escape to Andrea's."

"Okay, so you like, feel sorry for Brett?" I was trying to put what she said into a box, for later reflection.

"Kinda. I hate that he's mean to me. But, at the bus stop, the other kids didn't know what to do to help him. His dad was über-scary and their families were normal," she smiled and corrected herself, "more normal." She went on, "I knew what it felt like, how embarrassing it was to have a parent that out-of-control, the feeling of slippage. Like you're hangin' on to the edge of the cliff and some maniac has a hold of the rope and you have to hang on and hope they don't let go." A defeated little sigh escaped her before she continued, "I just wanted him to know that I was hangin' on to his rope too. That the maniac wasn't the only one that had a hold of it. So, we were friends. Then, for some reason, last year when we started going here," she gestured back in the direction of Kent Middle School behind us, "he started acting like he didn't know me." She shrugged. "I just sorta gave up. He and Carson became friends and that was the end of that."

Interesting.

We sat for a moment, chewing on what she had told me.

"I want you to come on Sunday," I said.

"I don't know, what if Carson and Brett get really mad and something bad happens? I don't like Brett getting it. It feels wrong. If it backfires, they'll be more determined to make sure the right adults find out what you can do."

"Speaking of that, tell me how you knew?"

She was wringing her hands a little then I covered one with my own.

"Just now, when you touched me I just got a really strong... impression," she paused struggling for clarity, "of concern and... love." She looked quickly to see if I was offended by the "L" word. I couldn't say I loved her yet but I cared. Maybe there wasn't as much of a difference between the two?

"Anyone can guesstimate, but I *know*. People can't lie to me. I know who likes me and who doesn't. And that's not so great, believe me. But what can I do? It is what it is," she said.

I felt the same way about what I did, it is what it is.

"That doesn't explain how you know that I'm AFTD."

"Well, each person has a 'flavor,' like ice cream," she perked up at the analogy, "... so there are paranormal flavors and I started to recognize the differences. Sometimes before they even know what they're going to have. Mostly, I just try to not touch anyone, I really don't want to know."

"Who else is AFTD?" I was stunned, I thought I was the only one, I don't know why, it could happen to anyone.

"That girl in PE."

Well that cleared it right up, thanks.

"Tiffany Weller." Jade's voice modulation rose, indicating, *do you know her?*

I thought about the name and then the face came to me. Kinda plain girl, could be an enraged cow.

I nodded.

She went on, "About a month ago, she was sitting outside the school, crying. I don't know her. Anyway, I asked her what was wrong and she pointed to a dead bird just a few feet away."

I knew what she'd say next.

"She's got snot and tears leaking all over her face and she says something, but I can't hear because she's talking so soft. So I lean in real close and she says, 'it whispers,'. 'What whispers?' I asked her.

" 'Death,' she said, *'death whispers'.*"

"It was so fundamentally creepy that I sorta backed away real quick, but I lost my footing and my palm touched her back." Jade looked far away then.

I didn't push her for more.

The sun was starting to get low in the sky, a hot crimson ball on fire, balanced between the sky and the horizon. Seconds ticked by.

"I felt it all then. There was this echo," she paused here, "I could feel Tiffany's feelings of sadness and loss, but I could also feel, real faintly, the bird's images too." She shuddered then stared at me. "You're the same Caleb. But, it is so much more... you're so much more." She kept looking at me, frightened and finished, "... it's like static noise, there are so many voices."

The orb began to drown in the horizon, painting the sky blood red. The wash of color expanded like arms of light, reaching out for an embrace. I looked down at Jade and understood that she was horrified by what she could feel was going on with me, with everyone. It was always something I had to keep the iron fist of control over. Otherwise, it was simple misery.

The dead spoke, they spoke to me all the time.

CHAPTER 11

Mom pounced on me the minute I walked through the door. I hucked my backpack on the chair and she gave me the mom-glare. I sighed, trudging back out to the foyer and hung it up on a slick brass hook. Coming back in the house I followed my nose right into the kitchen, my stomach giving an appreciative rumble.

Mom spoke the dreaded sentence, "You have to eat supper first."

That sentence never failed to put me in a crappy mood. Mom had to know that I could probably eat the whole wonderful loaf of banana bread and still eat. I glanced over to the cook top where the last of the chicken was frying up. Three pieces of her chicken, plus mashed potatoes and I'd still have room for a dessert. I scanned the kitchen counter hopefully but knew that banana bread meant no dessert tonight.

Mom had been looking at me in a most critical way for the last minute.

"What?" I said.

"Your eyeballs are taller."

This was a long standing comment. In our house, with me being the shortest guy in the history of the world, Mom liked to notice me growing by saying my eyeballs were "taller" than whatever random day she had noticed before. Whatever, I decided to play along. After all, I was riding the happy wave of having been in the Presence of Jade.

"Huh."

"Yes, let's go measure you."

"Mom, don't you have some potatoes to mash or something?"

She gave me another death glare. The third one meant business so I stalked over to the bathroom door. There, on the casing that surrounded the door, were a lot of horizontal pencil marks cataloging my growth. A very small amount of growth.

I stood ramrod straight, kinda like I did in the locker room when we were all in there together, eesh... never pick up the soap. I put my heels against the molding, holding my shoulders up straight and back. Mom put a ruler on my head and made the new mark. A low whistle escaped her mouth and I turned around, the ruler lashing my cheek.

There, unbelievably, was a whole bunch more space since the last mark only three months ago. I hadn't noticed at all. Mom was measuring the distance with a tape measure.

"Two inches, Caleb. I knew it." Mom pumped her fist, which seemed eerily like Jonesy.

I looked at her like the screwball she was.

"So, how tall does that make me?" I leaned in to see the micro-writing; five-six now? Yeah, five-six.

Wow, five-six.

I turned my head, facing Mom. She looked down at me, but Not. By. Much. We grinned at each other until our faces hurt.

Dad walked in and Mom went back to the frying pan, turning the chicken. I knew the routine, it'd be in the oven in about five minutes.

"What's going on here?" Dad asked, looking at the two of us.

"Oh nothing much," Mom flung over her shoulder, then continued slyly, "but Caleb is two inches taller."

"Really?" Dad drawled. "Now you remember that statistically..."

I gave Dad the hand, "Okay, but you understand it's just a matter of time before you're all grown up." he said for the millionth time.

We smiled at each other as he put down his pulse-top carrier. It was super-slim, held all the biggies, his pulse, and that was a multi-pulse, which included his planner and all the scientific data he needed for his job. Dad extracted a small, deep orange bottle with a name label on it.

The cerebral inhibitor.

Dad gave the bottle a little shake, its cargo rattling. Mom slid the glass pan of chicken into the oven. I sat down at the kitchen table, its surface sunset-colored, from the setting sun.

Dad loosened his tie and silently passed the bottle to me. Which read, in part: Take one tablet in the morning after food, take with one full glass of water, take as prescribed.

I turned it over to the side which had all that scary crap that can happen after you take it. It said: may cause disorientation. I glanced at Dad and lifted an eyebrow, he looked steadily back at me with his chin in his hand. I read on: slurred speech, listless responsiveness and possible dizziness.

"Dad, I won't be able to do well on the AP tests. I'm gonna be a moron."

Mom gave me the glare, *again*. She hated the use of "bigotry" names. She thinks the retards (I self-corrected), differently-abled, need to *not* be identified in a negative way. Overweight people and anyone that were looked down on all fell under Mom's treat equally category.

Which meant everyone in the world.

Dad took a quick, peripheral glance at Mom and rushed on while she grunted her annoyance in the background.

"No, I can give you a half dose, Caleb."

Dad opened his fingers, flexing them back and forth to indicate he wanted it back. I passed the bottle back, its shadow a dark blot over the fading orange light of the table.

Dad studied it as mom sat down on her throne.

Mom was never one to let silences drag on. "Kyle, you're sure that this stuff won't," she paused for a second, "permanently harm him?"

Dad rolled his eyes and Mom scowled.

"No. Even buying us some time to figure this thing out would not be sufficient reason for taking chances with Caleb."

Mom seemed to decide something. "Good."

"So, let's talk about the dog." I said into the sudden quiet.

Mom and Dad looked at each other significantly.

Mom began, "We've thought about it and decided that after this whole mess is over," her smile said the mess wasn't my fault, "we will try to transition the dog into our family."

A large breath of air escaped that I hadn't realized I was holding.

Dad watched my obvious relief.

"Your mom has taken the time to call Sergeant Garcia and find out where the dog is being held and gone to see him."

Wow, I was really surprised by this. There had always been a no pets rule in the house. I looked at Mom and she smiled; she was a little smug about it all.

"Mom, you didn't tell me."

"I know, but there's been a lot going on, with Jade, Carson, Brett and now the testing. It just seemed you didn't need another thing to worry about. And your unusual," she looked up for a moment, thinking about the word, "*connection*, with the dog seemed a touchstone of comfort for you."

Dad was nodding at her phrasing, they'd discussed it.

"Where is he?" I sat up straighter, my butt bones kinda squawking.

"He's at the King County Animal Sanctuary," she said.

I slumped in my seat. Good. They had a non-euthanize policy. I allowed just the smallest amount of the iron-fist-of-control to loosen and a wash of confused emotions filtered through.

Wow. The dog's emotions/impressions were all over the place. Thirst (I thought that was odd), and above all, he knew on some level, I was in his head and that gave him a sense of peace. He also had some memory of another Boy, but it was faded, like a shirt washed many times. I closed up the small link that had allowed the brief connection. I felt fatigued. I didn't know if I was tired from the effort of *not* releasing all that pressing, eager energy that was always there, or if just allowing a small amount had taken more control than I had.

My parents were both leaning in with identical expressions of concern on their faces.

I smiled, releasing a big breath. "I'm okay."

They both leaned back in their respective seats.

Dad asked, "What was that?"

"What?"

"That whole... fugue," Dad said.

"Oh, is that what it seemed like?"

"Yes, you didn't respond when I snapped my fingers right in front of your face," Mom said.

Well, that was weird. I had been aware of my parents, but then I thought about it, really thought about it and although I had been *aware* of their presence, I had been utterly engaged with the dog.

"I can feel the dog if I," and like earlier with Jade I hated trying to explain psychic stuff to someone that wasn't, "let some of it go, just a little."

"And Caleb, that's it, that is exactly what I wish to explore," Dad said.

I thought he'd say something like that.

"I know you guys want to know how I do it. But there is really no way to explain it. I mean, the first few times it was a complete accident. It just happened. Now, I'm trying to control it, at least all the whispering and voices." Another speech for me, it was trend.

"Did you read anything about the Parker kid? Did he have these same manifestations?"

"Same," I repeated.

Dad rubbed his chin.

Mom said, "I want to peruse those papers that John brought over so we're on the same page, no pun intended," she laughed. "Your father has already done some independent research, uncovering some possibilities. But people are so unpredictably unique that there's always new abilities with each individual. We're wondering what will be in store for you."

"Well, Dad and I have discussed the possibilities." Dad and I exchanged a look.

Mom's eyebrows shot up. "So what's the consensus fellas?"

"We think, from the Parker kid's testimonial, that Caleb may be able to control hauntings as his skill set becomes more advanced."

"Hauntings?" Mom asked, rhetorically.

"Yeah, Mom, ya know... ghosts."

She gave me a look like, *duh*.

The timer beeped and Mom stood up to retrieve the chicken from the oven. She began dumping cream onto the potatoes along with a generous half cube of butter, rounding out a murderously cholesterol rich meal. She set the corn in the microwave where it spun in a lazy circle, steaming it to perfection. The minutes ticked by and Dad and I discussed Jade while Mom beat the taters into submission until they were smooth, white mountain peaks.

I told Dad Jade felt uncomfortable with them knowing her family situation.

"She is a separate person and will be treated as such. No one chooses who they are born to."

I nodded, I got it. Being an Empath, I couldn't say that was a huge improvement. If anything it made her situation more complicated.

The microwave timer beeped. Mom put an oven mitt on, scooping the dish out and transferring it to the table. She flicked a pat of butter inside, mixing it in through the cut corn. Dad and I watched.

Mount Rainier sat before him on the plate. Mom laughed. "Too much?" she asked with a grin.

"I think... yes," Dad said with a smile of his own.

I heaped my plate full of mashed potatoes, then put some corn on top and mixed the whole mess up with my spoon. Next came two pieces of the best fried chicken in the world. No gross skin to give it that squishy feeling in my mouth. Mom watched the whole event with that look on her face she had every time I ate.

"What?" my parents asked at the same time. Jinx, I thought.

"Just thinking about the justice that the Js could do to this meal, Mom."

"Hmp! That's an understatement," she grunted.

Mom knew what the Js could do to a meal.

We cleared our dishes and I got the Homework Question, a ritual I could do without.

I jogged over to the stairs to ascend into what the Js called the "bat cave." My room was nothing more than a hole under the eaves of the half story of our house. It was dark and had a separate place where the Js and I could game and hang.

I jerked the door open, making that pleasant sucking air sound and flung myself on my bed, whipping it shut as I was in the air. I flopped over on my back and read some more from where I left off about Parker:

...we were unaware, of the ramifications of this particular ability. Parker's abilities were the first true, full-scale five-point AFTD abilities we've seen since the inception of the inoculations in 2015 and even into the present day. Now, we have seen many AFTD children manifest one of the five commonly known characteristics or "points" for this category.

"Dr. Daniels, please explain to this readership exactly what Affinity for the Dead means? I have to assume, that like myself, there are many people out there that assume teens which manifest this ability are mainly able to communicate with the dead. But, if what you're saying is true, there may be quite a bit more to it than just communication."

"You're right, Tim. The five, main sub-categories for AFTD are as follows: Cadaver-manipulation, Hauntings, Medium/communication, Cadaver-control, Murder/traumatic victim location, and Death Impressions. Now the first and third

abilities are obviously linked, with the last being the most common manifestation of this ability. The Parker child manifested all five categories. I cannot overemphasize the rarity of all five points of a little understood ability such as this being a part of one person's skill set. We didn't realize just how rare that was until ten years later; there has not been another case that encompassed all five."

"Beside having all five categories, is there anything else that makes Parker special?" Anderson asked.

Laughs *"Yes, Parker is an extraordinarily rare case. Most importantly, since his assimilation into our military, we have not been able to study his abilities further, which is a national tragedy. I **am** at liberty to say that. He works in a capacity that has not been explained and is under a top secret umbrella that even the scientific community cannot breach."*

"Why can't we all *know what Parker is up to? Don't we have a right to know?" Anderson queried.*

"I am not at liberty to answer that. However, I can say that if there were another 'Parker', his or her outlook would not be broad. He or she would almost certainly, in theory, be a very interesting commodity for certain groups."

"Which groups?" Anderson asked.

"Any group in which raising cadavers was politically advantageous."

I put the papers down on my chest and rubbed my eyes. I felt the full flesh crawl march up my body and settle uncomfortably at the base of my neck, where the short hairs like to stand on end. Mom called that "getting the creeps."

Yeah... those.

I was afraid of this. My parents were afraid of this. Dad putting me on meds, going against the rule-follower I knew him to be, scared the crap out of me. Making a fist with my hand under my chin I rolled over on my stomach. I thought about Jade and the dog. Sighing, I got up, swinging my legs onto the floor. I stood up and walked over to my pulse-top. Plunking down on my chair, I pressed my thumb onto the pad.

Hello, Caleb Hart... accessing...
I *thought*: *subject; murder, AFTD-related.*

The display lit up with news and one article struck as soon as I saw it; although it was older:

Twenty-year old AFTD Policewoman Bobbi Gale "Discovers" Murder Victim Leading to the Arrest of Pierce Dickson

by Tim Anderson

Boy, that Anderson guy gets around, I thought. I read on:

Another police deterrent slash victory in what can only be classified as a paranormal ability, which is labeled as the most misunderstood of all, is now taking a foothold as post-inoculation children come-of-age and enter the workforce in occupations that showcase these unique skills. In this instance, Ms. Gale, after testing as a two-point in the AFTD category (in the nationwide Aptitude Tests given eighth graders), excelled in the subsequent, specialized school she attended and upon graduation was given a coveted role in the police department of her choice.

This trend of using people in important capacities such as law-enforcement cannot be a bad one. Considering that paranormal ability is not just given to people driven to do the right thing. There are criminals out there, as Ms. Gale, when asked to speak for this article, is quoted as saying, '...Are now our most powerful criminals, using all their talents for evil...'"

Wow...I hadn't considered what it would be like if, say, a *Carson* showed up with paranormal skills. I shuddered thinking about the trouble that dickhead could make. Of course, it was possible. I threw that errant thought aside and bent to do more reading.

Ms. Gale was quoted as saying, when asked how she was able to find these criminals, she responded with, "It's a difficult ability to quantify."

No kidding, I thought, *duh.*
   "But, I'd have to say it's the dead... they *speak to me. It seems that when someone dies violently, there is a 'footprint' they leave,*

an impression of who they were. I follow that trail and sometimes, I get lucky and can put it all together."

When Gale was asked if she was satisfied with her work, she responded with an emphatic, "yes," but added that she was very, "... glad that she didn't have all the categories of AFTD."

When asked why, she responded simply that it was, "..more than she wanted to deal with."

I depressed my thumb on the pad and *thought*: *writing.*

A blank page asserted itself in the middle of my monitor which hung suspended above my desk. I tapped my fingers on the desk, struggling to write. This was my least favorite homework; writing. I guess one paragraph I could manage. History was second period and I needed to do a paragraph per day synopsis. *Thought* and *pulsed* to the school before second period Monday through Friday. Mr. Peterson was cool but current event stuff sucked. Who cared what was happening, seriously? I had to care more than I wanted and was pissed about it.

I sat thinking about what to write in my paragraph, struggling with the spelling, as usual. My desk had a built in thumb pad so I just laid my thumb on it and *thought*: *this sucks ass* **guffaws**

The phrase lit up on the screen and I howled, slapping my knee, comic relief. I finally got a grip and thought: *erase phrase.* It disappeared. That last phrase *may* have affected my grade. I felt giddy at the prospect. I tapped my fingers again and thought:

Copy & Paste header. The article header lit up.
I amended: *and include author.*
Anderson's name glowed on the screen.

I *thought*: *This past event is about a girl cop that has the paranormal ability, AFTD (Affinity for the Dead). This ability usually means that somebody can communicate with the dead. She uses her ability to find criminals that have murdered people.*

I paused, taking my thumb off the pad a second, then laid it on the pad again, and *resumed thought*: *She says that she can hear impressions from people who've died, that if they were murdered she can feel a trail of their emotions. Sounds like this is damn handy.*

Huh... *thought*: *erase profanity.* "Damn," disappeared.

Thought: *Pulse to Mr. William "Billy" Peterson, History teacher at Kent Middle School.*

That done, I glanced at the illuminated numbers on the bottom of the computer screen. I depressed my thumb, very lightly. Mom would kill me, literally, if I put my thumb through another pad and *thought*: *sleep.*

The screen became dark, only the green clock numbers continued to glow in the lower right corner.

Nine-thirty already, time to pulse John. Weird that I hadn't heard from Jonesy today, he was always pulsing.

My pulse was stuffed in my back pocket and digging into my ass. I whipped it out and pressed the pad. The pads for the pulse-cells were a lot tougher to wreck I thought with satisfaction, and *thought*: John Terran.

Green letters appeared: *Initializing.*

Then: *Hey butt-wipe, finally got around to pulsing. Busy with Jade?* **Laughs** John Terran

No, numb-nuts, if you must know, I just finished my PE! CH

Past Event? Yeah, I figured you'd finally get your butt kicked and do homework- John Terran

Are you ever gonna edit your name to initials like everybody else does so I don't have to see your whole, stinkin' name? **Smirks** CH

I like it this way, it irritates everyone **sarcasm-much-** John Terran

*Off-topic-*CH

K- John Terran

I was talking with Jade and we may do better to rein Jonesy in with doing the thing at the cemetery with the ass-clowns- CH

Why? John Terran

She knows Brett, or did, and says she thinks he'd never let it go, be bent on big-time payback, baby- CH

How does she know Brett? Besides, ya know Jonesy, he's got this thing buzzing around in his head and he'll want to see it through- John Terran

sighs *Yeah, I was afraid you'd say that-* CH

She and Brett were actually friends a couple of years ago. I guess his dick-headed-ness is a more recent development- CH

Huh... really? John Terran

Yeah, I guess his dad makes her dad look normal- CH

*No, **profanity block!*** John Terran

*Yeah, no **profanity block!*** CH

Well, I guess, we'll just have to tone Jonesy down as much as possible just in case he gets out of control- CH

***laughs** okay Caleb, good luck with that-* John Terran

Hey, where is Jonesy? I haven't heard from him- CH

*He got his **profanity block!** busted over homework and can't pulse-* John Terran.

How do you know if he can't pulse? CH

Because I pulsed him and his mom answered- John Terran

***ouch** well that blows.-*CH

Yeah- John Terran

*Okay, see ya tomorrow-*CH

K, see ya- John Terran

I touched my pad and *thought*: *sleep.*

It powered down instantly. I looked at my suspended monitor, as slim as my pulse and the glowing numbers stared back at me, ten-forty four.

As if by magic, Mom hollered up the stairs, "Caleb! Bed!"

"K!" I hollered back. In the morning it was *school*, at night it was *bed*. I rolled over on my back, realizing that my clothes were on.

I undressed quickly and threw the whole lot on the floor. I looked down at them and shrugged, picked them up and made a tight ball, making a basket into my dirty laundry hamper, thinking, have I ever used that? I didn't know. I flopped back down on my bed and grabbed my book. I liked to read before I fell asleep. Not the lame stuff the school assigned but cool authors, like Stephen King. Now that was a tight author. I began reading and didn't think about the other stuff until the next day at school where I was reminded by a surprise source.

Did I say I liked surprises?

CHAPTER 12

Something was... something was wet. Gross! I lifted my head off the pillow and I swear, there was the Lake Erie of drool. I did an abbreviated push-up and hopped out of bed, swaying a little as the blood rushed to my head. I surveyed the mess, looking for some clothes. I glanced at the alarm and my hand flashed out and flat palmed it just before it went off. Couldn't believe I had not slept past the alarm. I dug around in the clothes pile on the floor and leaned over the laundry hamper and looked in at last night's clothes that were in there. Huh, I grunted to myself, Jade would certainly notice if I wore the same thing two days in a row.

Dejected, I stalked out of the room in nothing but boxers. I thudded down the stairs where I encountered Mom, leaning with one hand against the counter top and the other holding a steaming cup of java.

"Hey now, you look a little rough." She smiled. I thought that was rich coming from her, miss queen-o'-beauty and light in the morning. I threw her a sullen look and made my unsteady way to the laundry room. Mom followed.

"Caleb, don't go back there and start rifling around, foraging for clean clothes. If you'd actually wash some, this would not be an issue."

I ignored that and plowed forward. There, in a dim little corner were all the mismatched clothes. I rifled through the whole thing and got a vintage AC/DC T-shirt that was littered with the fine holes on the bottom (a theme with my shirts), and threw that on.

Mom put out her hand and quietly said, "Maybe a shower would liven you up."

I scowled harder, then a vision of Jade popped into my head. She showed up smelling like a vanilla bean and I was there smelling like... like... a kid that woke up in a pool of drool. Life just seemed complicated now. Where were the days when you could just *be?* I grabbed some mismatched socks, the last pair of boxer briefs, no free-ballin' for me and took off for the shower.

I took an extra-long time in the shower and even cleaned my feet. Feeling super spiffy and primed I glanced in the mirror. It was fogged up so swiped it with my arm. I searched carefully for signs of my impending manhood. Seeing nothing (I think I had, like, three armpit hairs), I left the steam pit of a bathroom.

I sat down in front of a fried egg sandwich. "Huh, what gives?" I asked Mom.

"I thought you could use a little pick-me-up."

For today she was absolved of her sins.

Dad strolled in. "Hey Pal."

"Hey."

"You showered!"

I scowled, showering was an event that warranted comment? Parents.

"Caleb, I was thinking that we try some experimentation in the cemetery, in a controlled atmosphere, one in which there isn't a charged, emotional dynamic."

Dad looked at my expression.

"Don't worry about how you do, son. It's about gaining some control over this ability."

I wondered if having the Js with me would make it easier or harder? I deliberated. I decided it would be easier with the Js than without. After all, it had been them from the beginning of this whole mess.

Mom put her hands on hips encased in pajamas, her favorite outfit, and added, "I want to be included too. The Js get to go."

Sliding onto the bench beside me, she gave me a level stare.

"I read most of the papers that John gave me." I told her. "The main scientist, Daniels-something..."

"Byron, Byron Daniels," Dad interjected.

"Yeah. He said that if there were another Parker, that the kid would be limited to what certain groups wanted."

Mom sent Dad the *oh shit* look and he gave a minute shake of his head, *later.*

"You know this Dr. Daniels?" I asked Dad.

"I know *of* him. He works in related fields."

I looked at the clock and stood up, Mom gave me a hug.

"I haven't died mom," I said, pulling away.

"I understand," she commented, "but sometimes moms just want to squeeze their boys."

"I know," I said and took off for the door, whipping my hair out of my face. I turned and walked out the door, jerking my backpack off the chair as I went. I stuffed my feet into my shoes, closing the door behind me. I was looking forward to another day with Jade and my best jamming day of the week. Little did I know that the day would start off weird and just get stranger as it wore on.

****

The school commons was in the center of a humungous room with circular tables. Lockers flanked the entire room and bled down into the halls leading to our classes. Eighth graders had the commons lockers and the sixth and seventh (sevies) graders dealt with the jostling hallway. We all hung out in the commons and stalked each other's activities. I had time before Morginstern's class and could hang with the Js before and if I was really lucky, Jade.

I spotted Jonesy right away, his dark face a chocolate dot in the crowd. He raised a finger in salute and looking around I didn't see John or Jade. Sucked.

Jonesy wore that expectant expression I knew so well. "Hey man, what's up?"

"I heard you got nailed for skipping homework."

"Yeah, I had to make up, like, ten CE's."

My mouth hung open. "My parents would've *executed* me for that many missing current events."

Jonesy looked down and shuffled his feet, then looked up with a sheepish expression. "Yeah, no pulse for now..."

"No pulse?"

Incredible.

"Yeah, but my mom knows I am going to hang with you all day Sunday so I either didn't do that," NOT an option for The Instigator to be absent, "*or* no pulse for a week." Spreading his hands out, *sacrifices must be made for the greater good.*

Right. "Well," I clapped him on the back, "thanks for that."

"No problem."

Carson and Brett strolled by. Carson paused and said, "Hey Queers, how's it hangin'?"

Brett looked at Carson, and said, "Dumb question Carson, that's all they know, how each other is hangin'." They laughed at their brilliance.

Jonesy gave me that knowing smile. I was tired of them. I hoped Jonesy got them good. Jade appeared, making a wide berth around the chumps. She put her small hand in my bigger one, turning to look (contemptuous expression) at Carson and Brett who were   unsuccessfully containing their glee.

I was distracted. Jade did actually smell like a vanilla bean. Then Brett interrupted my sniffing.

"Not exciting enough for ya? Gotta use Jade as a cover?"

"A cover for what?" she asked.

"Their *fagness*, obviously," Carson claimed.

Jade did a smooth roll-her-eyes up in her beautiful head look.

Girls were uniquely talented in the rolling eyes department.

"I'm not a cover for anything. By the way: listen up, dumb asses, haven't you figured out that you guys aren't important enough to worry about covering for?" she said, hands on hips, head tilted, that hot considering look painted on her face.

Nice... feisty! Suddenly, Brett was standing not two inches from Jade's nose and she stepped back.

"Hey!" I yelled, shoving Jade behind me.

Brett was in *my* face now (that was just fine), poking his finger in my chest. We stood eye to eye, that small growth spurt putting me right where I needed to be.

"Keep your slut in line there, pal, or I will."

I grabbed his finger and twisted it while I said, "She isn't a slut, mouth-breather," and gave him a hard shove.

 He stumbled into Carson but rebounded fast, coming for me. Things slowed down. Feeling Jade's presence at my back, I got ready to abuse and then Carson said, "Cool it Brett, Morginstern's coming."

"What's going on here young men and woman?" he nodded at Jade, including her in his political correctness. My heart was still hammering in my chest with the post adrenalin surge.

Brett and Carson wore sullen expressions, which didn't faze Morginstern one bit.

"John told me you were having an issue out here and may be late to class. You know that I frown on the first period 'slouch'." A dissatisfied furrow formed between his eyes.

Huh, clever-John had been cookin' up a way to get us out of this little disaster. Nice.

"I wasn't trying to be late, honest. I got distracted by Carson and Brett's interesting dialogue." I threw a glance their way, digging their identical expressions of confused dumbness. Jade smirked. She was definitely getting it.

Morginstern folded his arms across his chest and stared at us.

Pointing a finger at Jade, then Carson and Brett, "You go *now* to your respective classes." He watched them walk away and I saw Jade turn around to look back at me. I smiled back.

Morginstern gave his attention to Jonesy and me. "I think I caught sight of a skunk and smelled a skunk so there must *be* a skunk." I had heard that before from Gramps. It was time to purposely misunderstand the expression.

"What do you mean, Mr. Morginstern?" I asked.

Jonesy was busy giving me the wide-eyed, *figure this out*.

Morginstern's eyes narrowed, looking right into mine, I held his gaze. "I think you know exactly what I mean. I have to go teach class now, with the two of you, but," he stabbed a finger in my direction, "I know there is discord between you, Carson Hamilton and Brett Mason. I know."

The laser eye fell on Jonesy (equal-opportunity lecture), "... and *you*... you're always around when these situations erupt."

Jonesy made some vague effort to look innocent but I had to admit, he almost always looked guilty.

"Get to class boys and no more loitering, I'll be watching." He walked back to class and we followed, our tails tucked between our legs.

We went through the door, the last bell already rung and every kids' eyes on us. John was making strangling motions around his neck when our eyes connected. I gave him the slashing index finger across the throat gesture, *can it*, I mimed.

Jonesy and I sat at the round table and Morginstern went to the front of the room explaining that he was unexpectedly delayed due to an incident out in the commons that needed his personal attention.

All eyes swiveled to us. I hated that.

I was in a foul mood because of the rough start. Jonesy caught my grumpiness like a cold and gave it to John. All three of us grumped together in silence, sanding our boxes.

Finally, John said, "Listen... I know it wasn't cool for Morginstern to break that up but would it have gone to plan if you guys had let it fall apart before the cemetery?"

No, it would definitely not have been cool, it would have ruined the Aqua Net Payback.

Jonesy looked abashed. "I *so* want to do this on Sunday."

"I knew that, it's why I made an executive decision," John said.

"A what?" Jonesy asked.

"He means he decided, on his own, what was best for our group." I looked at John as if to say, *come on.*

"No, you guys have to learn idioms."

Jonesy was utterly confused. I was gonna show off.

"It's not really an idiom, ya know."

"Yeah, it is," John shot back.

"No, an idiom is an expression that is not literal to its meaning." Mom was a word-freakazoid and had drilled this stuff into me.

John looked perplexed but rallied. "Okay... so what you're saying is that I really am the executive of the group and my decision was allowable."

Uh-oh. I hadn't thought about the consequence of taking on John's Undeniable Logic.

"Well, Jonesy and I," Jonesy nodded solemnly as if he understood and was in complete agreement with my thought process, "have not appointed *you* the executive formally." I hesitated here, "but the expression, executive decision is not opposite to its real meaning."

I then leaned back in my chair, mirroring Johns crossed arms.

A slow grin spread over John's face.

He began nodding. "Pretty damn clever, Hart."

We bumped fists and that sealed our coolness. We resumed the Dreaded Sanding.

Friday droned on without further incident. Jade and I hung with the Js while eating lunch. Jonesy got Carson on board, giving him the time to meet Sunday. We whipped out our pulses and set our reminder chimes, synchronized and ready or kinda ready.

The speakers began blaring out a message about the upcoming tests. Mrs. Calvert was reminding us that all eighth grade students' Aptitude Testing would begin on Monday morning so, "... be sure to get a good night's sleep and a proper," who ever said that, I wondered, "breakfast."

We rolled our eyes. I was the only kid that actually ate breakfast. Most of the kids would show up on Monday morning starving big time.

I gave Jade a hug as she walked off to her class and watched her progress. The Js watched me watch her.

Jonesy shook his head. "Man, you got it bad."

John nodded in agreement. "Yeah he does."

I was kinda disgusted with them.

"Oh and you two are going to be different when you like somebody?" I dismissed them with a wave of my hand, heading to class.

After suffering through English and PE, we were ready to jam. It was lame I really couldn't talk to Jade in those classes. Even Miss Rodriguez's hotness didn't entice. Now that Jade was the GF, it was so just English now, except when she pulled out all the stops with a righteous outfit.

I told John this and he looked at me in horror.

"Miss Rodriguez is still completely hot. You having a girlfriend so does not change that," he said with real reproach.

"Well, maybe she *is* still pretty hot," John gave me the, *ya think?* Look.

I rolled my eyes, "... but, there is Jade and she's plenty distracting. I bet all I'll pull out of that dumb class is a 'B'."

"Yeah, your parents will have a shitfit if you get a 'C'."

John was laughing but I didn't think it was that funny, not all of us could just have a heartbeat in class and get an 'A'." I mentioned that most obvious fact and he shrugged. That was John, he wasn't going to admit he was smart, no-oh.

Mr. Cole came over and asked John to play a measure or two on the piano to see if he could sub for Alex sucking at a measure. John stared at the sheet music and began playing and I listened. The adults called John a natural.

The notes floated out, he used all the dynamics, gaining volume and softening at the correct times. When he approached the fifth measure, Cole stopped him with a hand.

"Okay, today I want you to work with Alex, he needs some fine tuning."

John went over to where Alex was sitting and they looked over the sheet music. Meanwhile, I bent over my piece and got my fingers in position to play my chords.

I was jammin' out a good set and then that cop from the accident walked in. My heart began hammering in my throat, blood rushing to my head making a faint roaring in my ears. What in the hell was this? John looked up from helping Alex and saw Garcia and about crawled up his own corn cob. My fingers stilled.

I set the guitar down and stood.

Garcia went right to Cole and said, "Hey Tony, I just wanted to borrow Caleb for a sec." His voice formed the question like it was a request but I didn't think so.

"Sure thing Officer Garcia," he winked.

They're friends, swell.

Garcia looked at me, crooking a finger. I left my stuff where it was and followed him out the door into the parking lot

He faced me. "So, how are you, Caleb?"

"Since last week, fine." I mean, we just saw each other. We were alone, without anyone hearing what was said, I was gonna be careful.

"You remember that I said that I'd keep an eye on you?"

I nodded.

"Well, it's come to my attention that there's a couple of young men that are becoming a problem at the school."

I so didn't need this.

"There's no problem," I rushed out. Calm down Caleb.

Garcia raised a brow. "Really, because I've heard different reports."

Ah-huh, somebody had diarrhea of the mouth. "We're not great friends or anything, that's for sure."

Garcia switched topics, tricky bastard. "Doesn't," he looked down at his notepad, he still wrote stuff down instead of pulse-pad, "Jade LeClerc live fairly close to the Mason boy?"

Yes and why did Garcia care? I was liking this less and less. He was doing more than keeping an eye on me.

"Yeah."

"There's a situation that has been escalating in that neighborhood that you need to be aware of."

Was he warning me... or *warning* me?

He waited while bees droned lazily, the sun warming our faces.

Garcia sighed. "Listen, Caleb, I'm here to help, not run your life."

I waited.

"Okay, I have a feeling about you and I'm going out on a limb. I know the Mason kid is under tremendous pressure at home."

I just bet he is.

"Miss LeClerc has escaped, by a slim margin, a similar background, but not the same can be said for Mr. Mason," he intoned solemnly. "I was hoping, when there's a huge potential trauma for kids realizing some form of paranormal ability, if you might restrain yourself from exacerbating this situation."

He lost me, what?

Garcia sighed again. "Listen, don't spin Brett up like a top right now, he's like a bomb waiting for detonation."

"Gotcha." The bomb reference I understood.

Garcia's shoulders relaxed and a lopsided smile appeared.

"Maybe you can mention this to the Js."

Sunday. At. The. Cemetery.

I clamped down on my expression, but a little leaked out. Sergeant Raul Garcia's smile slipped. Him calling John and Jonesy the "Js" struck me as odd too. I didn't like it.

"Yeah, okay," I responded.

The bell shrilled and Garcia glanced down at his watch. We had that one thing in common. Everyone else had a pulse, all pulse technology kept world time perfectly.

John lurched out the door, coming to stand by me. He and Garcia were about eyeball to eyeball, John was gonna be tall I thought for the millionth time. But Garcia was all-that-is-man, broad shoulders (he hit the gym pretty hard), with bulging forearms.

John looked sorta unfinished. That was okay, we were still boys, we didn't have to be men yet.

I didn't know this then, but soon boyhood would slip away and manhood would arrive like a thief in the night. Inch, by insidious inch.

****

95

Jade came up as Garcia was leaving and gave me the look that I was already beginning to love, where she *looked* thoughts at me and I knew what she was thinking. No paranormal skills necessary.

I pressed her head against my chest in a tight hug. "Yeah, it's the same cop from the accident."

Jade bent her head back from me, her hands grasping my forearms. "Garcia?"

I nodded. John stared at Garcia's car as it became a white dot in the distance.

"What did he want?" John asked, still staring.

"He wants us to lay off Brett."

John looked at me, then at Jade, then back to me again.

"Really," I said.

"That's *so* not going to work!"

"Yeah," I agreed.

I looked down at Jade. "He mentioned you too."

"What? Why?"

"Garcia is keeping track of us. Somebody blabbed and now he knows we're fighting. He knows about Jade's dad, Brett's family, that they live in the same neighborhood..." I trailed off.

A cop's interest in our lives couldn't be a good thing, whatever angle you look from.

"We need to get the twins off our backs, at least distract them." John shrugged, his palms outstretched, *what else could we do?*

Jade restated the facts, "I sure don't like Garcia being this interested in our lives."

Yeah, ditto.

We stood in the warm sunlight, thinking about it.

John broke the heavy silence, "I guess there isn't much more we can do. The plan's set, Jonesy will never back down and it would make things *way* worse if we didn't meet Brett and Carson. They'll think we're cowards if we don't, un.bear.a.ble." John enunciated each syllable, like a guillotine to the head. I smiled, visualizing.

"Right. I hear that, but everyone knows what I think," Jade said.

We had to be brutal with Carson and Brett, so we could be free from their daily crap. She'd handle it differently.

"We know, but trust us, if there was an easier way to shut those two down, we'd have done it. Some guys need a two-by-four to the head before they understand we aren't tolerating their bullshit."

Jade's mind-wheels were turning. "I'll be there."

That's my girl. I almost did a fist bump with John but played it cool.

John smirked, he saw my thinly veiled glee. We were trying to survive until Tuesday.

That reminded me! "I get the dog on Tuesday," I blurted out.

John said, "Wow, I didn't think that was gonna happen!"

"Me either, but the Parental Unit caved! They think I've been traumatized by this whole AFTD thing... so, I get him!"

"Have you been 'traumatized'?" Jade asked with a trace of sarcasm.

"Yeah... really, *really* bad. And I'm gonna need a lot of sympathy and attention." I looked down at her with a perfectly straight face.

She looked up at me, her face breaking into a full grin. "Good luck with that."

John started howling, slapping his knee. "Yeah, that was priceless, you traumatized, yeah right!"

I was miffed. I mean, what if I *had,* ya know*, been traumatized?*

My face stiffened. That made John howl louder and traitor that she was, Jade joined in. And where-the-hell was the unspoken girlfriend-boyfriend code of honor? As if things couldn't get any funnier, Jonesy walked up.

"What's so funny?"

John and Jade were in the throes of laughter, at my expense, I thought moodily. I turned to Jonesy and said, "They don't think I've suffered a trauma."

"What... *you*? Hell, no! You're the man, you don't need sympathy for anything." Jonesy looked around for support but John and Jade were busy busting a gut.

"What's with them?" Jonesy jerked his thumb at the offending duo.

"I don't know," I huffed. They quieted themselves down to a couple of random hiccups, then looked at each other and another hysterical bubble of laughter escaped.

Jonesy looked perplexed.

"You had to be here, I guess," I said... or not, narrowing my eyes and giving them the look they deserved.

Jade and John finally managed to quit laughing. While we walked away, I filled Jonesy in on the whole cop-showing-up-at-the-school thing.

Jonesy said, "That's easy for him to say. It's not his ass during school catching crap all the time."

He had a point. Maybe Garcia was okay, but I wasn't trusting anyone right now. I told them and we agreed that Garcia was just another thing to worry about.

Enough with the gloom, I shook it off with an effort, it was Friday! Time for Jade to meet The Parents.

"You guys want to come and hang at the house?" I asked.

Jade hesitated for a second, "I guess I have to meet your parents sometime, huh?"

"They're great! Ali makes the best food," Jade looked at him like a bug, but typical Jonesy he kept talking, unawares, "...and Kyle is pretty cool."

John watched the interplay, having whipped out his pulse and gotten hold of one of his parents. "I can."

The rest of us joined in a silent pulse parade of contacting respective parents and Aunt Andrea.

Everybody could.

I wondered how Jonesy had managed to get his pulse back early?

"It's not mine," he said by way of explanation.

Just then Alex walked up to our small group with palm extended. Jonesy turned and gave the pulse to Alex, who ran his thumb over it, blanking it.

"I borrowed Alex's pulse for ten minutes."

"Couldn't live without it?" I asked.

"Dude! It's been diabolical without it; pure torture!"

Jade rolled her eyes.

John came over to Alex, who was where I was a couple of months ago, short. He looked like a sixth grader masquerading as eighth and asked how he managed that.

"I did a delayed ID protocol."

John was enthralled. We'd never get away once John started talking tech with another tech-freak.

"How?" John asked.

"See here," Alex pulled out his pulse and after a quick thumb-pass, he *thought*: *settings*: then; *timer/ID,* "... after that, there's only three different timed settings to choose from."

Bor-ing, I thought.

John was nodding, obviously *feeling it.*

"John," I said, breaking up the tech-fest.

John looked over, *let's go*, I mouthed.

He turned back to Alex. "I want to know more but I gotta book."

Alex gave John a mock salute and we headed to my house. Geeks, I thought, not without admiration.

I walked with my hand entwined with Jade's and noticed Jonesy was keeping an unusual silence.

Just when I thought he had to be sick or something he said, "Heard it's gonna rain this weekend."

John stopped and looked at him. He threw his hands up in the air at a perfect sky. He looked at Jonesy again. "From this to rain*?*"

"Yeah, man. My mom is totally into NOAA, she keeps up on the weather. She says, and he swung his butt around, making airquotes, "... that a 'system' is moving in."

John was nodding. "That means the barometric pressure should be dropping soon, giving rise to storms."

Wow, that sounded creepily adult like. I told him and he smiled.

"It'll just make things more dumb for Sunday,"John said.

Duh, Pacific Northwest, it's an obligation to rain here.

"Oh, I don't know, maybe Carson's gonna have to stick his head further in that pipe. Too bad it can't work in a toilet." Jonesy contemplated the logistics of making some kind of toilet episode happen with the jackass twins. Finally, he waved that thread of conjecture away and got back on topic. "Doesn't matter. He will still get his, rain or shine," Jonesy said with finality.

Nothing derailed Jonesy.

Jade had been quiet, she didn't just talk to hear herself. We started walking again, a light breeze bringing fresh smells, somewhere between warm earth and floral. Jade would like our deck with the lilac bushes in bloom. The Js wouldn't care as long as mom was the food-bearer and Fridays meant pizza.

We turned off the main road, making a left into my neighborhood. We passed the swampy stand of trees where the bench stood, my house was last in a row of about eight. I could just make out the arches. A false street lay on the north side, where a fence stretched right behind our backyard, running the entire length of our neighborhood. We walked through the atrium.

Jade paused, looking around. I forgot, she'd never seen our house. I looked around, taking it in from her perspective. A Japanese Maple spread its delicate canopy over the pebbled cement walkway, umbrella-like, its shady green leaves translucent with fiery red veining. All around, flower beds burst with shade loving plants, ferns, Hostas and Astilbe.

Jade looked over at me, her face alight. The Js looked like they would sleep as they stood there, but God love 'em, they were waiting it out. Now that was true friendship.

"What is this?" she asked, gently running her hand over an Astilbe that sat like a purple feather on top of its delicate leaves.

"An Astilbe," I answered.

The Js made kissy faces at me behind Jade's back. Jonesy made the knife to the wrist motion, This meant morgue, he had explained at one point, whereas horizontal meant hospital. What a dumb ass. *Not* helpful.

Mom saved everyone from the flower worship situation by opening the door. "This must be Jade."

"Hi Mrs. Hart." Jade smiled back.

"Oh no, please don't, I look around for Kyle's mom when someone calls me that. Just Ali, nice to meet you."

"You too."

Mom was pretty good at avoiding awkward turtle moments. "Hey guys, I made banana bread today."

The Js looked at her as if she were an angel. They raced into the house, shoving each other out of the way as they went. Mom and Jade rolled their eyes, laughing.

I cut up four pieces for each of us. It never occurred to me that Jade wouldn't like banana bread and I slathered butter over hers and mine. Jade looked at the slab and didn't seem sure what to do with all of it. It looked about the right size.

Mom saw the whole thing and stepped in. "Here," she took the small, fish-shaped plate, cutting the bread in half, "this may be a little more manageable."

How do girls stay alive? A mystery for another day.

Mom said, "You guys go get your crumbs all over the place outside, eh?"

"Good idea, Mom," I said with a tone.

"Do you have a tone, Caleb?"

How do parents always hear a tone?

"No, we're pretty neat, is all."

Mom looked at me as if us being neat was an impossibility. I grabbed the gallon of milk from the fridge and told John to get some cups. Like a good minion, he went straight over to the dishwasher he knew the drill, but Mom stopped him. "Those are still hot, just get some cups out of the cabinet." Switching gears, he snagged four cups from the cabinet.

We sat on our deck which was bordered by a built-in bench. Jade pulled a lilac branch close to her, its flowers so deep a violet they looked bruised, smelling its powdery sweetness. The Js were inhaling their banana bread but Jade was taking little bites of hers. Her awe at our small patch of garden told me that she didn't have anything like it.

Jonesy was licking the crumbs off his fingers when I realized what I'd missed! I told everyone to hold on a sec, running inside to get a napkin, but Mom had one in her hand.

I winked. "No youngheimer's for you Mom."

She frowned.

Alzheimer's was that freakish disease old farts got that caused their brains to turn to mush or was that mad cow? I don't know, I liked to use the non-politically correct terms to get Mom worked up. I could see her steaming in the kitchen, thinking about all the old people I had made fun of.

Jade smiled, taking the napkin and using it to wipe her mouth and hands. John wiped his hands on his jeans which was what I normally did. Jade saved me from these dire choices by handing me the *other* napkin. I looked back at Mom, pretty sly.

A movie would be great. My pulse said four-forty-nine, pretty close to supper.

"Mom," I bellowed.

Mom cracked the window open. "Caleb, I loathe yelling, as you well know, come in here or next to the window."

I sighed, getting up and closing the distance. "Can everybody stay for supper and watch a movie on pulsevision?"

Before she could respond I asked, "Wait, what's for supper?" Not all my friends were gonna like some fish thing.

"What day is this?" Mom asked matter-of-factly.

"Ah... Friday."

Oh... duh. "Pizza," I said, answering my own question.

Jonesy, always a good one for hearing anything food-related shouted, "Pizza!" double-fisting his excitement in the air.

Mom looked over at him then back at me, that's settled. I told everyone to pulse the world and see if it was cool. Once again, everyone jerked out their pulses and after a few silent minutes of *thoughts,* the pulses were tucked away for the night.

****

The movie was righteous with zombies chasing everyone around (the irony was not lost on me, the Js giving me sly looks), the heroes saved the world and fell in love. Jade liked the love story and the rest of us guys were diggin' on the gore. The parents allowed four Pay-for-Pulse movies per month. It wasn't too expensive. It was a little like the Netflix fad that mailed (unbelievable) people movies and video games back around when I was born. It all seems like a lot of work to me.

Mom made two pizzas and all that was left were a couple of crusts. Jade had one slice and we feasted on the rest, re-feasting once a few well-concealed burps made additional room. She'd set out a ginormous bowl of popcorn and we all got special, bottled root beer. A perfect night.

Dad popped his head inside the door right in the middle of The Quintessential Zombie Moment where it gets an arm torn off and uses it to beat the tar out of an enemy. Impervious to pain, zombies!

He shook his head, backing out.

The parents weren't big zombie fans.

Finally, the night had to end. All of us were rubbing our eyes and trying not to show how tired we were. The Js took off together and Jade and I stood at the door. I didn't like her walking home by herself but didn't know if she liked being independent and would be pissed and stuff?

I asked anyway, "Do you want me to walk you home?"

"Nah, you don't have to."

Well... okay, huh.

"Is it okay? Or do you really not want me to?"

"It's okay," she said with a small grin.

Ah-huh, so she dug it. Girl-speak was sorta hard to figure out, definitely a learned skill.

The parents told me to take my pulse. I held it up, its metallic black exterior glinting under the porch light.

Jade's neighborhood was a fifteen minute walk one way to the East Hill area. Most of the houses were seventy-five years old, built in the 1950s. They were in various states of disrepair. Looking around, it was a little depressing. There were crappy looking junipers on the edge of decaying lawns, outlawed now unless they were grandfathered.

Mom was a big one for the No-Lawns Act that was passed; mental eye-roll. Don't even get started with the Indigenous Plants Proposal.

Walking deeper into the rows of houses, my sense of foreboding came on line. Jade's mouth made a little "O".

"You feel that?" she asked.

"I feel something."

I sure wasn't needing anything besides the AFTD.

"Don't worry, it's probably me, spilling on you."

"Spilling?" I quizzed.

"Yeah, sometimes when Sophie and me hang, I can 'leak' some of the stuff I pick up onto her. She says it's major creepy."

Okay. "Why do you feel..." I struggled here, not wanting to sound dumb, but thinking the adult words my parents used might sound weird, "... anxious?" There, better than foreboding.

"Anxious?" she giggled.

My lip jutted out, I did pretty good with that. She saw my semi-pout, putting her hand over her mouth, stifling more insensitive giggling.

I frowned. "You've been laughing at me a lot today."

"Oh come on, Caleb, you can be really funny!"

Yeah, hilarious.

She began to slow in front of an especially gross house. Paint peeled like ribbons of decay off the trim. Once white, it was now a grim shade of bone-gray. The lawn, if you could call it that, started from some underground place near the house which teemed with a riot of overgrown bushes and became one with the sidewalk. It was a dirty brown, somewhere between poop and mud. Strange mounds of dirt were sprinkled all over it like big pimples in an ugly face.

"This is Brett's house," Jade said quietly.

Oh. I didn't really know what to say. The thought that it looked like an unhappy, lonely place did cross my mind. I couldn't help but compare it to my house. The atrium, backyard and the comfort smells of my home seemed like a dim light, shining a mill on miles away when faced with this.

We heard raised voices.

Jade grabbed my hand. "Quick, hide!"

I whipped my head around looking for a spot but she knew right where to go and dragged me to an overgrown hedge that we hid behind. Our sides were pressed together, eyes peering forward, seeing only silhouettes.

A booming male voice was screaming words, bad ones. The F-bomb was flying, with some accuracy. Jade flinched each time an "F" flew.

"You worthless turd. You wouldn't know sense if it knocked your dumb teeth out. Get the fuck outta here."

I saw Brett, I assumed it was him, he was shorter than the monster that stood opposite him.

"Don't hit mom!" Brett screamed. Even through the hedge I could see that his fists were clenched, definitely a Mason family theme. Hell, the dad was beating on the mom?

The dad raised his fist up and I knew he was gonna clock Brett, and I just couldn't not do anything.

Jade grabbed me. "No don't," she begged.

I shook my head. I couldn't stand cowards. He'd have to beat my ass too. In that moment I didn't care that it was Brett. The whispering that was always there grew in volume and a dull, static roar filled my head. It felt good, throbbing with my heartbeat.

"Stay here," I told Jade, never turning.

She watched me clear the hedge as Brett's dad's fist connected square with Brett's chest. It made a meaty thumping sound, Brett staggering back. The dad came right after him with purpose.

Brett was making alarming wheezing sounds, trying to recapture air that had been knocked out.

"Hey!" I yelled, startling them both.

Brett turned toward me, still wheezing, arms flailing, the elder Mason with a comical expression of surprise.

He recovered with a wonderful, "Who the fuck are you?" in a snarl.

Ignoring his question, saying more calmly than I felt, "You're not supposed to be beating on people."

Brett gave a spastic shake of his head, holding his chest with both hands, almost catching his breath now, looking at me with clear warning. There was no love lost between the two of us but he thought I was insane to take on his dad.

Me too.

The Dad turned to face me, Brett forgotten. He was tall like my dad. Clearly, when he was younger he may have been athletic, but it was submerged underneath the hundred pounds he had on me. His fists were loosely clenched but ready for action, his gut hanging over stained blue jeans with a matching T-shirt, equally disgusting.

A prize to be won.

I let that thing that was always curled tight inside me out. I didn't mean to, but like a caged animal let loose, it responded to my distress signal. I was in trouble with no plan whatsoever except that I didn't want to watch some kid my age, even a dickhead like Brett, get the shit beat out of him by his dad.

He stalked toward me, all shadow and menace. Then, all the little dirt mounds in the lawn exploding, dirt geysered like miniature volcanoes erupting; raining back down on all of us.

Brett's arms fell to his side and he sorta landed on his butt right where he was. The breath I was holding slid out of me in a long line of relief. The whispering had stopped and the lawn had blown up and... I was feeling... *fine*.

I heard a noise behind me and it was Jade.

"What. Are. You. Doing?" I asked, clearly vexed that she was in sight now! Double-duh!

"Look." She pointed.

All around the lawn, moles (big ones) were standing at attention, there reflective eyes like small suns, staring at me. Brett's dad just got angrier.

"I killed all you," he shrieked at them. "You're dead!"

Priceless, of course they were dead, you dolt. I could hear their thoughts, waiting for me to tell them something, a directive I intuited.

Before I had time to do anything, the dad switched his attention from the Army of Moles, to Jade.

"Aren't you that upstart LeClerc girl? The one that gave her daddy all the trouble with them cops?" He glared at her and she shrank away behind me.

The slug started making his way to where Jade and I were standing at the edge of the split and cracked sidewalk. Moles stood vigil, their collective eyes watching me.

He was almost on us and Brett gave one more effort to deflect what he saw as a Big Problem by shouting for us to run. My heart was a jack hammer in my chest. I wasn't gonna run from this guy.

Jade's hand clenched and bunched on the back of my hoodie, a lifeline.

"Sounds to me like you two are in my boy's class; losers," he said with certainty. "And I know how to take care of that, yes indeedy I do, I'll clean that attitude right out of ya both."

He moved forward as if to grab the two of us, and I let a little juice funnel through the moles, which looked exactly like big-ass rats with pointy faces. Wait a second, these weren't moles I thought: as they literally *swam* across the grass as one unit, their fur a slick and deep chocolate tipped with a smoke-gray against the vomit-lawn. These were... I searched for the name, *gophers.*

Jerked out of my reverie by a hand clenching my shirt together with my hoodie and my toes clearing the sidewalk, I didn't struggle but hung like a dead weight as Jade squealed and pulled me back. I appreciated her efforts but this guy had the manic strength that only the truly drunk have. I was betting he would be hella sore tomorrow, but for beating up teenagers, he was about inebriated enough to make a go of it.

A gopher sailed across the remaining two feet flying like a bat with wings, landing on the vulnerable back of the neck area, making a tight "C" shape with its body. He bit The Dad's neck as it made purchase.

Brett's dad dropped me like a box of rocks, trying to do a quick release by jerking the gopher off his neck with his hands. I could feel its mind, with solitary purpose: *to protect me.* All *it* knew was that I was master and it would be torn asunder rather than allow harm.

I turned. Like an invisible string my power slid down that line, finding eager recipients, the remaining gophers launching themselves at various parts of The Dad. He did a little dance, round and round he hopped trying to divest himself of the troublesome gophers. They were single-minded, biting, nipping and defleshing Mr. Mason.

I stood swaying, feeling like I held a great baseball in my hand with the absolute knowledge that the perfect pitch was within reach. Jade's hand was pressed against the small of my back, the gophers making satisfied mewling sounds as their teeth connected with flesh.

"Caleb... *stop it*," Jade said, voice raised above the crunching and gnashing of teeth, "you'll kill him."

Instead of being filled with the expected horror of The Dad's death at the hands of my gophers, there was a distinct satisfaction. I knew that his life hung in the balance of my action and it wasn't worth it.

Brett was suddenly beside me. "Please," he said, one hand still on his chest where his dad had hit him, "he's bad but he's still my dad."

Brett the poet.

I felt the power leaking out into and through all the gophers and made the ginormous effort to rein it in. For a moment...nothing happened. I was suddenly scared that this thing I had was bigger than I could manage, unwieldy. Then something clicked into place and I was in control again. The gophers looked at me, some of their teeth glistening wetly black with The Dad's blood.

Rest, I thought, and gave a mental shove of "juice" that felt like turning off a big, humming battery.

The gophers, my gophers, swung their heads to consider me one last time before swarming back to their mounds, sinking into them, like water finding a cleft in a rock.

Jade, Brett and I walked over to where Brett's dad lay, groaning. Blood pooled around his body, pretty much everywhere. I stood, without sympathy, the lingering emotion of wanting to end his existence still there, still waiting.

I knew that I could call them back.

"Thanks," Brett said in an hollow voice.

"What do you think, Caleb?" Jade asked.

"He'll live," I said.

I looked at Brett, all out out of words. Jade and I walked off together.

I turned around just as we were almost out of sight and saw Brett standing there, over his dad's body, staring at me as if he'd seen a ghost.

CHAPTER 13

I woke up naturally, that means no-damn-alarm. Throwing my hands behind my head, a long sigh escaped me. Oh joy, the weekend was here and I didn't have a thing to do today. Okay, not true, I did have some ridiculously insignificant homework.

Last night came crashing down on me a minute later. Brett, his psycho dad and the gophers. I'd pulse the Js later, update them on the newest mess. Did this change things for tomorrow? Maybe that was the bigger thing.

I heard Mom-sounds coming from downstairs. I glanced at my suspended monitor, the glowing numbers read ten-forty. Huh, I didn't sleep in too late today. I stood up too fast and swayed, dizzy. Pancakes were the cure for that!

I stumbled over to my door, kicking the clothes out of the way so it would open.

Mom looked up from the griddle as I rounded the corner.

"Hey pal," she greeted.

"Hey."

Mom gave me a sideways glance. "Little rough today?"

I smiled. "Yeah."

"So how did it go last night?" I knew she meant about walking Jade home.

Dad walked in, wearing pajama bottoms that looked a lot like mine.

He plopped down opposite me, resting his head in both hands. We looked at each other and he gave a chuckle. Family telepathy, I guess.

"Yes, how did things go?"

I threw out what happened. "Brett's dad was beating on him and I got in the middle by raising an Army of Gophers."

Mom put the plate of pancakes in front of me without a word. I poured hot syrup over the top, then passed it to Dad.

The parents considered me, I stared back. They didn't look shocked anymore, maybe they had passed on to the numb stage. I bet they wished they had a kid that had low level psychokinesis. Ya know, somebody that could shut a door that was left open or some random thing. But they had me instead.

I told them everything, we'd have to deal with it. The obedience of the gophers intrigued Dad. Mom was a little shocked at my indifference about Brett's dad's life.

"Why should I care?" I asked, unruffled.

"You've been raised to think of others, Caleb."

"Mom's right. We cannot condone willful sabotage of life Caleb."

Here comes the but.

Dad looked at Mom for a long moment. She sat down at the kitchen table, resting her elbows on its beaten surface.

"I understand you intervened because your friend was in trouble."

"He isn't my friend," I clarified.

"Yes, true, but, he was someone that was in danger. I commend your," Dad paused here, "...bravery in the face of danger."

Mom rolled her eyes.

Dad gave her a quick look but she was unimpressed.

"It was a good thing, what you did, but, you could have killed him." She spread her hands out, fingers splayed, *right?*

I couldn't argue with her there. I had felt what it was to control the dead, I knew what they wanted, what I wanted of them.

"Is his dad going to be okay, do you think?" Mom asked and Dad nodded.

I shrugged. "He was the one beating on his kid and from what I heard Brett say, the mom too. If he goes to the cops, how will he explain it?"

"Yes," Dad said in a relieved tone. "A conundrum to be sure."

When I looked unsure, Dad explained, "A puzzler. You may have gotten that contextually."

"Yeah, but I wanted to know for sure. Just the words around it aren't always enough."

"I like that you ask, son."

Once in awhile I was slick.

"So... it would stand to reason that we need some target practice, the sooner the better," Dad said. "Especially in light of recent events."

"What?" I asked.

"You know, we go out and practice, and you gain control"

Okay. "When? Today?" I asked.

"No better time than the present. I don't have anything on my schedule." He gestured to his casual pajama attire.

Mom was wearing hers too. She'd wear them all the time if she could. I'd be hotter than hell if I wore mine all the time.

I took a bite of the still-steaming pancakes and Dad waited for my response. I just nodded, my cheek distended into a sideways hill with pancakes. I gulped a huge swallow of milk, the whole great ball o' food slid down to the cavern.

Mom got up and flipped Dad's pancakes.

I raised my eyebrows. "I'm going all out," he said.

Dad didn't usually have pancakes, he didn't want the dreaded shelf. I looked at his gut and thought it was okay, for an old guy. I told him so.

"Thanks, Caleb, you know just what to say to make me feel better." Mom and he smiled at each other.

What did I say?

****

The car ride to the cemetery didn't take long. Hell, the Js and I could walk it pretty fast. Dad had his pulse to document... whatever. I was nervous. I had never tried to make anything happen. It always just jumped out in the middle of some psychotic event. But after thinking about it, I do remember using the gophers to hurt The Dad, Brett's dad. I frowned. I had made them rise but that had not been on purpose. The rest I had kinda steered, trying not to crash.

Mom turned around in the front seat. "Penny for your thoughts."

"I don't know if I can, ya know, make anything happen."

Dad's eyes met mine in the rear view mirror, the brown eyes a mirror of my own. "Don't be nervous, Caleb." His eyes traveled back to the road as he was driving, the trees rushed past us like a green highway in the sky.

"I just don't want you guys to go to all this trouble, and I can't..." I struggled with the word.

"Perform?" Dad asked.

"Yeah. That covers it."

"Don't worry about us, Caleb, we're not the enemy," Mom paused, glancing at Dad then looking back at me, "we just want you to gain control of this... quickly. "

I got that, but what if I couldn't do anything? It was broad daylight for God's sake! Dad laughed and told me he didn't think the setting needed to be creepy for things to happen. Mom smiled, I relaxed and looked out the window at the gray day.

Dad took a left into Scenic Hill Cemetery. The same scrolling gate from that first night framed the entrance; it was not so eerie in the daytime. As much as a mile away the whispering had grown louder. At the gate it was a dull roar. Like a washing machine you had to scream over.

Mom asked what was happening and I told her.

"So it's like 'whispering'?" she asked.

"Yes and no. I don't know, it's hard to describe. It's like that thing that you and Dad talk about... white noise?" Dad had the car parked, thumbing off the pulse ignition, powering the car down. "But you guys say that noise is like a *good* thing."

"You're saying the quality is different?" Dad asked.

"If you mean type, then yeah. It's way different. Like something is going to happen, that something needs to escape."

Dad looked at me with that somber expression, Word of the day baby, somber means gloomy, depressing, dismal). But I knew from experience that he was definitely just serious, not sad.

"This seems wrong on a lot of levels, Kyle," Mom said.

"Yes, it probably is. But I can't have our son running around raising creatures for his personal killing army. There needs to be some control, some lessons learned. Better that he practices, with our supervision, than become truly threatened at some future point and not have the tools in which to effectively deter the problem. Or, an irrevocable consequence."

My zombies killing the populace at large.

Mom didn't have a rebuttal for Dad. He was the logic-man.

Dad circled to the back, pulsing open the trunk. He grabbed his pulse and turned to me. His pulse was a specialty version. A tri-pulse that could record, interact and take stills, I bet it could wipe your butt if you asked it to.

"I thought we'd start with the familiar and see if you could raise someone we knew."

Okay... surreal, but okay.

Mom's hand flew to her heart. "Oh God, Kyle, are you kidding?"

He didn't look like he was.

"I just hadn't really thought about using a *relative.*"

I watched her gulp like it hurt.

I did a rare thing, putting a hand on her shoulder, our eyes so close. "It's *me* having to do it Mom, not you. Better that it's somebody we knew, right?"

Her hand cupped the side of my face, a smile breaking through like sun sliding out from behind clouds. "You're being the brave one and me being anxious isn't helpful."

"But your fear is not his fear, right Caleb?" Dad said.

"No, I'm not afraid of using it. It feels good... *that's* scary." I wiped off my sweating palms on my jeans, glancing around I saw that we were all wearing the same thing, uniforms for dead people raising! A cackle of laughter escaped me and the parents gave me an odd look.

"Sorry, the whole thing seems a little..." I trailed off and Mom finished, "surreal?"

I nodded. "Yeah... that."

Dad smiled and with the tri-pulse in hand we headed over the path of stones and winding road that led to our family plot.

We arrived at a slight knoll. I had visited before when I was little but it'd been awhile and it felt fuzzy in my mind. Like a dandelion seed that once chased and captured, blows away, leaving not a trace behind.

I looked at the granite markers in front of me. My hair tumbled into my eyes and I flipped it back, where it instantly settled back into position. Mom frowned. I broke the stare, looking at the headstones again.

Mom sank down to her knees and ran her right hand over the engraved lettering:

Margaret "Maggie" Doyle, Beloved Wife-Mother-Grandmother, RIP; born 1935, died 2015, aged 80 years.

Huh, she died the year I was born.

A tear escaped and she withdrew her hand. "Gran was a good woman."

Dad agreed, "Yes she was."

The power swelled, one whisper above all the rest.

"She wants to be free of the ground," I said.

"What?" Mom's head whipped around, hair falling in her eyes. "She's *speaking* to you?"

I hated explaining the weird stuff to people that didn't have it, but it was her gran and all. "No... yes, not exactly." I sighed. "I guess it's more of an impression of needs or wants or feelings, I don't know."

"Well, I guess the dead make choices too," Dad said.

That was the first smart thing I'd heard anyone say. Actually, that was exactly it. I was the thing allowing them that need, or whatever it was, release, expression.

"Yeah, it's not just me, they want to be free, and say things and have one more chance or something. I'm somebody that can help them help themselves."

"You're a facilitator. Fascinating," Dad murmured, hand on chin.

"Kyle," Mom hissed, "this is no time to ruminate about the schematics. This is *Gran* we're disturbing."

Mom stood up, looking up at Dad, who was quite a bit taller. But Mom never looks short, she always looks vital.

"Listen buster," she pointed a finger at Dad, oh-no the dreaded tone, "this is NOT one of your science experiments, this is Caleb and Gran."

She crossed her arms over her chest, all intense eyes and huffy body stance.

"I don't know another way to be Alicia."

Huh, Dad used mom's real name, he meant business.

"Well, tone it down, would you?"

He slowly grinned. "I'll make a supreme effort."

Mom looked like that would be the last thing he did.

The whisper from Gran was a steady thing, it had a vibration all its own. I was starting to get a signature from different people. Everyone was different and now I could sense those differences. Gran's had a familiar quality about it, I didn't know exactly what or why. I honed in on that and let a tendril of my power uncoil. It felt a little like the gophers but different, more complex. Their minds had been one mind to me, simple. Hers felt like it had a complicated series of thoughts and distractions. A dead brain... but somehow alive.

I gave it a good shove and thought, *come here*.

I felt like a great weight had lifted from my head, there was a feeling of vertigo, a shifting. My vision doubled and I was fuzzy around the edges. Ah-oh, I'm gonna pass out and the parents are going to be stuck with dead granny. Then my vision cleared, stabilizing.

Nothing happened.

Dad took a photo of me... unhelpful-much. I blinked at the pulse-flash and felt something cold hit the back of my head. We looked up and the clouds that had threatened were now roiling above our heads. Great smoky-colored plumes lashed back and forth like an angry sea.

Dad looked at me.

I shrugged. "I don't know what..."

A hand burst forth through the earth, softened by recent rain. It was awful looking. Some nails were gone and finger joints were visible. Oh boy, Mom was gonna see her Gran looking pretty disgusting. I gave Dad the it's too late look and watched the train wreck happen.

Inch by slow inch the ground revealed Gran, as a fossil being excavated, climbing through the ground to exit her grave. Her silver hair hung in huge rope-like strands from a scalp with bare patches, shining like an eggshell in the dimming light.

Her head was lowered (she was on all fours), her hand reached out toward me and said, "More," in the barest of whispers. Without all the whispering in my head it felt blissfully clear.

I mouthed, *more?*

Energy, she whispered in my head, like a thread of silk, worming its way through my brain. I shuddered. That was an intrusive feeling. Disgusting as hell.

I grubbed down inside myself, where that sleeping monster lay, scraping what was left and hurled it down that connection, the thing that tethered the two of us together.

She suddenly flung herself backward, her back bent awkwardly behind her knees. Both claw-like hands clung to the remnants of a blouse of some kind, its fine print of flowers a spray beneath the tendons and sinew of what she used every day to work with, touch, love.

She straightened as suddenly as she was backwards, standing. Ripples crossed her face and like watching a movie rewind, the face knitted together before our eyes, skin flowing over and filling holes. Not perfect, no, but better. The joints in her hands were covered now and a few nails had righted themselves.

I was relieved until I looked at Mom, white as a sheet, clutching Dad's shirt, looking somewhere between barfing and fainting. Made me feel like a loser. Dad was fussing with the tripulse, trying not to let Mom topple and get a still of Gran-the-corpse.

He got my attention and winked! My dad winked at me. Nothing rattled him.

It had its intended affect, I felt a little calmer, not so frantic.

The corpse/Gran turned to me, ignoring her granddaughter entirely.

"Caleb," she croaked.

Her voice sounded full of mush.

I took a deep breath. "Hi Gran."

"Am I free of this?" she turned to gesture at the grave. Her skeletal fingers caressing the air.

"Right now you are."

She frowned. I could tell that she wasn't clear on where she was at exactly.

Comprehension slowly dawned on her face.

"I am dead. Really and truly dead."

This was the hard part. "Yes."

"And you are a," she struggled to think, being dead fifteen years would put a crimp on that, "necromancer?"

I had actually looked up that word after the first corpse called me that. I guess they knew what I was... somehow.

I would keep it simple. I was certainly more (and different) than that. "Yes, Gran."

"You have questions of me. I hear them."

That was new. I guess the communication was a two-way street.

She stepped toward me and I fought the urge to step back. That was all in my head. This new thing I could do, this ability, did not feel sickened or grossed out with Gran. Actually, I felt a sense of ownership over the dead, *mine*, it intoned, *mine*.

Standing my ground until she was about eighteen inches away, in my peripheral vision I could see my mom step away from my dad. He pulled her in against him, watching me, all the while murmuring something in her ear. He looked at me, giving me the barest of nods. I refocused on Gran.

"I want to know what this is."

She tilted her head to the side, like I had asked an important question that eluded her grasp.

"Why... this is you, Caleb. *You* have caused this."

Her arms, with the sleeves in ribbons loosely swaying in the slight breeze, clung and whipped around her like a cape.

"I mean," I was frustrated here, dad was taking stills in the background and it was distracting. I gave him a look, he stopped.

"What did you hear?" I asked her.

"Your summons, dear boy, your summons."

Oh. "You heard me calling you?"

"Yes, your voice telling me to come to you. You *did* call me to you. For your bidding."

Wow, this was definitely big-time-in-my-pants-creeper status, she looked at me raptly, waiting for some command. No wonder Parker was in trouble. If he had anything close to this, he would be like a king amongst robots. Not a cool thought. I was starting to understand why Dad had been so fast to get me hooked up with the happy med. The, we're-gonna-hide-what-you-can-do pill.

"Ah, no. I don't have a job. I just have some questions. Actually, I'm worried I can't control this so my dad thought it would be good if we came here and practiced."

Saying it out loud made it sound super dumb. Don't worry Gran, just a little corpse-raising and then we'll tuck ya back in your grave-bed and be on our way. Geez. Practice makes perfect.

She looked puzzled. "You're just practicing this gift? With me?"

I gulped and I heard a dull click, my throat dry as a desert. "Yeah, that's about it." I would have killed puppies for a glass of water about now.

She finally took the time to turn around and look at my parents. She stood there, with her hips facing me and her torso almost fully turned to them, reluctant to turn away from me and fully face them. I heard disgusting sounds when she turned and realized it was her spine, wetly cracking.

Mom's face was flaming when Gran looked at her. But my dad just stared back. Whatever he was thinking, he wasn't swayed by emotion. As he would say, the nuts and bolts of preparing me was the critical thing. He knew what Gran was, Mom didn't. That was the difference. Mom still thought of Gran as *Gran.* But she wasn't anymore, she was Gran but she was *other* too.

"Gran."

She turned from my parents without a backwards glance or a word. Mom looked at Dad and he shrugged.

Gran looked at me, waiting.

"Who are those people behind you?"

"My granddaughter and her husband," she said, just restating the facts. Pretty clinical for a corpse.

"Do you want to talk to them?" I asked.

"Do you wish for me to?" she asked, her eyeballs, which had not filled in all the way, (better not to think on that too long), rolled around in the eye sockets with a little too much room.

"No. I wish for us to discuss things." Copying her words.

She relaxed. As if a corpse could relax.

"I am here to serve you."

I gave Dad a panicked look.

Okay. I needed to get a grip, figure out some stuff and put great-grandma back in the ground.

"Is there anything you need?" I asked.

"Yes, it would give me great peace if you would tell my son, if he lives, that I am sorry."

"For what?"

"He will know. Will you?"

Mom nodded her head. "Yes, I will."

She turned, inclining her head. "Thank you."

"What am I here to do? I mean, what good can I do? How can I help people?"

"Only you know those answers, Caleb. Doing that one errand of mercy for me will be something of worth, to be sure."

She talked funny!

"Some of us can tell you a portent of your future."

That was news. I heard mom gasp her surprise in the background but Gran remained focused. My eyes met dad's and he just nodded again.

I was thinking fast. Portent... a forewarning.

"Do you wish to know what role you have in this life?"

"Yes."

Her eyes rolled up in her head, her hands lifted above it, reaching for the sky. Thunder clapped and I jumped. Fat drops of rain splattered on our skin while Gran, her gray skin looking like paper stretched tight like a drum over bones, swayed in place, hearing a rhythm that only she could.

The rain was getting its teeth in it, starting to come down in earnest. Gran's head snapped down and she stared into my eyes, a strange light illuminating hers. All movement stopped and she pointed a finger at me.

"You will need protection. Surround yourself with your own kind and others who have skills that are unusual but more common now. Do not be deceived by people that would use you for evil. There is a young girl, with a name of stone, who will be your greatest ally. You must protect her, she will be your salvation."

With that, Gran sank down to her knees and looked up at me. A great toll had been taken for this fortune telling thing. Great hollows had begun to cave in her face. I realized that all this being alive again took energy. I could feel that power in me right now, very low, like a spent tank of gas. Did I have enough to put her back? My energy faltered.

She gave me a small smile. Kinda wish she hadn't done that, there were about three teeth in a mouth that was black with decay and a bit of tongue.

I smiled back anyway, brave-much.

"You can put me away, I need to rest now." She spared a glance for my parents, her eyes resting briefly on my mom.

She looked at me. "Tell Alicia what is different. Only you matter in this time, this world."

"I understand." And I did. I wasn't comfortable with it, but it didn't matter. It was what it was.

My parents came over and stood on either side of me.

I didn't look at them. But said, mainly to Dad, "I'm really tired."

"What can I do, Caleb?"

"I gotta put her back." Gran stared up at me, her gaze unwavering. No pressure... damn. Out of nowhere, I heard voices behind us. What in the Sam Hill?

Witnesses.

Dad turned and put his body directly in front of Gran, who being on the ground, prone, could still be seen. Mom flanked Dad and I was in the middle, behind them.

I turned around and gave Gran the index finger over my lips, the universal sign for *quiet*. This couldn't get any weirder.

She understood, I could *hear it*.

There were three kids from school. The middle girl I knew, there was something about her. My power flared, recognizing hers.

She was like me.

Her eyes widened and she said to her friends, "Let's get out of here."

My parents relaxed.

I came around Mom's side and said, "No!"

What was her stupid name? We had just been talking about other kids that had AFTD. Let me think... *Tiffany-something!*

"Tiffany, no... stop. Help me do this," I said.

She stiffened, slowly turning. My first thought was, wow, she could be pretty. She stood there with a purple hoodie, brown hair peeking out from the hood, which half covered her face, just a sliver showing. She had dark eyes, color unknown. I spared the briefest of glances at the other kids, dismissing them, their faces familiar. But right now, blowing any cover in the whole world, I was going to ask for help. I knew I didn't have the energy to put Gran back, not for certain. I was pretty sure I didn't need blood, or something catastrophic to make it work. I needed energy, death-energy.

"What?" kinda pissed.

"I have AFTD, like you."

"Ya think?" sullen.

So she loved it as much as me, fine. Like we had a choice? Not for the first time I wondered if the adults that made the drugs, unlocking our paranormal potentials were really that smart.

She glanced at her friends, a guy and girl. They were taking turns looking nervously between my parents and me.

The boy looked at Tiffany. "I thought you said there wouldn't be any other people?"

She gave him, what I considered to be, one of the best girl eye-rolls ever. He pursed his lips and crossed his arms across a barrel chest.

She jerked her head to the left and said, "This is my brother, Bry." Oh, that explains the dynamic between those two.

Back to the mess.

"Listen, I kinda raised my great-Gran," I began.

"What-the-hell?" she all but screamed.

Mom humphed in the background, unappreciative of the colorful wording.

We ignored that.

"No... *no*, I can't help with anything that big," she said.

A voice that sounded like gravel crunching under tires said, "Yes, you can, seer."

The corpse speaks. Brother.

"What is that?" Tiffany asked.

"That's Gran."

Mom and Dad had moved away from me, revealing Gran. She looked worse for wear but not bad for a corpse who had accomplished a bit of precognitive forecasting.

"That," she pointed without an ounce of reverence, "is not your great-Grandma, "it's an *it*."

I casually turned around to see Gran. Yeah, I guess she wasn't really Gran anymore.

Gran stared back at Tiffany.

"Hey," Mom piped in without a hesitation, "that's *my* Gran you're dismissing you brat." Nice. Mom had regressed to name calling, a first.

"Mom, I got this."

Dad gave Mom a look, *let him handle this.*

She huffed her displeasure, crossing her arms, silently stewing.

"Yeah, she's not really Gran anymore, but she *still* has to go back."

"You're the smart one that raised her. *You* put her back." Tiffany crossed her arms, so unhelpful.

The sun broke through the clouds, a light drizzle continued to fall making the whole scene glow with an eerie luminescence. Gran came forward in an awkward shuffle.

"You will do as this one says. He is a ruler amongst your kind."

That partial tongue does odd crap to speech.

Tiffany was staring at Gran in the strangest way. I didn't have enough juice to force her help. In fact, I didn't think I could make her do anything, not with that humongous brother standing there and a girl (another body with a pulse to deal with), helping in the fracas if things got ugly. I didn't want to fight her but things were gonna go bad if I didn't get Gran back.

I could feel it.

"Make me. I'm not gonna help out. I wanna get out of here. Period. End of discussion."

Gran looked at me, her rotting face inches from mine. The smell was gag-worthy but having been in the boys' locker room, I could take it.

"What is your will, boy?" Gran asked, solemn.

"I want you to be put back to rest," I said.

Later, I wish I'd realized what that request meant, because I would have handled it differently.

Zombies were terribly literal.

Gran stepped toward Tiffany, all shuffling determination.

Oh crap.

Mom turned to Dad and said, "Kyle?" What's happening?

Dad surged forward and Gran turned, very smoothly for a zombie. Geez, and put the flat of her palm on his chest and shoved for all she was worth.

Quite a lot, apparently.

One of Dad's slip-on shoes flew off and smacked Gran's tombstone with an audible thud while he traveled, airborne, landing with a resounding smack on the grass.

The three kids looked at Dad, as he made the arc, then landing, he conked out, legs splayed in front of him.

Mom screamed his name, rushing over and crouched down beside him. While Mom was panicking, Gran was going for the gold. She had wrapped her hand in Tiffany's hair, hood completely gone, using her fist twined in her hair like a handle, dragging her over to where I was.

As I stood mesmerized by the scene, Bry leaped on Gran's back. She reached behind with her free hand, the other hand busy in Tiffany's hair, and plucked him off like a worrisome gnat, throwing him in the direction she had shoved Dad. He promptly landed on his ass, his mouth closing with a snap. Blood spewed from his mouth. That was the first clue he'd bitten some of his tongue off. Oh boy, I thought wildly, he can loan that to Gran.

No longer frozen in panic, I was moved to action and gave Gran a new command:

"Let her go!" I yelled.

Gran complied, instantly dropping Tiffany on her face with a dull crunch. Shit-in-a-sack, did she break her nose?

Gran straightened and turned to me, hand hovering over the girl. Bry took his palms to the ground, blood spilling out of his mouth like a fountain said, "I thont are aut oo re."

Redoubling his efforts, since speech was *so* not working, he engaged in a frontal assault on Gran. Both of them tumbled to the ground. Rolling to a stop on another grave, Bry's hands circled Gran's neck and he began thumping her head into the ground, gray strips of hair flying back and forth.

Her hand shot out and grabbed him in the balls as he straddled her. She tightened her grip and he yelped (sympathy grimace). Releasing his grip on her throat, she used that lull, holding his crotch in one hand, grabbing his neck with the other and heaved him--again.

Dad came to, moaning, his head in Mom's lap. His eyes grew wide when he saw the two broken kids laying in separate heaps.

From his prone position he asked, "Caleb, what's going on?"

Looks like granny's getting her groove on, I thought. Hysteria pressed in on the edges of my consciousness.

Tiffany was coming out of a near catatonic state. Flinching away from Gran's hand, which was back to hovering again, she held her nose with her left hand and glared up at me over the top of it.

"You think you can help me now?" I asked with just a tiny bit of sarcasm.

"Yes," she hissed through clenched teeth, glancing covertly at her brother, who lay on the ground, observing everyone in various states of hurt. The other girl had long since run off. Probably straight to the police, I thought dismally.

Wonderful.

Gran hauled Tiffany to her feet none too gently, using her arm that was holding the nose, Tiffany gave a girl yelp. I almost felt sorry for her but this is where her lack of cooperation had taken us. I was ready for a little grave closure myself.

Dad was rising shakily to his feet, not every day a person gets knocked out by a corpse, and making his cautious way toward us, Mom on his heels.

Gran looked speculatively at him.

I gave Dad the *stay back* look. He stared back at me, *you got this, Caleb?* I shrugged, I just didn't know but them getting the potatoes beat out of them by Gran wouldn't help.

Tiffany glared down at my Gran. Yeah, down, Gran was small, not that size mattered. Bry was on his feet too. Holding his crotch that was probably throbbing like hell.

Gran waited. Tiffany waited, eying each other warily.

I did what I thought would work. I released what I had left. It wasn't much, little more than a drop of water in a glass. It found its mark and hit Tiffany running.

Like knew like.

Naked goosebumps began at her wrists, making their way up her arms, hoodie long-gone in the midst of the scuffle with Gran.

Tiffany threw her head back, her mouth open, like catching snowflakes on our tongues when we were little.

She said, "it feels good... *it feels good*, why didn't you tell me it would feel good?"

"Because I didn't know," I replied softly.

Her head righted itself and she stepped away from Gran who kept a wary eye on Bry and my parents as they walked toward me. Tiffany's eyes were a deep, hazel green I noticed as she got closer. Not the brilliant shade that Jade had, but pretty in a mysterious way. Dried blood edged her nostrils delicately.

She held her hand out, momentarily forgetting Gran was right there, shuffling behind her. I reached out to take it, having never touched another AFTD and two things happened at once; I felt an instant injection of juice and the whispering grew in volume. The voices and their distinct signatures...*clearer.*

As if in slow motion, Tiffany turned to me, looking me in the eyes. "Is it always like this?"

"What?"

"The voices."

"For me... yeah."

Her eyes widened. "It's so loud."

"It's louder with us touching."

"Oh."

We turned as one mind, one intent.

Gran had shambled over to her grave, looking rattier by the moment. Somehow, she had super-zombie strength.

My juice was okay now. I could feel Tiffany's energy or power, complementing mine.

I looked into Gran's eyes, and for a moment, there was some spark or something, I didn't know what. Tiffany and I both noticed and reacted. It felt slimy and evil.

She looked at me, scared.

I looked back, a little shake to my voice, "Ready?"

We both knew I wasn't asking.

I let my power shift to Tiffany at the same time I squeezed her hand and it flowed between us and I thought, *rest.* A mental muscle flexed, the strength of my will chased the thread that connected me to Gran from when she gave up her place in the ground.

Tiffany's hand convulsed around mine. "Oh."

It was so simple it was criminal. Speaking of which, I could hear sirens in the background. There was no explaining our way out of this mess.

Gran gave one last heave of her chest, seeming to suck in real air for the last time, the breath rattling hollowly as it left her lungs, then she laid down on the grave. The dirt flowed over her, engulfing her body.

Tiffany and I watched. When it was done, the grave was undisturbed, like it had never happened. But as Tiffany and I released each other's hand, that spark between us fading, we surveyed the bloodied people around us. We knew it had been real.

The first police car arrived and Garcia stepped out, a smile of satisfaction on his face.

Perfect.

****

Garcia sauntered over, that wide smile stretched over his face.

Tiffany stayed where she was, Bry walking over to stand beside her. I had to assume it had been Tiffany's snitch friend that had blabbed to the police. Sure enough, she exited Garcia's police car.

With the hood covering her face I hadn't really noticed her that much, kinda busy with Gran-the-corpse and Tiffany's rather problematic older brother.

She had weird-colored hair and that's how I'd remember her later when I filled the Js in. It was somewhere between dishwater blond and red. Mom would know the color right away. Her face was all tight and pinched. From the guilt I was betting, morbidly pleased.

She looked warily from Tiffany to Bry then me. She took in all of us standing together and the lack of a zombie running around and flushed a fine, true red.

Good, let her feel embarrassed. The evidence was gone and just some blood hanging around. My parents were at my back (literally). I was absolutely sure Dad had figured out what to say unless Gran had knocked something important loose on his trip to the tombstone.

Garcia stood facing us, legs wide, considerable arms folded across his chest. He looked at the Weller kids then my parents.

Then... me.

"Well, Caleb, what do we have here?"

Just a tiny bit of corpse-raising.

Dad interjected, I knew he would, "Sergeant Garcia, good to see you again."

"Hello, Mr. Hart. No offense, but I was talking to Caleb." his eyes got back to boring into mine.

I felt steady. I hated to admit it, but I felt more solid with Dad here.

"And he's a minor," Dad added.

Garcia's head swiveled back to Dad, his eyes narrowing. "I don't have to be reminded of that Mr. Hart."

Their gazes held.

"We were here, conducting some experiments, and these kids," Dad gestured to the Weller kids and then gave a nod in the direction of girl unknown, "happened upon us."

Dad put his hands out to each side then shrugged like, *no big deal, just a family hanging around the graveyard on a Saturday...* riiiggghht. That was gonna fly.

Garcia put his hand on his chin, rubbing it.

Mom hiccuped behind me. Oh great, she always got those when she was nervous. Loud ones, too, from her gut.

I rolled my eyes and Tiffany gave Mom a look like, *what now?* Mom went ahead and did another one. Garcia's eyebrows shot up but he said nothing. Dad squeezed Mom's shoulder. Geez.

The other cop joined Garcia. He was all business, with a short, military haircut. It was so blond that he looked bald. He was short, barely taller than me, with deep set eyes, never stopping their back and forth restless movement. Shifty bastard, he made me nervous.

Garcia glanced casually at him and said, "This is my partner, Officer McGraw."

This guy was big time Aryan nation, white bread in his pants, all blond and light compared to Garcia's tall darkness.

But he was scarier.

I could feel this guy's potential and it didn't feel good. What I wouldn't have done for a dose of Jade's Empath skills about now.

Garcia smiled during his introduction then got down to the meat of the matter. "The department is pairing mundane officers with a paranormal to better handle paranormal crime. After all, we need the paranormal presence to handle that element." Garcia finished.

He said *paranormal* like a curse. That, I-want-to-be-your-friend thing had been an act. Boy, was I glad I hadn't said too much during the dog incident.

McGraw let a cruel smile flash, then it was gone. I was guessing he was about Parker's age, one of the first group of kids that got the inoculation.

They weren't giving these guys good enough psych screenings.

What was he anyway? That would prove pretty useful to know in say, the next ten minutes.

I didn't have long to wait, this jerk was just dying to show off, who knew why? Because he could, like Carson.

"McGraw's an elemental." Garcia let the comment drop like a stone in a lake.

We-were-so-screwed.

The Elementals could manipulate the four elements and it was NOT weather dependent. Fire, water, earth and air. God help us if he was like, on my level, controlling all four in the way that I had all five "hit-points" of the AFTD.

He obviously did not have all his dogs barking so I was not interested in show and tell.

I looked at Dad, he was frowning. I did a mental face-palm: there were three more kids from school that knew and the cops were involved... swell.

"If anything gets out of hand here, I have perfect confidence that McGraw can handle it to the letter of the law."

Great, *I bet.*

Dad spoke up, "I don't think any of us will be unreasonable. There is no need for posturing." Oh boy.

Garcia flipped open his notebook (*pulse it,* moron) and got a pen out. Who wrote anymore?

He turned to the girl, who's name floated just out of reach. "Miss Cote," (that was it!), "... why don't you reiterate what you told me at the police station."

Miss Cote came forward awkwardly, eyes downcast. "It's cot-A, ya know, a long 'A'," she corrected sullenly.

 Cops growing out of the ground and she's correcting their pronunciation.

"Okay... Miss Cot-*A,*" he emphasized. "Please repeat what you told us at the police station for these folks."

Cote looked at Tiffany, who shook her head, no.

So, Tiffany wasn't feeling like being outed either.

Cote rolled her lower lip, biting it with her teeth and staying silent. Garcia turned his whole body to face her, towering over her with his height, intimidating. She looked up at him, a shadow of doubt crossing her face.

"I thought I saw something over there by his parents." She pointed in the general direction of Gran's tombstone. "But it isn't here now."

"Now come on, you said a lot more than that," McGraw prompted.

Dad gave him an unfriendly look and Garcia gave it right back.

Cote glanced over his way and sighed.

Tiffany said, "Mia, no."

That was it! Mia. I hated forgetting peoples' names.

Mia went on, "We were just going to come out here and hang. And then we saw these guys," she gestured to my parents and I like a loose unit, "and saw something else too. It smelled," she said with distaste.

"What smelled?" McGraw asked.

"The dead woman," she said finally.

Garcia smiled with triumph. Well, good luck with finding any evidence, I thought with a stab of satisfaction.

"But where is the dead woman now?" Dad's arms spread out on either side of him, *no corpses here, guys.*

Garcia and McGraw left Mia where she stood. They began a tight search of the area, moving in between tombstones where tall Douglas fir trees grew in great clumps.

The cops separated, stepping on top of Gran's grave without a downward glance. When I said undisturbed, I meant it. Not a blade of grass was out of place. It looked perfect.

McGraw turned back to Mia. "Where did you see this dead woman?"

"Right there," she said.

He looked to where she was pointing, his eyes roving up to read the tombstone:

Here Lies Charles Doyle, beloved husband of Margaret "Maggie" Doyle. Born 1934, died 2000.

He read Gran's headstone next.

Don't ask Garcia, don't ask.

He asked, "One of your relatives, maybe? Doing a little visiting."

"No. Actually, we were conducting experiments, as I mentioned earlier," Dad repeated.

"Well, I did some looking." He tapped his pen to the side of his head, indicating some thinking too. "I have the last five generations of both your families in my little notebook, right here." He looked down then back up again. His eyes met Dad's in a direct challenge. "And here you all are, right at the family plot."

He snapped the notebook closed with a tight grinding sound that made me give a little involuntary jump. Dad put his other hand on my shoulder. "But from what Miss Cote tells us, you were doing more than experimenting."

I looked at Mia but she wouldn't look back.

The Weller kids had been quiet this whole time then Bry spoke up, "Caleb and I got into a fight, that's all. His dad tried to break it up when it got out of control."

McGraw looked openly skeptical but took in Dad's appearance; the disheveled hair, the grass stains on the seat of his pants. He looked at Mom next, who shrank behind Dad. That clinched it for me, she didn't like him any better than I did.

Garcia focused all his attention on Bry. Taking in the blood all over the front of his shirt, then looking at Tiffany, the dried blood from the ruckus with Gran, still congealing underneath her nose.

He looked back at me.

"But not a scratch on *you*." His eyes steady on my face.

"I guess I got lucky," I said with only a small tremor in my voice.

"But the," he opened his notebook, scanning with his index finger until he came up with the name, then tapped it once, "Weller boy, has what looks like a piece of his tongue missing. And the sister," he looked down again, "Tiffany, has sustained trauma to her nose." His eyes narrowed at me, barely more than slits.

"It's not Caleb's fault," Tiffany rushed into the space in the conversation. "I just got in the middle."

Silly me. I kept the surprise off my face, she was sure busy keeping things from the cops.

McGraw was openly scowling and Garcia looked thoughtful. They couldn't do anything. They'd have to chalk the whole thing up to a hysterical girl in a graveyard, thinking she saw things she didn't. Two boys getting in a fight, maybe over Tiffany. Duh, like that would happen but they didn't know that and a fight ensuing after Mia took off to rat on us.

The cops studied us as we calmly looked back.

Finally, Garcia turned to Mia. "Are you sure that you saw a dead woman? Or, are you willing to recant your testimony?"

"Recant?" Mia asked.

"Take it back. What you said. All of it."

"Yeah... yes... I recant. I don't know what I saw," she responded helplessly. No corpse and her two friends obviously siding with me. I almost felt sorry for her. Almost.

"I guess we'll have to be satisfied with that." Garcia said.

The wind had come up so much it was distracting, whipping my hair and lashing my face.

"But know this: I thought I smelled a skunk, saw a skunk so there must be one." Weird, just like Morginstern. Must be a contagious skunk fetish going around.

"You have my full attention Caleb, and for the record, I don't like being played. If I find out you're a Cadaver-Manipulator, we are lawfully bound to report that to the proper authorities. Don't let me find out you've been holding out on us."

His hand came to rest on the baton strapped to his utility belt. Well hell, threatening-much. Mom made a sound behind me, Dad drew her into his body.

McGraw let a huge smile settle on his face, a look of concentration sitting oddly askew. Raising his palm up he said, "Be still."

The wind that had been so annoying suddenly stopped. Yet, just about fifteen feet away it made the huge, low branches on the fir trees dance and move rhythmically. We were in some kind of eye of the storm. McGraw was showing his "juice" was working here; he was an air elemental (AE). Clyde-the-corpse's words, *to whom much is given, much is expected,* didn't apply to this guy. It was all about him.

Terrific.

"We'll see you again, Hart family. There *will* be a next time, and we'll be ready." He turned and gave a moment's attention to the Weller kids and Mia, committing them to memory.

With that charming goodbye, McGraw gave another small, tight smile, closing his open palm into a fist and drew it into his body. There was an audible pop and the wind rushed back, a reverse whirlpool, to lash our faces again.

Garcia lingered, staring at our group, then turned and joined his partner.

That didn't go well.

We watched the police cruisers drive off, knowing that some vague threat had been issued, a warning. I looked at my parents worried faces and saw identical expressions mirrored on the kids I had met today: we're screwed.

CHAPTER 14

Tiffany turned to Mia. "You're *such* an ass-potato!"

Mia looked around for support, getting none, she retaliated with, "It looked bad to me. The old, dead woman and all. I didn't know what to do!"

Mom and Dad were watching this interchange with interest.

Bry walked up to Tiffany. "Leave it Tiff, we all did the best we could. AFTD has been hard for you too."

I looked at their bloodied faces and felt responsible.

Dad turned to me. "Is this girl another AFTD?" he looked at Tiffany. "Just clarifying here."

"Yeah."

Tiffany looked at me. "I thought I was the only one."

If I'd known sooner, we wouldn't have needed to be alone.

"No. I just found out that I had it."

"How?"

I gestured to the grave behind me, Gran's grave. "It was an accident the first time. I told Carson and Brett," I paused here, our school was big enough...maybe she didn't know them? But she gave me a gagging finger down the throat, she knew them, "...that I could hear the dead. Actually, John did."

"Why would you guys tell them? They're dickheads." She caught Mom's look and rephrased to soften the swearing some. "They're jerks to everybody."

I nodded, perfect assessment. I'd agreed with the first one too.

"Because, I knew from Biology and some other stuff." The roadkill came to mind and all the fun with the insects, also in Biology. "That I had AFTD... the frogs..." I shuddered where I stood, "that I may have enough," I thought for a second, making airquotes, " 'power' to prove that I wasn't some kind of coward."

"Who the he... *heck*," she looked at Mom, "cares what they think?"

"They were being jerks to me and I was tired of it. Jonesy," Tiffany rolled her eyes, she really *was* good at that and Bry chuckled, "thought it'd be a good idea to show them what I had, that I wasn't a poser."

"Does that seem like a good idea now?" she asked.

"No way." I smiled, I couldn't help it.

Dad clapped his hands together, we all jumped. "This is all well and good but we need to discuss what happened, the possibilities."

Tiffany and I looked at Dad with puzzled expressions. What were we supposed to think about? Gran was back, she helped out and I wasn't on my own with AFTD.

Dad turned to Tiffany. "Can you raise cadavers?"

"Zombies? No." She looked at me for clarity.

She could do some other stuff, but not The Biggie.

"Sometimes I know where murdered people are. And," she looked my way. "I can sense the dead."

She must mean hear them, ya know, *hear* them. I told her so.

She shivered. "No, it's not like those loud voices you hear." She looked at me with a grudging admiration, "that'd be bad."

"It's like impressions of their feelings or thoughts, I don't know, it's hard to explain."

We shared a moment of complete understanding.

"Jade told me about that bird thing outside of gym."

Tiffany looked confused for a second then did an *ah-huh*. "Oh yeah! I almost forgot about that, LeClerc, right? Aren't you guys going out?"

"Yeah, that's the girl."

Was there another Jade in our entire school? Totally rare name. Then a whisper wafted through my head: a girl with a "...*name of stone.*" That's right, Gran had said I needed to protect her. She must've been talking about Jade.

Tiffany was snapping her fingers in front of my face. "Hello, wake up!"

"Sorry," I said. "Just thinking." Geez, pushy thing.

I glanced at my parents. Mom said, "We have some things to talk about."

"We do but I wanna," I grabbed my pulse out of my back pocket, Tiffany did too, "add Tiffany to my pulse-contact before I forget."

I thumbed my pulse and thought, *add contact.*

Tiffany walked over and laid her thumb on the pad and her contact info. appeared:

555.455.9830: Tiff Weller

"Tiff?" I asked.

"Yeah, I hate 'Tiffany'."

"Why? Tiffany is a swell name," Dad commented.

We both looked at him. I gave him the double-lame parent stare. Tiffany looked equally disgusted.

Dad said, "Alright... brother, chillax!"

"Dad, don't try okay?"

A ridiculous lack of coolness.

Tiffany recovered and looked around for the scraps of her hoodie. Seeing that the hood and armpits of her hoodie were beyond repair, I took mine off (the teenage uniform, hoodie, jeans and tennis shoes), handing it to her.

"Thanks."

"No problem. I'll get it back on Monday."

"I don't know, we may not test in the same building."

That was true. It was alphabetical. Hart, Weller; probably not.

"Tuesday then."

"Okay."

"So, I have a huge favor to ask," I began.

"What?" she asked with barely contained skepticism.

"Can you guys keep this thing a secret?" I gave her time to think.

She nodded slowly. "Yeah, you worried you're gonna have to go away, to that special school?"

I nodded. She knew what the deal was.

"Like Parker, right," she expounded.

"Yeah, like that."

She shuddered. "I'm *so* glad that I don't have the effed-up corpse-raising to deal with."

We stood silently, thinking how much it sucked that I did.

"That was pretty cool that you raised your grandma."

"Great-grandma."

"Did ya know her?"

"No, she died the year I was born."

"It was pretty tight how strong she was." Bry rubbed his mouth.

"Yes, she showed remarkable strength," Dad agreed.

"What grade are you in?" I asked Bry.

"Sophomore."

I nodded.

"What did you do on your AP Test?" I was sorta curious to see what he had, being Tiff's brother and all.

"Math-Science," Bry said.

"What focus?" Dad asked.

"Abstractions and Patterns."

Dad palmed his chin thoughtfully, "Really... hmm."

"Dad..."

"Right! Back on task," Dad said.

Tiff had wandered over to the grave to get a closer look, shaking her head.

"I've seen this on the pulsevision, but to see it done in front of you, how we put her back and now it looks like it never happened." She turned to Mia, silent all this time, "Come over here and check this out."

"I'm not going over there." Mia folded her arms across her chest, fuming.

Tiff sighed, "Okay, I am sorry I called you an ass..."

"... potato..." Mia supplied.

"... right... you pissed me off, bailing like that."

She turned to me with that top shelf eye rolling routine she did. I struggled not to laugh. She was kinda funny, tomboyish... smart too. The story that Jade told me didn't agree with this Tiff that I had met.

"What had you all emo about the bird?"

She looked my way, then off into space for a second. "It was the first time I *heard* them. And the whispering," she looked back at me, "it's nothin' like what you hear, but it was pretty creepy."

I nodded, that made more sense, I was freaked out the first time too. Can anyone say, Biology? Über-disgusting class. I suppressed a shudder. I knew I wouldn't be getting a good grade out of that.

We looked a little longer at Gran's perfect grave. Mia stayed away. The day had blown itself out and the wind was gone, leaving behind a pregnant stillness.

We said our goodbyes with assurances of not telling anyone about my issue. The parents didn't have to tell me that the more people that knew I had all five points of AFTD, the sooner I would get attention from the wrong people.

We left the cemetery, Mom giving a final glance at Gran's grave. Her Gran was truly lost, not just to death, but with a different memory superimposed over the old.

CHAPTER 15

Riding in the car seemed longer because Dad wanted to discuss everything to death.

"I suppose it isn't too redundant I mention the timing was less than ideal when Officers Garcia and McGraw made an appearance."

Mom answered, "Yes, that was the worst of luck."

A puzzled expression dominated Dad's face. "What intrigued me was they didn't ask any pertinent questions regarding what experiments I may be conducting." He drove on, thoughtful and silent.

"It terrifies me to think that those two are hanging around like sharks, scenting blood, waiting for any confirmation that Caleb exhibits AFTD. I mean, corpse-raising."

I had her there. "Mom..." I raised my eyebrows, "... is that the politically correct word?"

Mom blushed. "Cadaver-Manipulator."

Those words had the ring of finality.

Dad turned to her, surprised. I wasn't, she came up with the most obscure crap on the planet.

"I have been doing some reading on the subject. What little I could find, doesn't seem to be much available. There isn't that much more written than what John gave Caleb," she said.

Dad gave me eye contact in the rear view mirror then his eyes fell away as he turned on the left hand turn signal. I'd pulse Jade when we got home, the Js needed to know too. Another complication... they just keep on coming. Questions pinged around in my head speeding up, unanswered: could I put something back I raised? I'd done it before and it hadn't been this huge-ass problem. For the first time I thought that it would have been awesome to be able to talk to Jeffrey Parker. He would definitely have answers.

The car glided smoothly into the stall as the door folded down behind us. The engine purred to a stop and Dad turned around in his seat, all of our harnesses automatically unlocking and retracting simultaneously.

137

His face was oh so serious. "What you have here, Caleb, is too big to go untrained. I don't know who to trust but we need someone to help you hone your skills."

I barked out some laughter. The Parents started.

"No offense, Dad, but who even knows anything? I mean, who *can* we trust? I know they'll send me to the Kent Paranormal High but what good will that do if I am hiding what I can fully do? You heard Garcia." I looked down at my hands, clenched and tightly folded. I loosened them purposely, the tension tightly coiled. "He said that he had to, by law, turn me in."

Mom and Dad felt the weight of my words, their message reflected on their faces.

Dad said, "I have read the percentage of the student population for the paranormals in the high school you'll be attending. I assume you'll be attending," he flung a hand out, *of course* I would be there, "and the AFTDs are the smallest in number."

I looked at Dad *and? so?*

"The point is, there will be others like you and they have a trained AFTD teacher that can help you gain a measure of control. They have detailed literature..."

I broke in, "... how does that help me? I mean, if I can't tell anyone what I can do?"

"The why is very important. Knowledge is power, Caleb. Just learning some practical application can speed the process of discipline and control."

Logical as always.

He continued, "The officers, well that is another matter entirely. An unrelated matter."

Mom opened the door and we followed.

Walking into the house I was struck by how odd it seemed. The parents stood completely still, the fine hairs on my body rising.

Dad turned his face to mine, his eyes too wide in their sockets, wild, and shook his head, no noise.

I nodded.

That's when I noticed, everything was overturned and messy. What the Sam Hill was this?

Dad grabbed the baseball bat to the left of the door that leads from the garage to the inside of the house. He held it tightly in his left hand, his knuckles showing white in a bloodless grip, keeping it close and slightly behind his body.

Mom and I stayed behind Dad. He coasted along, his butt to the wall, just turning the corner his body stopped blocking our line of sight, and the living room came into view.

We should have worried about intruders but the room was in such disarray we were stopped in our tracks.

My eyes roamed the mess, some things destroyed. All Mom's indoor plants drooped like sad streamers from a party, discarded.

Mom started to rush forward and Dad clotheslined her and the breath fell out of her in a whoosh. "No Ali, it's not safe," he said, apologetic but firm.

Mom's hands were wrapped around Dad's forearm where it was still barring her way. He looked into her eyes, big as fifty cent pieces, and she straightened up, his arm falling away.

Dad's briefcase and pulse-top were apart and papers were strewn about like confetti. His pulse-top lay open, the blue screen-of-death staring blankly back, a winking eye that never closed. Dad's mouth tightened into a hard line.

"Wait here," he said, walking off down the hallway.

It was the longest five minutes of my life.

Mom and I stood together while Dad cruised the house, searching for the A-holes that had violated our house. What could I do to protect Mom?

Finally, Dad came back, face grim.

"They're not here, but we're not staying here tonight."

"We'll have to pulse the police." Mom walked over to the Fam-pulse.

"Wait!" Mom's thumb wavered above the touch pad, one eyeball hidden by a stray clump of hair.

"What if Garcia comes?" I asked.

"Yes, most interesting," Dad said and Mom humphed at that. "What I mean is, we have done nothing wrong. It chronicles that we may be the ones in danger, not the people hiding things or perpetuating crimes."

"Smart," Mom agreed, her noodle no longer in a twist.

"Sometimes," Dad agreed.

"What about," and I gestured to the house being torn apart, "our house?"

Dad nodded to Mom and she hit the touch pad.

I walked over and stood behind her shoulder watching the words assert themselves on the screen.

911, your emergency? 911 Dispatch
My house has been vandalized. Alicia Hart
Your house number is 26503, Kensington Heights, is this accurate? 911 Dispatch
Yes. Alicia Hart.
Our sensors do not indicate bodily damage. Is there need for an ambulance at your dwelling? 911 Dispatch.
No. Alicia Hart.
Police response will arrive momentarily. 911 Dispatch.
Please stay on your pulse-phone in case intruders re-enter dwelling. 911 Dispatch.

Mom rolled her eyes. She hated all the automation.

She thought again, *Connected-* Alicia Hart. This would allow mom to move around.

"Mom, it's a pulse conversation."

"I'm just that old-fashioned," she said.

Made no sense to me. Who cared, as long as the information was being conveyed.

Dad was hanging on to the bat loosely. I mentioned the bat could go away. He looked down at it blankly, forgetting he'd ever had it. Nodding, he put it back in the garage. That's all we needed, Garcia and the goon squad showing up and getting a load of dad with bat in hand.

Then it struck me; *my room.*

Racing up my coffin step staircase I flung open the door, heaving a big sigh of relief. Everything looked exactly as it normally did.

Dad and Mom came up behind me, staring at my room, as if for the first time. Dad made a gasping noise, like a fish out of water. "Is this," his eyes landed on one mess to the next, a frog leaping from lily pad to lily pad, "normal?"

I nodded vigorously. "Yeah, doesn't look like they made it this far."

Dad kinda had a spacey, buzzed look.

"What?"

Dad looked at Mom. "He really... his room..." Dad paused, uncertain how to continue.

Mom saved him. "Yes honey, I have told you he never listens about cleaning."

"I thought you were just..." he trailed off.

I helpfully supplied the word, "ranting?"

Mom squinted her eyes at me. "Watch it, pal."

I surveyed my room, the pillowcase for my bed in a tightly wadded ball at the corner with the bare pillow bunched up next to it. I had a fake wood floor but my clothes were all over it so no décor to worry about. My desk was at the end of the room, like a dark exclamation point, where the ceiling and eave junction met. A precariously balanced mess of candy wrappers, pizza boxes and different varieties of soda pop cans all neatly crushed and waiting to run out of space so I would then be forced to throw them away. I frowned, thinking that may have to be addressed soon. My dirty clothes hamper was empty of clothes but was a great holder for anything that was not actual trash or laundry. Last months' completed homework, that was never turned in, resided in the graveyard of my hamper.

Dad looked an unspoken question to Mom. "Yep, he's ours."

Dad shook his head again, walking out of my room and downstairs without word.

"What's the matter with Dad?"

"He's had a shock honey."

"Yeah, the losers that wrecked our house."

"Well I think it's a toss up between what happened in our house and him discovering that your room looks like it was ransacked."

"But my room wasn't messed with." I didn't get it.

"I think that may be the shock. That this is the normal state of your room."

Huh. Parents.

Suddenly, I heard the pulse-chime, the cops.

Show time.

I came downstairs and two new cops were in our foyer, guns standing naked in their hands. That one thing made me more nervous than anything could.

When Mom and I appeared, they turned, their guns at the ready.

Dad said, "... Whoa guys, it's just the family."

The woman cop, who was tiny, looked reluctant to re-holster her weapon. She turned to Dad with a husky voice that didn't match her, "Sir, we need to secure the house."

"Of course, go ahead," Dad replied.

She of the small build and tough attitude gave a curt nod to her partner. Her gaze lingered on me for a second, then they went down the hall, guns drawn.

We watched them as they reappeared around corners, magically disappearing again, exploring every part of the house, finally coming to stand in front of us. An awkward silence ensued.

Dad filled it, "So Ali and Caleb, this is," Dad nodded toward the male police officer, "Officer Ward."

"Chuck," he corrected in an automatic way, winking. I gave a slight smile, duly noted, turned to the woman, struck again by how young she looked, "and Officer Roberta Gale."

She didn't correct us.

Officer Gale stepped forward, toward me. I stepped back. Dad turned a puzzled expression her way.

She smiled, but not like she meant it.

"What are you?" she asked.

Huh? "What do you mean?"

Then she let me have it, which wasn't anything like it had been with Tiff. With her it was a soft breeze, a gentle thing. This was like someone took my heart and squeezed it until it burst through their fingers, the breath left my body, I sagged to my knees, sucker punched.

Mom screamed, "Caleb!"

She reached out to grab me, I held out my palm, warding her off... *damn.*

With her extra creepy running through me I reached down where that special power always lay and prayed for enough to deal with this.

The power rose to my call, a life force welling up inside, pouring out of my body like a vessel. I Visualized a spear and aimed it at tough chick Gale. It left me and I let it. I'd never used it as a weapon, but she'd hurt me and I was going to defend myself.

She flew bodily from the floor as if shoved by an invisible hand, landed flat against the wall. A high-pitched whistle escaping in a rush, leaving her mouth opening and closing like a trout out of water.

Officer Ward's gun cleared the holster, again, pointing it at me. He said out of the side of his mouth, eyes never leaving my face, "Bobbi, what's this about? Tell me *right now*, so I don't have to hold my gun on a teenager. I hate this paranormal crap," he muttered.

Officer Gale wasn't talking just then, thank you very much. But her eyes were on my face, her hands pressed to her chest, as if I had shot her. We kept serious eye contact and finally she spoke.

"He's AFTD," she gasped out.

"Didn't I say I hate that paranormal crap?"

If she was like me, why'd she do that? I used my knees as leverage and got to my feet, Dad's hand on my elbow. My parents were looking at Officer Gale like an alien had landed and told us I was their new pet.

The good news was that AFTD, for me, was a rechargeable battery, I was good as new an hour after the cemetery, good to know.

I gave her wary eyes, so did my parents.

"Put the gun away, it was a test," she said.

"Great, think you could warn me next time," Ward said as he holstered his weapon, giving her a nice glare with hard eyes, cop eyes.

The tension eased down a notch.

"I'm sorry, I wasn't expecting this kind of reaction. It was what I was trained to do when I encounter another paranormal, an AFTD paranormal in particular."

"What, suck the life out of me?" I asked with a touch more sarcasm than I intended.

She lowered her eyes, staring at the ground. "I wasn't expecting it to be quite like this." I asked her how she'd known.

"It's hard to explain but it's like when you know someone is American?" I nodded, there were so many foreigners living in the U.S. that it was getting harder, but I knew what she meant. There was a look, an arrangement of features. I knew it when I saw it.

"Or, it's similar to a scent in the air," she bowed her head for a second, "or a taste."

"But you," she emphasized, her eyes meeting mine, "I haven't encountered that before."

Dad interjected, "Isn't it standard procedure to pair a non-paranormal with a paranormal?"

"Not yet," Ward responded. "Soon it'll be a mandate. It's difficult for us to protect the public, when part of the public are paranormals. Informally, we're already pairing."

Ward laughed and pushed away from the wall. I didn't see what was funny.

"Let's face it, people that can set fires by mind control alone, manipulate air, earth, water, raise the dead," Gale looked at me and I kept my face blank, "can, if on the wrong side of the law, be problematic." he shrugged.

Problematic... *ya think*? It was my turn to laugh. I'm sure the cops were busy with the paranormals that were into a life-o'-crime. Did the pharmaceutical tycoons consider that before they released the drugs that gave us the cool skills? *No way.*

Gale regarded me with eyes that reflected nothing. Something about her name clicked. Roberta Gale... ah-huh! She was the chick that used her AFTD to find murder victims and help the police.

Bobbi Gale.

"Aren't you the one that did that article about AFTD?" I asked.

She cocked her head, birdlike, an expression of realization overcame her face. The first true emotion I'd seen so far.

"Oh yeah, that. Well, at that time I was the only AFTD on the force."

"There's more?"

She nodded. "Not many, we're so rare."

"Maybe that's natural selection," I said, more to myself than anyone.

Dad looked at me in surprise.

I grinned. "Sometimes I listen to you."

He grinned back, turning to Gale. "Okay, now that you're done with the theatrics, can we figure out what this," he swept his hand around, "violation means?"

Gale, by this time recovered, took out her pulse-pad. All thoughts and notes transferred as she automatically thought them. Those were cool, gimme, gimme, gimme. I bet most cops had them. Except for Garcia.

She took her thumb off the pad. "Can we talk after we get your statements?"

Mom replied for me, "No more 'testing'."

"Yeah, I promise. I followed protocol exactly. I apologize that it backfired." shaking her head.

"Sure, okay." I was acting cool but I wanted to talk to her if she didn't pull another whammy.

Officer Ward broke in, "Okay, let's go over what happened."

The cops asked my parents a series of questions. Was the house pulse-alarm activated? Had there been suspicious activity? Were there any known enemies? Boring. Like who would remotely care about our family?

Finally, they wrapped up the whole thing, saying they'd make an official report. Automatic police surveillance would be given.

"For how long?" I asked.

Gale looked up from her pulse-pad. "It'll be random, so the perpetrators can't anticipate our moves. Typically, we give about five days."

"This area usually doesn't have this kind of crime," Ward paused, "you sure there isn't someone who has an agenda, a motive?"

He looked at us.

It felt like it was way too much of a coincidence for this to happen as all my voodoo death stuff was coming online. It felt like connected trouble. If I was thinking that, my parents sure were.

Mom and Dad shook their heads the silence swelling like a balloon. They wouldn't have shared anyway, especially after Garcia had said he was law bound to turn in corpse-raisers.

"Okay." She powered down her pulse-pad. "That'll be all for now." Ward gave her a strange look but she was focused on us. He obviously expected more but she had deliberately shut the meeting down.

She turned to me. "Still up for talking?"

Cautious. "Yeah."

"You can use the kitchen table," Mom said.

We walked out of the foyer, through the kitchen, making our way around the breakfast bar, sitting down on the long bench. Gale kept walking, past me, then sat in the queen's chair. I could hear the parents and Officer Ward speaking quietly out in the foyer. It was weird to see her in Mom's chair.

Gale stared at me "Spill it."

I lowered my voice, " 'Spill' what?"

"I know you're more than a two or three-point, AFTD. I have never felt anyone as powerful as you." She rubbed her arms up and down as a person will when they're cold; but she wasn't cold. Mom always had the heat cranked to I'm-going-to-die-in-this-oven temperature. Gale was that creeped out.

I was having that effect on a lot of people lately.

I shrugged. Like I'd admit anything to a cop, look what happened with Garcia?

"I've felt plenty of AFTDs..." she waved her hand at me, "..you're something unique."

I wasn't ready to answer. I decided to ask her some questions.

"How do you know when someone is paranormal?"

She sighed. "It's like I told you before, it's a feeling, a difference. It feels like a low level, electrical buzz."

Like sticking your finger in an pulse socket?

I'm friends with Jonesy.

"Is that what they taught you at the school? How to identify paranormals?"

"Yes, some of it. You'll go to the same school I did. I'm a local girl, ya know." she grinned.

I dug local, they knew the deal, the people, all that jazz.

"What was it like, the school?"

"It's like regular high school, but you're with people that can do amazing things. We're the most rare, but fire-starters are running a close second."

"You mean like the book?"

"The what?"

"The book by Stephen King."

"Who's he?"

"Only the greatest writer globally!"

"Well, I'm not much of a reader but the name rings a bell. What's his story about? Pyrokenetics?"

"Yeah, but it's more. Back then, it was just an idea, fiction. No one ever thought it'd be this." I gestured to include her and I as part of the the paranormal equation.

I leaned forward, she did too. "What do they make you do?" I asked in an almost-whisper.

"Math and English."

Huh, that sucked.

She saw my expression and laughed. "It's not *all* dead stuff and fun! You still have to do core."

"You study Animation of the Dead. That's an actual class, 'Animation of the Dead in Theory'."

"Wait a second, who's in that class? I thought all the corpse, I mean, Cadaver-Manipulator's were so rare..." I let my sentence trail off.

She looked down at her hands for a second time. "Have you heard of Jeffrey Parker?"

Had I heard of Jeffrey Parker? Geez, duh. I nodded my head, checking the sarcasm at the door like a coat.

"We were some of the first, he was ahead of me. A senior when I was a freshman," she paused, a troubled knot between her brows, "he wasn't treated that well. You can understand there would be some prejudice toward him."

Yeah, that.

"Well, he was the first, in the first group of AFTDs. They didn't know what to do with us, *him*. He was more than they were prepared for. Before him, I don't think anyone knew cadaver-renewal was possible. It was just theory. When Jeffrey Parker started to raise things accidentally..."

"What... accidentally, really?" Gee, imagine *that*. My new mantra: control, control, control.

"Yeah, accidentally. In fact, one of the teachers was killed in a car accident, and shuffled to his job the next day."

Well that would have been something.

"But how did they know it was Jeffrey? For sure, I mean. It could have been any of you guys."

She nodded, plausible.

"Because the," she paused here, "... teacher, *dead* teacher," she emphasized, "... shambled over to Jeff and said, 'I am here to serve you'. Not exactly what he would have done in life. The statement was directed at Jeff, not the few other AFTDs in class. Jeff could control him."

Boy, that would be great, raising your teacher for a personal slave.

A fantasy come true. I got a dreamy look.

"Snap out of it. You weren't there, it's not remotely cool." She rolled her eyes. Girls must take eye rolling classes in kindergarten.

"Well, there's a short list of teachers that I want to do My Bidding." I laughed. The Js were getting a full report.

She didn't laugh. Kinda humorless.

"Anyway." she glared at me, well sor-ry. "The AFTD teacher knew that we had ourselves a real, live, Cadaver-Manipulator. No one had ever manifested the five points before. They had a heck of a time figuring out how to put it back."

I bet they did, remembering the fun of getting granny back-in-box. Back-in-coffin?

"What did they do?"

"It was a big deal. The principal came to our class with the Empath Professor." I thought briefly of Jade. "Of course, we had our AFTD professor as well. He was one of the first professors to theorize about the potential for cadaver-renewal," she paused, "it had never been well-received. Then Jeff proved it *could* be done. And he hadn't even tried."

We turned at the same time, hearing the murmurings of the conversation wrapping up in the foyer. Gale dug around in her uniform pocket until she came up with a business card.

It had a big dollop of coffee on it, obscuring the last four numbers of her pulse-phone.

"Ah the heck with it. Do you have your pulse?"

I nodded, turning it in her direction. I put my thumb on the pad and thought; *new contact*.

She looked at me, I nodded as I lifted my thumb.

Gale replaced it with hers. She stared for a second, the green characters illuminated on the screen:

Gale, Bobbi 206.631.6312.

"My direct line, not the Department's 'general'."

"How'd you get that area code? Is it Kent?"

She smiled. "Yeah, it was my grandmother's number. When she passed I inherited it. When Pulse Technology came on board, I transferred it to my pulse."

Officer Ward and my parents walked in and Gale stood. We shook hands. When we touched I'll be damned if there wasn't a sorta low, voltage-type buzz. I didn't let it show on my face, but her eyes widened, too weird.

We trailed the cops into the foyer. Gale mentioned she'd be available if I needed anything, day or night. I'd heard *that* before. She knew *way* more than she let on, her partner included. They left and Mom closed the door behind them softly.

"Major strange," Mom said.

"I wasn't real pleased with the 'testing' of Caleb. It seemed odd," Dad replied.

"I don't trust Garcia much. I liked her better," I said.

"Yes, that was a troubling turn of events at the cemetery."

Troubling? Yeah.

Mom got the broom and dustpan, starting the clean up on the shattered debris of her beloved pots and plants.

"Caleb, go fetch me some of the picnic glasses and we'll get my babies in some water."

Brother...Mom. But when I took in her long, sad face I just turned without a word and went into the pantry, digging through the mess of the closet until I found the recycled plastic goblets, like big colored jewels that sparkled in the light.

"These ones?"

"Yes, those ones."

I walked to the kitchen sink, opening the tap, setting it to *gray water*. I filled each glass about three quarters, arranging them on the windowsill. Low-slanting sunlight streamed through the window, catching them in a kaleidoscope of colors, which lay like jagged pieces on the floor behind us.

Shaking off the dirt in the compost can under the sink, I placed the four plants that would be saved in their respective glasses. I turned to hold the dustpan for Mom.

I cruised the living room, throwing afghans on the back of couches, closing drawers and straightening pillows.

Mom came out from her bedroom. "Nothing has been stolen. Mom's necklace, my fancy bracelet with real diamonds."

Dad looked up, puzzled. "Nothing?"

She shook her head.

"What about your pulse-top, Kyle?"

"The mainframe shut it down the instant someone tried to hack it."

"Did they? Try, I mean."

"They most certainly did. When I return to work on Monday, we'll do an analysis of what files they breached, if any. In the meantime, I won't be able to recover anything, it's locked down. It's for the best, if they return..." Mom startled, her hand flying to her chest.

"We have to consider the possibility."

"I thought the police were watching," I said.

"True, but they don't have the manpower to be here twenty-four hours a day, son."

That blows. Out loud I said, "That doesn't seem safe enough. I mean, they didn't rob us, but somehow, they got in even with pulse-security." I turned to Dad and he nodded. "So they can get in again."

"I'll change the pulse-code," he said.

"But, what I'm saying is, how did they get in to begin with? The cops said there were no signs of forced entry."

Dad rested his chin on his hand. "That's the best I can do. Also, it provides a fail-safe."

"A what?" I asked.

"A way to find out who or what may know sensitive information, like our pulse-code," Mom said.

"So that means if someone got in here again, it's an inside job?" I clarified.

"Exactly," Dad agreed.

"Can't we just assume that now?" Mom asked.

"I'd like to, but the scientist in me insists that it may have been some malfunction, or someone using one of the many pulse tools out there to neutralize settings."

"Thereby allowing them to assign a new pulse-code," Mom finished.

"Right," Dad said.

The clean-up continued its silent course for the next hour. Four o'clock came around and Mom started to do her thing in the kitchen. It was magical. She disappeared in the kitchen, looked inside our empty fridge, pulled a few things out and ta-da! a meal was ready. Now, if I were to try that same thing, looking in the freezer and pantry for good measure, which I often did as a ritual, there would not be anything popping off the shelves saying something cool like, eat me.

"What's for supper Mom?"

Mom turned around, looking lost. Dad noticed, their eyes meeting.

"How about a McDonald's run?" he asked the two of us.

Huh? Could I get this lucky?

"Alright!" I said, doing a Jonesy-style fist pump.

Mom's shoulders slumped a little. Don't ruin it Mom, I silently begged. Dad closed the distance, taking her by the shoulders and they stared into each others eyes. About this time was my cue to take off... but I stayed. We were in this whole mess together, this was not a gross-out parents moment.

He ran his hands up and down her arms, sort of caressing her. "It's been a tough day on all of us. Just... let's go out."

Mom opened her mouth, to protest I think. But Dad put a finger to her lips. "Let me take care of you and Caleb tonight. I know you like to make the suppers, but let's get some food in us and a good night's rest. Things will look better tomorrow."

She smiled, a wan thing, not her usual, full toothed grin. "Hey, that's my line buster." She playfully punched him. He released her, his hands sliding down her bare arms.

A caress, I thought, definitely a caress.

****

McDonald's was always an act of self-restraint. I had a fantasy, where, I walked up to the counter (glided up to the counter), and began with, I'll have one of everything.

Unfortunately, the reality was more like Dad finding a place to sit and Mom selecting the food. As Dad put it, "She's the health nut of the house, son."

That meant that I usually couldn't get a milkshake. It didn't matter if they were made with seaweed or not. I had tried that argument with Mom and she didn't buy it.

Imagine my surprise when she came to the table with not two but *three* shakes!

That meant it had been a Really Bad Day.

Mom slid into the booth and put the tray on the glaring orange Formica table top. "It's been a really bad day," she said as she sat down next to me.

Yay for ransackers! I guess it was too much for a family to go through for milkshakes, but it was a near thing.

I tore the lid off, sighing with pleasure at the chocolaty goodness.

Mom opened hers and threw in a straw which stood up in the center of the cup in a satisfying way. I liked to slurp and Mom hadn't bothered to get me a straw. She had strawberry and Dad had vanilla.

Neapolitan family.

Dad thought that someone suspected me but without proof they had fished around, hoping to find confirmation of my Cadaver-Manipulator status.

"Caleb," she said, swallowing a mouthful of fry, then chasing it with some shake. "What about those papers that John gave you?"

Ah! I had forgotten all about those.

"Maybe they're in my locker at school?" I said hopefully.

"Really? Why would you have taken them there?" Mom asked.

She knew organizing wasn't a strong point of mine.

Mom's half eaten meal was before her. I slid her tray over to my side and started polishing off was left. Her shake was also made available. To all the germ-naysayers out there, I stand by the "family cootie" mantra of we're all exposed to each other's germs anyway so a little shared shake wasn't going to take away my fun. I slurped and gulped, quietly, as to not get nailed, listening to the parents figure out our next move. Trays were emptied in the separator and we piled back into the car, the seat harnesses locking after Dad pulsed the car ignition.

It was a silent drive on the way home. Dad glided back into his spot in the garage but turned to us. "You guys stay here and let me look inside."

Our days of just roaring in and out of the house were behind us. No longer did I feel safe.

Mom and I waited in silence. The first thing I was gonna do was pulse Jade, then the Js. A bright spot in the week was picking up black dog on Tuesday. If I survived that long, I thought morbidly.

Dad gave the thumbs up. Mom and I got out, walking into the house. She paused just inside the door and I almost piled into the back of her. She sighed, then headed for the kitchen. Dad came over to her and gave her a side hug and she leaned into him, her head tucking almost into his armpit. I got out of there. Dad could deal with Mom and the house would survive. Whether we would, now that was another story.

I rushed to my room flipping my hair out of my eyes as I went and jerking my pulse out of my pocket. I flew into the air and back-landed onto the bed. Home sweet home. I pressed my thumb onto the pad and thought: *Jade.*

Green letters appeared: *Hey.-*JLeC
What's up with you? CH
*Nothing much, Sophie's here.-*JLeC
*Oh. Well, our house was broken into and the cops came.-*CH
*What?! **gasp** Are you guys okay? Why was it broken into? Did Garcia come?* JLeC
*Ya know why. No, he didn't; some other cops.-*CH
You think? JLeC
*I do. I think it's all about that.-*CH
Well, Sophie's here (I can't really talk much) so I better go. Are we still meeting at your house tomorrow? JLeC
*Yeah. Say, three o'clock or around there.-*CH
*Okay, I'll be there.-*JLeC
*Can't wait to see ya.-*CH
***smiles**, Caleb?-*JLeC
Yeah? CH
*Be careful.-*JLeC
*Okay **smiles**-*CH

Next stop, the Js. I pressed my thumb back on the pad *disconnect* and thought the command: *three-way: Jonesy and John Terran.*

*Hey dill weed.-*MJ
*Hi.-*John Terran
*Hey-*CH
Thinkin' about tomorrow Caleb? MJ
*Yeah, ya know I am. But, something happened today that is freaking me out, big time.-*CH
What happened? John Terran
Some losers came through the house and tore it up, broke mom's plants, tried to hack my dad's pulse-top. It was bad. Then the cops showed.- CH
Garcia? MJ
*No.-*CH

You think they're looking for the 'goods'? John Terran

smiles slyly... good one John. Maybe. That's what Dad and I think.-CH

laughs it's not funny, but you have the dumbest luck.-John Terran

They couldn't find anything anyway.-MJ

Probably not...but.-CH

The papers I gave you distress! John Terran

nodding... right.-CH

*Profanity block! That's right, John gave you the corpse papers...*MJ

Yeah sighs.-CH

Are those at school... maybe? John Terran

Well, I hope they are but I'm not much for organizing my locker. The only thing I hope is, they looked at my room and figured it'd be too much time to search laughs.-CH

guffaws you got that goin' on Caleb! MJ

So, are you guys staying at the house? I mean, is it safe? John Terran

Yeah, the cops said they'd do random surveillance.-CH

Okay, we'll talk about this more tomorrow. Let me think about it more. Maybe we can figure out who did it, or why? What about Jade? Can she do anything with her mojo? John Terran

Mojo, John? Laughs, I don't know but let me ask her, alright? CH

Get over yourself, Caleb, we won't frisk the girlfriend.-MJ

Yeah, you chumps just follow my lead.-CH

Pushy bastard! MJ

*Just for you laughs.-*CH

You guys come over about three o'clock.-CH

Okay, what are you telling your parents? MJ

That we're gonna hang out.-CH

That's so not going to work if you have another corpse day.-John Terran

*Well... actually...*CH

You... what, did it again? MJ

Yeah. Today Dad thought it would be a good idea to visit the cemetery and experiment with my 'growing abilities'.-CH

Well, profanity block! How'd that go? John Terran

Not real well. But I got granny back in the ground.-CH

WTF?! MJ

You raised your dead grandmother? John Terran

Yeah, I meant to, but she sorta got out of control, and then Tiff Weller and I... CH

WHAT?! John Terran

You don't even know Tiff Weller. Wait a sec...what was she even doing in the cemetery? MJ

Hang on to your shorts guys, I will tell you the whole thing tomorrow. I don't want this on our pulses, you feel me? CH

silence

Okay- John Terran

Yeah, I got ya, but you're killin' me dude. MJ

Three o'clock, right? John Terran

Okay, see ya. -CH

I powered down my pulse to sleep mode and was immediately lost in my thoughts. The Js were gonna have to know about the lovely graveyard mess, then the house break in. Was it getting dangerous for my friends to know some of this stuff? For Jade? I just didn't have any answers anymore. Like I had all the answers anyway, duh. Things felt like they were spinning out of control.

It was all in motion now, too late to turn back.

CHAPTER 16

I didn't sleep well. Every noise, every scrape of a branch against a windowpane was cause for wakefulness. At one point, I sorta gave up and sat up on my knees, turning to the window and looking out, confident that I could not be seen.

The street stood quietly, a breeze lifting a tree branch now and then. The moon cast shadows under the streetlights, pools of light bordered by inky blackness.

As I watched, a police cruiser slowly pulled up. Idling for a few seconds, an officer got out, then a second from the other side, Garcia and McGraw! What were they doing here? I sure didn't feel safer with them guarding the house. No siree. My hands gripped the windowsill, leaning forward, I pressed my nose pressed to the glass, careful not to fog up the window with my breath.

Garcia turned suddenly as if McGraw had said something, bending to hear him. Surreptitious whispering ensued, their heads pressed together, one blond, the other so dark it blended with the night.

They looked up at my room at that precise moment. It took a whole lot for me not to jump down underneath the window.

But I wasn't noticed.

A sigh of relief escaped me into the hushed silence of my room.

Just as they were finishing their covert conversation, another cruiser pulled up. Officers Gale and Ward got out.

Now this was interesting.

I was certain we didn't need four cops. I rested my butt cheeks against my heels, perching for the duration.

Even in the gloom it was easy to tell which cop was Gale. She was clearly the smallest, a whole head and then-some shorter than Garcia, he being the tallest and Ward a little shorter. As obsessed with growing as I was, I noticed people's heights. Bobbi Gale was around Jade's height, but built bigger, solid, like she worked out.

There was some arm flailing going on with Gale gesturing to our house and then throwing her hands up in the air. Ward had his arms crossed across his chest, not pleased. McGraw was mirroring Ward's stance and Garcia was nose to nose with Gale. Their height difference didn't really allow for that but she was right in his face, her's craning up to make eye contact.

Finally, McGraw touched Garcia's shoulder and he stepped back... away from Gale. I could see his shoulders hike up in an exaggerated shrug, with a wave of his hand he dismissed our house and walked over to his cruiser. McGraw followed, turning once to give a considering look at Gale. Even from my vantage point I could see her glower at him.

She was pissed. It was in the set of her shoulders, the way tension sang along them. I would've loved to heard what they said.

The two cops got into their car, pulling away into the night. Gale and Ward looked after them, then they got in their cruiser, backing up into the space that McGraw and Garcia had vacated.

That was odd as hell, what were they arguing about? I knew it wasn't a shift change thing because Gale and Ward said random. Could it be that McGraw and Garcia were not supposed to be here and showed up? Showed up for what, my mind asked the obvious. I just didn't know.

I stared for a couple more minutes, barely making them out in the gloom. Gale in the driver's seat and Ward beside her, gesturing and talking, a badge twinkling in the dim light cast by the streetlight. I laid back down, crossing my arms behind my head and thinking. I tossed and turned, but sleep evaded. Finally, I fell into a fitful sleep, unconsciousness pulling me under like a pebble in a river.

CHAPTER 17

I was swimming, the sun shining through the water, me at the bottom looking through layers of grayish-green, a great pale orb shining dimly above me. It was important that I reach it.

Moving a hand in front of my face, it floated there like a dead, pale fish. I moved my body, feeling the resistance and rose determinedly toward the surface, my hands knifing through the water. As I gained speed, the heat grew, the light intensifying. The coolness of the water retreating as I surfaced. Breaking through I opened my eyes.

I was in my room.

I became aware of things in stages, as if still dreaming and unable to wake up. I pinched myself, yup, that hurt, definitely awake. A red crescent appeared where I'd self-damaged.

The Js and Jade would be here in three hours. Sitting up, I moved my neck in a loose circle, definitely stiff from the shitty night's sleep.

Last night! I sat up on my knees, pulling the curtain aside. The cops were gone and any evidence of their presence wiped away. I looked at the sky, noticing storm clouds brewing, a brisk breeze hammering them through. Perfect cemetery weather. I was trying for optimistic. The ass-twins would get good and distracted, I'd get some space before the AP Test tomorrow and we'd pick up black dog.

Leaning across the bed I cracked the window. The May heat would buzz up here, making it eighty degrees by nighttime. Getting off the bed, I kicked a pile of junk out of the way of the door and headed downstairs.

Dad was downstairs in his fave chair working with his pulse-top. Reading the news, the most boring use of time. Mom wore her apron finishing pancakes. Music swam around the room on low volume, while she put the fixings on the table, butter, the cow, the milk, and syrup. Dad was gonna succumb. He tried to limit pancakes because he was O.L.D and didn't want to get F.A.T.

I plopped down in my seat and Mom gave me the eye.

"Kinda late getting up this morning, pal."

"Did you hear the cops?" I asked.

Mom rolled her eyes and Dad looked up from his pulse-top, closing it.

"I thought you said that was shut down Dad?"

"It is, I was just putting it through some security paces."

I looked at him.

"Security protocol," he said in way of explanation. "Rudimentary procedure before I have one of our tech people go through it."

"Oh. I thought maybe you got it fixed and were reading the boring news or something," I said.

Dad smiled. "That 'boring news', keeps me up-to-date on world events, Caleb."

Ah-huh.

"I didn't hear a thing," Mom said.

"I was awake when they came around midnight," Dad said.

"Oh. I didn't hear that time, just the four a.m. run when Garcia and McGraw came."

"That makes me all warm and fuzzy," Mom said.

Yeah.

Dad had chipmunk cheeks, but after a few chews he stated, "I flat-out don't like Garcia and McGraw showing up."

I nodded. Mom was quiet, a rare thing.

"They looked like they were arguing out there."

"Who?" Dad asked.

"Ward and Gale were there too."

"What? That's bizarre. They don't need that much show of force to deter a criminal revisit," he said.

"I guess it's too much to ask what they were arguing over," Mom said.

"Yeah, but the girl..."

"Officer Gale?" Mom asked.

"Yeah, she looked pretty pissed." Mom made a face. "She was using a lot of hand gestures, right up in Garcia's face."

"Based on how they looked, what do you speculate they were talking about?" Dad asked.

Judging on how different Garcia had been at the cemetery I had a feeling that I had his full attention, and not the good kind. Gale knew I was AFTD like her. She suspected I was something unique, but wasn't ready to out me to anyone. I got a sense of protectiveness from her that I wasn't getting from Garcia. I told the parents that, I also told them I thought she had argued about why they felt they needed to show up. As far as we knew, Garcia and McGraw weren't on this case.

After a moment, Dad said, "I think that Garcia has our house, you...all of us," his finger having encompassed us, flagged in some way. If anything happens here of any importance, he's alerted."

"I don't like it," Mom said.

Dad shrugged. "I am concerned about Garcia's watchfulness. It's not a matter of *if*, but when he finds out Caleb is a C-M."

They were solemn. I kept wolfing down my pancakes. Talk of my discovery as a corpse-raiser does not interfere with The Appetite. The parents would allow possible government exploit, espionage, capture and imprisonment to effect theirs. Huh.

"What can we do legally, Kyle, to stop this interference? He's just a kid, a minor for goodness sake." As she lowered her chin, her hair fell forward.

Dad tucked a strand behind her ear, where it curled around the lobe."I've been looking into that. We'll go to the press if it comes to that. If he gets noticed, and they try to pull a 'Parker', we'll see how uncomfortable we can make them. They managed to stuff a lot of the press about the Parker boy, but there is heightened awareness now. Awareness of Paranormals and awareness of the AFTDs."

I didn't like the sound of that. I'd be famous, like Dad, but not because I was a brainiac. Because I was a freak. Nobody wants to be famous for weirdness. Infamous.

"Why does everyone think AFTDs are weirdos?"

Mom said, "You're not a weirdo Caleb." Her gaze steady on my face.

"*I* know that I'm not. But the kids at school think other paranormal abilities are cool. Everyone is grossed out about AFTD and they don't even know. Well, not all of them." I thought of Bry and Tiff Weller, Mia and the A-hole pair. Some kids knew. The Js and Jade didn't count.

"I know you're not keen on people on a larger scale, knowing of your unique ability. But the alternative is not acceptable. Do you think anyone thought that this would be the outcome? That mapping the genome and its subsequent use to unveil these abilities in the human race was going to be without uncertainty, challenges, danger?" Dad asked.

He was right. The other scientists, who took up where he and his team left off, didn't consider the consequence of their actions. Now we had people my age through mid-twenties that could do some pretty extraordinary things. And there wasn't always a counter to that, except for psychic Nulls and those weren't common. Some paranormals were committing crimes, and our police were chasing their asses trying to keep up with that.

He shrugged. "Hearing the officers concede that they were switching to paired mundanes/paranormals was a good thing. They need it."

"Why do they break the law?" I asked.

Mom muttered, "Because they can."

Dad looked at her. "There will always be people making the wrong choice, it's human nature."

"The world spins," Mom said.

I admired her sense of justice but I just couldn't, as she would say, embrace it.

I glanced at the clock, straight up one o'clock. "The Js are coming over with Jade at three."

"You know, Jade is a 'J' too," Mom said.

"Yeah, I guess, but she's not. Ya know, she's her own thing."

"Autonomous," Dad said. "Independent from the Js."

"Oh! Well that's true." I blushed, Jade was so *not* like the Js.

My parents pretended not to notice how awkward the whole Jade conversation was.

"So, what's the plan at three?" Mom asked, neatly changing the subject. My parents were mainly cool.

"We're gonna go hang out."

"Where?" Dad asked, trying to find butter on his plate with the last bite of pancake.

"We're just gonna walk around." The parents would have cattle if they knew I was gonna go to Scenic Hill Cemetery. It occurred to me that I might have wanted to get Tiff up there for back up. Huh. Kinda late for that.

"Okay," Dad said, giving me some space.

I gave a mental sigh of relief, they'd bought it.

I needed to get the twins off my back and the J-Man had the plan... I hoped.

CHAPTER 18

Everyone showed up on time; for Jonesy that was nothing short of a miracle, time management was not a priority. Scheming was (we all had our talents). As in now, scheming five seconds out the door.

Jade walked beside me on my left, absolutely mouth-watering in a pink hoodie, faded jeans with strategic holes, and pink high top All Star basketball shoes. Did she play, I had asked her at one point? No, she just thought they looked tight. And they did... on her. Her hair, which usually flowed around her face like dark water was pulled up in a ponytail, the end making a black sweep in the valley of her shoulders.

I casually held her hand, not fingers entwined but cupped around it fully. I loved feeling its smallness. One of the many things I liked about Jade, other than her utter coolness as a person, was how physically small she was. It didn't diminish her. She didn't have some complex about it. She knew who she was and that was very cool.

Jonesy had been talking the whole time since we left and I started tuning in, even with the distraction of Jade.

The bag full of gear rattled as he walked animatedly beside John, who was between us.

"Anyway, like I was saying, I snagged the can of Aqua Net a couple of weeks ago out of my mom's separator and the lighter..."

"How'd you manage the lighter?" John asked.

"My dad registered it for BBQ-ing," Jonesy said automatically.

Lighters were like guns now. With the explosion of paranormals, there was also that small group within the paranormals, the fire-starters. Not a fully PC term, it was sorta like corpse-raiser. Any accelerant: lighters, matches, fuel, had to be registered like guns. Now that we had the Pyrokenetics, they could use anything like that as a deadly weapon. Some really talented ones didn't need anything. They were the weapon. And I thought

being an AFTD was something. Starting fires would be the coolest!
I told the Js that.

"No way," John said automatically. "Think about the control
and all the adults up your ass all the time. Ah... no, that would suck
dude, big time."

"I like it. I could think of about a million things to torch!
Starting with the school!" Jonesy fist-pumped.

He had us grinning like fools.

Jonesy was busy outlining the plan but stopped midway with,
"You're not gonna like, make something pop out of the ground,
Caleb?"

I laughed. I got a picture of a Jack-in-the-Box, or, as it were,
Jack-in-the-Coffin, a grin spreading across my face with the visual.
"Nah, that's totally not the plan." Jade squeezed my hand and I
squeezed back.

John, all seriousness said, "But you just had that deal with
your grandma at the cemetery."

"Great-grandma."

John shrugged, *whoever*.

"You didn't need blood? To like, put her back?" Jonesy asked
before I could answer John.

"No. I've been thinking about that. Maybe it was coincidence
the blood happened to be part of it last time. Gran rose without any
of that."

But a knot of unease had begun to build in my chest. What
if... what if there was something special I needed to do to get a
corpse back to rest? I mean, Tiff had been there and saved my ass
yesterday, but what if she hadn't?

"Okay, so we don't have to worry about an accident?" John
asked, placing stress on that last word.

Like potty-training, nice.

Jonesy hooted, "Accidental corpse-raising!"

"No, I don't having any corpse-raising plans today."

Jade spoke up for the first time, "Why are we meeting them at
the cemetery then? Why here?" Her opposite hand swept in the
general direction of the cemetery that wasn't quite in view yet.

Jonesy rolled his eyes and I gave him the look.

"That's *our* turf. Caleb pulled the creep-out card there and
they'll feel all, off-base. Plus," he pointed to the side of his head

and tapped his temple, "The Master," clearly indicating himself, "needs a proper environment."

John's eyebrows shot up. Usually, John was the brains of the operation. Jonesy was in his element, scheming.

It must have showed on our faces because Jonesy said, "Hey, I know that I'm not brilliant but I've got rockin' good ideas, and I'm rollin' with that program." We laughed, there was no denying he had a program.

We crested the hill, the gates of the cemetery loomed, framing the cemetery beyond. I gave a little shudder, the sensory memory playing through my body like a discordant instrument. Jade looked a question at me and I shook my head. Hard thing to explain. Had to be there or in her case, *not*.

The weather hadn't improved, in fact, it looked like it was working up a head of steam, a late spring storm. The clouds boiled above our heads like giant pewter boulders.

John saw where I was looking and said, "Might rain."

Jonesy shrugged. "We'll get Carson and Brett all lit up before the sky opens."

I looked at my beat up watch, it was riding at four o'clock. Getting late but probably wouldn't be dark until almost nine.

"What time is it?" John asked.

"Time for the ass-clowns to show," Jonesy muttered.

Jade covered her mouth, hiding a smile but Jonesy caught it, joining in.

And just like that, the duo in question rounded the hill behind us as if conjured. Their blond heads glowed in the dim light of an overcast sky. The two of them climbed the hill with determination, dual expressions of purpose... *a bad one.*

****

Carson and Brett stopped just in front of our group, Brett making a point of staring down Jade. I wondered if he had told Carson about the other night with his dad's meltdown and the gopher attack.

Ah-*no*.

The breeze had come up and it was windy. The great trees inside the cemetery stood sentinel, their sweeping branches moved by invisible puppet strings.

Jonesy came forward with his bag of goodies swinging into his legs as he did. Carson met him.

They stared at each other. "I've got this experiment all planned out for ya. Me and the guys tried it last year and it turned out *cool*."

Even to me it sounded suspicious, but Carson looked interested. The only reason he'd be motivated to try something that was connected with the three of us (four, I guess, since Jade was starting to be part of the group), was a way to prove how much of a mondo-stud he was.

Typical.

Carson leaned forward, trying to scope what was in the bag. Jonesy pulled the bag back using a back and forth motion with his finger, *no-oh.... not yet.*

"Come on Carson, this is some kinda game, let's get outta here," Brett said.

Jade and I were silent. We knew what had gone down and now I was feeling unsure about making Brett pay, but Carson...that was okay. The Js and I had decided that if Carson was taught a lesson, Brett would lay off too, following his lead. I liked it better because Carson just acted like an anus cause he could. He didn't have worries, the ass-hat.

"Nah, I want to see what Jonesy's got that's so special."

"Let's take a walk," Jonesy said.

We followed Jonesy with his bag of mayhem into the cemetery. As soon as I crossed the threshold, the buzzing of their voices rose to a fever-pitch, like the low droning of bees. That was with me trying to tune it out. I should have been able to hear the dead even further away. But there was something about actually being *in* the cemetery that seemed to make it resonate deeper.

I stalled a little and Jade slowed beside me, her eyes widening and I knew she was getting a little feedback.

She confirmed this when she whispered, "Are those the voices?"

I nodded.

"Is it like this all the time?"

"Not always, but this close to a big nest o' corpses, oh yeah."

Everyone turned to look at us and we began to walk again. Jade and I stopped holding hands. She didn't need the overlap and I was straining for control. This was a bad place, I thought belatedly.

This much dead were just impossible to ignore for me. Now that Jade wasn't touching me, it was a little better. She was like a radio antenna, she amplified their signal. Kinda like Tiff. Interesting. But Jade wasn't AFTD. Something to consider.

Jonesy and Carson stood close with Jonesy taking out each item for the science experiment. It looked like a strange hodgepodge to me. Jade shared the same expression. But as I remember, when Jonesy pulled this on *us*, we had fallen for it. If I was guessing right, he had improved on his original idea.

Jonesy was all seriousness. The first clue that this whole thing was an absolute farce. He said to Carson, "You take this tube-thingey," he pulled a bizarre, corrugated tube that looked like something Dad had put by the foundation of our house and Jonesy then pointed to Brett, "holds the other end, while you," and he mimed depressing the small spray tip of the hairspray can, "spray this crap inside the tube."

"Why is it duct taped on this side?" Carson asked.

Jonesy did a long, slow blink at Carson.

Wow, he had the IQ of a shovel.

"It's to keep the Aqua Net inside the tube, Carson." Jonesy elaborated slowly.

Carson tried to save face. "I knew that," he countered.

Right.

John sorta turned away and laughed into his hand, pretending to cough. Brett glared in his direction.

Brett asked the first smart question of the night, "What's the lighter for? How'd you get it?"

Jonesy smiled. "Swiped it from my dad."

I was sorta drowning in the voices but making a colossal effort to quiet them. Gotta get through this. I just wanted these two to figure out that we weren't gonna be messed with, to leave us all alone.

Carson asked, "You guys did this, right?"

We all nodded, I gritted my teeth, *get on with it.*

Then, just to sweeten the deal I asked, "Scared?"

Carson lowered his chin like a bull before a red flag, fists clenching and said through gritted teeth, "We can do anything you ass-wipes can do."

Resolute, his chin rose and he crossed his arms across his chest.

Going to plan.

Almost like it was choreographed, Jonesy motioned Brett over, handing the tube with the duct tape out to him. Carson stalked to Jonesy and tore the can of hairspray out of Jonesy's hand. The top spun off from the force and became a bright pink exclamation point on top of a grave marker. Nice. Jade watched with fascinated horror.

I sorta knew it wouldn't end well, but it was like the chocolate with the mystery stuff on the inside. I suspected it would taste bad but there might be something about it I liked.

Jonesy ignored Carson's crap and opened the palm that held the lighter. A ghost of a smile formed on Carson's lips. I wasn't liking that development. He shouldn't have been smiling.

He leaned forward and delicately plucked the lighter out of Jonesy's hand.

Jonesy backed away, a little uncertain. "So... Brett holds the duct tape end and you like," he mimed depressing the sprayer gizmo again, "spray a bunch in there until that's all you can smell, then light the lighter just as you stop the stream."

Brett had an expression on his face that might have been some sort of thought process.

John immediately saw the dilemma and took it in hand, seeing that the whole thing could go sideways."Look, you guys, if you're chickenshit or something, you don't have to do it. We won't hold it against you," John said, all sincere-like with a hand laying over his heart.

We all nodded our agreement that we would definitely not be inclined to spread crap about them in school. Riiiggghhhttt. I could see how John's cleverness was going to work this kink right out.

"No, we'll do it. I can't see any of you guys not saying anything." Carson looked at each one of us, lingering on Jade longest. Who stared defiantly back at him.

"You just remember, we," he included Brett in this, "have the goods on you, Hart. We know what you are, what you can do. We know who to call..."

"Ghostbusters?" Jonesy asked, eye alight.

We laughed, they glared.

Standing just inside the gate, with unspoken consensus, we moved over to a stand of fir trees, away from direct line-of-sight.

Avoid prying adult eyes at all costs.

Brett held the tube up. The black exterior looked very much like the old-fashioned accordions, with the duct tape end facing him, his hands circling it like a steering wheel. Carson readied the can, carefully facing the spray nozzle away from his face and sprayed into the tube.

Even from a few feet away I could see the mist and smell the God-awful cosmetic smell wafting around. How did women wear that? It meant something that you could set it on fire... ah, hello?

Carson positioned the lighter, depressing the ignite button just inside the tube. Exactly like what happened to us a year ago, there was a sucking noise. What I didn't remember was that nothing happened at first.

Then....

Flames burst out of the open end in an orange tangle, licking along the sides and traveling toward Brett's hands. Just before Brett dropped the tube, Carson leaned *into* the flames.

John and I had about exactly three seconds to exchange a look, *what-the-hell?*

But when we glanced back at Carson, we saw what the problem really was. The fire hovered like a lover, all around Carson's face but leaving him untouched.

Jonesy, never one for internal dialogue said, "What the hell is this?"

That about covered it.

Brett was backing up, backing away from Carson, who turned to us with an evil grin. Fire was still moving around his face in a wave. He held out his hand and a small flame swept down his arm, blue in its center, burning just above his palm.

"So, you were saying Hart? You want to go chew some glass? Sounds like a good plan to me."

Beautiful, Carson the Comedian.

We stood speechless.

Holy hell.

I guess Carson had the fire thing goin' on and Jonesy, the Plan-Man, hadn't counted on this.

Zero contingency plan; nada, zilch, zip.

Shit.

Brett was well and far away from Carson with a stunned expression. A surprise ability apparently.

John stepped in, the voice of reason. "Listen, it was just a joke, you've been up Caleb's ass since forever and it was just a little payback. You don't need to torch us."

John put his hands out like, *just all fun-and-games here.*

"I'm not gonna torch you guys... just him."

And with that delightful objective, he did just that, putting his hand back, readying to throw the ball o' fire.

Everything happened in slow motion. I heard Jade gasp beside me and I gave her a hard shove to get her out of the literal line of fire.

Jonesy shrieked, "Hey!"

But it was John that shocked me, stepping right into Carson, the two of them colliding, the fire halting mid-throw. There was a crazy flame floating, suspended between myself and Carson. It moved neither backward or forward, but sputtering and flickering, trying to go out.

With a roar, Carson leaped forward trying to recapture the flame but John drop-tackled his ass and they both went down. Once John nailed Carson, the flame died out completely.

"Get off me Terran!" Carson roared, grabbing John by his frizzy mass of hair, pulling him off his legs by his scalp. Now that the fire was out, John had started to get up but Carson, typical jerk-off that he was, just *had* to get into with John.

"Hey! Let go!" John gave him an elbow to the nose and a spray of blood erupted. Carson howled and grabbed his nose, kicking John right in the kneecap. John went down holding his knee.

Well... damn.

I ran over to break it up before the whole world figured out that something was going on besides a practical joke.

And was interrupted by Jade's dad.

He appeared at the entrance of the cemetery, the wind lifting his sweating hair off his forehead. Fists clenched and breathing heavy, his chest rising and falling, swooping in great lungfuls of air. I was struck by how much he moved and looked like Brett's dad; he was in a lot better shape.

His timing blew.

I swung my head in Jade's direction and, prone on her butt (oops, shoved harder than I meant) she gave me the I'm-caught-rabbit-stare.

He hollered, "Jade... what in the blue hell are you doin' hanging out with this pack of boys?" His face had flushed an alarming purple color as he began making his way toward us.

He scared me to death, a fine tremble coursed through my body. I called Jade over; she scrambled to her feet and ran. His momentum was carrying him, he was gonna put a hurt on us and I wasn't gonna let it be Jade.

My next move was as natural as breathing. Instantly remembering that Jade and I worked like complements, I grabbed her hand and flung out every bit of my power over the dead. Mr. Scary was wading through graves, his fists like great meaty hammers, coming to nail us.

Like a great flowing river, the power left my body: a vessel fully released of its contents.

I looked over at Jade and she was breathing rapidly. Her eyes so wide the whites showed, the startling green irises standing out, burning like emeralds on fire.

Like before, nothing happened, then... chaos reigned.

The graves in front of him burst upward, sod and dirt exploding in every direction. Hands followed; two, three, no... five graves shifting and opening to allow the dead to rise.

My dead.

Starting from my toes, the full flesh crawl climbed my body.

Jade was saying something real soft, "no, no, no." I released her hand.

"I think I can take it from here," I said, stepping away. So much for not raising the dead.

Like a freight train, Jade's dad hesitated at the junction, not sure what track to choose.

"What the hell is this?" He flung his arms wide, including the corpses.

Violence wasn't the only thing that Brett and Jade's fathers had in common. The smell of alcohol preceded him by a mile. Brother, what a loser.

I had a collection of corpses now standing. Their eyes vacant, waiting for direction, purpose. I stepped forward and they all swung their heads to me.

"Protect us from him." I pointed a finger at Jade's dad.

Her dad wasn't drunk enough to *not* understand the potential for self-preservation.

"Come here Jade. You don't need to be hanging out with them losers," he said.

That was a joke. Him calling us losers. I looked back at the ass-potatoes, Carson and Brett. Excluding them, maybe he *was* onto something with them.

"No daddy. I won't ever come back," Jade said, stepping forward as if to speak with him. I grabbed her arm. She wasn't going near him.

She turned to me and shook her head, like, *it's okay.*

I redoubled my hold and shook my head back. "No fucking way Jade."

The corpses started to get agitated. One in particular. He shambled forward, keeping his eye on Jade's dad, who had begun to inch closer.

The corpses closed in on him, a tide wave of death to shore.

Oh geez. This is the one I had raised before... Clyde. Fluke of flukes. In the whole graveyard I couldn't raise a new corpse? I bet raising zombies more than once wasn't a good thing.

"I have risen again," Clyde said, his voice full of the dirt-sound I was getting used to. "For what purpose, necromancer...for what purpose."

The other zombies, in various stages of rot, stared at me.

"I'm sorry," I rushed out. "This guy is going to put a serious pounding on us and I need help."

The corpses turned their attention to Jade's dad.

"A bunch of dead people ain't gonna matter to me boy! I'm gettin' my girl back and there ain't shit from shinola you can do about it!"

He lunged forward to grab Jade and I felt intent form in my mind, I didn't have one moment to say anything, but the corpses knew.

They knew what needed doing.

We were of one mind, the zombies and I.

The twice-raised zombie (my guy-in-charge, I thought wildly), swung its arm in the path of Jade's dad, clotheslining him.

His progress effectively halted, he turned, wading into the batch of corpses. He threw a punch into Clyde and all he got for his trouble was some black ooze from the impact with the corpse's face whose teeth gleamed through his cheek.

Clyde-the-Corpse took the beating, placing a hand on either side of Jade's dad's head, boxing his ears. He howled, kneeing Clyde in the gut. Clyde obligingly rolled down the small knoll, just out of sight.

Holy shit.

Jade's dad hissed a sound of fierce triumph and turned to grab his prize, Jade leaning backward in avoidance. The other four corpses took their cue, moving forward as a single unit, laying their collective hands on him.

An awkward dance began, Jade's dad swinging corpses. They would get up again, restraining him. Meanwhile, Clyde shambled up the hill, steady and slow, making his way toward Jade's dad.

It was almost funny, Jade's dad on the bare earth, looking like he was drowning in a sea of dead people. He flailed his arms about, trying to grab solid ground and hoist himself to his feet, while a determined zombie would then weigh him back down.

I let him battle the zombies. When the Js walked up and John said, apprehensively looking at the spectacle of dead bodies, "Shouldn't we, like, get outta here? And, while we're at it, can you get them, you know, back?" pointing to the ground under our feet.

I spared a glance at the spectacle of struggling. I could hear grunting and some colorful swear words.

"Are they going to hurt him?" Jade asked.

I shook my head. "Nah, not unless I tell them."

"Hey dude, you sure on that, cuz they seem kinda enthusiastic," Jonesy said, tilting his head in the direction of the ruckus.

The zombies had taken things to heart and one was banging Mr. Scary's head on the grass.

"Hey! Quit that! No head-banging," I said.

The zombie slowed the head-banging with a dissatisfied grunt that sounded a little muffled.

No tongue.

Carson and Brett were wearing identical expressions of fascinated surprise. It was like a train wreck, you know you don't want to be on the train, but you wanna see what happens. Morons.

Priorities, priorities...

"Okay, you two," I looked at John and Jonesy. "Get Jade home, fast."

"What about..." John rolled his eyes in the direction of the dopes.

Yeah, them.

I walked over to Carson with the zombie noise part of the background melee.

I hollered back to Jonesy, "Keep an eye on my zombies."

Jonesy's eyes became like saucers. "Who me?" he squeaked out. "Have John do it, he's good at that."

John turned to him with a glare. "So I've done so much zombie-sitting, right?"

I sighed, kinda busy here. "Both of you then, just till I'm done talking to these guys."

I gave the *come over here* look to Jade. She came, casting nervous glances behind where her dad was buried under a pile of death.

I felt better once she was next to me.

Carson gave me a smug smile. "Having some trouble with the girlfriend's family?"

"No, just handling things Carson. We're even now," I said.

"How do ya figure?" he asked, Brett's beady eyes following us back and forth, back and forth.

"As I see it, people knowing you're a Pyro will get you big-time attention from some key people," I reminded him logically.

"That's bullshit, Hart. You're a damn corpse-raiser." He gestured behind him to the squall that was the fight behind me. My friends nervously shifted their feet, John making the hand signal, *come on, hurry up.*

"We all know what *you* are now." I looked at Brett, remembering that he'd found out tonight with the rest of us. "Playing with fire is a pretty important skill pal and you're doing a fine job of managing it," I said.

Throwing fire balls had to be illegal somewhere.

"Let's get outta here, Carson, let him figure his own crap out," Brett said.

"Yeah, I was done here anyway. Have fun with that," he said, motioning to the zombie brawl.

"See ya, Hart... *Jade.*" Carson puckered his lips and blew her a kiss.

"Go guzzle bleach, ya squirrel," Jade said.

My eyebrow rose; not just another pretty face.

We raced over to the zombie pile. It was getting bad, Jade's dad continued to try to pry himself out of the mountain of zombies and they would tumble away like bowling pins. Then Clyde would straddle him and it would start all over again.

"Stop," I said.

All the zombies stood stock still, awaiting the next command. One fell over in mid-struggle.

Cool. Über-cool. I like.

"Come *on*, Caleb," John urged.

Right, back to it.

Jade's dad lurched unsteadily to his feet, his considerable size a factor on smoothness, along with the booze.

Jade stayed close to me and the guys.

"You," I said and the zombies all looked at me. "Not you guys." I dismissed them with a hand but they continued to stare at me with steady devotion. *Uh*, creeper.

I turned back to Jade's dad. "You better just give up."

"I ain't givin' up, but I can see when things get challengin'," he said in a slur.

This guy... what a turd!

"You have one last chance, girlie, come with your daddy." He held his hand out to Jade.

"No," she said quietly.

"I see how you're gonna be. I'll fight that bitch sister of mine, and get my kid back where she belongs... under my roof!" He smacked a meaty fist into a meatier palm for emphasis.

Looking out at my army of dead, his gaze fell back on me like a weight. This close I could see his nose was slightly bulbous, with a fine spider webbing of broken capillaries.

"And *you*," he jabbed a thick finger right in front of my chest, which made the zombies tense. Geez, they were being my emotional barometer. "I won't forget what ya did to me today. You're not normal. This," he jerked his thumb in the direction of the zombies, "ain't normal. Sometime, when you're not lookin', I'll be there... waitin'. And there won't be no help from any of them," he said, pointing a finger at Team-Rot.

Special.

He straightened to his full height, inches taller than me, looking down his drunken nose at me and my friends.

At Jade.

He didn't intimidate me. It wasn't having the zombies around or false bravado. Here was a grown man, Dad's age for God's sake, who had been a bully in school, a drunk as an adult and a child-beating father. I didn't have a drop of respect for him.

I spoke in a furious, low tone, "don't you come near Jade. You don't *know* what I can do. You're not gonna hurt her... ever." My finger shook in front of *his* chest.

He could taste my beating on his tongue, but gave a furtive look to the group of patient zombies. He wasn't going to take *them* on again.

His eyes narrowed. "You haven't seen the last of me," he said to no one in particular. Staring a hole through Jade. "You especially, little lady." And with that, he stumbled off, weaving more or less in a straight line.

Playing with zombies will sober a person up.

****

That went well.

The only relief was Carson's ability was almost as troubling as mine. He would be looked at as a teach-and-contain for sure. And knowing that he hadn't even told his butt-buddy Brett? Well that was a surprise.

There the zombies stood, waiting for orders. I turned to Jade and said, "What do ya say, one more time. I gotta get these guys back in the ground."

She looked up at me with eyes shining with unshed tears, uh-oh.

The Js looked horrified: Girl crying! Girl crying!

"What's wrong?" I asked.

A fat tear rode a slow path down her face and she did one of those hitching breaths that people do when crying might make way to sobbing. "I'm so embarrassed!"

Ah... what?

Out loud I asked, "Why?"

"Because he's my dad, and he's drunk and so stupid."

Absolutely.

"Don't worry about him. He isn't going to do the right thing, ever. You worrying about it won't change the way he acts," I reassured her.

"Can't pick your family," Jonesy chimed in unhelpfully.

John sighed.

Jade surprised us all by drying her tears and saying a quiet, "You're right."

"See, that's what I'm talkin' about." Jonesy did a dance step to emphasize his point.

Jade's eyes narrowed. "Don't push it."

John smiled, I laughed and the moment passed.

"Let's get your zombies back in the dirt," Jade said.

I held out my hand to her and we clasped them in a tight grip. Two things happened at once, the zombies moved to their respective graves, and I felt a low buzzing. Not voices, but similar to an electrical current. Different than with Tiff, but related somehow. I gave a mental "flex" and the energy moved through me, swirling. Then it found the thread that couldn't be seen, the power moving as a conduit, connected as I was to the zombies.

With explosive sighs, the breath slid out of their bodies, permanently escaping. Clyde, the main zombie, lingered longest. An expression was in his eyes that went beyond devotion; bright intelligence burning there. I shoved the last of that lingering otherness down to them and thought, *die.*

The corpses collapsed on their graves, boneless, like puppets whose strings had been cut. The ground rolled noiselessly over them, like water poured backwards and they were hidden once again.

Jade released my hand and said, "That is such a weird sensation, it makes my teeth ache." She rubbed her hand on her jeans.

The whispering was back, but manageable. Feeding the power made it quiet down to a dull roar, even dead-center in the cemetery.

I walked over to Clyde's grave. There was something that was nagging at me, something that I should be thinking about but it escaped my consciousness. Too much had happened in too short of time. I was having a brain fart.

"Let's get outta here," Jonesy said.

Nobody had to ask me twice. Tomorrow was AP testing and drug-taking time. I was up for it.

I'd missed supper, a big, bad one in my house. I pulsed the parents on the way back to deflect The Wrath. The three of us had gotten our stories straight before going our separate ways.

Jade had protested me walking her home. But with Brett living in her neighborhood and her dad on a rampage, I'd believed him when he said he'd be watching. I told the parents we were just blowing off some steam with the AP Test coming up tomorrow. I'd headed off disaster and wasn't ready to tell them about all the other stuff: Jade's dad, the prank that went way-wrong with Carson. And best of all, that we had a fire-starter running amuck. Yeah, that.

Later, Dad and I put our heads together talking about how I had to have the inhibitor with food and all the stuff I already knew.

"Dad, are you telling me this because you're worried I won't get it and like OD or something? Or, are you telling me so you feel better in case I do the 'stupid'."

Dad laughed. "Caleb, you're funny."

I waited.

"The latter," Dad replied. That's what I thought, the second one.

"I knew that you were giving yourself an out."

Mom set the bowl of chili down in front of me with the yummy Mexican cheese on top and a huge hunk of cornbread. Time to pork.

"Dad just wants to remind you honey, since you're such an accomplished pill popper."

My eyes rolled up to meet hers with the spoon halfway to my open mouth. "How'd that go over with all the other adults? Pill popper? Nice."

"I guess I'll be serious about it when I have to be. Right now humor is the lesser of two evils."

"What's the other one?" I asked.

"Anxiety."

Oh. I guess I hadn't given a lot of thought to my parents being worried.

Okay, off topic. "The cops still cruising by?"

Dad nodded. "Yes, Officers Gale and Ward were just here as a matter of fact."

"You know Caleb," Mom began while my mouth was stuffed with chili, "you would probably do better to refer to the officers as such rather than cops."

Total word-Nazi.

Dad came to the rescue. "Yes, that's something to consider in the future Caleb. Words are powerful."

I took a big swig of milk and asked Mom for the jalapeños and some honey.

Mom passed the honey and I did an upside down dump.

The parents watched, fascinated, as my cornbread was obscured by a molten mass of goodness.

Dad said, "You having some cornbread with that honey, pal?"

I smiled and nodded

"Okay, so I want you to get up early for a good breakfast, take the pill, then you can scoot to school."

Dad told me he may halve the pill so I'm not in a daze and can actually get a decent result on the academics.

"Not gonna make me high, Dad?"

"Yes, that's the total idea." He smiled.

So far, except for jerking dead people out of the ground, I hadn't shown aptitude for much of anything. It was kinda funny if you thought about it.

"It's nicely ironic that Caleb doesn't appear to be blessed with a scientific aptitude but is talented nonetheless," Mom said, A Point Coming.

Dad frowned. "I know how you feel about all this, Ali. That we are all meant to be completely unique so the balance works for the cohesive whole. But," shaking his head as if fighting his own internal battle, "human nature is very predictable."

I stuck up for Mom here. "So, you could predict that I'd be a zombie-raiser?"

Mom automatically corrected me, "Cadaver-Manipulator."

So irritating, but accurate.

Dad got a little bit of a flushed face. Embarrassed? That would be something.

"No." He made a steeple with his fingers for his chin. "I certainly didn't anticipate this."

That made me stop eating.

"What did you *think* I would be?"

Mom shrugged and Dad said, "Your mother and I had a lot of theories. In the last few years, every parent waits for the Aptitude Tests or," he paused, giving me a steady look, "the manifestation of a talent to rear its head."

Loosening his hands he put his palms out as if to say, *that's the way it is for us all.*

"In your case, we didn't need the test."

"Thank goodness for that. What if it had been flushed out in the AP Test, then he'd have been whisked away or worse," Mom said.

"'Or worse'?" I asked.

I took another bite of the cornbread, resisting the urge to lick my fingers. I picked up a cloth napkin and started working over my fingers.

"Just look at the Parker boy," Mom said by way of explanation.

"What about him? I've never heard anything about him," I said.

"Exactly," Dad stated.

CHAPTER 19

My parents hadn't been thrilled when I unceremoniously stuffed the pill in my front pocket. The deal was, if anyone got a lame idea of checking people's backpacks they wouldn't find the pill. There wasn't a reason I could think of but they were adults and sometimes that *was* the reason.

Butt-munches.

I told my parents my thinking. Mom huffed and Dad mumbled something about my constitutional rights. Whatever, by the time I was able to yak about my rights, they'd be through my gear in a hot second. Especially with nothing allowed in the aptitude testing room.

Nothing.

Mom had made pancakes and bacon (thank you God). I was on my sixth pancake, having already plowed through half a pound of bacon.

Mom grimaced when I was unable to speak.

Dad looked over his papers, hiding a smile from Mom.

"Caleb, stop shoveling your food."

"Mom! Come have a pancake and stop panicking about etiquette." I took a swig of milk and the whole load slid down the pipe.

Mom rolled her eyes. It'd have been impressive but I'd seen Tiff Weller, no one could compete.

I finally had an empty mouth and told her, "Thanks for the breakfast Mom."

My hair fell into my eyes and I whipped my head back and it stayed there. Mom looked at me and my hair then back to my plate again. She gave a big sigh and turned around, getting the next batch of pancakes on a plate.

"Ah... hon?" Dad called.

Mom turned with an eyebrow raised. "I think I want something lighter," Dad patted his belly which was barely over the belt.

Was that the crap I was gonna worry about when I was old? That sucked.

I turned to Mom. "I'll suck those up Mom."

"Are you sure? You've had six already."

Was she kidding?

"Yeah, Mom, still hungry." I stood and jerked up my shirt, displaying my flat stomach and ribs.

Dad laughed aloud. "Wow, doing some dieting?"

"No, doing some growing, I think," Mom said, looking at me critically.

I put my dishes in the sink. Mom came over and gave me a tight hug which I ducked out of the moment I could and not hurt her feelings. Mom was cool but no touchy.

Dad gave me a hard clap on the shoulder and asked if I remembered the protocol for the pill taking. Yes, I told him. I figured forty times had been enough reminders for the next one hundred years.

"I didn't remind you that many times, Caleb."

Mom and I looked at each other, laughing. No, guffawed. That's what Jonesy called it.

Dad threw up his hands. "Okay, okay, I surrender. I guess I mentioned it a few times." We looked at him. "Ah... more than a few times."

I walked to the door, throwing my backpack on and launched myself outside. A drizzle settled over me through the cedar slats and I was instantly wet, freaky weather.

My thoughts crowded inside my head like cobwebs. The Js and Jade were gonna meet at my locker and then we had alphabetical buildings for the testing. Good thing that all the school buildings already had letter of the alphabet names I thought with disinterested sarcasm. I was feeling hyped.

I ripped open the school door and used my foot to prop it open as a hooded girl walked in right behind me. She let it slam behind her with a satisfying clatter. A tingle went through me and she looked up at me. It was Tiff, shoulda known.

"Hey Hart. Done any playing in the dirt lately?"

I grinned, and she grinned back. A vague bruise rimmed underneath her eyes like a shadow. I wonder how she'd explained that to her parents.

She read my face and said, "They don't know."

"Who?"

"My parents, bright one."

I looked around while kids surged back and forth, the constant noise of their talking in the background.

I leaned in. "Are you nervous?"

"Hell yeah. I don't want any attention for this. Maybe I'll just hit a couple of points. I'll get noticed but not *noticed*, if ya know what I mean."

I did.

"I was thinking about what happened. And, it was damn good that we're not testing in the same building. Since, we're like... a..." she gave a puzzled frown.

"Radio?" I supplied.

"Somethin' like that. Whatever it is, I don't want to pop some false-positive crap. Ya know, hit as an all-five-points just because you're in the room," her eyes narrowed. "Ya know Hart, you're okay... for a boy."

Thanks, I guess.

"But just because we're both," looking about her furtively, lowering her voice, "AFTD doesn't mean we have to be in the same frying pan."

She straightened, about to bolt.

"Wait... can I count on you?"

"Well, yeah. I just meant that I don't want to be corralled in some creepy place because of getting sucked into your undead drama."

Tell me how you *really* feel.

Out loud I said, "gotcha."

"See ya later and good luck." She flipped her hood back, skulking into the crowd.

I'd been so into my conversation I'd missed everyone standing by my locker. Three faces peered at me through the mess of kids. John had his usual expression of silent mode, the weather awakening his shock of orange hair into a tornado. Jonesy was smiling. The whites of his eyes two twin dots of ivory floating in his face, only to be joined by a brilliant slash of teeth as he caught sight of me coming toward him.

But it was Jade that made my breath catch in my throat like an errant bubble, captured. She wore coal black jeans and matching short-top All Stars, the laces as black as the jeans. A brilliant green camisole stole all attention inside the v-neck of a tight T-shirt that ended at the swell of her hips. Her hair hung there and as I looked, she gave a subtle flick of her head and one side swept away over a shoulder.

I realized I had stopped moving forward. With a low chuckle, I resumed my progress across the commons. Jade gave a little smile. Looks like she had sorta figured out I dug her. Maybe she already knew since she was an Empath and all. Go figure.

I walked up to the group. We all sorta shuffled around nervously. This meant a lot to all of us. We were all gonna find out, in the case of me and Jade, everyone else was gonna find out about us and it would change things. So far, I was the only one that had the big guns. Well, that wasn't completely accurate, Carson could burn the place down. Things were complicated. But he didn't have any cool drugs (I didn't think) that would buy him time. He was going away to the same school as all paranormals.

An evil idea began to take shape.

Jonesy picked up on it immediately. "You've thought of something cool." Leave it to him to scope the potential for trouble.

"Yeah. Here we were hoping to distract the dorks from making trouble for me but *Carson* has his own."

John stroked his chin thoughtfully, its narrowness perfectly fitting in between thumb and the curl of his index finger. John was all angles and bones, he was a skinny sucker.

"Let's play it cool today," John said looking at Jonesy.

Jonesy gave him The Look.

"Let's try not to make a ruckus," John clarified.

"A fracas," Jade added.

Jonesy was deeply confused now.

"What they mean is, don't blurt out anything in the middle of testing that will get us all in trouble," I said.

"Well, hell no. I wouldn't do that," Jonesy said, offended.

We all did a slave eye-roll. Yeah, that was *so* going to happen! Jonesy not talking out of turn! Jonesy following along and playing well with others.

Jonesy having a filter.

Jade intervened, "You're a great guy Jones but, I have noticed that you aren't always self-aware."

That was diplomatic.

He glared at her and she stared back, her face all open and innocent. Finally, defeated. "Okay, I guess I'll try to concentrate on the test," he grumbled.

"Well that's the concept," John said.

The principal walked out into the commons, manually ringing the class bell. This was it. Suddenly, my awesome bacon and pancake breakfast sat like a cold lump in my belly, waiting for expulsion. I got a grip.

Jade held out her hand and I took it, fingers closing around the whole of it. The Js glanced over at me nervously.

Principal Avers began in his monotonous voice saying, "people, listen closely to your building assignments, all pulse accessories are disallowed in the testing facilities. There will be mandatory breaks every fifty minutes..." he droned on about some other unimportant stuff, then we all sharpened right back up when he said, "...and finally, the following buildings will be assigned alphabetically as follows: last names beginning in A through H will test in Building Alpha, last names beginning in I through P will test in Building Bravo, and names beginning in Q through Z will test in Building Charlie."

I did the swift calculations in my head... Jade, Sophie, and Jonesy in Bravo. And Brett, my mind added. Jade was safe enough with a bunch of other kids and some staff. Let me see... me and Carson (oh joy) in Alpha and John and Tiff in Charlie.

My eyes met John's over Jade's head. He was thinking the same thing I was; Carson with me and Brett with the girls. Bad news.

Principal Avers added, "Disperse to your respective buildings. You have five minutes. Line up outside the door to be scanned."

That meant the disc that all of us had located behind our ear would be scanned for attendance, admittance, and later, tracking and information.

I jammed the pill inside my mouth and dry swallowed it. I used the commotion of everyone wandering around, acting like I was coughing in my hand. Dad had told me that I couldn't be *too* paranoid, maybe there were pulse sensors or pulse-digis recording all our moves. I did okay.

I turned to Jonesy. "Can you sit next to the girls?"

He nodded, serious for once. "Yeah, I know Brett's in there."

"I think it'll be okay but he's riding on the edge, I don't know what'll set him off."

"Will do," he said, nodding as he walked toward Bravo.

Jade gave me the press of her lips like butterfly wings on my cheek, then was gone. No PDAs in the school, but she chanced it anyway. I smiled down at her, squeezing her hand as her fingers slid slowly out of mine. I watched her walk away, Sophie flanking her out of nowhere.

John came up beside me. "She'll be okay."

That was one of those lies that I let John tell. A lie of comfort. I felt like nothing was going to be okay. We walked to our buildings, separating at the last minute. My friends were counting on me.

I was counting on me too.

"Good luck," John said.

"You too," I replied.

****

The slim paddle hovered behind my ear for about two seconds and the school nurse said, "Hart, cleared." like she'd said about the other fifty kids before me.

I was definitely feeling high. Or something, I'd never been high. If I really wanted to get high someday, I could wait until I turned twenty-one and jump into any of the drug bars and have at it. But, having a scientist for a father was an advantage. Dad had outlined drug use and consequence. I had a fuzzy warm feeling that was a blanket of tranquility. The buzzing from the dead was down to a manageable roar. Low frequency, that was a dead giveaway I was floating on the cerebral pond.

We sat in our assigned seats, everyone in attendance. Not surprising given it was mandatory by law that all children at age thirteen by August thirty-first of the current school year must take the AP Test; even the home schooled kids. I guess that guaranteed the puberty net would be flung wide. But the reality was, kids were slipping through. There had to be other kids that were starting to manifest (like me) their abilities sooner than August thirty-first.

Puberty had its own clock.

My floating cloud of warmth was momentarily interrupted as an AP Test supervisor handed out, with two assistants, slim pulse-pads. They same thickness of our pulse-phones, but the dimensions were the same as Mom's old-fashioned paperback books.

I stared at mine in front of me, just a blank screen with a thumb pad, my head filled with cotton.

Once all the pulse-pads were distributed, the testing supervisor instructed, "Please depress your thumb on the pad and *think* your identity and pertinent information. You have eight seconds, begin."

Great personality, this one.

I did as instructed:

Caleb Hart, Age 14, Kent Middle School, King County, Washington.

The screen lay black, then:

Confirmed.

I looked around, my thick brain swimming with the movement. I got a bearing on Carson. He was already looking at me, making sure none of the adults were watching, he gave me the middle finger salute.

So consistent.

I stared at him, such a moron. But... a powerful one. He'd spend the next four years in a fire-proofed classroom and I wouldn't be in it--I smiled.

That confused the dolt for a second, then the instructor spoke again, "You'll be asked a series of questions. All answers will be confirmed as valid. There is obviously no way to cheat." I was overwhelmed with an insane urge to laugh, high as a kite that I was, "and all areas of aptitude will be identified. Make your best effort to offer concise, short answers. Keep your thought processes clear of extraneous thinking."

Translation: don't think about anything fun or what you'd *rather* be doing.

"One more thing," she paused, she had our full attention, then said and odd thing, "there will be control questions inserted that must be answered even if they seem to be unrelated to the main body of testing."

What the hell did that mean?

I began digging into the test questions, *thinking* my responses. I felt decidedly dull. But Dad was right, the half dose allowed me to *think* and answer, so far...no-retard. I didn't have nervousness either. I could feel wanting to stress about my AFTD but the drug kept emotions under control. Sweet.

A lot of standard Math and Science questions answered, we began verbal. Then this question out of nowhere: *How do you feel about things that have died?*

That's one of the questions that didn't fit.

I had an instant stab of dread but *thought*: *Good.*

The moment I answered there was a burst of the buzzing that the dead emanate followed by what could only be described as a drain of energy.

The instructor came to my desk. I looked up.

Crap.

"We need you to change buildings."

I replied carefully, drug befuddled, "But this is the building for my name."

A condescending smile appeared. "We're aware of that, but some of your responses have alerted us that the remainder of your testing will be administered at an alternate location."

I wasn't the only kid. Carson and about ten other kids were herded by assistants, who must have leaked out of walls, because there were more than the original two.

I scanned the group of kids, now disrupted by our leaving, their faces wary.

The instructor, who remained nameless, addressed the class, "please continue with your questions, this interruption will be as brief as possible. Your first break will be in," she glanced at the pulse clock, which counted backwards, "five minutes."

I stood unsteadily, feeling woozy and she gave me a penetrating look. I gathered myself together to appear alert. She didn't know me well enough to determine if I was sleepy or there was more to it.

There was definitely more to it.

We were ushered back into the commons, pulse-pads in hand. There was another head honcho guy out there and I saw through my semi-drug fog two other instructors, one for Bravo and Charlie, and a butt-load of assistants.

"This group," waving dismissively at us, "will be escorted to Delta." It was taken totally for granted that everyone would cooperate with His Authority.

It made me want to do the opposite.

We followed the instructors in a loose group, the assistants flanking and following. Scanning the area I saw Tiff and John! I assumed that we pinged paranormal and that was why we were getting moved. What the hell was John doing here? We looked at each other and he jerked his shoulders up around his ears like, *I don't understand either.*

I didn't make an effort to hide my curiosity, looking around for Jade. I caught sight of her and a tight spot in my chest loosened, she smiled back. And Sophie! But Brett and Jonesy weren't a part of our group. Didn't matter, I was relieved to have John, Jade, and even Tiff in my sights. I didn't really know Sophie but figured she was okay because she was Jade's friend. I tried to remember with a brain made fuzzy if Jade had ever made any comment about her. I couldn't think of anything; another wild card.

We walked through Delta's doors, settling into a group of about seventy or so seats, filling only half of those.

We were arranged alphabetically. That put me real close to Carson with only one kid separating us. It was Alex. Alex of the bad piano playing. We gave the guy-nod.

Head Honcho turned to us. "I am the instructor for this building. You have all been moved here because your responses indicate paranormal aptitude."

Yeah, duh.

"We will resume your testing in," he looked at the pulse clock, "approximately three minutes and change."

Another inappropriate urge to laugh came over me, which I eliminated by biting the inside of my cheek until the copper taste of my own blood silenced it. I ducked my head, my hair sliding into my eyes. My cheek hurt like hell.

We took stock of each other. It was weird, the students knew it was a "sanctioned" thing, the testing, but the testers were super-spy about it; leaving a taste of underhandedness. It intensified my paranoia.

There was a skeletal guy leaning against a kids sized desk angled into the corner, drumming his long, tapered fingers against its edge, all dark planes with a complexion to match. His fingers were stained yellow with a grayish skin cast. He was rich (and don't forget dumb) or he wouldn't be smoking.

Head Honcho went to him, fingers nervously stroking his tie. Their heads were bent together, those fingers going up and down, up and down. They paused in conversation then looked up at our group. We weren't allowed to talk but some kids were nervously looking around, others looked bored. They seemed to stare straight at me but I knew that could have been Carson or Alex too. But somehow, I knew it was me. AFTD was so rare, I'd be the star of the show.

A chime sounded. Gaunt-man lounged in his corner and Head Honcho worked over his tie one more time, moving to the front where our desks were assembled.

"You've answered a satisfactory amount of academic questions and we have a strong idea of where each of you fall in these categories," he paused for effect. "This building is being utilized to further gauge your individual potentials for each paranormal ability you have manifested."

Creeper-factor of about ten.

"Each one of you will have a series of control questions interspersed with academic questions. These questions are tailored according to your individual gifts. Each year, we are always surprised by a new ability or 'branch'," he made airquotes, "which will manifest in a student, or one that is not easily quantified."

Blah, blah, blah, let's just get on with it, I thought sullenly. It didn't matter that he felt better about explaining things to us. I understood everything: they knew what each of us was. They were going to test us for that specific thing, and there may be some kid that gives them a whammy of surprise with a yet unknown ability.

Marvelous for them.

He finally shut up and our pulse-pads came back to life with a press of the thumb.

Useless question after question appeared. Most seemed standard but a few were funny:

<How do you feel about your parents/guardians?>:

<*they're alright*> I answered.

How dumb was that? What were you supposed to say? They need the tomahawk?

This was a control question. I bet they had people in windowless rooms without food that thought this crap up.

Another laughable one was:

<What are your thoughts about persons of authority?>

Real answer: *they suck, of course.*

But, I realized, even in my semi-stupor, that I had to play into what the adults wanted me to say but not be too obvious about it.

This was actually hard. Until most recently, I could have answered pretty honestly. Now, I didn't feel like all adults were to be trusted. I glanced at the clock, realizing this last part of the testing was almost over for lunch. Lunch would be served in the testing building. After all, they couldn't let us *teens* fraternize during testing day. Oh-no.

Finally, I answered:

<some are trustworthy.>

Cryptic but honest and not TMI.

I was deciding the last answer, thinking about changing it, but the pulse chimed. I depressed my thumb and my answer floated away to be cataloged as my response, for better or worse.

****

I was wrong, lunch wasn't served in the testing rooms, it was in the cafeteria, like usual. At every door stood what I was thinking of as "formula-people." They all wore the same adult get-up of tie and suit or skirt and sensible shoes.

The Js, Jade and Sophie had all shown up and we snagged one of the coveted round tables. These were best because I could see everyone when we talked and keep things private. Or more private, the noisier the better.

I did a room search for Carson, spying him with Brett and some other standard losers at a table opposite ours.

Jonesy unraveled his gigantic lunch, John and I watching with interest. His lunchbox was kinda like Dad's; a huge rectangular tin thing with a flat bottom. It had been red once but had faded to a dull, rust color.

First, the thermos came out with what I was sure was a quart of milk, then two sandwiches bursting with lunch meat, a half bag of these gross chips called Funyuns that made your breath reek like ass but tasted strangely good. Finally, the grand dessert finale was a fat brownie full of disgusting walnuts.

The girls watched this with various degrees of disgust. They had about the same lunch stuff as each other. Jade pulled out a small recyclable container that had some disgusting salad thing with tiny chunks of chicken mixed in. I looked over the top of it and quickly grabbed her spork and did a full search for anything substantial and couldn't find dick. Where was the dessert? Sophie had about the same thing but hers was some noodle-salad casserole that smelled like rotting mayonnaise.

John, after surveying the lunches said, "Jonesy, look at what the girls eat, maybe you could get a clue."

Jonesy sniffed Sophie's casserole. "I wouldn't eat that stuff if someone pressed a gun barrel to my head."

John nodded in approval, Jonesy would tell it.

Jade sniffed, replying with dignity, "Well, you go ahead and eat three meals in one. Sophie and I will eat healthy."

John looked down at his lunch, which mimicked Jonesy's, but no grodie nut-brownie, he had an awesome chocolate chip cookie, and shrugged.

I laughed, mealtime was interesting.

We all started eating and I asked John, "So what gives? You hit the radar as something, 'cuz you're in our building."

We looked expectantly at John.

A slow flush crept up his face, he wasn't used to the attention, but he rallied."I don't know. I thought there was a bunch of control questions, and academic questions, but there wasn't anything that I thought was paranormal."

What was he?

Then, our heads swiveled to Sophie, who had just shoveled a bite into her mouth, a small lump protruding from her cheek. We waited until she swallowed.

"What?" she asked.

"Well, what about you?" I inquired.

Jade gave a nervous glance her way.

She knew what Sophie was.

The Js were all curiosity when she admitted, "I guess I have some Astral-Projection."

"Some?" Jade stated.

Sophie glanced down, her tight curls cascading froward, almost brushing that nasty casserole.

"Maybe a little more than some," she mumbled.

Jade gave her a tense look, leaning forward she cupped her hand around her mouth and whispered something inside her ear.

Sophie looked around nervously then stared at each one of us.

"You can't tell anyone," she directed, looking pointedly at Jonesy.

"I'm not going to say anything!" he all-but-shrieked.

We all gave a big sigh.

Jonesy leaned forward. "So barf it out. If it's not so juicy you think I'll blab." A wide grin appeared in the middle of his chocolate colored face. He crossed his arms on his chest, but not before popping another one of the Funyuns in his mouth.

John breathed out, "Wow... Astral-Projection." Yeah, that was pretty cool I agreed mentally.

Sophie gave him a sharp look and he held out his palm out, *go ahead.*

"So, it's like this. About a month ago I started dreaming I was traveling to all these places, far away places," she looked at us all, "like Europe."

We stared back and shrugged, *so?*

"Remember in History class when a bunch of us came in with the CE about the assassination?"

John nodded. "I did my current event on that President."

"The French one?" Jade clarified.

"The Prime Minister," Sophie said, exasperated.

"Right, Prime Minister, my bad," John said, embarrassed. He of the Perfect Grade Point Average, making a mistake! Unheard of.

I cupped my hand over my mouth, hiding a grin. Jade smiled, letting it show all over her face while Sophie looked smug.

John's pale complexion flamed to life again. Being a known brain-iac only to be shown up by Sophie, a girl no less!

"Anyway," Sophie waved the awkward moment away with a hand, "I was *there*," she said in a low voice.

Jonesy leaned all the way forward. "You mean... there, *there*? Like, as in, Astral-Projection there?"

We held our breath. Sophie nodded, once.

"Well... damn, girl, no wonder you aced that CE! Cheater!" Jonesy said, throwing up his hands.

John and I nodded emphatically, it must've been an advantage.

We were quite for a moment, then John said, "But, they don't know who did it."

Jonesy yelled, "Do you?!"

"Shhh, Jonesy... God!" Jade said.

Jonesy looked right and left, making sure his yelling got sucked into the general din of cafeteria noise.

"Chillax, nobody heard." Jonesy leaned back in his seat, all relaxed and everything. The bigness of situations didn't impact the Jonester.

"We need to be circumspect," Sophie said.

Jonesy and I were confused, John nodded and Jade waited.

"Secretive and cautious," Sophie expounded.

"More big boy words for you Jonesy," I said.

"Can it, Hart, you didn't know what it meant either," Jonesy growled.

He had me there.

"Off topic guys," John said. "So... you *know*, Sophie?"

"Know what?"

"Who did it," Jade stated.

"Yeah."

"Who?" Jonesy leaned forward again.

"That's not important. It's what happened after."

John looked thoughtful, then shook his head. "I remember that the guy signed an important document into effect," he paused. "Sophie?"

She nodded enthusiastically, "Yeah, you're getting warmer. You remember all the adults were raging about how it would change the face of France?"

I remembered that, my parents had talked about it. "Yeah, so?"

"He didn't actually sign it. Well, he did and he didn't."

"Oh Sophie!" Jade said impatiently. "Just tell them, or I will."

Sophie glared at Jade then went on, "He was dead when he signed it. *Dead.*" She leaned back in her chair triumphantly, stabbing a helpless curlicue noodle and popping it into her mouth, chewing on it slowly while we all sat, mouths agape, digesting this latest disaster.

"Parker," I said.

Swallowed her bite, she pointed her fork at me. "Bingo."

John said, "So... if I am following this, Parker was used by somebody," John turned to me to confirm and I gave a terse nod, "and made sure that after the assassination, in which the Prime Minister was probably marked for death so he could not sign this document, he was then raised by Parker, who directed him to sign it and faked the nation out."

"What? Did the dude die twice?" Jonesy asked.

Jade sighed. "No, listen, there was an attempt to kill him. It worked, but the bad guys made it look like it hadn't. The prime minister signed the thing, as a zombie, then they made it look like he didn't make it after all."

"Ah-huh, well I did my CE on some Greenpeace thing."

No wonder he didn't have a clue.

"Ugh!" Sophie said, disgusted with the general ignorance that was Jonesy.

"Everybody knows I don't dig that civic crap."

"What-ev-er! It was kinda important," Jade said.

Jonesy shrugged, completely unconcerned.

"The bottom line is, Parker changed history," I said.

We were all quiet at that revelation.

"You're in deep shit," Jonesy said.

"Ya think?" I replied. He had put that together, at least.

"I do," Jonesy nodded.

Wonderful.

Sophie said, "Listen, I'm a witness, what do you think about that? Imagine the trouble I'd be in if *they* knew that *I* knew, huh?"

More silence. Our little group was becoming quite a threat. I cast a secretive (or circumspect... ha,ha) glance around us, the formula-people were still by the doors. The pulse clock was counting down, only five minutes, forty-seven seconds left until the rest of the AP Test.

"We need some kind of plan, an objective," John said.

"A what?" Jonesy asked.

John just looked at him; we did a lot of that.

"Listen, have any of you freaks-o-nature considered that the Jones-Man here doesn't have any cool stuff at my awesome disposal?"

He was right. He was a mundane in a pond of paranormals.

John ducked his head, shamed. "You're right, I'll try to be more patient. After all, you get stuff done."

"Yeah! Damn straight! I'm accomplished, I'm legitimate, I'm..."

"Okay, Jonesy, we know your importance," Sophie conceded, suppressing an eye roll.

"Listen, let's not get distracted. We've got," I glanced at the pulse clock, "less than three minutes to formulate a plan. And, let me just restate the obvious, we still don't know what the blue hell John is."

"That's true, Caleb. But we have bigger problems than just that, like Carson and Brett and getting through this test," John said.

"Well I, for one, want to meet somewhere and figure it out," Sophie said.

"Where?" Jade asked, glancing at the clock again.

Jonesy let a slow grin spread over his face.

I started to shake my head. "NO-oh, don't you even think it."

Jade joined in, "No way, Jonesy."

"Yes way, sista!"

"Oh crap," John moaned, doing a face-palm.

"What?" Sophie asked, confused.

"The Cemetery!" Jonesy clapped his hands together gleefully, barely containing his joy.

We hung our heads, while Sophie looked confused at Jonesy's triumph. He was in his element, let the games begin.

The pulse clock chimed; it was back to AP Testing. We were almost done and hopefully I'd be just a two or three pointer, not a Parker-worthy five pointer.

A glimmer of hope sparkled in my mind's eye, wrapping a fist around it. I held it tight like the world depended on it.

Maybe it did.

CHAPTER 20

The testing wrapped at the end of school. A damn good thing, as after lunch, I could feel myself "sharpening right up." As we filed out of Delta, we were scanned again for dismissal. This time, our pulse pad's results were scanned as well.

Now, and forevermore, the committee of "they" would know what our collective aptitudes were, paranormal or otherwise. We would all know what each other was. The results would determine the next four years of our education and where we'd receive it.

After I was scanned, I could only hope that the drug's effect had lasted long enough that the remainder of the questions were answered and completed without giving myself away.

No pressure.

I grabbed my backpack out of my locker, noticing that it was not in the place that I'd left it. Huh, I looked around, unconsciously looking for the formula-people, none were in sight.

They were top on my list of suspects. Lurking around doorways and such, not doing much of anything. Didn't like it.

Just then, Jade strolled up in all her blackness, looking dark and mysterious.

Hotness.

"Hi."

I smiled, smitten as usual. Then I had a thought.

"Before we go, would you," I gave her the helpless look and her eyes narrowed, huh, better ask straight out, "do a 'feelie' on my locker?"

"A which?"

"Ya know, touch my locker and see who's been in it."

Jade put her hands on her hips (still hot). Then she got that look, ya know the one, where the girl may go all emo on you. So I rushed in with some explaining.

"The thing is, I always hang my backpack here," I pointed to the double hook on the left side.

Okay... her look said.

"And I hang my cap on the right."

"Which you never wear," she noted.

"True, but my mom makes me take it to school in case I get cold."

"You never get cold."

"Right, but *my mom* feels better about it. And when she asks, I can say it's in my locker just in case."

"Okay?"

"Anyways, when I came back from the AP Testing, the backpack was on the right and the cap on the left."

That cute little frown between her eyes made an appearance. She was thinking it through; no cluttering up the moment with chatter. Love that.

Jade came to some decision. Reaching forward with her hand, she touched the hook, wrapping delicately built fingers around the cool metal.

I had a moment when I didn't think anything would happen and then her body stiffened, her eyes taking on a glazed expression. I didn't like where this was going, getting up close behind her. Just as her eyelids fluttered and she started to sway, I moved in against her, cradling her small body against my larger one.

"I think I'm gonna be sick," she said, eyes still closed.

Like... right here?

The Js charged up out of nowhere.

"What's wrong with Jade?" John asked.

"I don't know. Jonesy, get my water in there, no... in the backpack."

Jonesy tore through my backpack, jerking out my water bottle. John grabbed a chair from one of the commons' tables and put it next to Jade. I carefully lowered her down on the seat, a fragile commodity.

"Jade, can you hear me?" John asked.

"Yeah," she whispered.

"Put your head between your knees."

Jade did it. Jonesy hopped from one foot to the other, not knowing what to do with the water.

John looked at me, the flat of his palm on Jade's back.

"What's going on, Caleb?"

"I don't know, I had her do the whammy on my locker because someone's been messin' around in there, and she had like, I don't know, a moment or something and got all dizzy."

"The whammy?" Jonesy asked.

"She used her Empath powers to find out who infiltrated Caleb's locker," John translated, using his fancy vocab.

Jonesy surprised us all with, "someone rippin' off your crap?"

Accurate for Jonesy.

"Nothing's missing, but someone was in here."

"But... it's a pulse lock." Jonesy's look said double-duh... fingerprint security.

Pulse security.

John nodded slowly, Jade began to raise her head. Jonesy gave her the water, which she uncapped.

"Just sip that Jade, no gulping," John said.

She nodded.

"That means a manual by-pass," John said.

Jonesy smiled. "Bringin' up that civic crap again. That bores me 'til I weep, dude."

"How do you figure?" I asked.

"Because, who is going to be able to by-pass a pulse lock unless they're 'The Government'?"

"Not bad Jonesy, not bad at all," John said.

Jade looked scared.

"He's right. They're total posers."

"Who are posers Jade?" John asked.

"The formula-people," she replied.

I sucked in a big breath. Hell, that had been the name I gave those people when I saw them. But, that wasn't their real name. It's just what I thought of them as.

"I know what *you* thought Caleb. You touched the hook too," she said.

"How can you tell it's me and not them thinking?"

Jade did a huge eye roll. Definitely feeling better now.

She lowered her voice and we all leaned in to hear, "How do you know one zombie from another?"

Well, that was easy, they just, felt different. It was like hearing a voice, no two were alike. Some of what I thought must have shown on my face.

She leaned back in the chair, satisfied.

"See, it's like that," she said.

"So, you knew it was me. As if it was my voice talking?"

"That's not completely accurate, but it'll do," Jade said.

"It's like a signature?" John asked.

"I guess. It's hard to explain this stuff to someone that doesn't do it," she shrugged.

I noticed the death volume wasn't loud for me at this moment and mentioned that. The drug was definitely flushed by now.

"It's kinda random now anyway, right?" Jonesy asked.

Yeah, now that I thought about it, sometimes the voices were loud, sometimes hardly there. I couldn't figure out why it came and went but it was a recent development.

"Who was it Jade?"

"I don't know who they are but I know *what* they are."

"What?" Jonesy asked.

"They're government alright, just not the government that we know about. They're like a subdivision of a subdivision."

That sounded bad. I thought of my ransacked house, where nothing had been stolen but everything had been looked at, touched, moved.

"Let's split. I don't want to talk about this here," John said, looking around.

Good idea. We gathered our crap up and started to walk away.

"Wait," Jade said.

I turned toward her. "You okay?"

She nodded. "Getting there. Let me go find Sophie first."

Jonesy made a face. Uh-oh. Jade put her hands back on her hips and marched over to Jonesy.

Almost nose to nose but she was still shorter. "You got a problem with Sophie?" she demanded, her face fierce.

"No, no problem," Jonesy sputtered, caving.

"You looked like you had one."

"It's just, we used to be an all-guy thing, and now... well, we may be getting too many hens in the chicken coop."

"Oh... please! You bunch of roosters need all the help you can get. Be grateful!"

And with that parting shot she pivoted on her heel and went off in search of Sophie. Sophie of the Astral-Projection persuasion.

We stood silently looking after Jade.

"You handled that well, Jonester," John said.

"Yeah," he said glumly.

"Maybe next time just let the girls come," I said.

"Yeah," John said.

"This mundane thing blows goats. And the girls are taking over the world," Jonesy stated.

"Not *yet,*" I said, winking.

Jonesy smiled and we walked out the door into the school parking lot where cars swarmed everywhere. We hiked over to a small grassy knoll, waiting for the girls. I threw my backpack behind my head and laid down, my head balancing on a lump of junk. Jonesy and John flanked me.

We waited as the sunlight warmed our bodies. Almost summer, I thought. Not hot and crummy yet, still spring.

"We have to find out what these..."

"Formula-people," I supplied.

"Yeah them. What they really want from you," John said.

"They're just rooting around, hoping to come up with something," I said.

"Good thing you didn't put that pill bottle in your backpack," Jonesy said.

"Right. Isn't that the truth," John said.

We thought about who was watching.

We were lying there all languid when two shadows fell over our bodies. All three of us put our hands up to shield our eyes from the sun. It was the girls; Sophie's shadow, completely shading my body, Jade's covering Jonesy up to the neck.

"Let's go," Sophie said.

"Where?" Jade asked.

"The cemetery," Jonesy said.

"No," I said.

"Oh, come on Hart! You can clean house if anyone shows up!"

Jonesy sat up, shaking off the languor and pantomiming punching.

"I don't want to. Every time I go to the cemetery a bunch of crap rains down on our heads! *No.*"

"What could happen?" Sophie asked.

We looked at her. She laughed. "It's that bad?"

"Yeah," we said in unison.

"But it is the safest, the most private. They can't hear us." Jade reasoned.

I thought about it, wavering. There really wasn't a very good alternative.

I made a decision. "Okay, everybody pulse the parental authority, get the go ahead, and let's book to the graveyard."

"Wait," everyone's attention turned to John. "Let's have a look-out. We don't want to be followed."

"Brilliant. I'll do it," Sophie said.

I nodded and we dug out our pulses, getting the parents handled.

Jade's face fell.

"What?" I asked, my hand landing on her shoulder and giving it a gentle squeeze.

"Aunt Andrea says I need to go home and check in," Jade made airquotes.

John said, "I don't like it."

That made two of us.

"Not normal Jade."

"I know, right?"

"You don't think it's your crazy-ass dad?" Jonesy asked delicately.

I glared at him. Jade saw and said, "It's okay, he's crazier than a shit-house rat."

Sophie barked a very un-girl like shout of laughter.

"Where did you get that one?" she asked.

"Andrea."

"I guess she's good for something."

"Sophie, she really tries. They were raised in the same family ya know."

"I know," her hand squeezed the opposite shoulder. Now we both had our hands on our girl. Sophie's eyes met mine, Jade was fragile and we loved her. A fierce grip of possession blossomed in me and I felt a new focus for my life.

She gave us that radiant smile reserved for us; me and her best friend, I'd take that.

CHAPTER 21

Any graveyard always affected me the same way. As I got closer the voices grew louder. It was Jade and I in front with Sophie slightly behind, the Js pulling up the rear. Voices of the dead droned; I hadn't missed their absence (internal sigh).

Jade and I, our hands held tightly as we swept under the arch of scrolling metal, looked up at me with questions. Touching me like she was, I was tuned to the frequency of the dead. Brave girl, her hand was still dry.

John trotted up to us and the whispering dimmed. "So, where do you want to go?"

That was easy. "Let's head over to Clyde's grave."

"Clyde?"

"Yeah, he's by far my favorite corpse."

Jade laughed. "Ah... okay, whatever you say."

"I've never seen the fun, so I'll assume being in the cemetery is kinda risky," Sophie said.

Jonesy caught up with us, hearing the last comment. "Hell yeah! That's the full throttle of hanging out with us! It's the way we roll," Jonesy said, folding his arms across a muscular chest.

Sophie looked at him. "Well, good for you," she snarked, turning to Jade, eyebrows shooting up. Gee, how did we ever live without them?

I figured Sophie had about five and a half minutes before she succumbed to Jonesy's charms.

The Js did a high five to cement the moment and I grinned. The friends were it, they just flat were. Sophie gave them a look, knowing her presence was not going to change our supreme maleness.

We made our way to Clyde's grave... ole' twice-raised Clyde. He looked a little "smart" on that last run and I'd felt uneasy. No guts, no glory. Jerking corpses out of the ground more than once, I pondered that. Nope, I really wanted to know.

We plopped down in a semi-circle around his grave. The thrumming of the dead sounded very low in the background. I just couldn't make sense of that. They should be shrieking with me being in the cemetery and all. Jade was on my left, John on my right. Jonesy and Sophie had an unspoken truce, sitting together. Jonesy had his legs splayed out in front of him with his elbows locked behind him and Sophie sat legs crossed, elbows on knees and palms holding her chin.

"Okay we're here, now what?" Sophie asked.

"I want to talk more about the testing," I said.

Jonesy frowned "What's to talk about? I mean, I'm a mundane, you guys have the juice, end of discussion."

Maybe he was jealous. He was the only one that hadn't pinged paranormal. Didn't matter to me, Jonesy was always gonna be Jonesy. It just was.

John looked at him. "Remember, you get things done."

My thoughts exactly, Jonesy was our main man.

"Yeah, I'm feeling that," Jonesy said.

"Don't wanna take you guys away from your love fest or anything but I want Jade to let us in on this spy crap."

Jade laughed. "It's not a 'spy thing,' it's more like a government within our government."

"Okay, we've got that. What's their objective?"

Silence.

"You know, what's their goal?" John clarified.

John was gonna be my dad when he grew up.

"What I felt was they're trying to identify kids that have rare paranormal abilities and are also powerful."

"Why were they looking in my locker?"

She looked down at her hands, twisting and untwisting. "They suspect you."

"Why?"

"The dog. Garcia saw what you did with the dog."

I looked at Sophie, big-eyed. "You're sworn to secrecy."

"Ah... okay."

"But I didn't raise the dog, the dog wasn't dead yet."

"Come on Caleb, that's what my parents call splitting hairs." That's like saying you're almost pregnant," John said.

Sophie and Jade laughed, mutual amusement.

I guess he had a point, dammit.

"Okay, so I did some AFTD crap, he saw it and... what?"

"I felt, that they have fingers of their group within the police department," Jade finished.

"Haven't we figured out that Garcia is dirty?" Jonesy asked.

I wasn't absolutely sure but it was circling the drain of possibility.

"What was that cop that showed up when you raised granny?" John asked.

I thought about that... McCain? McRaw...

"McGraw!" I remembered.

"Yeah, him. You said he pulled some scary shit."

"He did; gave us a little elemental show," I said.

"Didn't he cause, what, a mini-tornado?" Jonesy asked.

"Not really, it was more like we were all in the eye of the storm."

"Was it righteous?" Jonesy asked, eyes alive.

"No, it was an intimidation thing. And he's Garcia's partner. Two plus two equals four, pal."

Sophie shook her head, ringlets bouncing. "Whatever. We have dirty cops and adults that are lurking around looking for ways to force us to do their dirty work. All good news! What's the plan?"

John was the thinker, Jonesy the schemer and I was becoming the leader. Not a role I thought I'd be in.

"One thing is obvious: they all know what we are. In Caleb's case, they don't know how much he is, but that's a matter of time. Too many people know that he can corpse-raise. Jade's dad knows!" John said.

That was true, but...

"He won't say anything," I said with conviction.

"Why not?" John asked.

"Because, A) he'd look bad, B) he would have to explain why he was there and what happened."

"Caleb's right, he doesn't like to look bad. He wants to be right all the time," Jade said.

I hugged her to me, stuffing her face in my neck, silently thanking God that I had worn cologne, "It's okay, he's not gonna hurt you, ever."

She pulled away, her tears shimmering like diamonds on her lower lashes.

The Js looked away, feeling uncomfortable.

Sophie saved it. "We still haven't figured out a plan."

"I've been thinking," Jonesy started, we all groaned, a typical Jonesy Plan included us all getting our asses in a sling.

He held up a hand. "Hear me out," he looked at us all. "I think we need a hideout."

Cool! That's *just* what we needed.

"A safe house," John said.

Jonesy looked at John. "That's what I said."

Sophie said, "I think we need a labor force."

"What do you mean exactly?" Jade asked.

"Caleb, you can raise the dead, right?"

I think we determined that. I nodded.

"Slaves," John breathed.

"Slaves," Jonesy repeated.

Sophie nodded.

"Isn't this one of those moral things adults are always blabbing about?" Jade asked.

Yeah it was.

"To recap then, you want me to raise zombies, to what? Work on a hideout?"

"Safe house," John corrected.

"Whatever!" I yelled.

This was wrong on about a hundred different levels. Yet, it did have a practical feel to it.

Sophie said, "Do you not see the logic, Caleb?"

I did.

"But, I haven't really tried to raise anyone (except Gran... oops), this would be really, really..."

"Premeditated," John said.

Jonesy looked at him.

"CSI," John expounded.

"The crime show, what, in their twentieth season?"

"Yeah, they use walkers now!" Jade said.

"Okay," Sophie made the cut-the-neck gesture with her finger, "focus, guys." They looked at her, shrugging.

She directed her attention back to me. "I'm just saying, if you could, like, raise two or three zombies. Then make them construct a lair..."

"Lair?" Jade repeated.

"A secret place," Jonesy said, then added, "maybe underground?" He pulled his shoulders up close to his ears in an exaggerated shrug.

This was actually sounding pretty cool, in theory anyway.

"I don't know," Jade hesitated, "is it wrong to make them work for us, like slaves."

Those words hung in the air, sitting there.

John finally broke the silence, "I don't think so. I mean, we need a place to go. We don't know if Caleb is going to *have* to go into hiding." I looked at him with skepticism. He saw me and continued, "You never know, Caleb. Also, there are the dumb-asses at school, this government agency," he looked at Jade, who nodded, "and the random parent who shows up and freaks. No offense Jade."

"It's okay."

"John and Sophie are right, Caleb. We need a place they'd *never* think to look," Jonesy implored.

"I don't like it, but there's degrees of morality and we are just going to have to be more moral than the guys that are plotting on using us," Jade said, adding, "what about the city dump?"

We all looked at her. The dump?

"Yeah, it's where I went when my dad got..." she looked at Sophie, "bad."

Her eyes sought mine like a compass. I held her a little tighter. I was starting to hate her dad. Someday, he and I would come to an understanding and that day was coming.

"I like it," Jonesy said.

"How far is it from here?" Sophie asked.

I remembered that Sophie didn't know Kent like the back of her hand. She hadn't always lived here like the rest of us.

"It's walkable," John said.

Jonesy hopped up, brushing the grass off his butt. "Let's do it!"

The rest of us stood. I noticed again the voices were hardly more than a murmur. Weird. I told the others.

"Shouldn't they be almost screaming? Right in the damn middle of corpse-ville?" Jonesy asked, twirling around.

"Yes, they definitely should," John said slowly, considering.

John snapped his head and looked at me, I stared back.

The girls said, "What?" at the same time.

Everything suddenly fell into place. *I knew what John was. Psychic Null.*

Every ability was negated when he was around. That's why I couldn't hear the voices!

John grinned so hugely I thought he'd push the freckles right off his face.

"What gives?" Jonesy asked.

"I cancel everyone's powers," John said, pride creeping into his voice.

"You're a Null?" Sophie asked, incredulous.

"What!" Jonesy shrieked. "How does that help us?"

"In a word... Carson," Jade replied.

"And everyone else," I said, stating the obvious.

Jonesy's face took on a life of its own. "Fantastic! That blows their juice all to hell!" he clapped his hands together for emphasis.

"Try to raise a corpse, Caleb!" Jonesy cried.

"Right now? That wasn't really the plan."

"We've gotta see!" Jonesy shouted.

"Shh!" Sophie said.

"Right, sorry," he said, chastised for three seconds.

Jonesy said in a normal voice (translation: still loud), "Try it."

John said, "I don't know, whenever you say: I wanna see, I wanna do it... something bad happens."

John was right on that, maybe we should find out if our speculation was on. Could John zero-out my abilities? Could he, if things flat-lined, protect us from one of these freaks that were working for that government agency? Good questions. I wanted answers, knowledge is power, Gramps always said.

"Jonesy is a little enthusiastic with experimentation. But, it'd be good to know," I said.

"Remember the last time he wanted to 'see'?" John asked.

Yeah, that hadn't worked out real great. The whole Carson-pulling-a-can-of-fire-whoop-ass on all of us. Geez. Internal cringe.

"Let's try it," Jade said.

How could I say no when my girlfriend was willing to be brave.

Ah, hell. Okay.

"Alright," I said out loud.

We looked around us, our pulses read almost five o'clock. We had to get hot because parents were expecting us to come home and eat soon. Crap.

John stood closer, looking down at me, his bony elbows standing at attention. "I'm ready."

"How does this work? I mean, do you know?"

John shook his head. "Not really, I mean, we just put it together that I may be a Null. We still don't know for sure. But, it would explain some stuff."

Like all the times the voices had been bearable in the five classes we had together. Not for Biology though.

John read my mind. "I don't think I've had it long."

That would mean that it fully came on line just recently. Would have been sweet to miss the whole frog dissection catastrophe.

"Okay, you two just stand where you are. Caleb, you let your," Sophie moved her hand back and forth, "stuff go and we'll see if something happens. And! If it doesn't, we'll know," she finished.

"Wait a sec. Shouldn't we see how far away John has to be before Caleb can use his powers again?" Jade asked.

Good point.

I stood facing Clyde's grave. Again. John stood beside me and I felt his nervousness like a cloak. It floated around me on the wind and settled uncomfortably on my shoulders. I sighed, breathing out deeply, trying to relax.

The fist that was my power loosened inside my body. Fingers lengthened until they became tendrils, a ghostly octopus, reaching out to the ground, stroking the grave like a lover.

Then, without warning, they choked up like vomit up a throat. It was as if a steel wall, high and impenetrable had been erected. They swirled and sought, looking for a small hole, any opening, a way to invade. There was nothing.

I looked up at my best friend, who was grinning like he won the lottery.

Putz.

Jonesy was rubbing his hands together. "Now *that's* what we're talkin' about!"

Jade was rubbing her hands up and down her arms, it was *that* intense.

"Move a couple of feet away," Sophie said.

We parted a little.

"No, I think it's gonna have to be," Jonesy moved us away from each other, his grip vise-like.

"Hey!" I said.

"Sorry... Caleb, stand here." Now I was on top of Clyde's grave.

"That's not right," Jade said, looking ill.

"Quiet," Jonesy said and I looked like I would deck him. He looked back at Jade. "Please," he added.

He looked at me like, *happy?* I nodded, better.

Now we were ten feet away from each other.

I tried again. John looked at me and grinned.

Kinda frustrating. But, I had to admit, useful.

John recovered first. "Okay, we've got that I can cancel out Caleb." He turned to Jade. "What about you?"

Jade scowled. She wasn't really "feeling" her power. That was the main reason people had the wrong impression of her. She stayed away, because she *didn't* want contact.

"Come on Jade, just use me, touch me and then we'll get John into play," I wheedled.

She began to relent.

"Everybody knows that a Null negates all paranormal talents," Sophie said.

"That's what they say, but I want to know for fact," John said.

"Yeah, what he said," Jonesy supplied.

Jade gripped my forearm and gooseflesh ran up from the point of contact.

When she was using her power, it was total weirdness. John moved toward us in slow motion. His arms swinging like windshield wipers, frizzy hair bouncing on his head, late afternoon sun lighting his head on fire, torch-boy.

The moment became surreal, climbing power crawling over my skin like fire ants biting, sizzling electricity building, building; John touched my other arm. An electric spark shot off between us, we jumped, then... nothing.

Jade made a perfect "o" with her mouth, looking at John in wonderment.

"That was great," she said. "Finally... silence."

John was nodding his head. "That's just how cool I am." He took a small bow.

I punched him on his bicep. "Chill the self-love Terran."

"Hey! You're stealing my moment." John made a face.

"Let's congratulate ourselves later." Jonesy grinned, *he* was definitely digging this new turn of events.

We stepped off Clyde's grave, walking away to our separate houses, the graveyard at my back.

For once, the dead still resting.

CHAPTER 22

"How did it go today?" Dad asked.

My mouth was full of Mom's baked salmon. I held up my index finger, *hang on a sec.*

Dad and Mom watched me.

I swigged a gulp of milk down the hatch and replied, "It was okay."

"Did I gauge the dose okay?"

I smiled. "Dad, I was still kinda high."

Mom laughed and Dad looked puzzled.

"I based it on your weight, age and all the other parameters. Doesn't make sense. Wait... how much did you say you weighed?"

"One thirty-five."

"I thought you said one forty-five..."

"Nice Dad, you overdosed me!"

"Kyle, aren't you the scientist?" Mom asked, teasing.

Dad ducked his head then regained the "dad composure." "I am not a pharmaceutical representative, that's for sure."

"Well, let's not make this a trend," I said, feeling like I had tagged him on this one. How often was that gonna happen? I was taking full advantage!

Dad looked at me, nonplussed. "Humph!" he grunted. "I'll make a supreme effort." Picking up his fork, he stabbed a chunk of fish, throwing it into his mouth, chewing aggressively. Mom chuckled, enjoying his discomfort, she had an evil streak.

"We received your results in pulse-mail," Mom informed me.

I put my fork down, waiting.

Dad looked at me, smug. Okay, so I was high but maybe, just maybe, it had worked. Of course it had! I mean, the choppers weren't showing up with guys-in-black, dangling from ropes in kidnap mode.

"Two points," Dad said, triumphant.

"Really? Hot damn!" I jumped up and aimed my hand towards Dad's. A resounding high five sounded.

Mom didn't, miraculously, correct my language, she thought it was great too.

Mom nodded. "The drug worked."

"It did. But," Dad waggled a finger at me, "we're not out of the woods yet."

I looked a question at him.

"The threat is still there, but isn't immediate," Mom expounded.

Right. I got that.

I explained how we'd all gotten separated from the other kids; paranormals in Delta Building and mundanes in the other buildings.

"Sounds standard, Caleb," Dad said.

"Yeah... I guess. But there were these creepers that I named 'formula-people'."

"Creepers?" Dad inquired.

"People that lurk about and generally give a sinister vibe," Mom explained.

"Ah-huh, okay. Go on."

"Well, they all wore the same clothes and stood by all the doorways."

"Like uniforms?" Mom asked.

"Not exactly, more like, the same but different. And! They wore sunglasses... inside. How weird is that?"

The parents looked at each other in an uneasy silence.

The food stilled in my throat, a lump petrified. I swallowed through the hardness of it.

Dad put his fork on his plate with a clatter.

"*That's* not standard."

"What are your thoughts, Kyle?" Mom asked.

"My thoughts are... that this thing is its own machine. That there are forces working that we don't know or understand."

"Like I've been saying," I said.

They looked at me as if, *explain that*.

"Dad, come on, remember McGraw and Garcia at the cemetery when I raised Gran?"

He nodded, somber.

"Well, then there's Parker. All the signs are pointing to something bigger," I said.

I recounted what Jade had felt from the people who had dug through my locker. That Carson was a Pyrokenetic, that John was a Null. That Jonesy wasn't anything. Well, he was a math whiz, I guess that was something. But he couldn't bludgeon with equations!

Mom looked shocked. "I guess there are some blessings."

I raised my eyebrows.

Dad pretended to wipe sweat off his brow. "Jonesy doesn't have a power."

I laughed. "There is that."

"Yes, Jonesy with an ability would be..." Mom searched for the word.

"Explosive..." I supplied.

"I don't know if that covers it, Caleb," Dad said, getting a visual of the Potential that was Jonesy.

We all loved Jonesy, but he was an immoveable object. Regardless of what was going on, he was him, sometimes that worked, other times, not.

Usually not.

"The officers came by today to let us know they're discontinuing surveillance," Mom said.

Good, I thought. I liked Gale and Ward but Gale had gotten too close for comfort. I sure-as-hell didn't want McGraw and Garcia sniffing around either.

"When?" I asked.

"When you were running around with your posse," Mom said.

"Huh, they still don't have a clue, right?"

"No, so far, they haven't been able to ascertain a motive for the break-in. Nothing was stolen, some things broken and touched. Of course, there's the matter of my pulse-top compromise. However, we did a full diagnostic at the lab and everything is in order." Dad shrugged.

"I think it was the formula-people," I said flatly.

"So suspicious," Mom clucked.

"Somebody's got to be," I replied.

The parents frowned.

"Well? It's pretty obvious someone knows more about me than we want them to. Why all the interest? As you'd say, Dad, things aren't 'adding up'."

"Caleb's got a point, but, that doesn't mean we live in fear."

"You're concerned, Dad, or you wouldn't have dosed me."

"Caleb, would you stop saying that, please?" Mom asked.

"Dose, dose, dose, double-dose..." I chanted.

"Caleb..." Dad warned.

"Oh... okay. Geez, you guys!"

"Anyway, Gale is suspicious. She had your results as a two-pointer." I raised my eyebrows. "She could have sworn you were *much* more. The last time she got a reaction like the one you gave her, it was from Parker."

Swell.

"But, we had the proof." Mom's relief palpable.

"Thank God for small favors," Dad said.

We sat quietly for a second. Then I asked the important question, "What about the dog?"

Mom smiled "We'll get him after school tomorrow. Now the Aptitude Test is finished and that stress is behind us, we'll move forward."

"Are you going to come, Dad?"

"No, I don't think I need to. I can let you and Mom get him." he smiled.

Finally, I was going to get the dog. What to name him? He was black like night, really dark. I wondered...

"What about a name?" I asked.

"I've been thinking about that," Mom said.

Of course, Mom the Word Queen!

I waited.

"Onyx!"

Mom had it... much better than "Inky." Or, the dreaded, "Blackie."

"Nice, Ali," Dad said.

"I thought so," she said, twirling away to refill my milk glass.

I slurped down the rest of my milk and cleared away my dishes. Mom would pick me up from school tomorrow and I would have a new dog, Onyx.

Things were looking up.

CHAPTER 23

The school was abuzz over the paranormals who were "outed" by the AP Testing. I got a lot of, "corpse-lover," and my personal favorite, "Doin' any corpses lately?" All of them, *so* clever. Dunces.

John was acting incognito (ultra-cool vocab word: to conceal a real identity) by not telling anyone he was a Null but having a great time running around, getting close to some of the paranormals. They'd try to put their groove on and... nothing.

Evil for John. I liked it.

Jade was planning to come over to the house to help us pick up Onyx and formally meet him. I couldn't wait, it was the silver lining in today's cloud.

The classes droned by as usual. I was itching to get home and get Onyx. I knew there were other things to think about, like class, but that didn't matter today. Summer break was coming and my head was engaged with ideas of playing basketball, fishing, and especially, extra time with Jade.

Finally, the pulse clock chimed and sixth period ended. I raced to Building D, feeling a fleeting sense of déjà vu.

Mr. Cole was perched on the windowsill like a cat in the sun. I mentally crossed my fingers and took a deep breath.

"Hey Mr. Cole..." I rushed on, throwing out all my words at once so my chances would be better.

"My mom and I are going to get a new dog today and I was hoping I could make up band this Friday?"

I was out of breath but recovering.

Cole took off the glasses, bending his head as he polished them on his T-shirt, layered under an adult, button up shirt. I think that was required for adults. I figured Dad had about three hundred.

Geez. Then he put them up directly in the sunlight, checking for dirt. His glasses didn't look dirty to me.

He slowly looked over at me. Please say yes, please.

He smiled back. "I guess that would be okay. But you'll have to make it up Friday for sure, Caleb." He gave me a mock stern look. But Cole, besides my shop teacher, Morginstern, was cool. They were the best teachers.

I breathed a sigh of relief and seeing my expression he laughed.

"Cool! Thanks, Mr. C!" I sprang up, taking off for the door as John came in.

"Whoa! Where ya going?" he asked.

"I get the dog today, Onyx, remember?"

In a low voice John said, "Cole let ya go?"

"Yeah, but I gotta make it up Friday."

John pantomimed choking himself with his hands. "Ooh, the torture! Extra band practice."

I punched him in the arm. "Shut up, Terran. You're gonna stay too."

John rubbed his arm and glared at me. "I don't know... Friday... may have plans." he grinned.

"Stuff it, ya putz. You know you've got plans, with Jonesy and me. That's your plans."

John grinned wider. "Yeah, now that I'm cool like you."

"You think you're cool like me. Listen, I don't have time for clever repartee, I gotta split and get the pooch."

"Fancy words don't intimidate me!" John mocked swordplay in my gut.

"I thought you needed to get going Caleb?" Cole asked.

"Yeah, I do! See ya!" I gave John a salute, taking off.

I checked my watch, damn, forgot to wind it.

I ripped my pulse out of my pocket; three-ten. Okay, Jade was meeting me at three-thirty, better book. I began a slow jog, working up a good sweat by the time I threw open the front door, instantly smelling Mom's banana bread.

Decisions, decisions... shower or food. Sighing, I slogged off to the bathroom. "Mom, be out in a sec. Jade's coming over to pick up the dog with us!" Yelling over the kitchen noise.

"Thanks for the head's up!"

I ran the shower super hot like I liked. Finishing up, I got out, toweled off, and resigned myself to having to floss. This hygiene thing was a pain-in-my-ass, but I smelled better. Jade was a motivator!

I opened the bathroom door, having had just enough thought process to grab a clean T-shirt and Jade was here. I listened to Mom doing the hostess-goddess routine. They were getting along, good.

I rounded the corner, Jade looked up and our eyes connected in that I-dig-you-but-a-parent-is-around-so-play-it-cool. It sucked but was as automatic as breathing.

"You ready?" Mom asked.

"Yeah, just had to de-scuzz."

"De-scuzz?" Jade asked.

"Yeah, got to smell fresh." I flipped my long bangs out of the way, still damp from the shower.

Jade laughed, comic relief.

We walked to the garage, our shoulders touching.

Mom got into the driver's seat and Jade and I were in the rear where I figured Mom would be too distracted with that driving thing to notice us holding hands.

Jade leaned her head onto my shoulder. Her hair smelled like a big piece of fruit, nice. I wanted to touch it but knew that was pushing it.

We pulled up front and I listened with that part of me that hears the dead. In the case of Onyx, we had already done that psychic dance, *he recognized me.* I felt him in my head. We walked through the big glass doors, Jade and Mom in front, me bringing up the rear.

****

The Dog knew when the Boy entered the place-where-he-lived and howled joyously. He sniffed at the metal tubes which made seeing more difficult. He held the liquid that smelled interesting inside his body because the People-who-fed-him took him to a good smelling place to let the liquid go. The Dog held it but not without effort.

The Dog heard the voices of the People coming with the Boy, who was special, the Dog knew because the Boy called him in a special way, soundlessly. The Dog liked the Boy. The Boy would throw the soft, round thing. The Boy was... was... using those people sounds in his head.

I'm here Onyx, you'll come home with me.

The people-sounds were very exciting and the Dog could feel a little liquid come out.
Bad Dog, Bad Dog... he must hold the liquid.
The Dog saw the Boy and his People come to the bars and look down at him. He was a Bad Dog because of the liquid Accident but the Boy did not notice. The Dog was relieved and moved his tail, hoping the Boy would be pleased.

"Good dog, Onyx," The Boy said.

The Dog wagged his tail harder, the end hitting the metal tubes. The Boy had said a word that was important that he did not know. He recognized some words.
He pressed his nose to the metal tubes, they were cold against his nose but he needed to smell the Boy and his People. The small female smelled like not-right-garbage and was excited to see him; so he wagged his tail harder. The older female smelled like the Boy. They were pack to each other. Would this be a pack like his other Boy? There was a sharp pang of sadness when the Dog remembered his other Boy, but he shoved it away because the New Boy was making the sounds from his mouth and he must listen.

"That's a good dog, Onyx." The Boy said.

The Dog jumped up on the metal tubes and the Boy stuck his hand through and the Dog gave him one lick. The Dog understood some people did not like a lot of the wet thing in his mouth that was so good for all kinds of things.
One of the people-who-fed-him approached and he was a Good Dog and sat down. He continued wagging his tail because the small female put her delicious hand on top of his head and moved it in a most pleasant way.
The alpha female of the Boy's pack made new sounds out of her mouth and the Dog understood she had a tonal quality similar to the Boy...

"Arlene, is there any more paperwork to fill out before we take Onyx home?"

"No, Mrs. Hart, just sign this form attesting to pick-up." She showed Mom where and Mom bent over the 'X', marking out a quick signature.

"Thank you. By the way, we're sure glad that he's going to a good family."

The Dog saw the person-who-fed-him make dominant eye contact and he shifted his eyes away politely then looked back.

"We'll miss him around here." she smiled.

The Dog heard the sounds, good dog, which was his signal to begin to wag his tail again. Which he did; thunk, thunk, thunk. He also heard that strange sound, Onyx, which meant something important. He would try to remember, for the Boy.

"Okay Onyx, let's go!"

The strange sound again, thunk, thunk, thunk.

"Caleb, he probably needs to go out to the potty area and do his business," Arlene said.
"Oh right, K. Jade, let's go," I said.

The Dog heard the sounds, potty area, and the liquid wanted to rush out, but he held it in. The Dog bounded around, hoping the Boy and his people would notice that he was a Good Dog and needed to let the liquid go.
The Boy and the small female went toward the doors where holes appeared to the place-that-smells-very-interesting.
He burst through when the holes appeared and lifted his nose in utter bliss. So many different liquid smells here! Where to start?
The person-who-fed-him came and said the sounds, "go hurry up." He wished to impress the Boy with how quickly he could let the liquid go.
He trotted over to an especially good smelling corner and let the liquid rush out and was very happy when it covered the other liquid smell.

"Good Onyx, good hurry up," *the Boy said.*

He wagged his tail, the Boy was using the happy tone with him because he was a Good Dog.

He followed the Boy, who took him to the fresh place where there were no holes to think about and he could run and run and run. The Dog hesitated. He wished to run but the Boy had no soft, round thing that he could grab, and the pack had a calm, unhurried posture.

He waited.

The pack made noises with the person-who-fed him, then opened a metal box with holes on top and with foul smelling round shapes on the bottom.

The Boy gestured that he wanted the Dog to get in. But the Dog felt a disquiet with the box. He remembered that it was a Bad Thing. The pack got into the big metal box that smelled like the Boy's pack. He sniffed it suspiciously and looked at the Boy for direction.

The Boy reached for him and scooped up the Dog. He gave a lick with the wet thing in his mouth in appreciation. The Boy tasted like a Good Boy, not the good of-not-quite-right-trash smell of the small female, but still good. He liked his new pack and wagged his tail.

****

Onyx explored every, tiny corner of our house, spending an especially long time in my room, stumbling over all the crap on the floor, deciding it was good and rolling around on top of it. Perfect, now that's a good dog!

Jade had gone home a few minutes after Onyx arrived. I was feeling righteous: the testing was over, the government hadn't come *yet* to kidnap me, Jade and I were together and Onyx was finally here!

Mom had done some crock pot thing... chili, so we could just scoop and pork. I liked that.

The front door opened and Dad came through, looking a little frazzled. Onyx gave a small growl.

It's okay, Onyx, it's just Dad. I let that thought float out through whatever allowed me to talk to the dead. And that was the frequency the dog was on.

Onyx sat up straighter and cautiously approached Dad.

Dad sat down on his haunches, putting his hand out. Onyx sniffed his hand, doing an exaggerated lean with his neck, slowly wagging his tail.

The male was Alpha, he smelled very much like the boy but not at all like the Alpha female. The Boy smelled like both of them. The Dog made his tail move to show he liked this new pack member...thunk, thunk, thunk.

A part of the male's body was out, the Dog leaned forward cautiously... smells like older male, like the Boy... he shows respect by making himself smaller. The Dog likes the Alpha Male. The Dog shows respect by lying down.

I watched Onyx lie down, showing his belly. Dad was petting him on his belly and Onyx wagged his tail. Good, everybody was friends now.

Suddenly, Onyx flipped over and stood, trotting back over to me, where he turned and sat down next to my chair.

Dad stood, stretching, arching his back and standing on tiptoe.

"You stiff?" Mom asked.

"Some... been in a chair all day."

Dad turned to me. "Feel like one on one today?"

That sounded great. "Yeah, it's been forever since we played."

"Now that the immediate crises are over, we can resume our lives," Dad said.

"It *has* been stressful," Mom said.

"How do you like your new dog?" Dad asked.

"Onyx is awesome!"

Mom looked critically at Onyx, who stared back at her expectantly, his brown eyes a pool of liquid in his black face. "He sure is black, like an ink spot that barks."

It was the first supper we'd had in what seemed like forever where we just talked about normal stuff. No government threats, break-ins, bullies at school or raising dead stuff. Almost normal.

Time for more chaos.

After supper, Dad and I were cranking it up on our cement basketball court. I was guarding him like a cheap suit and he was huffing and puffing around me. I jumped up just as he was shooting and slapped the basketball right out of his hands.

The Js came walking up then, taking off their hoodies as they strode, piling them up just outside the court.

"Hey Kyle!" Jonesy yelled.

John inclined his head to Dad.

Jonesy ran over and we ganged up on Dad. After all, he was all-that-was-man *and* six-foot one, he had to man-up.

We tore around the court, Dad driving the ball toward the basket, Jonesy accelerating and me trying to steal, John getting in the way of all of us. It was the absolute best.

We horsed around till the light faded so much that we couldn't see the basket. Bounding up the steps we threw the door open. Mom was in her pajamas with two pitchers of iced tea. Jonesy rushed over, grabbed the biggest cup out of the cupboard he could find, filled it to the brim and chugged it down while we watched. Finally, he wiped his mouth with the back of his hand.

He saw us all watching him. "What?"

"Hey, Mrs. H., what do ya say about some banana bread?" He waggled his eyebrows in that charming Jonesy-way of his.

Mom laughed. "You bet, it's right over there," while pointing to the right of the bread box. A large slab was left out from yesterday.

Mom said, "Looks like someone wants to meet your friends."

Onyx had come to sit patiently in the corner of the room, eying my friends with curiosity.

"Hey boy!" John extolled.

"That's right! You got him today..." Jonesy said. "So this is the famous dog?"

"That's him," I said proudly.

We all looked at him and his tail started to wag.

"Mom, is it okay that he sleeps in my room?"

"It's okay, but I think that he may want his own space," Dad said.

I felt a lecture coming on.

"Kyle means that you have to move all your junk on the floor, to some other spot so he has a place to be," John said.

Oh, that made sense. But, maybe he would like the smell of my stuff on the floor I told them.

Mom shook her head. "No, Caleb, he can't just lie on your clothes." A cool idea foiled!

John's hair was standing straight up because he was always pushing it out of his eyes and a combination of boy-grime and sweat had acted as... I don't know, some kind of gel, I guess. Jonesy's hair was cut close to his scalp and seemed to dry instantly when he was sweating. We all thought that was really cool. Mine hung in strings. We all needed showers but I wanted to get my room in shape for Onyx.

"Hey guys, let's get a space for Onyx," I said.

John shrugged.

Jonesy said, "Sounds like a plan."

I looked at Onyx and he was just there. Cool.

We climbed the stairs, opened my door and surveyed The Cave.

"Crap Caleb, it's a mess in here," Jonesy said.

"Oh, I don't know, it looks a lot like your room Jonesy," John said, cocking and eyebrow.

Jonesy gave John a dirty look. "It's not this bad," he protested, waving his hand around.

"Whatever. This isn't getting a spot for Onyx figured out."

"Caleb's right, let's get to work," John agreed.

We started picking up all the clothes off the floor, heaving them all in a pile on top of my bed that soon became a mountain. John looked at my garbage stack, I shook my head.

Jonesy, seeing the direction of where I was looking said, "No man, the dog can't sleep on the desk..."

That was my logic.

John frowned, he was thinking we would clean the whole room. Out of a scale of interest from one through ten, with ten being the highest, cleaning my room was a negative number.

"Where do the clothes go?" John asked reasonably. Then, "This clothes hamper here? Are these dirty or clean?" he asked, pointing to the pile on the bed.

I shrugged, who knew? If they smelled bad, I didn't wear them.

John folded his arms across his chest. "This is your closet?"

"No. This is my closet." I opened the bi-fold doors and a bunch of crap rolled out at our feet.

Jonesy surveyed stuff. "Look, there's my History text from last year! I had to pay a fine!" He glared at me.

I shrugged again.

John threw up his hands. "Okay... the plan is, dump the junk in the dirty clothes hamper upside-down, then put the dirty clothes in the hamper, then, put the clean clothes in the closet." He looked over at the closet, "and I guess stack all that crap in the bottom."

Damn.

"I hate to say it Caleb, but, I think you're gonna have to go downstairs and get a trash sack," John looked at the closet again, "not those weak ones that your mom uses for kitchen trash, but *yard* waste."

"Can't dude, we compost."

John face-palmed. "I forgot your mom doesn't believe in trash."

"My Dad does."

"Really?" Jonesy asked.

"Yeah, but don't tell my mom. She thinks trash is very uncool," I said with feeling.

"Jonesy, minion, go fetch trash receptacle," John said.

Jonesy gave a sharp salute and beat it downstairs.

Onyx stood patiently waiting for us people to figure it out.

Jonesy came back up and we put the trash pile in the bag. Actually, John did. Somehow, I think he was offended by it.

We started into the closet.

"Do we give the school back the History book?" John asked.

Jonesy and I looked at it and at the same time said, "Nah."

"Jinx!" Jonesy said as we grinned at each other.

John sighed again, into the trash it went.

An hour later, the bag couldn't fit any more and I noticed that there was a lot of floor space to choose a spot for Onyx.

After a ass-load of discussion, we decided that Onyx needed to be at the foot of my bed, but close to the computer desk, on the right. I had a sudden idea and decided to search around in the closet, moving all the non-trash items. Mom's Stephen King collection was carefully put aside. I found just the thing, Gran's afghan. It was a bunch of bright-colored squares all stitched together to make a huge blanket. It was itchy. Mom said it was made of wool. She didn't like synthetic fibers since they were made with petroleum products. I folded it in half, then half again, placing it in the new spot.

I thought in Onyx's head, *here's your new spot.*

He walked over, sniffed the scratchy thing, and laid down on it.

"Good dog."

He wagged his tail.

"He sure *seems* like a good dog," Jonesy said. Hearing that, Onyx wagged his tail harder.

Smart too.

John turned his attention back to the closet, poking at my stack of books with a toe "Why don't you use a dedicated reader?"

"It's like the watch, isn't it?" Jonesy said.

"Caleb *is* a little outdated," John remarked.

"No. I just think that it's important to use some stuff that isn't modern. I mean, think about our dependence on Brain Impulse Technology? If everything went stupid, and suddenly that junk didn't work, just think about the chaos, even if it was only for an hour; people would melt down."

John looked thoughtful. "You have a point."

Jonesy looked at my watch. "It's not even LED," he nearly wailed.

I looked down at the funky thing, scratched and old looking. It had been Dad's first watch and I liked it.

John bent his head over it and grunted, "It's a winder."

"A what?" Jonesy asked.

"You have to wind it every day to keep time."

Jonesy looked baffled.

John shrugged. "I gotta split. Let's get this stuff back in the closet."

We threw all the stuff back in there, stacking the books carefully, and shut the thing. Jonesy looked relieved that the doors could close.

Onyx sat on the blanket watching us.

Jonesy whispered, "He's kinda creepy, Caleb, the way he just stares at us."

We all looked at him.

"He's something," John said.

Be right back... stay, I thought at Onyx.

The Boy made the people noises in the Dog's head. But, the noises weren't as clear as the flavor. The Dog thought about how the Boy put a smell inside his head, all different types of smells, and they made a message. The Boy was very easy to understand. He was different from the Others. The Dog would stay on this, (he dropped his nose to smell)... soft thing that smelled like old pack female...in the Boy's den. He closed his eyes, feeling something that was familiar... a sense of home. The Dog was happy.

His memories of the other Boy were dimming.

CHAPTER 24

The rest of the week dragged by. Go to school, daydream about it ending, then rush home to see Onyx, eat some food, hang with the posse and Jade and do it all again. All of us were getting so tired of school. The end of the year loomed large.

Hadn't seen much of Carson and Brett but I knew we'd probably go to the same high school next year as freshman, Kent Paranormal High, KPH. That's where all paranormals went. At the regular (mundane) high schools in town everyone with different academic aptitudes would go to the high school that specialized in that aptitude. Jonesy had shown Math/Science aptitude so that's where he was headed, Kent Lake High. The rest of the gang was going to KPH. I was gonna really miss the Jonester, it seemed wrong somehow.

Friday finally rolled around and it was the sixth of June. Jonesy, ever mindful with scheming said he thought the last day of school would be a blast.

"Ya see... it's a special day." We were all at the lunch table festering about the possibilities of government plots, hiding what we were and such; ya know, normal conversation.

We waited expectantly for him to continue. Jonesy always had cool and bizarre ideas. Sometimes, like the disastrous cemetery plot with Carson, they didn't work out but it was interesting to see.

"It's Friday the Thirteenth," he said, clearly satisfied with himself.

Sophie rolled her eyes. "So?"

Jonesy grinned back at her, smug. "It's an unlucky day. Stuff that's bad, that's gonna happen, happens then."

Sophie stared at him.

"He is amusing," Jade said.

"He's right," John agreed, showing guy-support.

Tiff strolled up just then, hands jammed into the pocket of her hoodie, the hood pulled all the way up, a sliver of her face revealed. "Whatcha doin'?"

"Hey Tiff," I said.

The Js nodded, the girls said hey.

"What's he sayin'?" Tiff asked.

Sophie said, "Jonesy thinks the last day of school is going to be riddled with bad luck because it's Friday the Thirteenth."

Tiff said without preamble, "That's a load of horseshit."

Right.

Out loud I said, "Ya never know, it could go okay. It's just supposed to be a warning, right?" I looked at John, who nodded.

"I know some bad stuff that's happened on that day," Jonesy said in a creep-you-out voice.

"Yeah... what?" Tiff said, plunking herself down between Sophie and Jade, who gave her a miffed look. She didn't have girl radar or she'd have seen the problem with that move.

Tiff put her head in the cradle of both her hands, clearly bored and waving the red flag before the proverbial bull.

Jonesy obligingly said, "There's this haunted house...ya know, the one where that old cemetery is, it's just a shack. I heard there was a kid that went in there and never came out." he was nodding his head the whole time.

"Who told you that lame-ass story?" Tiff said skeptically.

"One of the teachers," Jonesy said triumphantly.

That got everyone's attention. Jade took a bite of apple and John fussed with some Cheetos, putting a couple up his nose and wiggling it. It was comical with a Cheeto sticking out of each nostril. Sophie was unimpressed.

"You're gonna eat those now, aren't ya?" Tiff said, smacking her gum.

Jade sighed. "Boys."

"Hey!" I exclaimed.

"Not you." She fluttered her eyelashes at me and I was instantly smitten again.

"Listen up chumps!" Jonesy redirected.

The girls gave dissatisfied grunts, John took the Cheetos out, peering at the ends that had been in his nose... *nice*.

"This is the plan," oh, here we go, John looked cautious. The girls were clearly interested but they didn't know Jonesy *that* well.

"Jonesy..." John started.

He held up a palm, warding him off. "Hear me out. We're gonna go to this shack..."

"That's by a cemetery... smart," said Tiff in a droll way.

"Yeah, and I have the ghost-buster team here with me to take care of everything," Jonesy said with confidence.

Tiff and I sighed.

"So, we're gonna go there and *see*."

"See what, Jonesy?" Jade asked.

"I don't know... somethin', whatever."

"Well that clears things up a lot," Sophie said.

"Jonesy's consistent," John said neutrally.

Jonesy gave John a speculative look and continued, "It's a half-day but I'm thinking we have to wait until dark?"

I was figuring Jonesy for a full dark, check-out-the-haunted-house kinda guy.

"Hell yeah! This is the best part, it won't be dark until late, like ten, so we have plenty of time to rebel-rouse before."

"Rebel-rouse?" Tiff asked.

"Rouse means 'to wake' and rebel, well... you gotta know what that means," Jonesy said.

A sneaking seed of suspicion started to take hold.

"You're not thinking of some cemetery shit again?" I asked.

"Who, me?" he asked, all innocence.

Tiff's eyes narrowed into slits. "We don't need the spotlight, Jones. We need to stay underground."

She was right, even if her way with words was not real smooth.

"That wasn't The Plan," he paused. "But if something cool were to happen..." he spread his arms wide, w*hat's the problem?*

The voice of reason spoke up. "Let's stick to checking out the old place and seeing what's in it; no cemeteries," John finished.

Jonesy looked embarrassed. Uh-oh, something was up.

"Spill it," Tiff said.

"Well, there's something I forgot to mention," he said, putting his thumb and index fingers almost together, a paper's width from touching.

John spun his hand like a wheel, *go on*, and Jonesy finished with, "You gotta walk through the cemetery to get to the house."

"I knew it!" Sophie said, Jade making a face.

Tiff and I looked at each other.

"I guess it's okay. Carson and Brett don't know we're going," I said slowly.

I looked at Jonesy who would tell The World if he felt it would help The Cause, he shook his head; he hadn't said anything... yet.

Tiff interjected with, "And it's a bonus your Gran isn't buried there. Wait, do you have any *other* relatives buried there?"

"No, they're all at Scenic."

"Well thank God," Sophie mumbled.

"Okay, I'm in," Tiff said, leaning back and crossing her feet at the ankles. "Can Bry come?"

"Ah-huh..." I thought about that more. "He's not gonna kick my ass, is he?" Didn't want to set myself up for the fall *and* with my girlfriend as the audience.

"Nah... he's over it."

"Is he the cute one?" Sophie asked.

Jonesy glared at that. Interesting.

"How should I know? He's my brother, gross."

The pulse clock chimed and we stood, separating our trash. The Js trailed behind as Jade and I walked to our next class.

"What do you think you'll get out of Biology?" Jade asked. "It was kind of a cluster with the frog thing."

Yeah it was.

"Maybe I softened him up, knowing stuff about flowers."

Jade's eyebrows shot up.

I nodded. "Yeah, my mom makes me do gardening chores."

"That's why you knew about the plant names when I came over." She smiled up at me.

Huh, bonus point.

"It beats cleaning toilets," I said.

"Yeah, that's a gross job. I'd rather learn about plants," she said wistfully.

She had the chores I hated and I had made a big deal out of it. Geez, Hart, good going.

"This summer you can come over and we'll do gardening together. I bet my mom would love the help!"

"Alright, cool!"

We stopped in front of Biology. "Have fuuuunnn!" she teased.

"Oh, yeah and monkeys will fly outta my butt!" I said.

She giggled and I laid a kiss on her full mouth that felt like crushed velvet (sensory overload!).

I entered the classroom thinking about the weekend stretched before me. Last week of school, a plan for creepy Friday the

Thirteenth, a new dog and a hot girlfriend; life was rocking about now.

CHAPTER 25

I was splitting my time between the Js and Jade and it was a job. The guys wanted to hang at Jonesy's tonight. I called Jade and she told me it would be okay to see me Saturday night instead. I pulsed the Js and told them we were on for tonight. Mom asked what Jonesy's mom was having for supper. I didn't know, like it mattered? Knowing Jonesy, we'd forage in the pantry and come up with something good. Mom decided to make a pizza and send it with me.

I jetted over to Jonesy's on Dad's old one-speed Schwinn. I was sure I'd hear about that from Jonesy, *Caleb is outdated, Caleb is... blah, blah, blah.*

I didn't care, I loved the old stuff.

The pizza dangled from the handle bars in a most undignified way. Mom had cut the pizza, so I was riding around with eight slices of homemade pizza. The bag swung and whacked. It thunked as I rode along, passing all the familiar milestones: 7-Eleven to my left, QFC Grocery to my right... there it was, Meridian Villa. My dad grew up there. The houses were just the next step older than my neighborhood. Jonesy's parents had actually bought the house that Jonesy's dad had lived in as a kid.

Swinging my leg off the pedal and around to the other side as the bike slowed I came to a complete stop at the top of their circular driveway. I grabbed the bag of pizza and approached the front door, checking out the house. Jonesy's house was cooler than mine, it had a basement. Dad called those man-caves. The house was really flat looking and hugged the knoll it lounged on. Small windows that looked like eyes lined the point where the basement met the flower beds. Jonesy's dad, Bill, had a very small lawn. By the looks of it, barely within legal limits. Seemed like some dudes just had to have a lawn. Mom would have never allowed it at our house, not *Eco*-enough. Mom thought lawns were for outdoor sports fields, period. I loved the lawn. It was an emerald slash of green that anchored the flower beds. Jonesy's mom wasn't a garden-Nazi like my mom but she made it look nice.

I climbed the three, broad, concrete steps, ringing the bell.

Helen came to the door, grinning. "Hey Caleb! Long time no see!" Her impenetrable hair stood at stiff attention (and looked like a rat lived on top).

Aqua Net Queen.

I smiled back, she had Jonesy's grin exactly. "Hi, Mrs. Jones."

A frown appeared. "I mean... Helen," I corrected.

"That's better," Helen said, ruffling my hair. Geez, no touchy!

I ducked my head and threw over my shoulder, "My mom made some pizza."

"Good deal, we'll add it to mine."

Great, more pizza, happy Friday! I rounded the corner, walking down a long hallway painted McDonald's yellow. With such a neutral exterior, the yellow was a shocker. But Mrs. Jones (Helen), said with our gloomy Pacific Northwest days that she needed the sun inside her house.

As I came down the hall I could hear the guys before I got to Jonesy's room.

I opened the door, surveying the room. Jonesy sat on the floor, pulsing through his dedicated reader, John likewise absorbed. I walked over and sat on my haunches, they were looking at comics. We were nuts over the super hero comics. Especially now that some people's paranormal skills echoed what was once considered impossible.

"Look at this dude... hell, to be him, huh?" Jonesy said to no one in particular.

"You got that. I'm just a Null," a disgruntled John said.

"At least you're something, you ingrate," Jonesy replied.

"Hey, look at this." I pointed to a spot behind the guy lifting the car off the person.

We put our heads together, and saw a small boy in the background with big eyes, watching the rescue of... I think his brother, from under the car. But, he had one finger on the bumper.

"Is that kid doing it or the guy in the cape?"

That was the $64,000,000 question.

John studied it. "Hold on!" He leapt up and ran out of the room. In the distance I heard voices.

"What's he doing?" I asked Jonesy.

"I don't know," he shrugged.

John rushed back in with a funny looking thing with a black plastic stem and a round piece of glass on the top.

"What's that?"

"It's my mom's magnifying glass," Jonesy said.

"This will do the trick!" John said.

We all bent forward again, the high resolution in the reader giving a sharper image as the convex shaped glass flowed over the top, expanding and defining.

"Hell yeah!" Jonesy punched air.

"Jonesy! Language!" Helen yelled a reprimand.

"Sorry mom!" Jonesy yelled back.

Jonesy repeated quietly, "Hell yeah!"

John and I smiled.

"Okay, so the kid is holding up part of the car? So what, it's a comic," I said.

"That's where you're wrong," John replied with gravity.

I looked a question at him.

"You remember Alex?" John asked.

"The bad piano player?"

"Yeah," he waved that opinion away impatiently. "He told me that there were hidden messages in the comics. That if we looked closely, we could find things in the images, the artwork, that when strung together means something."

"Are you shitting me?"

"No, would I?" John asked.

We both looked at Jonesy.

"What?" he asked, oblivious.

We shook our heads. John wouldn't make it up, too weird.

"Alright, so what does it mean?" I asked.

"Well, that's what we've been trying to decipher with just this months' worth of comics."

"What does Alex *say* it means?"

"He thinks there are allies of the paranormals that have been shut down by the government and there's subtle messages in the comics that talk about what is going on, what they're doing. Maybe even where they might be located."

"And... Alex got this all from, what? He pulled it out of his ass?" Jonesy asked.

I had a visual of Alex, who was such a nerd it hurt me to look at him, but he was truly smart. Maybe there was something to this.

Jonesy turned off his DR. "That's for when we have more time. I have a plan."

Oh joy.

John asked, "What now? I thought we were going to talk about the comic messages?"

"Later. Besides, you've already agreed to this," Jonesy said.

"What?" I asked, impatient.

"Let's figure out the hideaway. While there's no chicks around to ruin it," Jonesy answered.

"Jade wouldn't ruin it," I defended.

"She wouldn't *mean* to but, she still distracts you. She's like the 'shiny thing'. She moves and you follow."

I really couldn't argue with that. I looked at John for support.

John just shook his head. "He's right Caleb, you're kinda gone on her."

"I'm here tonight though, aren't I?" I asked, indignant.

"Yeah, but we're not getting together as much as we were. It's okay, I'm just sayin'."

"Okay. I want to find a place to have a safe zone. Somewhere we can go if the government gets wind of me," I said.

"That's what I'm talkin' about, Caleb," Jonesy said like, *duh.*

I still felt uncomfortable doing the zombie slave labor.

"Come on Caleb, we need them," Jonesy said, seeing my face.

"Yeah, I have been thinking of a way for us to use the zombies and get them back without being noticed," John said.

I held up my hand. "Let's just wait and see if we even need to use them. Maybe we'll find a really cool place in the old dump and it will be perfect, without..."

"Improvements," John supplied.

"Right."

"Let's go tonight, right now," Jonesy said.

"I gotta have some food first," John said.

Right on cue, my stomach did a huge rumble.

"That's a sign," Jonesy said.

We walked out to the kitchen and plopped down in front of a huge thing that my parents called a breakfast bar. The Js and I pulled out the stools. Jonesy's mom poured us out three pops, Big Red. Helen believed sugar was a food group, that made me happy on a deep level.

She put a plate in front of each of us with four slices. My mom's pizza was demolished during round one. Jonesy and I were okay after that but John had to have two more. Helen said she still had a whole pizza left.

"I don't wanna walk, Caleb," Jonesy said through a mound of food crammed into one side of his mouth.

"Listen, mister, don't talk with your mouth full," Helen said.

"Sorry, mom," Jonesy said, and smiled, the pizza guts showing through his teeth. Helen shook her head and started a load of dishes.

"Why not?" I asked.

"Because, I think it will be fun to just watch you ride on that old bike of yours, I need a laugh."

John smiled.

Helen said, "Jonesy, that is a perfectly adequate bike."

"Mom, have you looked at it? Really looked at it? It's pathetic. It's a one-speed."

"Those are classic instruments for the development of large motor skills," she elaborated.

"Huh?" Jonesy asked.

"Mrs. Jones is talking about your butt," John said.

It was Helen's turn to grin.

"Let me explain. There are no gears, right?"

"Right," Jonesy agreed.

"So, it forces you to use the booty gear."

"Precisely, John, and I thank you for clarifying," Helen replied.

"You're just not gonna admit that it's not as cool as my Raleigh Scout, mom," Jonesy stated.

"Not on your life, big-for-your-britches."

John and I barked out an appreciative laugh. The DNA train wasn't far from the track with his smart-ass behavior.

Jonesy glowered at his mom but she didn't even flinch; tough-as-nails, loved it.

We grabbed our bikes, my tires the monsters of the group and were on our way. The old, abandoned dump was really close to Scenic Hill Cemetery so we parked our bikes there and walked over. It wouldn't be good for some observant adult to see a bunch of kids' bikes loitering in front of a dump.

We looked up at the sign, "Kent Refuse, Authorized Personnel Only, Trespassing Prohibited, Hours of Operation: Mon-Fri: 10:00-4:00. Then, over the top of that was the haphazard lettering, *Closed.* Our gaze traveled to the top of the chain link fence where barbed wire swirled lazily in a spiral. That would take some doing.

I turned to John. "What do ya think..."

He pulled out two pair of gloves.

Jonesy's eyebrows shot up. "Great! Good thinking,Terran!"

John, always prepared.

"You first," I said to Jonesy.

Jonesy grunted, threw on the gloves and climbed. Fine muscles bunched and moved in his forearms as he finessed his way up the links, John keeping an eye on the road for adults.

"Hurry," John said.

"I am. Can it!"

Finally, Jonesy got to the top and pushing down the barbed wire with one hand, straddled it in preparation for swinging his leg over to the other side.

"Hey!" I yelled.

"What? Kinda busy, ya moron."

"Why don't you stay awhile?"

"Shut up Caleb, it's your turn next," Jonesy said, giving a nervous look at his balls, millimeters above the barbs.

Jonesy carefully swept his left leg over, securing a foothold on the opposite side. He removed one glove at a time with his teeth, throwing them one-handed over the top of the fence for John and I.

I struggled the gloves on while Jonesy climbed down the other side. I got them on and stood facing Jonesy. Jonesy smiled and did an elaborate middle finger. John laughed.

"Have fun with that, Hart."

A knot of anxiety was like a ball in my stomach. I was gonna do this.

I was definitely not scared of heights.

I took a deep breath and started to climb. It was pretty easy until I was just about to the top and my arms started to shake. Jonesy hadn't mentioned that part. Maybe it hadn't made him tired. He was shorter, but muscular.

I used the same tramp-down-the-barbed wire technique as Jonesy, hovering precariously over the top in complete terror that my arm strength would give way just at that moment. But the threat of a testicle free life kept me stable. Swinging the other leg over the top, I hung there at the top of the other side, catching my breath.

"Somebody needs to do some push-ups!" Jonesy sang.

Jerk.

I climbed down and stood by Jonesy on the right side of the fence.

"I do push-ups."

Jonesy grunted, "Maybe do some more."

John was still staring at the road.

"Let's get going," Jonesy said through the fence.

John sighed, looking one more time at the locked gate. "Just a sec," he said, jogging over to the gate.

"It's locked John, you're gonna have to climb," Jonesy called out smugly.

John stood staring at the gate, which was a huge chain link affair with a padlock the size of my fist.

"It's got a numbered entry," John called.

Jonesy shrugged, *so?*

"It's pre-pulse," I explained.

"Whatever. John, just climb, you're wasting time."

John started to spin the numbers on the lock, jerking it experimentally. Finally, after a minute of messing around with it and Jonesy grumbling, it opened, like magic.

John looked over at us and grinned triumphantly. "I guess I'll just open the gate, and *walk* in," he said.

Oh brother.

And he did; walking right in and right over to us.

Jonesy had his hands on his hips. "What-the-hell, Terran? Why didn't you try that from the start?"

"I didn't think about it until it was my turn to climb," John tapped his head and continued, "Work smarter, not harder."

Nice.

"Okay, smart-ass, go close the gate so adults don't check it out."

John sauntered over to the gate, carefully arranging the lock so it would appear locked.

He came back over and we started to search for the perfect spot.

The dump was an interesting place. I was thinking it was gonna smell trashy. There was some of that, but the acute trash smell was long-gone. The refuse station had been closed since I was little back when recycling became mandatory, with trash penalties and stuff. There just weren't that many dumps in service anymore.

There was a butt-load of tires and old cars and the appliances! It was insane!

Jonesy was thrilled with everything, touching and opening all of it.

John and I let Jonesy explore, while we stayed on a semi-clear path that meandered and wound through huge hills of broken and beaten cars. Old appliances lined the "road" on either side.

He looked inside a huge, commercial style freezer. "Hold on a sec... I've got an idea."

"What?" I asked.

"I think... that if these cars," he looked up from our vantage point of being at the base of the "hill" of cars, "weren't compressed all the way, we may be able to make a 'doorway'," he made a large rectangular outline with his fingers of a doorway, "using one of these old fridges, kick the back out and find some space behind it that we can use."

He folded his arms across his chest and let me think it through. I looked over at the long line of appliances. Maybe one didn't even have a back anymore? I slowly nodded.

"Good, huh?"

"Yeah, let's get the Jonester over here and lay it on him."

"Jonesy," I yelled.

"What?!" came the muffled reply.

I turned to John. "Where is he?"

John shrugged.

Suddenly, a head popped out of an old car.

"Come on, stop dickin' around and get over here."

Jonesy shot his leg out and booted the car door open, its protesting creak piercing the quiet with a squealing groan.

John cringed at Jonesy's subtlety.

Jonesy trotted over and rubbed a hand over his face, covering it with grime. I looked closer. It was like grease, great.

"You've got grease on your face now," John said.

"I do? Oh well, whatever. I've got soap at home."

I told Jonesy the plan.

"Hot damn! What are we waiting for? Let's tear these babies open!"

We separated, searching each one. Finally, there was an ugly pink fridge with a clear handle, that looked to have a car emblem embedded in the handle. Weird.

John looked critically at it, circling around the thirty percent that showed.

"Good size," he stroked the top that he could barely reach. It was a behemoth, bigger than some of the fancy fridges that were in restaurants. John whistled at Jonesy and he walked over from inspecting an avocado-colored beauty.

John slowly opened the fridge; it was deep, probably two feet plus. A perimeter of internal rust edged the interior all along the back. Rust-like lace spread out from the corners in a spider web of burnt orange. Jonesy stepped forward and tore out the two shelves that hung cattywampus inside, making them sail like Frisbees over John's head.

"Hey! Watch it," John said, ducking.

"Hold your shorts, Terran, you'll live."

"Kick out the back Jonesy," I said.

He turned his head and looked at me. "Duh."

Jonesy did a super graceful dance kick where he sorta hops, then jumps, bending his knee and swinging it out at the same time. A ripple appeared where his foot had struck, the back buckling.

Jonesy did another strike and the buckle widened from top to bottom.

"Come on Jonesy, I thought you were all-that-is-boy," John antagonized.

"I," kick, thunk, whack, "am!" The whole back gave, splitting open into the dark.

John, of the ever-prepared, whipped out his LED light, where a dim spiral wove a murky path through the gloom.

"Come on, let's go."

And in we went.

There was only enough room to crawl, it was dusty and we were a sneezing, wheezing mess. I crawled about another eight feet, turning my head. "This isn't going to work."

John lit a match. "If there isn't enough oxygen, this match won't stay lit."

We all stared at the light of the match, wavering and uncertain, but burning bright, like a beacon.

"Okay so what now?" Jonesy asked.

"There's enough oxygen this far back that I think this tunnel here might open up into a bigger space. Keep moving."

Jonesy and I crawled forward on our hands and knees, for about three more minutes. I was losing track of how long it had been when it narrowed. I belly crawled and twisted through the last bit and...it opened up enough for me to stand up, the LED light gripped firmly between my teeth. Slowly, I took it out and looked around. It was big... real big.

John said, "Wow."

That about covered it. Everywhere around us were cars that were compacted in huge stacks. Several were precariously perched above our heads, acting like a ceiling. I wasn't worried, I figured they'd been like that for a decade and they weren't ever gonna come down.

"Come on morons, stop gawking and haul me out of here!"

John and I turned around, and sure enough, Jonesy was wedged in the part of the "tunnel" that had been a real twister to get out of. John barked out a laugh that made Jonesy do a death glare.

"I like it," John said.

"We can't get out if he's in the way, smart one," I said.

John sighed. "You're right, but it was fun while it lasted."

We each pulled one arm, counted to three and jerked him out like an eel out of an oil can.

Jonesy grabbed his knees and stood up, brushing the dirt off his jeans.

"Thanks for the help, guys," Jonesy delivered sarcastically.

He looked around appreciatively. "This is just the guy-cave we had in mind."

John took out another LED light and turned it on to join mine.

"Where are you getting all the lights," Jonesy asked. "And how did you know the combo for the lock?"

"Yeah, what he said."

"I read some documentary about pre-pulse security. They said sometimes at commercial sites the numbered addresses were used backwards, or the last for digits of the phone number."

"You mean, ding-a-ling?"

"Yeah, Jonesy, actual non-pulse phones," John said.

"Why is this here?" I asked, indicating the big bubble room of forgotten cars.

"It's like I was hoping. There would be a pocket of space that was trapped, something they missed," John said.

"The workers missed?" Jonesy asked.

"Yeah. Just think of that job; all day long smashing cars, trying to remember where you did it last. It'd be a bitch to keep track of, thinking you're at the bottom. When, really, you missed a spot."

"How would you know?" Jonesy asked.

"I didn't, I guessed. When Caleb wanted to do the hideout here I thought it might be a possibility."

"How do the girls get back here?" I asked.

"Girls!"

"Come off it Jonesy, Jade, Sophie and Tiff are included."

"There's Bry and maybe Alex too."

Huh, we were getting a *group* I told them.

"We can do it," John said.

"Does your mom still have that camping gear?" John asked Jonesy.

"Yeah, we haven't camped much, why?"

"Light?" I said, guessing.

"Yeah. I don't think we need heat, but if we can get a lantern and propane bottle we could have a halfway decent place." John fingered his chin thoughtfully.

He looked at me.

"What now?"

Jonesy grinned. "I think John is thinking we need some zombie action."

Geez.

"What do we have to do?"

"We need to widen this some. No big deal," Jonesy said easily.

Jonesy's ideas were always a big deal.

"I agree with Jonesy, we just widen this tight spot," John pointed to the squeeze that had stymied Jonesy's progress, "and we put them back."

I put them back.

He twisted his upper body, turning toward Jonesy. "What do you think, it's a one or two zombie job?"

"Hey! Don't ask him, they're my zombies," I said.

John turned away, smiling. He got down in the mouth of the entrance to the tunnel, turning the LED light on, checking it out. Then he turned it off, standing, "We leave LEDs here so as soon as we return we can set up our stuff."

John told us we'd need a lantern, propane, a couple of blankets and some milk crates.

"Where are we gonna get those?" Jonesy asked.

I didn't have a clear picture of what a milk crate was.

"Here. It's a dump, after all."

"What are those gonna be for?" Jonesy asked.

"Tables, chairs, storage, whatever," John said.

"Okay, let's get out of here before it gets too late," I said.

We crawled out of the tight tunnel the way we came in: slowly.

Jonesy had the most trouble.

He finally climbed out, arching his back.

"We gotta remember that these old freezers are not safe, they self-lock."

"What do ya mean?" Jonesy asked.

"We close the door from the inside and we're screwed."

We looked at him.

"Back in the day, kids would play hide-and-seek, hide inside, accidentally close the door... and..."

"I never heard of that," I said.

"Yeah, you wouldn't. We don't have bogus stuff like that now. Hell, they make up committees of people just to think up safety features," John said. "Anyway, we gotta put a door stop in there so we don't lock ourselves in and get busy dying."

Nice, John. Don't say that in front of the girls.

"Okay, whatever but," and Jonesy laid his finger up, almost in John's face, "we need to keep it open in a way people don't notice."

"Right," John conceded.

We stood there quietly.

"Let's just use a piece of cardboard, slam it into the door and the..." I waved my hand around, "jamb-thing won't self-lock."

John nodded. "It's not complicated. We make an escape hatch that doesn't make our hideaway a big coffin."

We agreed.

"I gotta get home and take care of Onyx."

"Yeah, let's not get the parents all interested in what we're doing," Jonesy said.

"My parent's don't give a crap as long as that 4.0 GPA is still there," John said.

I guess I was lucky that Dad wasn't bringing the hammer down on me since I barely got "C's."

We walked out of the dump and through the gate.

Jonesy stopped outside of the gate and looked at John. "You're kinda a putz not to let us know about the lock thing."

John grinned. "Yeah, but I wanted to see if you'd climb it. Even Caleb did."

It wasn't easy.

Jonesy said, "Remember: A) we have a hideaway now, B) we have a plan for next Friday, D) we have girls to protect from..."

"That would be C, Jonesy," John interjected.

"Whatever. And *C*," he nodded to John, "we have Girls to Protect."

"Protect from what?" I asked.

"I don't know... whatever."

"You get kinda squirrely when we get in tight spots," I reminded.

"Right, but you have to remember that I'll protect the chicks. *You*... you're on your own."

"Gee... thanks," John said, without surprise.

We separated, biking to our respective houses.

Onyx knew I was coming and met me at the door.

His tail wagged like an ink spot in the middle of the doorway, eyes softly glowing in the twilight. He trotted to me as I came forward. I rubbed the bridge of his nose.

The Boy has returned and is pleased because he is a Good Dog. I will lick the Boy's hand.

Onyx gave a lick that was wet and slimy, he looked so happy I didn't have the heart to wipe the nasty dog goo off.

The Dog pressed his nose to the Boy's body and smelled very interesting smells; smells of real trash (tantalizing) and foul-smelling things that are on the metal boxes, earth and something old. Such good smells. He also smelled the other Boys. What had the Boy done?

"Good dog. Gooooood dog," I said, scratching the sweet spot. Wag, thunk, wag.

I walked in through the door, greeting The Parents. Mom had her nose buried in her dedicated reader and Dad was taking notes (with a pen!) from his pulse-top.

They looked up while Onyx trotted past, taking an experimental whiff of his food bowl, he didn't look sure.

Where is the person-who-feeds him, the Dog wondered? The food is here all the time. The Dog paused... was this a New Thing? He surveyed the pack. They did not seem to be interested in the food. This new thing was confusing. He would wait and see what the pack did.

I noticed that Onyx went and laid down on one of Gran's blankets. Mom had an endless supply of those.

"What were you up to all this time, pal?"

Going to the dump, exploring it illegally, finding a dangerous boy-cave so we could hide from the authorities.

Out loud I said, "Just screwing around, exploring."

"That sounds about right," Mom said, smiling.

"Sounds like the heat may be abating for the interim, Caleb."

Mom looked on with interest but I wondered what Dad meant. Their expressions sometimes stumped me.

"I think, what Dad's saying is the government may no longer be interested in you."

"That's not what interim means," I said, guessing temporary.

"You're right, Caleb, I don't have a crystal ball. I don't know that they'll always *not* be interested. For now, we have a reprieve. But, if they find out you're not a two-point we're back to square one."

"We agreed to take one day at a time, Kyle."

"I agree, Hun, but let's be prepared for the inevitable."

"They'll eventually find out," I said.

Mom nodded, Dad said simply, "Yes."

Oh well. "What's for dessert?"

Mom laughed. "Nothing stops the unmovable object."

"What...?"

"Your appetite." Dad laughed, *obviously*.

I didn't understand what was funny. I had to eat all the time, it's just the way it was.

"So... what's your plan for the weekend?" Mom asked.

I swallowed a huge mouthful of chocolate pudding. "I'm going to hang with Jade tomorrow night." I looked up, thinking. "I guess not much Sunday. Oh! The Js and I are gonna explore..."

"...going to..." Mom corrected.

"...*going* to." Brother, anyway, "Check out this cool, haunted house."

That got Dad's full attention, the haunted word.

Dad stared at me for a second. Mom was doing the fish thing, her mouth opening and closing, gasping for air. I had that effect on my parents sometimes.

"This is not keeping a low profile, Caleb."

"It was Jonesy's idea." To cover for my friends I added, "but it doesn't mean cemeteries."

Not really.

"Well, that may be; you're aware you can control ghosts. Haunting is another issue to contend with."

I wasn't sure what the problem was, but I wasn't going to raise zombies so I figured it would be okay.

"Jonesy has some... interesting ideas," Mom said.

She didn't know the half of it.

"But, he doesn't seem to think things through."

Really?

"Just be careful, Caleb. We trust you. Keep in mind how wrong things went at Scenic with Gran," Dad said.

I wouldn't forget that. Licking the spoon clean as I walked the dish over to the sink, I filled it with gray water to let it soak until Mom did dishes.

Onyx stood, shadowing me as I went to my bedroom. I flopped up on my bed, grabbing one of Mom's old books. It laid on my chest, unopened. Ideas whirled through my head. I needed to think of something for Jade and I to do tomorrow. This girlfriend thing was complicated and school was ending. We were gonna find out where we'd be next year this Monday. I knew we'd be going to KPH, but what about Jonesy? And Brett? I guess Kent Lake.

But...*what* was Alex? After Carson's pyro show, I didn't want any more surprises.

I cracked open the book, feeling its hefty weight in my hands like a promise spoken, kept and realized.

CHAPTER 26

I woke up with something pressing into my rib cage, I pushed it onto the floor where it made a clunking sound. What? I looked at my floor, blurry-eyed, and saw that it was the book, which would normally have been cushioned by the fall with the clothes all over, but we had cleaned for cripe's sake, so now it had fallen like a bomb.

I lay back, groaning, my hand flung over my eyes. Suddenly, Onyx was there beside my bed his wet nose pressed against my face. A single lick. Gross.

The Boy seemed sad about something... the Dog restrained himself and gave the Boy a single lick, right after stuffing his nose on his Boy's face, inhaling the fragrant Boy smell. He would wag his tail and the Boy would notice and tell him the Good Word... he was sure.

I didn't want to hurt Onyx's feelings so I didn't wipe the dog-goo off. "That's a good dog, Onyx," petting his soft head. That got his tail wagging, echoing on the wood floor. I laughed. "Okay, boy, okay." and *thought, you're a good dog.*

The Boy had put the word-smells in his head and it sounded like the Good Word. The Dog wagged.

If Onyx wagged any harder it would take his butt off.

I swung my legs around and put them on the cold floor. Geez, maybe I needed a rug. Onyx stood, wagging. I searched the floor for something to wear. Looking around, I realized a crucial fact: being organized meant I couldn't find anything. Finally, in a drawer, I found one pair of clean socks. Eureka! I sighed, looking at the dirty clothes, which were now actually in the dirty clothes hamper (John's fault). I sorted through the thing, silently thanking Mom for not getting me anything white anymore, sorting colors was for fools. I mounded a huge pile of dirty clothes in my arms,

Onyx rushing ahead. I stumbled down the steps, looking around the mound in my arms to keep my footing.

"What are you doing... oh! Laundry? Miracles never cease," Mom exclaimed with mucho sarcasm. "Don't forget to take Onyx out."

Like he'd let me. I glanced at Onyx patiently waiting by the back door.

I heaved the whole bundle on the laundry room floor and opened the wash basin. Getting soap, I threw what I thought was the correct amount in. Who knew? I couldn't remember between washings.

Mom rounded the corner. "Did you remember how much soap to put in?"

Busted.

"Ah... I put in this much." I made a space about two inches wide with my index and thumb apart.

"No! You're going to wash the world, honey, scoop some out."

Geez.

"Okay."

I scooped, setting the knob to on.

Running to the back door, I let Onyx out.

I watched Onyx running around the "potty area." It was the lamest name for it in the world. But the lady from the animal shelter (Arlene? Barbara? Whatever) said calling the place where he did his "business" the same name as the shelter used would keep things "consistent" for Onyx. I think he would have taken a growler just about anywhere, being as it was his absolute favorite thing to do. As I thought this he did the old hunch-back, laying a steamer there on the gravel. A prize to be scooped up later, by me, of course.

Opening the door, Onyx rushed in ahead as I closed it behind me. I could smell the pancakes cooking, Dad was on his pulse-top reading boring news or looking at stocks (a fresh hell of unspeakable proportions). I plopped down in my seat, whipping my pulse out to say good morning to Jade. I pressed my thumb to the pad:

Initiated: *Hey Hotness,* -CH
Hi! **grins** *Whatcha doin'?* JLeC
Just sittin' here waiting for the deelish pancakes! CH.

Jealous! Are they fruit pancakes? JLeC
Profanity-block!-no! They're regular.-CH
What do you have against fruit, it's good for you! JLeC
That.-CH
What? That it's good for you? JLeC
Yeah, **laughs.**-CH
Okay **resigned.** *What's the plan?* JLeC
I want to show you the new place.-CH
Are we being careful here? JLeC
Always.-CH
Okay... what time? JLeC
Say... three o'clock, I'll pick you up.-CH
*Idk, do ya think it's good for you to come to the
neighborhood?* JLeC
Yeah. Are there more problems with your dad? CH
*Not atm but he goes off in random rages, he's definitely not
predictable.*-JLeC
thinking*...doesn't matter, I won't hide.*-CH
I know, that's why you're so special.-JLeC
You're special too, ya know.-CH
smiles *thank you, see ya later.*-JLeC
See ya.-CH

"Who's that?" Mom asked, putting a stack of pancakes down
in front of me.

"Jade."

"No more pulsing at the table," Dad said. "What are you guys
doing later this evening?" Dad asked, putting his pulse-top down,
walking over to the kitchen table.

Third degree. "Ah...we're just going to walk around and stuff."

They looked at each other, parental radar detection system on
line.

Mom started in, "You two are welcome to be here at the
house."

"I know, we just want to walk around, it's warm now," I said.

"Yes, school's out...?" Dad queried.

"Friday," Mom said. She was the keeper-of-the-social/house-
stuff-in-order goddess.

"Right," he did a mondo swallow. "The summer stretches
before one, shimmering in its ethereal beauty..."

Mom and I stared.

Dad shrugged. "Just waxing poetic."

"Well... don't, Dad."

Mom burst out laughing, batting her eyelashes.

Dad smiled back.

Geez.

I stood up, giving Onyx a secret wad of pancake.

The Boy handed the Dog some wonderful food stuff, full-of-life and not the dead food that he was accustomed to eating from the building-full-of-dogs. It was because he was a Good Dog. The Boy's word-smells filled his head and the Dog was happy and wagged his tail.

Onyx did a subtle wolf-down of the pancake and wagged his tail. He was a great dog. Dad caught the whole food thing and gave me the look that Mom should NOT find out. I nodded. Mom turned around and saw my plate in my hands, the milk cup with my used fork inside.

"Use the gray water," Mom said.

"I know." Like I'd forget that.

"Just a reminder."

I headed for the bathroom to complete the shower hassle. Although, I had gotten used to being clean and didn't like the grimy feel anymore. Not that I would admit that to the Js or anything. Dudes on hygiene... *no*.

I stepped out of the shower, did a swish over the mirror, closely examining my face. Jade would be up-close-and-personal. No zits, check, no unsightly man-hair on the face, check, hair in face... check. Wait a sec, I leaned in, critically looking at my hair. I needed a haircut.

I exited the bathroom telling Mom the dreaded words: "I need a haircut."

"I'll give you a buzz, son," Dad volunteered. Ya see, that was what I was afraid of.

"Okay. Can you not make me look like a retarded nerd?"

"Caleb..." Mom started.

"That's an oxymoron, it's not technically a put-down," I said cleverly, using yet another vocab word.

Dad tried not to grin and failed.

"I guess I'll give you that, but you understand I loathe the whole retard talk. I thought we had moved past that."

"Apparently not!" Dad howled, slapping his leg.

"Okay... *not* funny! You goons do the male bonding thing," Mom huffed out of the room.

"Nice Dad."

"Once in awhile I have a moment of clarity," he said, all teeth. "I'll have to sweet talk her later."

The buzz lasted for what seemed like forever. Dad said he needed to "taper" it for styling. I just itched and my feet got hot.

"What about the little hairs getting all over and inside your clothes?" she asked, moving back into the room and surveying the pile of hair growing on the floor.

I shrugged. I'd get through it somehow. Didn't want to repeat the whole shower routine.

"Done!" Dad exclaimed.

I got up, brushing hair off, looking at the "creature" on the floor. Onyx went over to the pile and gave it a sniff, whimpering.

The Dog smelled the Boy, who was standing and a part of the Boy was also on the floor. It was confusing for the Dog. Was the Boy hurt? The Dog looked up at the Boy, the rest of the pack seemed untroubled by the pile of Boy-smelling stuff on the floor. The Dog backed away.

"It's okay, Onyx," I said, toeing the pile.

"Let me get a broom, don't move that, it'll get all over the house!"

Dad looked after mom running to get cleaning stuff, "Go check it out in the mirror."

I looked bald. I hoped Jade liked short hair. It made me look older and taller. That couldn't be all bad. I hated hair cuts. The top of my head felt like a million soft needles, poking my palm.

Mom was cleaning up the mess, Onyx looked like part of me was getting taken away and buried. He looked seriously troubled by the hair; funny.

I thought at Onyx, *it's okay, good dog.*

He looked at me and began to wag his tail. This connection thing was pretty frickin' awesome.

Dad looked at me expectantly, his skill wasn't in haircuts. I didn't want to hurt his feelings. You couldn't be great at everything, famous scientist or not.

"Thanks Dad."

"You like?"

"Yeah... it's alright."

"What do you think, Hun?" he asked Mom.

She looked critically at my nearly bald head. "It's... short!"

"Come on Mom, you're always bugging me about my hair," I said, defending Dad's skills.

She nodded. "That's true. You won't need one again soon."

Dad folded his arms, looking satisfied.

I took off to my room, Onyx on my heels. I threw myself on my bed and Onyx jumped on it too, settling at the end. I pulsed the Js and told them what Jade and I were doing:

We need the zombie work force, Caleb.-MJ

I don't normally agree with all of Jonesy's ideas, but he's right. A zombie in there could take care of the tunnel issue right away. John Terran.

We can't talk about all this stuff on pulse.-CH

You're right. Let's meet later.-John Terran

*No, **sighs**... you guys, I need to be with Jade tonight.*-CH

*We have nights now? Nights? It's like **profanity-block!** joint custody or something!* MJ

***laughs**-John Terran

Okay guys, okay. You jerks don't have gf's so you don't get it. Payback's a Profanity-block! CH

Tomorrow then, Romeo? MJ

Yeah.-CH

Deal.-John Terran

We signed off; time set, plans made, zombies-to-raise. Life was busy. I picked up my book again, killing time for the next few hours until I could pick up Jade.

****

I rounded the corner of her neighborhood entrance, giving the sign a cursory glance. *Valley Keys*, the lettering long-faded. I was in a "bad area" of Kent. I worried a little bit for Jade. I'd rode my bike because it was three or four miles. I'd pulsed that she'd need hers. I figured it was about the same distance to the dump.

I hopped off my bike, swinging my leg over and doing a little hop and jog to slow down. Engaging the kickstand, I set it up close to the fence, hitting the latch on the gate and walking up to the front door. Jade's Aunt's house was all white. White body, white trim and white door. Kinda creepy.

Jade stepped out the front door looking fan-tas-tic. She wore her super dark jeans that rode the line of looking black but were actually blue. Her hair was swept back in one of those elastic hair things in a neon green color, a few wisps escaping to frame those gorgeous eyes. A cami that matched the hair thing peeked out underneath a hot pink top, just a slip of the color showing. Jade was zipping up a hoodie that was as midnight blue as the jeans, silver hoops swaying as she talked to Andrea.

"Hey," she said to me smiling.

My mouth was a little dry. Whoever said beautiful girls were mouthwatering must not have had to actually *talk* to one.

I smiled, swallowing to conjure up some saliva.

"Hey back," I finally croaked out. Jade's smile turned into a grin. Great, so she knew that I was reacting to her so much it made me ache.

Andrea saved the awkward moment. "Where are you two going?"

I sure wasn't going to tell her the actual place, she'd tell Psycho-Daddy for sure.

"We're going to check out the ice cream shop."

Jade gave me a look. I looked back like, *don't blow it.*

"The one where the old Baskin-Robbins used to be?" she asked. I was struck by how much Jade looked like her. The eyes were wrong, Andrea's were like black velvet, you could hardly see the pupil in there. Jade's dad's eyes were the same, the creeper.

"Yeah, I guess. I mean, I was little when they got rid of it."

"What's the name now?" she asked. Man, she was goin' for the details.

Jade piped in, "Terhune's Ice Cream."

"Oh, right," she said, relaxing.

"When do you need to be home?" Andrea asked Jade.

"Ten."

She turned those dark eyes on me. "Be careful. You know you're welcome to be here too, Caleb."

"Thanks, I know."

Jade swung her leg up over her bike, standing with her sandal clad feet on either side of the bar between the seat and the handlebars. On girls' bikes you could do that, boys' bikes had the ball-buster feature. I walked out to the gate and held it open for Jade as she rode out, giving a guy salute to the aunt, who watched us until the gate shut.

Jade balanced on her seat, one foot hitting one side, then the other taking over. I swung up on my seat as I started to pedal with my left foot first, putting on that burst of speed just to get going. I looked around to see if Jade was close. She was but I slowed down, she was shorter and I didn't think she had that maneuver down that the Js and I did. But, I was wrong, she was right on my flank, no trouble at all.

We rode down Kent-Kangley, a dangerous stretch if you didn't pay close attention. My parents always said, "Caleb, pay close attention." I'd respond, "I won't get creamed today, guys."

Confidence inspiring.

We took the back route to Scenic Hill. We passed the cemetery on our left after cresting a long hill that at the bottom you think, *no problem.* But at the top you're like, *thank God that's over.*

It wasn't long until we were at the refuse place.

Jade looked at me, balanced precariously on her seat. "Okay...so this is the hideaway?"

I remembered that I didn't know the combo for the lock.

"Yes, this is it. Hold on a sec." I pulsed John:

Hey, what's up? John Terran

Yeah... I'm here with Jade and I forgot to get the combo from you.- CH

Nice... smooth, Hart, in front of the gf and the whole jazz.- John Terran

*I know, dill-weed, just give it to me.-*CH

*Look up there at the sign and just reverse the last four of the phone number.-*John Terran

Which part? CH

Didn't I just say? John Terran

*There are a bunch of numbers.-*CH

It's the one that begins with the area code in parentheses.-John Terran

I looked up, okay there it was, got it. To think that they used to have to dial all that.

I see it, thanks.-CH
Welcome. Are we still on for tomorrow for the "help?"-John Terran
I guess.-CH

So didn't want to do the zombie work party.

I'm choking on your enthusiasm, Caleb, try to rein it in.-John Terran
sighs, *I know we have to do it.*-CH
It'll be okay.-John Terran
K, pulse ya tomorrow.-CH
K, ttyl.-John Terran

Jade was looking at me. "John?"

"Yeah, he had to give me the combo for this," I jerked a thumb toward the massive lock.

I explained the whole thing about knowing the combo and how it was the phone number reversed, how we found a tunnel underneath a mound of cars.

Jade's face scrunched up in a cute way. "I don't want to sound like a lame adult here but, is it safe?"

Like I'd endanger the chicks, especially this chick.

"Of course it is! The Js and I went in there for a couple of hours and look." Jamming my thumbs into my chest, *I'm alive still.*

She didn't look entirely convinced, sliding off her seat and looking at me while straddling the girl bar.

"What I mean is, do you think the pile will collapse?"

I understood that but it brought to me a funny thought.

"No. But, I guess we'll see what's what when the zombies take care of some space issues."

"Space issues?"

"Yeah, there's a tight spot in there just before it opens up into the main room."

Jade's black eyebrows rose, arching prettily on that smooth forehead of hers.

Flicking her hair over her shoulder she said, "So... let me get this straight. The zombies are going to be a 'slave force' and if they get," she waved a smallish hand around, searching for the word, "stuck, in there," she pointed to the gate and the lair that lay beyond, "they're already dead so zero loss?"

It sounded bad put like that.

"Ah, I haven't really thought about it that much. Me and the Js," Jade threw up her hands.

"What?"

"Tell me. Was it Jonesy?"

"Well, yeah."

"His ideas always get everyone in trouble."

"Sometimes," I replied loyally.

"Usually," she replied with accuracy.

"Alright, I guess we'll just have to be careful with the zombies."

"Let's get a girl with some brains in on this too."

"John and I have brains."

"But somehow Jonesy comes up with all these," she paused, "schemes, and you and John bail everyone out with a shovel."

Yeah, that was it.

"Okay, who's the smart girl?"

"Well, we're all smart."

"Ah-huh."

"I was thinking Tiffany Weller," Jade said.

"Tiff... I don't know, sometimes things go weird."

"What if she can help? What if adults show up?"

I guess, besides her dad, we hadn't had a lot of that. I didn't say it though.

"Okay, you pulse Tiff and see if she wants to involve herself. She's already said yes to the haunted house thing."

"Another Jonesy idea," Jade said.

"Yeah."

"It does sound pretty cool," she admitted.

"Yeah."

Jade walked toward the gate with me following. I spun the numbers, and it clicked open smoothly, first time. We walked in and I adjusted it in the fake lock position.

"We can't stop living just because the government might be up-our-ass."

"Up *your* ass," she said, smiling.

"Right."

We walked together hand in hand until we came to the pink fridge. Jade walked around the part of it that she was able to, but the very back was more or less surrounded by pieces of cars, with a whole car on its nose (scrunched down) all along the left side. It was still bright daylight out but I knew it would be gloomy-as-hell inside. That wouldn't work and I bent down, grabbing a metal tool, about sixteen inches long, with two curved sides opposite each other. I think Dad called it a crow... something. I used it to prop the door open and explained the coffin theory. The look on her face! Geez! I gave her a fierce hug, putting my hand on the back of her neck, leaning her into me.

I'd never let anything happen to her.

She scared easy but she'd been brave with her dad. Scared of being trapped?

"What is it?" I asked, brushing a wisp of hair that had escaped her hair band and curling it behind her ear.

"I hate being trapped," she said. Like I thought.

"We won't be. It's just dark but we'll keep the door propped and that will let in light."

"Okay," she said without enthusiasm.

"Listen, I'll stay next to you and I'm just gonna say, it wouldn't be much of a hideout if it was easy."

"I know."

We went, me propping the door open behind me with the bar. I sorta wedged it in and pulled on it to make it grip the door jamb thing.

Satisfied, I turned and we traveled through the whole tunnel the way the Js and I had. It didn't seem to take nearly as long as it had yesterday. I came through the tight squeeze first and was turning to help Jade out when she just popped right out no problem. Huh.

I clicked the LED light on and let her just look at it all.

"Wow. You're right, this is perfect. It's a creep-factor, but it will be invisible to most adults."

I was the MAN after all.

"Can you pulse?"

That was a smart question, I thumbed the pad: *Pulse-signal impairment.*

"No, I can't get squat."

"Me either," she said.

We sighed in unison and I gave her a kiss on the cheek, but she turned just enough and our mouths collided softly. I hadn't actually had a chance to kiss Jade but had given it a lot of thought. I used one hand to palm my pulse inside my jeans pocket and folded Jade into my body as if she was always meant to fit perfectly. I worked my mouth over the top of her lips, barely lifting off its silky surface for even an instant. She tasted, wonderful. She stood on tiptoe to reach me, winding her slender arms around my neck, pressing her hand into the base of my skull as I clenched her body in against mine.

I broke away and looked down at her, our bodies just skimming each other. I watched her pulse thudding in the hollow of her throat, mine a mirror.

All I could think was she was *this* close to me, smelling great and this feeling of swimming need pressed down on my chest, suffocating me. It was a new sensation. I backed up a little, giving her some space.

"That was nice," she said.

"Yeah it was."

"Our first real kiss," she said, ducking her head.

I was dazed, but was up for a repeat performance. Yeah, I was into the whole practice-makes-perfect philosophy.

"Better get going or your aunt will freak out."

"Yeah, I guess. I could stay here with you all night."

"Not scared anymore?" I teased.

"Not so much, no." She smiled.

I put the LED back in its spot, making my way back to about the spot where I thought light should have been. But, it was still dark.

What-the-hell?

"Caleb?" Nervously.

"It's okay."

"No... *no it's not.*"

"What?" I turned to her, not able to see her face in the inky blackness.

"I think someone closed the door."

"What? Who?"

"Those jerks."

That narrowed it down.

"Carson and Brett."

No way. Did they follow us?

"How do you know?"

Duh.

"They've been in here, one of them," she paused. "Brett touched the same place where I was crawling."

Well-hell. No pulse, no way out, in the dark with my girlfriend.

Hey... *in the dark with my girlfriend*. Now that had possibilities.

"Caleb!" She sounded a little hysterical.

"I'll think of something."

My mind turned to the graveyard not two blocks away. I guess the zombie crew were going to have to start early.

We needed zombies, (and the Js suddenly appearing wouldn't be too bad either). Were Carson and Brett still out there? I was gonna have to deal with them. Doesn't look like Brett had softened toward me when I lent him a hand with his crazy-ass dad. Huh.

Jade was mashed up next to me, which was great, but she was my responsibility.

I had an idea.

"Are they still out there?"

"I think so."

Okay. I decided that if I just didn't fight all the calling the Dead were doing then they'd just come.

I let that thread of power slide out of me, visualizing one grave in particular, knowing that probably, in the Zombie Handbook, there was a rule about too many multiple raisings.

I called Clyde to me, *come*. Then threw a visual net, using it in my head like a lasso, tossing it around that one grave like a circle. I clenched it tightly, pulling it toward me.

"What are you doing?" Jade said, sensing something big.

I heard her voice as if far away, I felt them coming, heading toward the dump. Belatedly, it occurred to me that they may draw some attention.

I thought, *stay hidden...* I heard a response... *yeeeesss;* a hiss in my mind like a razor. I shuddered, the communion with the zombie felt like breathing. Natural and right.

My voice answered Jade, sounding as dead as what I called, "Getting help."

"I think they're here," she said.

Outside of the door I heard a scuffle, then shouting, "I told you he'd get those fuckin' dead creepers out of the ground. They're going right for the door," Brett screeched.

"Don't worry, I have this under control," Carson said.

He was going to burn my zombies, couldn't have that.

I yelled, "Clyde, rip the door off!" And put everything I had into it. A great bubble of power left me and I felt a moment of extreme vertigo, my skin feeling as if it would slide off my body. Then the world righted and sunlight streamed in, a rotting head poking in as the door hung crookedly off its hinges.

That solved the locking-us-in-the-hideaway problem, I thought wildly.

Jade yelped when Clyde poked his head in. Clyde wasn't a chatty guy, he just stared and I said (very literally; zombies were a task-oriented group): "Grab the kid named Carson, don't hurt him."

Carson saw Clyde coming and tried to throw a fire ball, which he held, suspended, in the palm of each hand. I noticed that one of my other zombies was frantically beating at the flames on its feet or what was left of its feet.

Carson was going to need work on his aim. But Clyde was fast-as-hell. Whoever said zombies only shambled, hadn't met *my* zombies, they could have serious speed.

I exited the broken freezer door, pulling Jade out as I went. I kept her behind me until I figured out this new mess. I saw something blurring toward me in the periphery.

Jade screamed, "Caleb, watch out!" and then Brett was on me, both of us rolling away from Jade, our hands swept apart.

I turned desperately, trying to keep sight of Jade and Brett belted me a good one in my jaw. Hell! I gave him a knee right in the crotch but it glanced off and got him in the stomach. Too bad the damn kidneys were around the back. We grappled. I got on top and punched him right in the head. I sprung up, trying to get to Jade who was very near Carson, but Clyde had Carson pinned to him, his back against Clyde's chest. Carson could move his hands and he was moving his hands... against Jade.

She stood with four zombies around her, tiny looking, them a rotting back drop, Carson preparing to torch her.

I didn't hesitate, "Move in front of her."

The zombies twitched as one, moving in front of Jade, the one with the burning feet, crawling to be in front of her. *Cripes!* I'd think about that later, right now Jade needed saving.

"Clyde, the hands!" I screamed.

Clyde looked at me, his eyeballs rolling wetly in my direction, a dark understanding lighting in them. Clyde folded one arm across both of Carson's, tightening it like a vise. The remains of one cuff of his sleeves waving small fingers of material in the light breeze, a cuff-link tenaciously hanging on, twinkling in the hazy sunlight.

"He's breaking my hand," Carson screamed at me with true alarm.

"Oh *well!*" Jade screamed back.

Huh.

Clyde was busying himself with bending Carson's hand back toward his wrist. "Now Clyde, don't break it off. *Yet.*"

"Yeah *Clyde*... how's he gonna scratch his ass?" Jonesy asked reasonably, taking a swing at the now-lunging Brett who had crept up behind me to finish our business together.

"It's about damn time!" I said, ducking out of the fray. "I thought I was going to do all the work."

Geez, that was close.

John followed Jonesy, who was in a full-on struggle with Brett. I turned my attention back to Carson. "Say 'uncle' you troublesome prick."

"Screw you, Hart."

I just looked at Clyde, who *got it*, exerting more pressure on old fire lover.

"Ouuuuuw... tell him to stop," Carson squealed like a pig.

"Clyde stop," I said like I didn't mean it.

Jonesy and Brett were still dueling it out behind me; distinctive meaty thumping sounds of fists swinging.

Interestingly enough, Clyde didn't stop.

"Stop him!"

"Okay Clyde, stop breaking Carson's hand, for right now." Clyde slowed his progress but let his skeletal hand linger over the top of Carson's palm, white from the pressure.

John came up behind me. "Not that this isn't terrific entertainment, but I want to mention that we're not exactly being subtle."

He had a point.

I looked over at Jade who looked a little shocky, huh, better shore her up. I walked over to her, the zombies marking my progress like it was the single most important thing in the world.

She fell into my arms. "I thought he was going to burn me Caleb!"

It was lesson-time for Carson.

I looked over at Brett and saw that Jonesy had him in an elbow lock. Nice. I guess we couldn't deliver them back all broken; the adults would ask about *that*.

"Jonesy, get off Brett."

"Ahhhh!"

"Just do it!"

Jonesy backed off Brett carefully, giving him full eye contact. That was really necessary with Brett, a proven weasel.

Brett was looking at us all sullenly.

I glanced at one of the zombies over the top of Jade's head, it was a girl zombie. But I was a believer after Gran and said, "Go watch him," I pointed to the pile of sullenness that was Brett. The zombie shuffled over there, oops, that was the one with the feet issue.

Brett stood up, fists clenched (I knew that look), and said, "Get your creepers away from me Hart."

"Ah... *no*, ass-wipe. You locked me and Jade in there then tried to beat on me." I looked over at Jonesy.

"No, *I* beat on him," Jonesy interrupted.

I finished with, "And Jonesy had to beat on you. Your butt can just stand there while we deal with Carson here." I jerked my head to where Clyde stood holding Carson.

The other three zombies stood there, blankly staring at me, waiting for the next directive. Their rotten smell clung to all of us like loose clothing.

I turned back to Carson. "Listen, I haven't done anything to you (except for the fire thing at the graveyard), but you..." I thought about it, "*insist* on driving me crazy, endangering my girlfriend, and hassling us all. Stop it or I'm gonna sic my zombies on you."

The zombies took a step toward Carson, Clyde giving an enthusiastic squeeze. "Not now guys, and girl," I hurriedly corrected, her eyes almost gone but somehow alive.

The zombie brigade, energetic bunch.

"Wow, they were going to make it happen there with Carson," John said.

"Yeah, nice," Jonesy agreed.

Jade was leaning against me but looking steadier.

My attention went to Brett.

"Not so easy, Hart. You need us."

Was he high?

"How do you figure, Mason?" Jonesy asked.

"Cuz, you've got this hideaway for a reason. I'm thinkin' you're all tryin' to hide from something... or someone. Looks like you're limited on how many of your creepers can help you, right?"

Damn. If he were really dumb, this would be easier.

John said, "Here's the thing, this is like a stalemate, like in chess. You're a mundane, Jonesy's a mundane. We're not," John indicated, sweeping his hand out to include me and Jade, "and Carson is a pyro. That's all of us against you. I think it's to your..." he thought, "benefit, to just go away."

"Yeah, don't go away mad, just go away," Jonesy said.

"Don't help Jonesy," I said, maybe I could negotiate.

"Don't even try Terran. You and your dip-shit friends don't stand a chance." He struggled against Clyde.

So not going to work.

Jade piped in, "Just go now and leave us alone. Find someone else to abuse." She looked directly at Brett. "You should know better, Caleb helped you," she said, referencing the fight with the manic gophers.

"You think he helped me?" Brett bit out. He barked out a laugh. "What do you think happened after you left?"

We were all quiet.

"He used me like a punching bag. You made it worse not better, Hart. You think you're so damn good. Because your dad's 'all-that'. Well, you're not. You need to be put in your place, like all the other jerks that think their shit doesn't stink."

I felt sick... his dad had beat him anyway.

"So your dad's a royal dickhead. You wanna be like him, he's so cool?" Jonesy asked.

John face-palmed.

"No!" Brett yelled.

"Then stop it Brett. Stop it now," Jade said quietly.

"Oh, you're all nice now that you're with him," Brett glared at me. "But you have bad taste in dudes Jade."

"Ah... how is this relevant?" John asked.

Right.

Carson squeezed out, "Make this," he rolled his eyes up to rotting-Clyde, "dead thing let me go and we'll leave you alone, for now."

"Not good enough. Leave us alone, forever," I said.

"Fine. Just so you know we're not gonna be friends, ever," Carson said.

"Yeah, I think we got the,'we're enemies' thing down," I looked at Clyde. "Let him go."

Clyde released Carson.

Carson stumbled and glared at Clyde, who unflinchingly stared back.

"They're not too smart, your zombies," Carson said.

"Smart enough," I replied.

"Nah, they're dumb. But that one," Brett said, motioning toward Clyde. "That one is something."

I had to agree with him there.

Carson was rubbing his arms with his hands like he was cold. But I knew it was, I-was-held-against-a-zombie and have *eau de* zombie cologne on now.

"Let's split. We'll leave the zombie-lover and his freak friends together. They can get it on in the cave back there in the dark."

Carson and he laughed. They're just a couple of comedians.

The zombies watched the two with dark intent. I was really betting that my residual feelings were leaking some on my zombie horde.

At the gate Carson turned and flipped us off.

"He's so consistent it's scary," John said.

"He's always a dick, if that's what you mean," Jonesy said.

"Yes, that's what I meant."

"Are we done yet?" Jade asked.

I looked down at her, her normally perfect face pale with purple smudges under her eyes like bruises. Maybe she wasn't up to all the zombie fun like the guys were.

"Ah, yeah. But I think, since we have a group assembled here that we should fix some stuff."

"Okay. But, now that they know where the hideaway is it's not a secret," John said.

"Secret enough. Carson's a coward and won't want to get mixed up in a thing where adults show up and he's around," I responded.

"True," John said.

"We got to hurry up because Jade needs to get back," I looked down at my watch, "real soon."

"Okay," Jonesy clapped his hands together, the zombie-posse turning to look at him. "Whoa! Hey Caleb, call the dogs off."

I laughed and John smiled. "I don't think they're gonna get ya," I said.

"Maybe. I don't want any special attention either," he said, gazing nervously at the zombies. Clyde seemed pretty sharp today.

Speaking of which. "You have need for us this day, master?" Clyde asked, his voice raspy.

Master?

"Ah... yes, Clyde. Maybe you and," I gestured vaguely at the others, "can help with our hideaway."

"This is what you would have of us?" Clyde asked, after I explained what needed doing.

"Yeah."

"This is a small thing, this that you require."

"Yeah."

Jade sorta stepped further behind me. There was a tone in Clyde's voice. I wasn't sure that there could be a different quality to a dead voice but here it was.

"This magic you have, necromancer, is not a small power. You must think on this thing that you wield."

He gave me that level stare, his dead eyes holding the weight of his words. I squirmed under that gaze, feeling uncomfortable.

"I think you need to give old Clyde here the sales pitch," Jonesy said.

"The what?"

"Tell him why," Jonesy said.

I turned to Clyde, I couldn't believe I was discussing things with a zombie, but I pressed on. "There's these government dudes that want to take me..."

"The young men that we dispatched?" Clyde asked. The zombies were reacting to Clyde too, splitting their attention between he and I.

"Ah-no. Actually, those guys just want to beat me up and make us all generally miserable."

A look of confusion came over Clyde's face, with like three teeth and a partial lip. I was pretty impressed to be able to interpret any facial emotion.

"They mean you harm without infraction on your part?"

That wasn't exactly accurate but I needed to speed this up.

"Kinda, I don't know. Listen, they're jerks and they don't like me and just enjoy causing trouble. Here's the thing, I need this place to hide in case these government guys are looking for me and I need to escape. Can you and them," I looked over at the patient zombies (would they just stand there all day and into the night?), "make the tunnel bigger."

"What, pray tell, do the 'government guys' wish from you?"

Persistent as hell.

John took over, "I think they want to use Caleb to do things for them that are bad, like spy-type stuff."

I guess that was pretty good as explanations went.

"Nefarious things?" Clyde clarified.

"Yes, exactly those things," John said, relieved.

Nefarious was a recent vocab word. They had a witch as the visual prompt from some lame old movie that had everyone singing in it. It meant wicked intent or something.

"What?" Jonesy asked.

"Later," I hissed.

Jonesy looked offended, he'd get over it.

"Very well," Clyde said, straightening the lapels of his coat, what there was of them.

He looked over at the zombie group silently for about a minute or two. I was just about ready to ask what he was doing when they all shambled over to the freezer.

"Now this is what I was talking about," Jonesy said.

The zombies did the GI Crawl back through the tunnel where I heard a general commotion of metal grinding.

"Are they lifting up those cars?" Jade asked.

"Yes," I replied.

"They're strong." she said it like it was a bad thing.

"Yeah they are."

She should have seen Gran.

We pondered zombie strength.

A sudden thought occurred to me. "I told you guys to piss off? How come you showed?"

John grinned.

"What?" I asked.

"You weren't answering your pulse, I knew something was wrong."

"We can't get pulse-signal in there," I said.

"For an hour?" John raised his eyebrows.

"Yeah, I guess that would have given me pause," I said, noticing that a fine blush had worked its way up Jade's face coloring her cheeks a delicate shell pink.

Jonesy, not one to let awkwardness pass unnoticed, said, "You guys getting all c.o.z.y in there!"

Jade wanted to die. I wanted to die. Jonesy... what an ass. But, he had saved the day. Choices, choices.

"*Anyway,*" John said. "Let's try to make good and go by the ice cream shop so we can make a pretense of having done what you said you were going to."

"First: this is the question we all need to ask ourselves," he paused for dramatic effect, we all looked at Jonesy, "am I the man, or am I *the man*?" He stomped his feet, bowing.

We laughed. Today he had definitely been The Man.

The zombies trudged back out, and we peered in, John had his LED with him again, God love him! The tunnel tightness was appreciably widened. Even stocky Jonesy could get through.

We stood up, brushing off our clothes. In the midst of our self-congratulating, Clyde turned his serious rotting eyes toward us and said, "Master,"(geez), "put us to rest now that we have completed this task."

I looked up at Clyde, who was a good shot taller than me, realizing that the rotting flesh smell wasn't affecting me much but my friends were at a respectful distance. I couldn't help but notice that Jade's hand was covering her nose and she was breathing out of her mouth.

I leaned in a little to Clyde, who met me in the middle, his neck making a disturbing sound as his face peered into mine from a hand's breadth away. "I may need you again, because things come up."

"What 'things' are you referencing?" Clyde asked through what sounded like mud. Maybe I could put him together better next time.

"Things like bad people showing up."

"Nefarious people?" Clyde reiterated.

"Yeah... them."

"Indeed," Clyde said, straightening.

Clyde looked solemnly at me. We needed to get outta here.

Jade, the Js and I walked toward the cemetery. Me, the pied piper, trooping ahead and the zombies following; skirting behind the tree line so the observant adult wouldn't get in an accident.

We entered Scenic Cemetery (felt like home now), traveling over to Clyde's grave. I turned around and had an unnerving moment in which Clyde was on a full sprint and the others were behind him, the one that had the unfortunate feet episode a little slower. They came directly for us. Jade didn't even pretend that she wasn't scared by the fleet of fluid zombies approaching at top speed, she moved behind me.

The Js backed up out of the way of the graves.

Clyde landed on his grave in a graceful, acrobatic move. The others laid down on top of theirs. I released the thread that held them to me, reaching out for Jade's hand as I did. Realizing I probably didn't need help, everything felt so much more real, organized...easier. I thought, *rest*.

And they did.

They appeared luminescent for just a moment, sunlight swirling around them, shimmering. Then, they leaked back into their graves as if they had never been.

Jonesy sighed, like he'd been holding his breath.

He clapped me on the back. "I'm *so* glad that you're my friend, dude."

"I hear that," John said.

"Me three," Jade said.

"Hey. How come you didn't whammy me?" I asked John.

John was pleased with himself.

"Yeah, John, what gives?" Jonesy asked.

"I read up on being a Null. I guess you can shield your abilities."

News to me.

"I have been practicing and this was my big trial run. Of course, it helped that they were all raised before I came. And," he paused, "I was standing away from you when you put them away."

We all looked at the undisturbed graves. Wild.

"How do you do it. The blocking?" Jade asked.

"Shielding," John clarified.

"Whatever, how?" Jonesy asked.

"I think about something completely different."

"Visualizing?" Jonesy asked.

John looked at him, surprised. "Yeah, that's it."

Jonesy broke out into a huge grin. I knew that John had stepped into some kind of trap.

John studied him.

"Whatcha thinkin' about John?"

"Ah-nothing, just something different."

"Riiiiggghhht. I am sure it's *really* different."

A bright blush rushed up John's face, playing off his orange hair. Jade stared. I stared. We waited.

"It's nothing," he mumbled, glaring at Jonesy.

"It's not nothing it's a some *one*," Jonesy said.

John's face looked on fire.

"It's okay John, I'm feelin' ya, bro," Jonesy said sympathetically. Jonesy was never sympathetic, something was up for sure.

"Come on, let's go get ice cream," John said, shooting Jonesy the evil eye.

Jonesy turned, winking at Jade and me. I was sure wondering what John was using to shut down the Null in him. It'd be interesting to find out. Jade looked at me, her eyebrows raised. I shrugged, I didn't know either. But I was gonna find out.

We hopped on our bikes and rode off toward the ice cream shop, the only tame thing we'd done tonight.

CHAPTER 27

We sat around a tall, round table surrounded by stools; more like perching than actual sitting. Jade had picked out what I thought of as "black-tongue" ice cream (licorice). Possibly the grossest flavor on the planet. I had the best flavor and so did the Js. Well, Jonesy insisted on half-ruining his scoop of bubblegum with another scoop of upside-down pineapple (disgusting), but insisted it was *the* tightest flavor. How could fruit elevate ice cream in any way?

"I'm going to pulse Andrea and let her know we ran into you guys and we're still at the ice cream shop."

"She gonna buy that?" Jonesy asked.

We all turned to Jade.

She nodded. "Yeah, she figures I'll sit here, staring at Caleb, then with you two showing up, we'd stay longer. And, the bonus is I don't have to lie. We did have ice cream, we did see you guys here."

" 'Stare', at me?"

"Yeah, it's like a joke. She thinks that I stare at you when you're around."

I felt a goofy grin on my face.

Jade staring at me. I could get used to that.

The Js ignored us, shoveling ice cream. Jade and I smiled at each other. Another weird girl thing: Jade got her ice cream in a cup. That was like against a religion. I didn't know whose, but somebody's.

We finished up, separating the trash and slipping out the door into the early summer heat.

"Wow, it's hot," Jonesy complained.

"No, it's just that they had the air conditioning in there set on *frigid*," Jade corrected.

The Js and I looked at each other.

"It was perfect in there," John said.

I nodded, that's what I thought.

"Well, I get cold easy and they had the air on and I was eating ice cream," Jade said, *see my logic?*

We didn't.

It felt like a raging inferno out here and decent in the ice cream shop.

We shrugged, girls.

The Js took off toward their houses and I got Jade back to hers, giving her a quick kiss. Actually, I let my mouth linger on hers just a little bit, then took off for my place.

Riding up to the front door I saw Onyx with his cold, wet nose pressed to the narrow window, tail wagging.

The Boy has returned and made the good word smells in my head. The Dog wagged his tail harder.

I tore open the door and closed it quietly behind me. Onyx was on my heels as I walked into the kitchen and Mom was there of course. She and Dad were talking in conspirator's tones. I gave Onyx's head a good rub.

Thunk, wag-wag.

They looked up as I strolled in. "Whatcha doing Parental Unit?" Snagging a peanut butter-chocolate chip cookie.

"Hey," Mom fumed. "Those haven't cooled for the jar."

I paused, cookie halfway to my mouth. "Okay and that makes what sense? Does it matter if I take it from the plate before it goes into the jar or after it's cooled and in it?"

Dad was grinning in the background. "I like the cookies to cool first," she emphasized. "Then, I've got more cookies to put in the jar. There are less cookies when you vacuum them off the plate before I can put them in their proper place."

Weird Mom-logic.

I sat there with the cookie in my hand.

"Ugh! Just eat it, but no more!"

Dad grabbed one off the plate before Mom could put them all in the jar. She glared at him but he was spared the "cookie jar speech."

Mom turned and opened the fat chef dude in blue cookie jar and carefully placed the cookies inside.

Dad gave me the look. "So what did you and the LeClerc girl do tonight?" he asked with interest.

That was easy.

"We went to the ice cream shop."

"On East Hill? Terhune's?"

"Yeah, that one."

"I liked it when it was Baskin-Robbins," Mom said.

"Remember Shakey's Pizza?" Dad asked to no one in particular.

Mom nodded. "Those were the days, all you can eat and we'd just walk over there from KM."

"Mom, that's a derelict school now."

"Caleb. You understand 'diversified' is appropriate."

"Yeah. But derelict sounds better."

"It depends on who's listening, I suppose. I'll admit it's a great adjective," Mom said.

Was Mom conceding my victory on a non-politically correct word?

"KM is Vo-Tech. now, right?" Dad asked Mom.

"Yes."

"Well, pal, I guess you won't have to worry about the 'derelicts' as you'll be attending KPH."

Mom frowned. Secretly, I think Dad really liked my sense of spontaneous language use.

After supper, I ran upstairs to my clean room, Onyx following. I had saved a cheeseburger chunk in my pocket. I got it out and looked at it. It was no longer plump, summarily squeezed down into a different size altogether, the ketchup and mayo oozing out.

It looked bad.

Onyx wagged his tail.

The Dog smelled something delicious from the Boy.

I shrugged, I was betting the looks wouldn't matter. It didn't, he engulfed it without a glance.

"Was that good, boy? Did you even taste it?" I laughed.

I fell asleep with a book on my chest and Onyx on the foot of my bed. He'd ignored the spot I had made for him. That was the way I liked it.

I fell asleep with Jade in my mind, choking out other thoughts.

CHAPTER 28

Monday arrived with all the kids milling around in the commons waiting to hear which high school assignments they'd have. Everyone was gathered in their tight groups whispering about who went where. Brett was the big topic of conversation as he was a mundane like Jonesy but wasn't going to Kent Lake High. If we were really lucky he'd go to KM; derelict central. He'd fit right in. Of course, there were the inevitable transfers. Some kids came "on-line" late and had to be reassigned. Their abilities had never even tripped the AP Test (that was rare). It felt wrong to split the three of us up, Jonesy was the glue of the group.

Tiff had strolled up and gave me the "guy-fist." She wore a flaming red hoodie, pulled halfway down her face, of course, and skin tight black jeans with black tennis shoes. She was leaning forward in earnest now. "It's a good thing that you figured out a hidey-hole for our coolness," she paused. "Otherwise, we'd be exposed to... The Man," she finished in a hushed voice.

"What?" Jonesy asked, baffled.

Tiff did a hard eye-roll. "Sort of a doofus," she said.

"Hey!" John huffed. We could call Jonesy any number of names but no one else could.

"Whatever," she waved our indignation away. "Are we still on for the haunted thing?"

Jonesy nodded thoughtfully. "Well... depends on your behavior. If, and I say, *If,* you treat me good, then you can come."

John and I nodded, we couldn't accept any dissing from the females.

"I think Tiff is just tired of explaining all her comments is all," Sophie piped in.

"Be clearer. The Man? What-the-hell is that?" I asked.

Jade clarified, "I've heard adults say it like 'the boss' or something."

Okay, that made sense.

"Yeah. 'The Man' is our government," Tiff repeated.

"If you say so. Anyway," Jonesy said real slowly. "We've got a place now..."

"That Brett and Carson know about," Jade added.

"Yeah," John said dejectedly.

"... and, 'The Man' isn't going to find it," I said.

"What if they lead them to our new spot?" Sophie asked.

"It's okay, between my skills and Team Dead, we'll be okay." Jonesy said with surety.

"Your 'skills'? What skills?" Tiff asked.

"Hey... I'm the one that comes up with the ideas, plans and other cool stuff to entertain everyone," Jonesy said.

John and I were wisely silent.

"Mostly you get us into trouble," Jade said.

Uh-oh.

"But it's a helluva lot of fun!" Jonesy said.

The secretary's voice came over the pulse speaker, "Eighth grade students, listen up: stand in line according to your last name in the same formation as Aptitude Testing."

We walked to our respective lines. Carson came out of nowhere and stood in my line, both H's, geez.

"Hey Carson," I said, feeling the waters.

"Don't talk to me, Hart, ya freak."

"You too," I said, a smart grin overtaking my face.

Carson glared at me. I turned away from him, I could ignore him.

Jade and Sophie were in line B, and John and Tiff were in line C. I was looking around for Brett and caught sight of him a few people behind *Jade*. My heart sped.

He saw me notice him and reached out a hand to touch Jade's hair. Sophie was talking to Jade and her eyes widened. Jade saw her reaction and turned as his hand brushed her face instead of her hair.

Jade cringed away from the small touch, stepping back. Her eyes found mine and I left the line, striding over to Brett.

"Don't touch her."

"Gets you all fired up, Hart," Brett smirked.

"Need another zombie lesson, Brett?"

Brett's eyes narrowed. "Ya know, someday, you're not gonna have Jonesy or one of your freak zombies around to save your ass, then what? Huh?"

He looked at Jade. "She lives by me and you're not always around."

Brett turned his attention to her. "Yeah, you're a freak like your boyfriend here," not sparing me a glance, keeping those beady eyes fixed on her. "It's okay if you know what I think. More than okay," he smiled. Jade shuddered and I put my arm around her.

Ms. Griswold strode up, arms pumping stoutly by her sides. "Hart, Mason...problem here?" she asked, her nasal voice shredding my eardrums.

"No problem," Brett responded.

Right.

"Mr. Hart, aren't you in the wrong line?"

"Ah," playing dumb, "I don't know."

"I think you do. Get going," she swung her clipboard to indicate line A, "over there."

She waited while I gave Jade a squeeze, crossing her arms over her ample chest and tapping her foot. I reentered my line where I had been.

Carson turned and said, "Nice going, dumbass."

"Shut up, Hamilton."

Carson turned away, a smile of triumph on his lips.

The line went on forever but finally I received my ticket which simply said:

Kent Paranormal High, appear for registration on September 2, 2025, between 7- 8AM for class roster.

Everyone got their tickets, comparing schools. Jonesy got Kent Lake High, Math and Science. That was expected but there was an addendum which stated:

Secondary Aptitude Testing for Paranormal abilities will be administered within the first two weeks of instruction.

We looked at each other, this was new. Once placed in the school which matched your aptitude, that was it.

John said, "There must be kids slipping notice."

We looked at him.

"There are kids that don't follow a 'puberty time-line," John made airquotes. "We're not all following the same schedule, you know."

That was true. "I thought the AP Tests picked up on" I paused, "that they were sensitive or something."

"They are but it's not an exact science."

Just what I'd been thinking about earlier.

Jonesy jumped around like his feet were on fire. "Ya think I may ping the test? Hot Damn!"

The girls watched the Jonesy-display.

John sighed. "I didn't say *you,* I've heard there have been a few kids that sometimes manifest later than the AP Testing."

"Weren't the drug companies promising that their shots would be..." Sophie started.

"Yeah. That everyone would manifest an ability by a certain time." Jade finished, and Tiff nodded. We'd heard the same spiel, straight out of their pulsemercials.

"That's what they thought but we're human beings," John rubbed his chin thoughtfully. "Individuals."

"What John's saying is we're all alike, but not exactly alike. The drug companies put us in the same box and some don't fit," I said.

"Generalizing the population," John restated.

"So... I may *ping* the test?" Jonesy asked again.

John threw up his hands. "I don't know! They'll see if you join us freaks at KPH."

"Nice. I knew I'd have extra skills."

"I thought you already had 'skills'?" Tiff asked.

"Yeah, I do, I said 'extra'."

"Whatever," Tiff said, exasperated.

Sophie's cheeks had a faint blush as she and Jade walked off to their class. Maybe she was diggin' on the Jonester.

"Hey!"

Jade turned. I jogged over to her, pulling her into my body as I slyly looked for adult radar and gave her a nice one right on that luscious mouth of hers.

"Miss ya," I whispered, pulling back a little and looking into the green pools of her eyes.

"Me too."

"Give me a break!" Jonesy said. "You guys will live until the end of the day."

I turned to him. "The question that you should ask yourself is whether you'll live."

Breaking away from Jade, I raced after Jonesy. Both of us flew down the hall, John trailing behind, slowed by his laughing.

CHAPTER 29

Finally, Friday arrived and we were doing all the field games which ended in a picnic. If we didn't go to school; no report card, they held it hostage. I knew mine would have a bunch of C's with a couple of B's plugged in there. John would have all A's or be shot when he arrived home. Jonesy always passed into the next grade but didn't do much of anything except Math.

I was scooping out the crap from my last period class when Jonesy piped in, "... Looks like your room Caleb."

I looked critically at the yawning hole that was my desk and saw that there was a treasure trove of pencils and other useful items back there. Well, that worked out.

John peered in, his face almost touching mine, the frizz of his hair spearing my nose. I could feel it coming on with no way to stop it, "Ahchoo!" I sneezed, blasting the inside of my desk.

"Hey!" John yelped in surprise, jerking his head up and instantly hitting the table top on his way.

"Ouch! That hurt like a bitch," John muttered, rubbing his head.

"Nice, Terran," Jonesy said, his eyes rolling to indicate adult radar had noticed his colorful wording. I stood up, just short of wiping my nose on my sleeve, I looked around, spying the tissue box on Ms. Rodriguez's desk and grabbed a couple of them, blowing the goodies where they belonged.

"Got any gold, Caleb?" Jonesy asked in front of the Hotness that was my English teacher.

I wanted to die, could a chasm open and suck me in?

But, thankfully Ms. Rodriguez was all eyes on John, who looked as though he would burst into flames.

Wonderful. I took that opportunity to notice that Ms. Rodriguez was dressed very summery today with stiletto heels, a tight, white skirt (very short) and a pale yellow blouse. A lacy cami in aqua flashed (a cleavage-hider, that), her hair all dark and flowing around a face that was... angry.

"You know very well the rules of decorum in this classroom, Mr. Terran."

"Yes, Ms. Rodriguez," John stammered.

"No vulgar language, understood?" Ms. Rodriguez arched a perfect black brow like a raven's wing.

John nodded.

Ms. Rodriguez turned her attention to us and I dry swallowed.

Jonesy looked ready to crawl up his own ass.

Rodriguez narrowed her eyes at me. "Mr. Hart... would you," she pointed a french-tipped nail at my desk, "gather the trash and food stuffs and get them where they belong?" She indicated the trash separator by her desk.

Sighing, I trudged back over to my desk. Jonesy looked like he had been struck between the eyes with a hammer. Funny, she sorta had that effect on me too. But, since Jade and I got together, not so much. She was still sweet looking, but didn't take my breath away like Jade.

John had recovered enough to peer back into my desk. He slid one lanky arm all the way back and came out with a colorful ball.

"A hackey-sack!" Jonesy chortled.

"A what?" John asked.

"See, you're not so smart."

"Give it, it's my Dad's," I said.

"I want a demo, Hart," Jonesy said, crossing his arms across his chest.

"Boys!" Ms Rodriguez almost yelled in warning.

I leaned forward. "Later..."

"Okay," Jonesy relented.

I stuffed the Hackey-sack in my jean pocket where it made a disturbing bulge.

"Hey Caleb," Jonesy looked down at my pocket. "You may want to put that in your back pocket."

"Right," John agreed.

I stuffed it in the back.

"Better," John said.

We went back to work, John using two pencils to excavate an unknown something.

It was slimy and gray... no, black. Gross.

"Caleb, that is truly disgusting," Jonesy said, awed.

"What is it?" John said eyeballing it.

"I don't know."

"I want to see," Jonesy said, leaning forward, giving it an experimental whiff; then he made a barfing noise, running over to the bin labeled Compost and heaved his breakfast into it.

Ms. Rodriguez left the room, squealing in disgust.

"That solves it, definitely a food item," John deduced.

From the well of the compost bin Jonesy said, "Banana!"

"Thanks for clearin' that up!"

John walked it over to the compost bin, giving it a proper burial.

"I'm going to the bathroom and rinse my mouth out," Jonesy said.

"Please," John said.

"Thanks for figuring that out. I'll sleep better tonight, now that the mystery is solved."

Jonesy waggled his brows. "Look at how I got rid of Rodriguez, huh?"

That was true.

Jonesy walked out, John and I scooping out the remaining stuff.

John said, "How can anyone get three English texts in here? You should be using your pulse-text."

"I just like holding the real book."

"Three of them?"

John stacked them in his arms, placing them on the bookshelf. We hardly had real textbooks, everything was pulse this and pulse that. On top were the dedicated pulse readers, all English.

Jonesy returned from the bathroom as we were leaving. "They're already playing baseball out in the field,"

"What are we waiting for?" I asked, all of us tearing out of there like our asses were on fire.

****

My belly was full of hot dogs, chips, and all the chocolate milks that were handed out after the games. Jonesy had got a home run and John had got to first base, tripping on the way there. I was busy staring at Jade and got nailed by a bad pitch right on my shin. My leg was throbbing in a distracting way.

"Look what I got," Jonesy said, making a loose fan of blow pops in one hand. He looked like one of those magicians who pulled coins from behind peoples ears. I grabbed a grape. Mom would have a turtle if she caught me with sugar. Sugar was evil.

I thought it tasted pretty good.

Jade grabbed sour apple. Disgusting, but she *did* like licorice ice cream.

John shook his head. "Two for me then!"

I glanced at Jade just as the sun slid behind a cloud reducing the luster of her hair to shimmering black oil. She caught me looking at her and smiled.

Jonesy snapped his fingers in front of my face. "Snap out of it, Hart!"

I swatted his hand away like a buzzing fly, smoothly changing subjects, "What's the haunted plan tonight?

"I think," Jonesy smirked, "you can just show up and scare all the ghosts with that haircut your dad gave you."

Jade gave me a sympathetic look.

"How do you know my dad gave me a haircut?" I asked.

Jonesy looked at me. "Are you really asking that question? Your dad always gives you The Haircut," he did airquotes.

"Is it that obvious?"

Everyone nodded.

Well hell.

I ran a hand over my super-short hair.

"I doubt my hair is going to be enough to scare anyone or anything."

"I don't know about that, Caleb," Jonesy said.

"Knock it off," I said.

"Caleb's right, what's the plan? I noticed it's Friday the 13th and nothing's happened," John said, hands spread.

"The day's young," Jonesy said. "There's plenty of crap that can still happen."

"And you want to *see*... right?"

He pointed his blow pop in Jade's direction. "She's quick to catch on."

"Yeah, Jade's been part of enough of your plans (read: schemes); she's figured out the potential," John said.

"Well, it's not any good to creep around and do scary stuff in broad daylight," Jonesy said, brandishing his sucker with a flourish. "So, I'm thinkin' we should meet around eight, at the cemetery, then weasel over to the shack about," his eyes rolled up in his head, the blow pop stuffed in his mouth, "say dusk, like ten."

John looked up at the sky, partly cloudy. "Maybe bringing my LEDs would be good."

Jonesy huffed. "Ah... nooooo... how is it gonna be creepy if you're wrecking it with LEDs? Think, my man!"

"He's got a point, kinda defeatist," I agreed.

"It seems safer though," Jade smoothly sided with John.

"What could go wrong?" Jonesy commented, popping a very small remaining sucker back in his mouth.

Jade gave him an astonished look. "Ah... everything," in the no-duh voice, crunching her sucker to reach the gum.

John said, "The gum loses flavor fast."

"Yeah," Jade and Jonesy said at the same time.

Jonesy and Jade grinned. The gum fell out of his mouth. Plop on the ground it went.

"Ah, damn," Jonesy said.

"Like I said, it loses flavor, no loss," John restated.

"I don't care, it pisses me off, I wanted to leech the flavor forever," he scowled.

"You'll live," I said.

They gave their sticks to me to put in the garbage separator with a plan for eight at the old cemetery. Jade and I leaned in and barely brushed lips, mindful of the Js.

Jonesy yelled, "Get a room!"

John gave the regular salute, Jonesy cackling.

After they walked off I said, "Why don't you pulse Andrea and see if you can stay for dinner?"

"Okay," she did the flash fingers and was pulsed and done in less than a minute.

"It's okay. But, did ya ask *your* parents?"

"Nah, my mom won't care. She'll think it's a vacation from the Js."

"They eat a lot?"

"Ah... yeah." Understatement!

Walking into the house, Jade leaned in, a fragrant chunk of hair brushing my cheek as we whispered together. "What's that funny smell?"

"Yeast."

"What's that?"

"It's some ingredient my mom puts in stuff that makes it get bigger, like bread and whatnot."

"Oh."

Mom walked through the pass-through that leads to the kitchen. "Oh... hi Jade."

"Hey Alicia."

"Is Jade staying for supper?"

"It's okay, right?"

"You bet. It'll be ready in," she turned to the pulse-clock, synchronized to Greenwich Mean Time, "fiveish, okay?"

"Yeah, we're gonna go up to my room."

"Doors open, Caleb."

Jade blushed, awkward-much. "Yeah Mom."

"Oh!" she paused, turning. "How was your last day of school?"

I thought about the rotting banana episode. Pass.

"It was good. Jonesy got a home run."

"Not surprising, he's pretty athletic, our Jonesy."

"Yeah he is," I said.

We all stood there. "Dad will be home shortly."

"Really?" That was different, Dad didn't usually get home until supper time.

"He knew it was your last day of school and thought it would be fun to play some ball or whatever."

That was great but I looked at Jade.

"Ah, I've got some stuff to do and then I can come back for dinner."

"I didn't mean to chase you off, Jade," Mom said.

"No," she laughed. "I'm *sure* my aunt has something for me to do since I'm going out with friends tonight."

"Oh?" Mom arched a brow, all-sharpness. Careful, she was really good at getting to the bottom of secret intent.

"Ah-huh, a group of us kids are going to explore and walk around," I said.

"Who?" Mom demanded, hands on hips, eyes intense.

"The Js," I nodded like, *of course,* "and Tiff."

"That tough girl from Scenic Cemetery?"

"Yeah, she's good to have around, Mom."

"Really? Why?"

"Because she is AFTD too. It just makes things better if some weird stuff comes up."

"Is there a plan for weird stuff?" Uh-oh, this was getting close to lying.

"No. But we didn't think anything bad was gonna happen at Scenic and look what happened there."

Mom looked thoughtful, absently correcting, "Going to."

"Right."

"Okay, who else?"

"Sophie and..."

"Bry Weller," Jade supplied.

"Who's he?"

"He's the older boy that was there."

"Oh... that was an unfortunate incident for him," Mom said, grimacing.

Unfortunate incident didn't cover it.

"Is there some issue with everyone in that Weller family shortening their names?" Mom asked suddenly.

Jade said, "Tiff thinks her name sounds," she paused, "too *girlie*."

"What about the boy?"

"I don't know about him," Jade admitted.

"Look at Jonesy. Why doesn't anyone call him Mark?"

We thought on that.

Finally, Mom said, "he doesn't seem like a Mark."

Yeah, Mark was so wrong for him.

"Yet, he is clearly Mark," I said.

Mom seemed to shake cobwebs away. "Okay, be back by around five and we'll have pizza and salad."

Disgusting. I'd drown it in ranch dressing.

Jade smiled. "I love salad."

"I know," Mom smiled.

Rabbit food.

Jade and I did a hug by the front door and she sauntered off. I looked after her, torn between walking her home but not wanting to be freaky overprotective.

Mom watched me. "You can't protect her all the time."

"I hate where she lives."

"No, you hate who she lives by."

"That too." I turned away and went to the bathroom to take a shower. I had a layer of baseball grime on me. I looked at the pulse-clock, almost two. Good, a few minutes of peace, then a Jonesy-plan for tonight, with pizza in the middle, a sandwich of anticipation.

Perfect.

CHAPTER 30

Jade and I arrived around eight at the cemetery, Onyx in tow. He seemed to know something exciting was going to happen and wanted to come. The whole group was already there. Bikes were piled up like sardines in a can. Tiff and Bry lived by Panther Lake, so they were there first.

I looked around, it wasn't dark yet but the shine was off the day. The sky had deepened to a polished azure, that color that only summer can claim.

Jade and I were holding hands and Onyx's tail would occasionally whack my leg.

Tiff and Bry had hoodies on (the Weller uniform). My stomach clenched as I caught sight of him. Our last encounter ended badly, he stood a half a head taller than his sister. He was John's height but had fifty pounds on John, definitely a jock. I swallowed nervously, Onyx lowered his head and I thought at him, *it's okay Onyx.*

The Boy has put the good sounds in the Dog's head but there was a nervousness that is not typical of the Boy. The Dog became watchful of this group, a foreign pack.

The Dog approached the big male that was still young, still smelled like boy and sniffed his hand, moving his nose to the female beside him. They were pack, but the others... not. This pack was not his *pack. He backed away cautiously, knowing that he must maintain his rude eye contact when his Boy was nervous with this pack of two. The Dog understood when the big male, that was still a boy, looked away that the Dog was dominant.*

This was good, he wagged his tail.

"It's okay Onyx."

"Doesn't seem like your dog likes me much, Hart," Bry said.

"Nah... just sizing ya up," I said because I knew.

Tiff said, "Hey Caleb."

"Hey."

286

Jonesy broke the ice on the awkward turtleness. "Let's get going,"

I looked at my watch, almost nine already. Looking at the sky, Venus shone faintly in sight, the sky a brilliant sapphire.

Bry came over and I tensed, Onyx omitting a soft growl. "We're cool," he said, giving me the guy clap on the back. Not the kind guys did to let you know they could kick your ass. The one they did when they wanted to hug you but that was totally not okay, no-homo, right?

The group relaxed, Bry setting the tone for the night. Cool, I instinctively liked him for setting it to rights.

The Dog understood the male and his Boy would not fight. That was good; thunk, wag, thunk.

We hiked up a steep knoll, Jonesy leading the pack and John, with his LED strapped to his side, following closely.

Sophie had arrived late, giving a coy glance to Jonesy, which oblivious-him, hadn't noticed. She was taller than Jonesy, what a weird pair they'd make.

"Ya know, you didn't need to bring a murse with all your safe crap," Jonesy said, eying up John's satchel-thing.

"What's that?" Bry asked.

I was an authority "A purse for dudes."

"It doesn't look like a purse," Bry said, eying it.

Jonesy turned. "Listen, if it has a strap and hangs off your body, it's a purse."

Bry said, all humor, "Jock-straps hang off your body."

We laughed and John said, "But those are mandatory."

He had a point.

Sophie let a lone giggle slip.

"Anyway," Jonesy said, drawing out each syllable, "John has the," he paused, "contingency crap in case something happens."

"What's gonna happen? We're here to see some ghosts, right?" Bry asked.

"Well... ya see, it's Friday the 13th... and..." Jonesy began. I waved him quiet.

"You remember Scenic, right Bry?" I quizzed.

"Unforgettable, my brother," he said.

"Right, stuff like that."

Sophie said, "It's okay, there aren't any more Caleb relatives here."

"Like that's going to matter?" John said.

"I don't know, Gran seemed pretty..."

"Enthusiastic," Jonesy finished.

"Yeah," Tiff agreed.

"Huh," Bry said.

We all looked up at the cemetery. I put my feelers out, there were some *old* dead here. They called to me like a satellite come to orbit, my teeth humming in response.

John looked down from his twenty feet away. "Hey Caleb," he said, just short of yelling, "how's your signal?"

"Fine, why?" The buzzing of the dead a dull roar in my skull.

Then... suddenly, a well-like silence filled the void where the dead had occupied. I looked up sharply at John.

"You doin' the whammy on me?"

"I am," John said.

Jonesy nodded. "...nice John."

I turned to Tiff. "Do ya feel that?"

"Not anymore," she said.

I turned to Jade, our hands locked together. "... and you?"

"Wonderful silence, nothing."

"Let go of my hand; touch Tiff." Jade moved away and touched Tiff. She shook her head. No Empath stuff there.

John watched us. "She a blank too?"

Jade nodded.

Well... damn.

Bry was around the base of the knoll, about twenty-five feet. Reconnaissance I guess.

"Hey Bry!" I shouted.

"Shhh! Don't be an idiot, remember, radar."

Bry said, "Yeah?"

"Jade's gonna come over there and see if she can get a read on you, see how far John's whammy extends."

"Ah... okay."

I turned my face back up to John, who by this time had his skinny ass leaning against a crooked tombstone, glowing like a soft beacon of whiteness in the dark that was closing in. "You still narrowed in on me?"

"Yeah."

"Okay Jade."

Jade walked over to Bry while I crushed a spark of jealousy.

She put a hand on his forearm and said, "I get something but..." she looked at John, "it's an echo of normal."

Okay, so we were working with maybe fifty feet.

"Are you fully juicing us John?"

"No, almost though."

"Give us all ya got," I commanded.

John made a strained face, I could see him struggle in the low light. He settled on a point between where Jade and Bry stood, about halfway around the base of the knoll, a loose arc.

Jade touched Bry again. "Nothing this time."

"Kill it John."

"Yeah, don't keep all amped-up or we won't have any cool shit happen," Jonesy huffed.

John visibly relaxed and the white noise of the dead rushed back in like waves to the shore. This close to the graveyard, it was a constant thing.

"I hear them a lot," Tiff said.

"Yeah, kinda hard to miss that whole group at the top of the hill," I said.

Tiff rolled her eyes at that.

Jade joined us with Bry.

Jonesy was impatient up there next to John.

"Let's do it," I said.

I half-pulled Jade up behind me as we laughed and talked about the baseball game.

"Jonesy got that last home run, right?" Sophie remarked.

"Yeah he did."

"Brett did too," Jade said.

"He'd be a really good athlete if he wasn't such an ass," John stated.

"It's too bad," Jade said.

"Come on, don't feel sorry for him. Look at what just happened at the hideout? I'll tell ya something. If either one of those jerks comes near you," I said, putting a finger under her chin, "they'll get a reckoning."

I wasn't doing forty pushes before bed for nothing.

Jonesy heard and said, "Yeah, I'm itching to get old pyro and Brett. That would be great!"

Nice to count on the Js.

We took a rest at the top, surveying the surroundings. The small hill overlooking Highway 167 had cars whizzing by, their progress creating constant noise. At least there wasn't the horrible auto smells anymore my parents described from when they were young. Pretty much, we were surrounded by a bunch of buildings with just a small oasis of trees adjacent to the graveyard. Which looked, well, untended.

Bry said, "My grandparents used to come here to make-out."

"Are you kidding? They *told* you that?" Sophie gasped.

"Yeah, they've been married forever and thought they could just, ya know, talk about everything."

"Wow, awkwardness," Jade said.

"Not a lot of privacy," I remarked, looking around.

"It was different back then. There was just the highway down there," he jerked his head in the direction of the cars moving on the ribbon of concrete. "And nothing was here but those houses up by Panther Lake. Small neighborhoods, nothing more, from the 1960s and a few farmhouses."

We tried to envision the Kent of sixty or seventy years ago; it didn't seem real. We moved forward into the center of the cemetery, looking at the tombstones, seeing that many of the etchings had worn away, only a few letters left.

Jade bent over to survey one, hair sweeping forward, her pert nose the only thing visible from the side. "Why is this one speckled?" she asked, running her hand over the polished surface, pressing a finger into a corner divot, worn smooth from many seasons.

I looked closer, some of the speckles seemed to sparkle in the pale light. I looked around me, there were similar tombstones with that speckled look. Small flecks caught the light, winking.

Night had descended, a velvet glove encasing our group while the moonlight speared through the trees, caressing a stone marker here and there, illuminating the areas between.

"I think it's granite," I said.

"No... pretty sure those are marble," John said.

"No, the all white ones are marble. My dad told me these were granite."

"He gives you the graveyard know-how?" Jonesy asked.

I laughed. "No, he knows some stuff about geology."

"I didn't think your dad did rocks and stuff."

"I thought your dad was bio-chemistry," John said.

"He is. But he had to study all kinds of sciences and I remember he told me once. They don't use granite like this as much anymore. They're using that recycled glass stuff now, ya know, the stuff that looks like quartz."

"It's pretty," Jade said.

I thought so too, but not out loud.

"Moving on... let's blow this Popsicle stand." Jonesy walked away in the direction of the shack.

We made our way carefully through the long, hay-like grass where the markers appeared to be stranded and drowning. Onyx's tail appeared like a shark's fin through the grass.

"Good thing it's a full moon, not a lot of need for the LED's," John said, slapping the one bouncing at his hip.

Jonesy was quite a ways ahead and held up a finger while still walking. "It adds to the vibe-of-creep I've been trying to establish, boys and girls!"

Tiff gave Jonesy a good natured middle finger salute, and without even breaking stride he said, "I saw that!"

Sophie giggled while Jonesy navigated the land mine that was the graveyard. Bry reefed his knee right into the corner of a tombstone and swore.

"Pull up your boxer briefs, bro," Tiff said.

"Put a cork in it," Bry replied, bringing up the rear with a small limp.

A broken fence marked what appeared to be one side of the cemetery, the slats of the fence crooked, standing up like swords. My sense of foreboding increased.

Jade whispered, "I have a bad feeling about this."

"We picked The Place for the scare factor." I looked around; I wasn't getting caught with my shorts down.

She didn't say anything but clung a little tighter to my hand, which I squeezed, the small bones moving under the pressure. She was fragile, such an interesting mix of girlness and toughness. I vowed to be hyper-aware of stuff around me, she was the one that needed protecting.

"There it is!" Jonesy whispered fiercely.

It was utterly different than I'd expected. For one, it was bigger. Jonesy said shack, but it was actually a small house.

It was super old-fashioned, a wide front porch that ran the length of the facade. The posts were square and stout, a bevel running up all four sides, softening the stern lines. One corner of the roof was drooping from post-collapse. It had an interesting window located dead center above the roof line in the gable peak, that looked like a dark unblinking eye. Not a happy architectural feature, that. From here the door looked like a gaping mouth, teeth unseen.

John, Jonesy, Tiff and Bry went forward. Jade and I lagging behind them and Sophie nervously bringing up the rear, her curly hair shoved behind her ears, the rest a cloud behind her.

"Hey, shouldn't we like, bring out the LED now?" Sophie asked, a bare tremor of fear coloring her voice.

"Not yet," Jonesy said, hesitating on her face for an extra second.

Interesting.

Jonesy put his foot on the top step and it shrieked in protest. We all jumped a mile.

"Holy-hell!" Jonesy stumbled back.

"It's a creaky step, brave one," Bry laughed.

"Okay, smart-ass, you tromp up there."

"Okay," Bry replied, all man of the hour.

"Wait," Tiff said.

Bry turned with a question on his face.

"Why don't you let us AFTDs check it out, hot-shit," Tiff said.

Bry crossed his ample arms. "Fine," putting his hand in front of him, palm extended, *go ahead.*

I moved away from Jade... changed my mind and took her with me. I didn't like her standing out here exposed. I was still remembering the hideout and how Carson and Brett had popped up like a couple of pieces of toast.

As Dad said, valor was sometimes masked as caution.

Jade moved in close, her torso following mine like a puzzle piece, to the side and slightly behind.

Tiff, on the other side turned. "Can you sense anything?"

"Nada."

We both looked at John.

"Oh! Yeah..." he gave us a sheepish look.

Suddenly, our senses came back online like a river covering stones.

Tiff turned to me and nodded.

We stepped forward, that feeling of naturalness with the dead and open door. A thought occurred to me. "Don't touch my skin, Jade. Just in case."

"Right," she nodded. That would be great to get her all deadified on accident.

"Do you know what's gonna happen?" Tiff asked.

"Just what I read in the papers John brought over," I replied.

"What did they say?"

"That not all AFTDs could *do* ghosts."

"I can. I hit for that," Tiff said. "They call me a two-point with a potential three."

I made the hand motion, *tell me more.*

"Remember Jade found me with the bird outside school?"

"Yeah."

Jade nodded , remembering.

"Well, I kinda freaked out, sensed what the bird, *dead* bird, had been feeling, knew where it was. So, the guy..."

"Who?"

"Later... anyway, he told me that I had a 'wrapped ability'. That means the abilities overlap or some crap."

"What does that mean right now?"

"It means that I'm not a full two-point or three point... that I have ..." she paused.

"Elements of both," John interjected.

"Yeah," she said, relieved of her burden.

"Okay while all of this is just fas-cin-a-ting..." Jonesy began, "can we see what the frick is in the shack?"

I gave him a look and he just shrugged, *please stop boring me.*

Ignoring Jonesy, Tiff said, "*Anyway,* as the five-point we all know you are, well... there's a lot of possibilities."

Bry started to ask a question, and Jonesy made an exasperated sound, "I know Jones-my-man, hold on to your jockstrap," he looked at me. "I never got the full scoop out of my sis, but what are all your points? It's not like I memorized it. I'm going to Kent Lake."

Math-Science, a mundane with an AFTD sister. Genetics, weird stuff.

John said, "I'll fill you in."

Jonesy threw up his hands, slapping his thighs. "Well hell," he muttered, walking back inside the fence and plunking his butt onto one of the tombstones constructed with a partial, flat "roof" on the top.

He put his elbow on his knee and cupped a hand on his chin, reluctantly listening.

Wait. "Did you read all those papers?" I asked John incredulously.

"Well, yeah."

"Huh, that's a lot of reading," I said, impressed.

"Yeah. What did *you* read?" John asked.

"Just the AFTD parts."

The girls rolled their eyes, John gave me The Look. What?

"Anyway, there are five-points possible for each, documented ability. Or, for a few... *levels*."

Jonesy interrupted, "Okay already, just throw out the AFTD stuff so we can get to the spooks."

We ignored him.

John ticked it off on his fingers, "Cadaver-Manipulation," John nodded at me, I mock-bowed, "spirit control (ghosts), communion with the dead," he nodded to Tiff, "victim location, and zombie control."

"Zombie control and Cadaver-Manipulation are two points that sorta overlap," he added.

That made me think of Onyx. Where was he anyway? A burst of panic started crawling up my throat. HWY one-sixty-seven was close by...

The Dog felt the Boy's fear and found him. There had been very interesting smells surrounding this old structure. Bad smells too; fear smells.

Onyx bounded up from behind the shack. A wave of relief flooded me. Maybe Onyx should stay home next time.

"Good boy, stay here." I petted his head, that felt too close.

"Life spark?" Jonesy asked.

"Yes, it's that thing that happened with Onyx. It's where an AFTD can..." his hand clasped his chin for a second, "call," he snapped his fingers, "that life spark back when death is close."

"So, some people can find bodies?" Tiff asked.

"Yeah, there are some AFTDs on the police force and they find murder victims, or traumatic death vics."

I thought of Gale and how it might be bad to raise murder victims.

John understood me. "It's a given, Caleb, that if you're raising zombies, you can do the other stuff."

"They don't really *know*, though," Jonesy began. "I mean, we've only been having the shots, what, ten years now? Uh-huh, there's gotta be more abilities, things they haven't thought about. What about mutations?"

Jonesy could sometimes astound.

"Jonesy's right," Sophie said. "They can't know everything. I'm A-P and they don't have all the levels figured out."

"True," John agreed. "Astral-Projection is about distance."

"I think they're figuring it out as they go and acting like they have a handle on it," Bry said.

Sounded like typical adult bravado to me.

"What if there's someone that has a completely new ability or is a higher level or a sixth point? Jonesy's right, they don't have it figured out. It's up to us now. The adults don't have abilities. The ones that do are the first group from 2015, the one Parker's in," Jade said.

Look where that got Jeffrey Parker.

After a minute or so I said, "Better to be mundane." I felt I could say that, Dad being a famous scientist. People always assumed that I would be something too. I couldn't find my way out of a paper bag in Math and Science.

Jonesy stood. "Okay, what I get from this is dead stuff can't get us with the freak duo here," Jonesy nodded to Tiff and I. "And possibly, my man Caleb, can find some violent corpses." Jonesy's teeth were a pale slash in his face, grinning.

John sighed. "That's not exactly accurate... Caleb is," John wavered, "may be some kind of anomaly."

"A what?" Jonesy asked.

"Something that doesn't meet normal patterns," Sophie said.

Jonesy's teeth disappeared and he was just a bulky shape at the edge of the fence, the moonlight slanting behind a cloud.

"Something new, something rare..." John expounded.

"A surprise!" Jonesy said, unfazed.

John just shook his head. "I don't know what could happen, Caleb," he turned to Tiff. "But we're in..." he thought, "uncharted territory."

"Perfect," Jonesy breathed out in a sigh.

Jade gave him an unfriendly look, which thankfully he missed in the dimness.

We went forward again, where yawning holes like chicken pox littered the porch decking. We moved around those, as the clouds cooperated by moving aside, a patch of moonlight lit the corner of the door. It was a faded red, a large square of glass in the middle, miraculously unbroken. Tiff wrapped her hand around an oval doorknob with perimeter beading hung askew from its cradle, glowing like a dirty gold egg in the failed light.

Our eyes met. "Ya scared?" she asked, all bravado.

I nodded.

Her shoulders fell a little. "Me too," she admitted in a whisper, "that's why we gotta."

I agreed.

Turning the knob, the door swung open silently as if inviting our motley crew inside.

I'd forgot about Onyx who shot past us, starting his exploration.

He was doing dog reconnaissance.

I cautiously looked around taking in a super-small house, definitely not a shack.

Jonesy, John, Bry and Sophie had followed us closely and Bry said, "It's a caretaker's cottage."

John asked Bry, "What's that?"

"Back in the day..."

"When?" Jade asked.

"You know, a hundred years ago... or more..."

"Oh."

"They used to have these little... houses for the dudes that would take care of these cemeteries."

"They *lived* here? Right here, next to all the dead bodies?" Sophie asked.

"It *is* a cemetery, that's where dead bodies go," John stated.

"Quiet neighbors," Jonesy said.

Funny.

"Okay, yuk, go on," Tiff said.

"Anyway, they would water the flowers people left at the graves, mow the lawn with this push-mower thing, paint the fence, you know, maintenance stuff."

"So... not a shack," Jonesy asked.

"No, more like quarters," John clarified.

We looked around, getting our bearings.

"Watch out, this place is a dump, there could be more holes in the floor," I said.

"Stay in pairs or more," Bry said.

Tiff, Jade and I took a few steps more and I turned to John. "Dude, I just can't see that great, give me the LED."

I could vaguely hear Jonesy in the back mumbling. But, with only meager moonlight finding its way through the dirty glass of the kitchen windows, it wasn't enough.

John slapped it into my palm, pressing my thumb on the push-button switch (something that wasn't Pulse-activated!). A brilliant swath of light slashed a path, illuminating the base of a staircase. The steps were narrow and tall, like a ladder, not true stairs.

I swung the light away from the stairs at the base of our feet, the girls shoes dwarfed by our surfboards. "Stairs last, let's check out the main floor."

Jonesy gave a lingering glance at the stairs. It was a democracy so he came along with the rest of us, but his fascination lay elsewhere.

As the reluctant leader, the call of the dead was a song in my soul, a resonating note which lingered. We explored.

We could've hear a pin drop it was so quiet.

"Ah hell, nothing's going to happen here," Jonesy said, dejected. He grabbed the flashlight out of my hands. "Hey!" I yelled.

He planted it under his face and started making the idiot grins people do under LEDs. Funny, he looked like the ghosts we weren't seeing. It was just the thing that cracked the group up, tension escaping like steam under a door.

Without warning, while Jonesy capered about, a green luminescent shape rose up over Jonesy, hovering for an instant above his head. Swooping down, it speared through his chest, Tiff and I leaping forward, my hand reaching for the vague shape.

Jonesy shrieked like he was being stabbed, "It's cold! It's a ghostsicle! Get it out off me!"

Tiff reached it before me, and I used the hand that wasn't now latched on to Jade to grab that opaque emerald. Instantly warmth bathed wherever I touched.

Tiff's eyes widened and held my gaze. "Pull!" I shouted over the chaos. Bry tried to wrench Tiff away while John and Sophie were reaching for Jonesy. My Empath girlfriend caught between and as green as the ghost.

Tiff understood and wrenched the ghost through Jonesy's chest where just a snippet of its form was. She wrapped it in her fist, with my left hand around her balled hand, my right wrapped around Jade. And we pulled, not with our hands but with our combined power.

The ghost made a popping sound as it was extracted through Jonesy like hot taffy, who collapsed on his butt. "It's a brain freeze, but in the body!" John and Sophie crouched beside him, but I had bigger fish to fry.

The ghost hovered about us, it looked like a man. I looked down and a part of it was like a rope to where our hands still held it. Tiff looked at me and we let it go. Like taffy, that rope snapped back into the ghost's form, making a sucking noise like water down a drain.

Onyx had been barking the whole time. "Quiet boy."

The Dog did not like this cold, dead-smelling thing. The Dog knew the Boy was dominant and he did not have to Protect, but the Dog did not like it.

Bry came up behind Tiff. "What is it?"

"A ghost, dumb-ass," Tiff whispered.

Tiff, so delicate with her wording. Bry gave her a glare, sibling love.

Onyx growled.

"Shh... Onyx."

The ghost seemed to know what I was, gliding forward.

My hand moved forward, looking up into the ghost's semblance of eyes and moved my hand through its form. It felt like bathwater, at once semi-solid and warm, right and good. Tiff tried, her eyes widening as she gazed up at the tall figure, its color shimmering in the ambient moonlight.

"So warm, like fur," Tiff said.

Our eyes met. "Like bath water," I said.

"It's the same, but different," John said. "You're AFTD but different people, your perceptions are different."

"That damn thing is not warm! It's cold as hell!"

"That's an oxymoron," Sophie said smugly.

"I know what I felt!" Jonesy huffed.

"Everyone knows hell is hot, dope," Bry said.

"Whatever! That thing is *cold as hell!*"

I turned back to the ghost and it swung its head toward Jonesy. I felt its agitation.

"I don't think it likes you," I said to Jonesy.

Jonesy backed up.

Jade leaned forward and I caught her hand. "Maybe not."

"I can't hide behind you all the time, Caleb."

"I don't mind." Leaning down, I kissed the tip of her nose, which coincided with her whipping her hand out and grabbing the ghost. It let out a shriek that reverberated in the house, she took it by surprise. Tiff and I reacted to that, the ghost jettisoning off straight up through the ceiling to the second floor.

Jade snatched her hand back, cradling it against her chest. "Not smart Jade!" Tiff yelled.

"God, you could have been hurt! We don't know what we're dealing with here!" I was scared, shaking her by the shoulders, what had she been thinking?

"I was."

"You were what?" I asked.

"It *did* hurt me."

"I wanna see," Jonesy said, rushing forward.

We all stood in a circle around Jade, she was the shortest one in the group so we all had a good view.

Slowly taking her hand away from her chest she showed us what looked like a burn, just shy of the blistering kind. It was the worst in the webbing which connects the thumb and index finger. I touched a finger lightly to the worst spot.

"Yeah, it's tender."

"Was it hot?" Jonesy asked.

Jade shook her head.

"Cold?" John guessed.

"Yeah... like colder than anything I've ever touched."

"Kinda like that time Carson put his wet tongue to that frozen utility pole," Jonesy smiled, remembering.

"And you pelted him with snowballs," John said.

"Ah-huh, that was the time," Jonesy said in that dreamy tone.

"Okay, so we know that they're dangerous," Bry said.

"Not to them," John said.

Everyone looked at Tiff and I. Awkwardness.

Tiff said, "That's good, right? I mean, that's the whole reason Jonesy thought we should come, we're the..."

"Contingency plan," I finished.

"Yeah, that," Tiff agreed.

I bent down and kissed Jade's hand and she smiled.

"All better," I said.

"Pretty angry looking," Sophie said, looking closely at it.

"Yeah, it's a war wound," Jonesy said, eyes cutting to the staircase.

"Ah-no, haven't we had enough excitement for tonight?" John asked.

"Never!" Jonesy enthused, running over to the base of the staircase, Onyx at his heels.

"Wait a sec.... where did that ghost go?" Tiff asked.

I pointed above my head and we all looked up at the ceiling.

Jade said, "I'm game but no touchy."

I squeezed her head underneath my chin, holding her. "It doesn't seem like the ghost meant to."

"No," Jonesy said. "It definitely *didn't* want to freeze my nuts off!"

Bry and John laughed.

Thanks Jonesy, so reassuring. "What I meant was, I think Jade took it.."

"... him," Tiff clarified.

Right, definitely male, "... *him*, by surprise. He gave her the ice blast because she startled him."

"It's a guy ghost ?" Sophie asked.

"Yeah," Tiff said.

"Wow, hate to see what he'd do to really freeze us," Jonesy said.

"He was warm to us," Tiff said.

John said, "It's the AFTD thing. You guys are like the same element or something."

"It was scared when I touched it," Jade said.

"Evil?" John asked.

"Not really but, it could be. He could be."

"I bet they got personalities!" Jonesy chortled.

"They do," Jade said.

He stopped laughing, John and Bry's smile slipping from their faces.

Tiff stepped forward. "They do?"

"*He* did," Jade said.

Whoa. "What did he think or whatever?" I asked.

"He didn't exactly think, I just got feelings about him being disturbed and then there were some random images of his life here."

"Wait a sec, Jade, you're not AFTD?" Tiff clarified.

"No, Empath."

"So how does she know anything about what it, okay, sorry, he thought?"

"I was holding her when she swiped the ghost. We've noticed in the past that I can put the zombies back into the ground better if I am touching Jade," I said.

"Back-in-box, back-in-box," Jonesy sang.

"Jonesy, come on," Bry said.

Bry stated his question, "His life here?"

"Yeah, he was the caretaker guy here," Jade said.

"Okay," I said. "Let's cruise the upstairs really fast then maybe we can rip by the hideaway after."

"I don't know, that's way across town," John said.

"Who doesn't have a bike?" I asked.

Jonesy raised his hand.

"Be a peg-rider, dude," Bry said.

"For five miles?" Jonesy asked.

"Who's driving?" John asked.

Our collective attention turned to Bry. He was the smart one that brought up the peg idea.

"Oh come on! He can't last five miles on my pegs."

"Can you?" A direct challenge from the sister.

Bry's eyes narrowed to slits. "Yeah, I can do it."

John clapped his hand together. "Settled then!"

Jonesy air-pumped. "Let's investigate!"

"Wait!" I said, arcing the LED in the air toward Jonesy, who smoothly caught it.

He took the steep steps two at a time never slowing down, Onyx at his heels.

Bry and John racing after him, John slipped and nailed a knee on the way up. "Ouch, damn," he said, cupping the offended joint, jumping up the rest in an ungainly frog hop.

Jade, Tiff and I climbed the steps with Sophie slightly ahead. It was dark and I held the railing in a death grip because the light was utterly non-existent here.

At the top of the staircase stood the gang, mouths agape, looking at the scene in front of them.

Wisps of luminescent figures twirled and sailed about, lighting the area with their phosphorescent glow, frantically gliding back and forth, agitated. There were "eye-windows" on either end of the eaves, caressing the floorboards, but the ceiling was really tall down the central section of the roof. We couldn't have touched it if we tried.

Jonesy looked less enthusiastic than earlier and inching closer to the staircase by the second. Our male ghost hovered in the middle, looking intimidating. But I wasn't worried, he hadn't been hostile to Tiff and me. But he'd hurt Jade and about frozen Jonesy's jewels off, caution was good.

Tiff looked at the agitated ghosts. "They're kids."

That made me stare. They were swirling so furiously that it was hard to tell... but, I thought she was right.

I didn't want to leave Jade. I looked at Bry, he nodded. Guy-speak, a wonderful thing.

He moved closer to Jade and I said, "Be right back."

Tiff followed me, turning around once to look at John. "I'm shielding," he said.

I kept approaching. The large male ghost was hovering and I was seeing more of him this time. Tiff looked at me with wide eyes, our hair starting to rise off our heads, floating with static electricity. The small ghosts hovered around us, slowing their frenetic spinning, calming. We stood in front of the one big ghost, it held out what had once been hands, and Tiff and I each took an opaque "hand."

Images flowed into our minds; reverse history. We saw his death, in broken images, like a kaleidoscope rapidly spinning backwards, colors and shapes, jagged loneliness and care-taking, feelings of accomplishing, then... a lonely death here in this house, with no one to take care of him.

"So sad," Tiff said through clenched teeth.

"Yes," I agreed.

But the images weren't done. We saw the ghost's pain as children were killed and he could do nothing. He took care of their spirits, that much he could do. He was still the caretaker for the dead.

He dropped our hands and floated back.

His message was clear, we could speak for these dead children.

We could do what he could not.

"Wow," Tiff said.

"Yeah."

We moved back and the ghosts returned to swirling again.

The evilness of his message began to sink in. Children had been murdered here. Kids. Like us. Tiff and I looked at each other.

Jonesy said, "What's the deal?"

I said slowly, "The deal is, he is the care-taker of a bunch of dead kids."

"Told you!" Jonesy said.

"What?" Bry asked.

"I told everyone that some boy had died here."

"Jonesy's right, he *did* say that a boy died here," John said.

Jonesy scowled at John. "And, there's a helluva lot more than just one." He indicated the ghosts floating and diving in the background, holographic in the moonlight.

We all looked at them, Sophie said, "Why are *we* seeing them?"

"I got this," Tiff said. "I did read all the stuff..."

You did? Sophie mouthed silently.

"Ah-huh, and us AFTDs," she looked at me and I shrugged, I didn't know, "give off an aura so others can see stuff like ghosts."

"So, if Caleb and you take off, then they disappear?"

"It sounds that way," John said.

"Shit, that's swift," Jonesy said, impressed.

The greater point of the murdered children was being lost to the jack-in-the-box ghosts.

Bry chuckled. "He does have a way with words."

"Yeah," I agreed but was thinking about all we'd seen. The horror of it felt like a splinter in my head.

"We'll have to do something about this," Tiff said.

"I know," I said, grabbing Jade's hand, comforted by the solidness of it after the creeping warmth of "our" ghost.

"I wanna see if they'll disappear, Caleb," Jonesy said.

"Jonesy, give it a rest," I said.

"Yeah, let's book. I want to check out this hideout you guys have," Bry said, glancing again at the ghosts.

John stood, mesmerized. "Not every day you see ghosts."

"Yeah, they're kinda pretty," Sophie said.

Jonesy raised both eyebrows, uncomprehending.

Jade nodded in agreement with Sophie.

Our group headed down the stairs. Jade, Tiff and I lingered. A palatable weight hung over us. Breaking contact, we climbed back down the stairs.

Walking through the door we shut it softly behind us, the sadness and horror clinging like smoke to our bodies.

CHAPTER 31

Coming out into the moonlight we sucked great gulps of fresh air into our lungs, trying to expunge the cloying feeling of claustrophobia the house had given us.

"Okay, so... let's shake that off," Jonesy said.

"Maybe you can but not me, not for awhile," Sophie shivered.

I agreed. It'd be awhile before Tiff and I would get over that.

Jade looked around, seeing the group lounging by the gate. "Let's pulse the adults."

Bry said, "Great idea, mom's going to have a kitten if we don't check in."

Tiff nodded, letting her brother pulse for the pair. One by one we shoved our pulses back into their respective spots and looked around.

Jonesy got a strange light in his eyes. "What do ya think..." he began.

"No." John said.

"Right. What he said," Jade agreed.

Bry said, "What, Jonesy?"

Tiff waggled a finger. "You don't know Jonesy that well Bry, he gets these ideas," she made the universal choking gesture with both hands around her throat, "that usually get us all in trouble."

"Oh, I don't know about that, so far the night's been pretty exciting," he said, smiling.

"See, *there's* a dude that knows how to keep the adventure rolling!" Jonesy said, giving Bry guy acknowledgment.

My watch said it was only eleven; felt like hours had passed.

"Looks like we got the green light to do more screwin' around. Let's see who we can jerk outta the pasture here Caleb." Jonesy said, thumb in the direction of the old graveyard at our backs.

"Nah, I don't want to. I've had enough for tonight. And with ghosts so close, I don't know. Things could go bad. Besides, it seems wrong to do it for sport or something."

"The element of surprise!" Jonesy said, ignoring me.

Bry blanched. "Would it be like Scenic?"

"May have been because Gran was a relative," I said.

"Well that one zombie, Chris, Claude..." Jade began.

"Clyde," I supplied.

"That's him!" she remembered.

"Yeah, he seems more aware," John said.

"What do you mean? I've never seen the zombie trick." Sophie said.

"It's not a trick," Tiff said, offended.

"I didn't mean anything by it, I'm just sayin'..."

"Caleb's raised this particular zombie, what, three times?" John looked at me for confirmation, I nodded. "So each time he comes back he seems to be..."

"Smarter," I said.

"Yes," John agreed.

"Last time he seemed to communicate with the other zombies like a captain or something," Jade said.

"Captain of the Zombie Guard!" Jonesy laughed.

Right... *so* funny, not-laughing.

"I don't want a repeat of the Gran Incident," Bry said.

"Yeah, that went pretty sideways," Tiff agreed.

"And then Garcia and his creepy partner showed up..." Bry began.

"McGraw," I added.

"Yeah, him," Bry said with gravity.

We were all quiet for a little bit.

"So Garcia's corrupt?" John speculated.

"It's lookin' that way, I don't know for sure. But they're pairing mundanes with paranormals now and McGraw was quick to show us he was an Elemental, sorta like a threat," I said.

"Wait, I hadn't heard they had decided that, pairing mundanes and paranormals," John said.

"They haven't, but Ward and Gale said that it was going to be a permanent rule or whatever soon," I said.

"A sanction?" Bry clarified.

I nodded.

"That makes sense. Look at what would happen if a bonehead like Carson decided to do crime professionally." Everyone nodded their agreement. "And two regular cops showed up?" Jade stated.

"Sish-kabobs! Cop-kabobs!" Jonesy yelled, making the up in flames noise.

Nice visual.

"The original human torch," Bry agreed.

"My point exactly. There's got to be a counter for that level of power, like a John," she said.

We all looked at him. "Bet there's a ton of Nulls on the force," Bry stated logically.

Sophie nodded. "Jade's right. Psychic Nulls would mean the negation of all those freak-a-zoids."

"Negation! Are you one of those smart girls?" Jonesy asked, eying Sophie.

"Sometimes," she smiled and even I saw the wink in the moonlight.

"Okay I give, what does that mean?" Jonesy asked.

"I can neutralize other paranormals' abilities."

"Oh yeah, I remember, you do the whammy and they can't zap us." Jonesy nodded, shaking a finger at John.

"That was alarmingly close to girl-speak, my friend," Bry said warningly.

"That's okay, I'm diversified, and consider my girl-speak to be my second language."

"Nice," Sophie said, unimpressed.

Jonesy grinned again, his teeth a pale sliver.

"That will count for college," John laughed.

Suddenly, Onyx emitted a soft growl of alarm at the same moment that Jade asked, "What's that noise?"

I looked around but didn't see anything. Then I heard it, a soft thump-thump-thump. If I hadn't known better, it sounded like a giant's heartbeat thumping through a pillowcase loaded with feathers. We frantically looked around but didn't see anything. Onyx gave a single sharp bark, looking up. The trees above us parted like a dark invitation, exposing a helicopter over our heads, over the graveyard, over our lives.

****

Jonesy stepped forward, legs planted wide apart, stabilizing his balance as the helicopter swept the trees in a silent hurricane, their tops bending back to accommodate it. The stealth helicopter descended like a black spider. The sky was its web, a fat body with chopper blades like legs ready to spring down.

307

Our loose group watched, Onyx outright growling with a random bark underscoring the oncoming threat.

Some spark of understanding swam to the surface and it was in that moment of self-realization that I felt responsible for more than just me and Jade.

I turned to the group, yelling over the wind tunnel noise of the chopper, its bulk blotting out the moonlight, "Get to the graveyard now!" I shouted out, "Bry!"

"Yeah!" he yelled back.

"Protect the girls, get them out of here!"

"Tiff, I need you!" She ran to me, her hoodie falling away from her face, leaving it exposed and vulnerable. I had a stab of guilt as she raced at me, but we needed to survive this, survive the *now*.

John and Jonesy gave me a profound stare; I was the leader here, whether I liked it or not.

"Stay with Jade and Sophie, Bry will help," I yelled.

Ropes dropped like snakes out of the belly of the helicopter; I counted: one, two, three. Resolve solidified into a tight knot of dread.

I would get us through this.

Tiff stood by me, her stance like Jonesy. I was counting on her being a guy right now, even though she looked *so* girl. Her slight body stood next to me, hands balled into fists. If things hadn't been so dire, I would've smiled.

The shadow of the chopper blades made her face a jagged dance of light. "We're in deep shit," she said.

"Yeah, it'll be okay." The closest to a lie I'd ever told.

"Take care of my sister, Caleb," Bry shouted.

We stared at each other across the space of the graveyard, he at the back with Sophie and Jade behind him and the Js in front, their bodies a shield.

"Yes!" I bellowed.

Onyx stood on all fours, his head lowered, as the three men dropped to the ground, the ropes loose and swinging.

The Bad Males had arrived and a grinding fear was covering the Boy, its smell permeating his nose like a coating of oil, slimy and alive.

He would protect the Boy.

Onyx crouched, preparing to lunge. "No!" I yelled, leaping at him, doing the superman, arms out in front.

"Not the boy!" the man in the center yelled over the noise of the chopper, their guns trained on me and Onyx.

Onyx and I rolled together and he sprang up. I got up on my knees and was greeted with the muzzle of a gun in my face. I was glad that my parents had been thorough in their potty training because I swear I felt my bowels hiccup.

"Easy there, young fella," Gun-Holder said.

It was an M-16, its black tip a solid circle in front of me. My eyes ran the length of the barrel, the spiral shape distorted, to lock gazes with Gun-Holder's lifeless eyes... killer's eyes.

The middle guy sauntered up to Gun-Holder and used his finger, pushing the end of the gun barrel up in the air toward the chopper.

"What the hell, Parker?" Gun-Holder said.

"We're not here to kill but to acquire, there is no threat in that, best to remember it."

My head snapped to the middle guy, who removed his knitted black ski-mask, and there he was.

I'd know him anywhere, *Jeffrey Parker*.

He looked the same except no glasses, the geek in him peeking through at the edges but inside a mid-twenties body that was hard and lean with a face to match. That unfinished quality that he had in the last photo I'd seen was gone forever.

"Stand up, Caleb," Parker spoke in a clear, ringing voice.

I did, but I was going to be in charge. This was not how I had thought I'd meet Parker, it was going to be on my terms. I glanced at the gun. Besides, they weren't here to kill me. They wanted me. That was almost worst.

It was my only leverage.

I turned around, sparing a glance for Tiff, who was standing with Man-Three a short guy as wide as I was tall, a gun trained on her.

This was going bad fast. Looking further back I spied the Js, Jade and the others still where I put them. Bry looked like the rock he was in the middle of the group. Jade's face was burning in my mind when I turned to face Parker.

"What do you want?" I yelled.

Man-Three, pressed a small voice-activated mike from his shoulder to his mouth, saying something quickly into it.

Suddenly, the noise of the helicopter toned way down like air leaving a balloon.

"There, that's better," Parker said. "Do you know who I am?"

"Yeah."

"Good, that saves time. We're here because we know what your potential is, Caleb."

"You're wasting your time, Parker. I tested out as a two-point."

He laughed, just short of braying; creepy and false. "Yes, we're aware of that. Our operatives were watching things very closely. We have high hopes for you, Caleb, and you won't disappoint."

I let the questions stand on my face. I was not going anywhere with this guy. He made all the hair on my body stand on end.

Like recognized like.

"Who do you think was in your house making a mess of your things? We know every conversation that has happened since that moment. We are very aware of what you and your clever father have been manufacturing for the sake of keeping your gift a secret," he explained patiently.

Like I wasn't going to get it.

I got it. "Here's the thing," I said. "I'm not going to be the government's bitch."

Parker smiled and said, "You'll be what we want you to be... to become."

He signaled to Gun-Holder. "Get the girl. We can use her to persuade Mr. Hart to our cause."

I turned to look at Tiff but Gun-Holder was jogging toward Jade.

Oh no, he would try to force me through Jade.

Everything slowed down then, I calculated how far Tiff was from me and she looked back at me, nodding. A gun tip like an arrow was pointed inches away from her head; I had to gamble with her life but we were all at stake.

I took two huge steps leaping for Tiff. She extended her arm as Man-Three whipped his gun around, using the stock as a weapon. She bent forward just as the butt whistled across her forehead, grazing it, a gash opening up as I touched her hand. She clasped the other one and we pulled toward each other as one, a mid-air waltz. We landed just the right side of the cemetery, our power shimmered together like a thing alive.

"No!" Parker shouted, realizing too late just what Tiff was.

Their intelligence needed work.

I craned my neck to look again at our group and Gun-Holder was within reach. Bry took the hand that he put forward for Jade in both of his, using the guy's own momentum to keep him moving. But he was an adult, a trained government assassin, and he took Bry with him for the ride.

"Move!" I screamed at Jade, as she flung herself out of reach and did the opposite of what the operative thought she would.

The operative was landing a solid beating on Bry (he never caught a break), and Jade ran through the tombstones, gray flags in the failing light.

"Shit! Get that girl," Parker yelled at Man-Three.

Man-three, who was the tallest of the group, ignored Tiff and me.

His fatal mistake, going for Jade.

Parker had been far enough away but was closing the distance between us fast, Tiff and I holding hands.

Jade had stopped right in the middle of the graveyard, the Js joining the scuffle to aid Bry. Sophie uncertainly moved forward after Jade while Man-Three paced her, mirroring her progress.

"Jade, run to me!" I screamed.

A violent anger for our situation, Jade being in danger, our friends in jeopardy rolled like a huge heaving animal in my body.

Man-Three roared like a lion, rushing forward those fifteen feet to grab Jade who took evasive action, leaping to the side, using her smallness to maneuver around a tombstone at the extreme left.

I let my power out of my body *that* fast, a precise laser sent straight in front of Jade, where a zombie exploded out of a grave. He was a macabre thing of beauty, his arms fully extended, knees bent up in the air, classic karate stance.

He appeared before her as a warrior and I screamed inside its head the command: *protect*.

My zombie landed directly in front of Man-Three who unceremoniously pressed the M-16's gun barrel to the zombie's chest, using a palm on the zombie's shoulder, jerking him closer and fired point blank.

"No!" I shouted, my zombie blown to smithereens before my eyes.

But Jade kept coming, my zombie's sacrifice there in her eyes and body as she moved to me. My zombie danced as the rounds penetrated its body. Bits of flesh arced from behind it, splattering tombstones, all the while leaning into the gun man, its arms rising as it was getting blasted, going for the throat.

Man-Three must have had twenty-round clips. As he clicked empty, my zombie's chest a hole that the starlight penetrated, its face a dark prison of blood and gore.

Protect, I thought at him. *Protect.*

A little slower due to damage, nevertheless, the zombie surged forward, tearing the butt of the M-16 from Man-Three's hands, tossing it like so much candy into one of the tombstones and cracking the corner off like a chipped tooth.

"God *dammit!* Take its head, fool! It'll keep coming," Parker screamed, reaching us.

A knife glinted in the dark and sailed out toward my zombie, embedding itself thickly in his neck, but not severing, black blood flying outward and hitting everything in its path.

I whipped my head around in time to see that Bry lay on the ground and Gun-Holder was making steady progress toward us. His arm tightened like a noose around Jonesy, who was flailing and struggling in his grasp. John and Sophie knelt by Bry, his other hand empty of the knife he'd just thrown.

Don't give up.

My zombie was slowing down, each wound more grievous than the last.

Gun-Holder was dragging my friend by the throat and Jade was not to me yet.

Parker was on our ass as we made our way to Jade, the zombie distracting Man-Three with Gun-Holder dragging Jonesy towards us.

More zombies, that's the ticket.

As if on deadly cue, Tiff and I got busy with a few more as Parker grabbed Tiff by her hood and zombies poured from the ground.

Gun-Holder stopped in his tracks, Jonesy giving him hell.

"Hold still or I'll choke you into unconsciousness, shithead." Jonesy did.

But he wouldn't do what he was told for long, he wasn't big on listening.

There were several zombies and now Parker held onto Tiff like a deathline. He sucked off our power, adding his to ours, it was numbing me.

The zombies looked at me, then turned to Parker.

Parker straightened arrogantly. "I am Master here."

The zombies moved toward Parker.

I jerked Tiff just about off her feet and slung her to my left and away from Parker. "Stop!" I flung out to them.

They turned to me and Tiff, some without eyes, staring darkly at the two of us.

Parker looked at me. "This will not work, I am more powerful then you, more experienced. You cannot prevail."

I wondered the same.

Never give up.

I turned with Tiff launching ourselves at Jade, running to the zombie with the knife in its neck. The first to answer our call, my call.

Jade's hand clutched solidly in mine, we tore through the zombies, moving like bowling pins as we wove between them, some stroking our bodies as we came through, bolstered by our combined power.

"Stop them!" Parker yelled, pushing zombies aside, knocking a few over.

Hands reached out and I said, "No." Their hands hesitated.

I reached my zombie just as Man-Three was taking the knife out, getting ready to plunge that blade home, killing my zombie for real. A sense of something lurked below the surface, just a feeling, and I went with it like a drowning man reaching for the lifeline, my last hope.

Jade and Tiff struggled to keep my pace as I landed next to my zombie, my knees sliding on the grass as my hand encircled the wrist that held the knife, Man-Three's eyes widening in surprise. I wasn't as strong, but I'd startled him, the element of surprise was enough.

My zombie understood, we were connected, his eyes glittering black diamonds, he snaked his hand out, grabbing my other wrist. The girls' hands fell away. Only the three of us connected now, the gun man, the zombie and me.

It took only a second to break his concentration and as he moved to finish the zombie taking my straining arm with him for the killing blow I thought, *die.*

A big sucking nothing happened for a heartbeat. Then Man-Three started shrieking, great gulping screams, one after another, as my power took from him.... and gave to my zombie.

It was watching a movie in reverse. My zombie started to fill out, the knife pushing out of his neck, falling to the ground. His cheeks filling in, the gaping hole of his chest filling in as I watched, the skin pooling together, flesh like water filling the void.

My eyes moved to Man-Three, the light in his eyes fading, his body growing stiller.

"Caleb, what are you doing?" Parker asked in a near whisper.

"Killing him," I replied dreamily. If felt good to use this thing, my zombie was mending itself and this bad guy, *very* bad guy... would... would be gone.

"Caleb!" Tiff shrieked in my face.

"Huh?" My head swam toward her.

"Stop! You're killing him!"

I released the two, reluctantly. I tried to feel bad about almost killing Man-Three, who had put a gun barrel to Tiff's head just moments ago, and couldn't.

We had bigger problems. Leaving Man-Three on the ground, I rose off my knees. Jade ran to me, pressing her face against my chest. We turned to look at Parker and Gun-Holder, who still had the choke hold on Jonesy. I could feel the presence of my healed zombie at my back, ready to do the same command.

A literal bunch, zombies.

"Let him go," I said to Gun-Holder.

Ten zombies looked in my direction. Of course he doesn't *have* to let Jonesy go.

I could make him.

Parker saw my thought process. "Don't, it'll be a stalemate," he said, his voice holding a slight tremor.

Something had taken that arrogance down a notch. The life-suck thing. I was sure *that* was not covered under the five-point standard.

I held Jade tighter.

He seemed to visibly collect himself. "We raised this group together, we both control them," he reasoned with me.

I wasn't feeling reasonable. "Yeah, maybe you guys didn't think this through when you were busy spying on American children," I said, watching him flinch.

Sophie joined our little group. *Where's John?* I mouthed.

"... with Bry," she answered.

Jonesy watched Sophie with concerned eyes. "Let him go or we'll see who owns who," I told Parker.

He nodded at Gun-Holder who let Jonesy go with a disgusted grunt. He glared at Parker, shoving Jonesy away.

"Dick," Jonesy muttered.

It was Parker's look that told me he was placating us. He had a plan and it didn't include us leaving.

Jonesy walked over to Sophie, giving her a hug. Their two-inch height difference allowed her curly hair to swarm around his like an embracing halo.

Gun-Holder spoke into his mike and the chopper noise was loud again, they had something up their sleeve, I knew it.

Parker stepped forward and I instinctively moved Jade back, taking Jade with me. "Don't get any closer, Parker."

But Gun-Holder grabbed at Jonesy again, who was to the side of Sophie and she got taken instead.

"No!" Jonesy roared, his lightning reflexes grabbing at Sophie, who yelped in surprise as his fingers slipped off her arm. Gun-holder smoothly took her and ran for the ropes hanging suspended under the roar of the chopper.

"Jonesy, no!" I yelled over the noise.

Of course Jonesy didn't listen.

Sophie was too stunned at first to believe that she was being carried like a sack of potatoes toward a government helicopter and began to fight in earnest, bucking and thumping her fists on Gun-Holder's back.

Jonesy was fast, overtaking Gun-Holder, who was weighed down with a body to carry, both of them reaching the ropes at exactly the same moment.

Jonesy leaped forward, grabbing onto Sophie's wrists, both outstretched, just as Gun-holder grabbed a rope.

Power surged in a blooming arc around us, all of us ducking, the feeling of it unfamiliar but vital. Pulsing once like a great light, searing and painful, then that big spider in the sky stopped making noise, dropping toward us in a black rush of crashing branches and trees.

Jonesy jerked Sophie off of Gun-holder who was scrambling for safety. The blades of the chopper cut great swaths in the sky, slowing down but coming closer. I ran with Jade and Tiff back to where Bry and John were.

Jonesy dragged Sophie to safety just as a chopper blade embedded itself in the ground, a guillotine meant for harm, two feet behind Jonesy, spearing a tombstone, which disintegrated on contact, shards of marble flying through the night like tiny missiles of destruction, the ground shaking with the force of impact.

I didn't look behind me but took great leaps between tombstones until I reached Bry and John. Turning, I saw Parker and the other two government men on the ground. I took stock of the group: Bry and John on the ground, Jade and Tiff with me, a grubby and tired Jonesy with Sophie and my human-looking zombie.

He looked down at me, completely unconcerned with the mayhem of the moment. It was all about the directive. That was a relief, some things never changed, I took a shaky breath.

In the distance the other group of zombies stood there, torn between masters, Parker staring back at me. "We're not done here, Caleb Hart."

"Yeah we are!" I shouted back.

"Tiff," I said.

She looked at me.

"Let's put him back before Parker gets his crap together," I said.

We all looked at my zombie, who stood unblinking, staring at me.

Unnerving.

"Rest," I said, unfurling that power again, just a stab of it directed at the zombie, Tiff's hand convulsing on mine.

He lingered, staring, and for one awful moment I thought maybe I'd used it up in all the chaos. But then he turned, running gracefully on fully formed legs. His clothes re-knitted to perfection, the stolen energy from another human being powering his effort. The grave opened like a crater to receive, swallowing him whole, the ground closing over him like a giant mouth.

"Let's go," I said quietly.

Parker watched us. The zombies around him stood like a small forest of corpse-trees, unmoving. He could lay them to rest. Besides, he said we were part owner.

Let him figure it out.

The government men laid at Parker's feet, the one I hadn't used up, hand rummaging around for that M-16 he dropped.

Time to get going.

Bry struggled to sit up, looking worse for wear. "Tell me to stay behind next time," he said, out of the fattest lip I'd ever seen.

Tiff said, "Let's go, *right now!*"

We hightailed it outta there, the graveyard and its inhabitants at our back.

CHAPTER 32

Our bikes stood at attention, hidden in the bushes at the beginning of a little used dirt road, which led to the main paved road. Instead of a clean escape a cop car stood parked, lights out, idling softly.

Jonesy swore with real feeling.

A dome light appeared inside the car as the cop got out, swinging it shut behind him, he turned his face and I recognized Garcia.

"Great, we're screwed. He's in it with *them*," Bry said, his voice thick with injury.

Jade seemed to sway next to me and I held her against my body. What else could go wrong?

He had the gun, the badge, and crooked friends.

John said, "I don't want to be *his* bitch either."

It was bad when John was swearing. "We're not going to be any kind of slaves for anybody," I said, stepping forward.

Garcia surprised us all, running forward. "You guys hurt?" he asked, all-concern.

We said nothing.

He sighed. "Listen, I don't have a lot of time here, they're calling in reinforcements as we speak. I have to get you kids out of here and somewhere safe."

"Wait a sec, we thought you were with them," Jonesy said, jerking his head in the direction we came.

"The Graysheets? Hell no, I'm deep undercover but won't be if we don't get your butts out of here."

"We can take him, form a rebellion if he gets outta line," Tiff said.

Everyone rolled their eyes at that, even me.

"Okay," I said, what choice did we have? But I didn't have to like it.

"What about our bikes?" John asked.

"Leave them," Garcia said. "We'll get them later, or somebody will, it sure won't be me," he said, looking around.

We piled into the cop car, all the girls stacked on top of us and Onyx, who had been oddly silent jumped in last, riding shotgun next to Garcia.

Garcia got in and put the squad car in drive, looking down at Onyx, who wagged his tail.

Garcia just shook his head at the dog and got rolling, the gravel crunching under the wheels of his cruiser.

We left the graveyard, surrendering our anonymity forever.

****

"So what's going on?" I asked

Garcia stared ahead at the road for a minute, I thought I'd have to repeat the question.

"Where to begin?" he said almost to himself.

Our group, with the Weller kids bashed up again, sat waiting to hear why he had the good fortune to be cop-on-the-spot. Even Onyx was looking at Garcia.

"Let's get where we're going, then we can talk."

"No, I don't want to go to someplace you want, I have a place, we have a place that we know is safe."

"Not the hideaway, Caleb. Maybe he can't be trusted," John said.

"Yeah, the hideaway, John. You think we can't take care of things if they get exciting?" I asked him, turning around in the seat where John was squished by Sophie, a sliver of his face showing behind her.

I turned to face Garcia, who did a quick check of my expression. "We have a place you can take us where we feel safe."

"I'll have to pulse Bobbi," he said.

"Gale?" My face was one Fat Dirty Look.

"Yes, Officer Gale," he said, noting my expression. "I guess I deserve that."

"No offense, but adults aren't really on our trust list right now," John said.

"Fair enough," Garcia responded.

I gave Garcia directions and he used his car-pulse to let Gale know where we would be.

She met us there in her civilian car, looking very weird in her regular clothes. I thought it was a little like meeting your teacher in the grocery store; they actually ate food?

We piled out of the car, stiff from being crammed together. I did a secret scan of Jade, making sure she looked okay. The cemetery had been a true threat. A threat to our freedom and in the end, a threat to our lives.

Garcia and Gale seemed amused by our breaking and entering of the old dump station. I thought for sure they'd be mad, but Garcia thought it was a clever contingency plan.

"You kids were thinking ahead after all," he said, looking around him at the inside of our hideaway.

"This is totally *not* safe," Bobbi Gale said, staring at all the smashed metal pieces from various cars making an uneven metal ceiling above our heads.

John replied, "It's been this way for ten years."

"It'll be okay," Jonesy agreed, his idea of true peril on a different level than the rest of us.

It was cramped with all the bodies in there but we pulled up milk crates and other things we collected for "chairs," and sat down.

John lit the propane lamp. A total throw-back but it worked.

"Where did you guys find this old thing?" Garcia flicked the lamp.

"My mom's old camping gear," Jonesy said.

"Better not use it for long in this enclosed space," Gale said. "It can get pretty toxic."

"We know," John said. "We'll have to eventually replace it with LED when we get the big bucks."

"Try pulsing your parents again guys, maybe the pulses will work here," Garcia said.

"No...we know they don't work in here," I swung my pulse around, "too much metal or something."

We went outside to pulse our parents (and aunt), letting them know we were hanging at the ice cream shop. I felt bad about the deception.

After settling back into the cavern-of-cars I told the story from the beginning,

Jonesy filled in the gaps, "... and then the helicopter just stopped working and crashed," he said. "And Soph and I almost got chopped!" Jonesy finished, doing a judo-chop to his hand, the smacking sound echoing in the space.

The cops were thoughtful. "That doesn't ring true to me," Gale said, looking at Garcia. "The Graysheets take all that time to acquire Caleb and blow it with a state of the art helicopter dying?" She shook her head, disbelieving.

"Tell us again exactly what you did, Jonesy," Garcia said.

Jonesy repeated what he had done, grabbing Sophie, then the chopper stopping.

"And our pulses didn't work either," John said.

"My car died about the time I heard the crash," Garcia added. "In fact, it began working about the time I saw you kids."

"It was idling when we saw you," Sophie said.

Garcia nodded. "Yeah, just at that moment I finally got it started. I was getting worried about how we'd get out of there." He and Gale looked at each other.

Something occurred to me. "John, you must have been holding back huge."

"Oh yeah, it was all I could do when Parker started his bullshit," John said.

"*He* turned out to be a monkey's ass," Jonesy said.

The cops laughed. "You guys sure have a way with colorful wording," Gale said.

"Yeah, Parker is a disappointment," Garcia agreed.

"Ya think?" Jonesy said, disgusted.

Gale changed the subject, "I have a first aid kit to take care of you two," she said, looking over at Tiff and Bry, holding up a small box with a red and white cross emblazoned on the front.

"I'll live," Bry said, his face telling a different tale.

"Come on Bry," Tiff said. "The parents aren't gonna buy us continuing to get beat up."

Sighing, Bry went over to where Gale was, heaving himself down on a crate.

"I got in a couple of good ones," Bry said.

"He was an adult, a bad one. You're lucky he didn't clean your clock," Garcia said.

All of us looked at him. "Sorry: a thorough job of beating the snot out of someone," he clarified.

"Eloquent, Raul," Gale laughed.

"So now what? It's obvious they want me. They put spy crap in my house so they know I can raise zombies, that I'm a full-on five-point," I said.

"I think what really needs to be addressed, Caleb, is what you did out there to the government guy," Gale said, dabbing antiseptic at the corner of Bry's eye. "That's not part of any five-point I've heard of," she said trailing off, gazing at me around Bry, everyone's eyes on me.

Gale got back to working on Bry's face, talking as she patched him up, "The scientists have theorized about that possibility, but they've never had any proof."

"You mean Caleb suckin' the life out of bad-ass, then juicing his zombie up?" Jonesy asked.

Garcia chuckled. "Yes, I think that's what Officer Gale was getting at."

"That will make you even more of a threat," she said.

"Does that mean you're a six-point?" Jade asked, through the veil of her hair.

She was cuddled up next to me, more on my crate than hers. I leaned closer, then put that hair that hid her eyes behind her ear, running a finger down the outside edge of her lobe. She rewarded me with a tiny shiver.

"Doubt it. I can't be a 'first' anything," I said with certainty.

"I'm AFTD, Caleb, and I know there is not one documented case of Life-Transference," Gale said. "Not one."

"Did that guy die?" Sophie asked.

"I don't know, but he deserved it," Jonesy said.

The cops were silent.

"Yeah he did. He had a gun pointed at sis," Bry said.

Bry looked at me. "Thanks for taking care of her, Caleb," he said.

"It almost wasn't enough," I said, feeling guilty.

Bry stood up and came over and clapped me on the shoulder. "But it was."

Garcia interrupted with, "I guess your best protection is your father, Caleb."

"Why?" I asked.

"His fame," he continued, "his son disappearing would be an inexplicable problem."

"Didn't seem to give them pause tonight," John said.

"Our source tells us they want to do experimentation, that they're not ready to take you forever," Garcia said.

Disquiet fell over the group.

"Comforting," Jade said.

"Those dicks don't get to have Caleb," Jonesy said.

"Yeah, what he said," Bry agreed.

Of course I agreed.

"How did Parker go from being like Caleb to working with them?" Sophie asked.

"We don't know what's happened this last ten years to form him."

"... shape him," Gale finished, nodding to Garcia.

"What was his family life like?" I asked

"It was bad. Sort of the opposite of yours. There was no one to advocate for Jeffrey Parker," Gale said.

"So, he's a tragic figure, now?" Sophie asked, arms crossed over her chest. "I don't know if I buy that. Doesn't he have a responsibility to choose the right thing now?"

"Who knows? Maybe they brainwashed him," Jonesy said.

"It doesn't matter. Caleb's AFTD, so is Tiff; he was going to hurt his own kind. He's shit, I don't care what way you color it, he's made his choice." Bry fumed.

We looked at each other over the hissing light of the lantern.

Finally, Garcia said, "We need to get these guys at their own game."

Gale nodded in agreement.

"You called them 'Graysheets,' what does that mean?" I asked.

"We don't actually know their real name, it's just a nickname Officer Gale and I gave them," Garcia said.

"What does it mean, though?" Jade asked, leaning in against me.

"It means that they don't understand black and white, right and wrong."

"Gray," John said.

"Right," Garcia pointed at John.

"Sheets?" Tiff asked.

"I got it!" Jonesy said. "They cover things up!" he air-pumped his fist with enthusiasm, breaking off to yawn.

"Don't tell me you're tired?" Bry asked.

"Nope. Just needed some O2 baby," Jonesy said.

I looked at my watch, which hadn't been affected by the whole electrical fall-out at the graveyard, couldn't see. I moved toward the lantern, sticking my wrist under the light, a fine fissure layered the crystal like ice. Damn, my watch got nailed in the fight. I couldn't really see the time.

"Ah-man, that sucks donkey dicks," Jonesy said.

I laughed, couldn't help it, John leaned in. "Maybe a jeweler could fix it?"

"Right, like anyone even has these anymore."

Everyone gathered around, Garcia, the tallest of us said, "My dad had one of those! Is it a winder?"

"It was," I said.

Garcia picked up my wrist, moving it beside his ear. "It's ticking, buddy."

"It is!?"

"Yes," he smiled.

Gale said, "I think I've patched up these guys as good as they're going to get."

We gave a critical stare at Bry. Tiff wasn't so bad, she could explain that away.

"You look like a pile of gnomes jumped you..." Jonesy said.

"... on your face," John finished.

"Gnomes are creepers," Tiff said.

I looked at her in surprise. She, the Unflappable Tiff, was scared of gnomes.

"Scared?" Jonesy said.

"No!"

"They make good prizes on Call of Duty," Bry said.

Sophie and Jade rolled their eyes. I guess they weren't big into pulse games.

"Let's get you guys home," Garcia said.

"What's the plan?" I asked.

"You're going to speak with your dad," Garcia responded.

"He's going to be righteously pissed," Jonesy said.

"Yeah. He'll be mad because I was screwing around in cemeteries," I said, dreading the whole thing.

"You're AFTD, that's like telling you not to swim if you had gills," Gale said.

"You're not the kid of a 'famous scientist'," I said with airquotes.

"Are you complaining? Seriously, I thought your dad is cool?" Sophie asked.

"He is," I sighed. "I just haven't been what my parents expected, I think."

"But you're hell on zombies!" Jonesy said. Yeah, that was my value, raising zombies.

Garcia slung an arm around my shoulders, "You've got a smart dad..."

... your clever father... Parker's words whispered through my mind...

I came back to what Garcia was saying, "... he'll think of a way to keep you safe."

Gale added, "A talent of your magnitude could help many people, Caleb."

I looked at her, letting my face ask the question.

Jade said, "AFTDs have pretty good success finding murder victims and stuff."

"What stuff?" Jonesy asked.

Gale answered, "Traumatic death."

"Can Caleb just, automatically find victims? He's got an unheard of six-point ability..." John said.

"We recruit people that test as sensitive to traumatic death," Gale said.

"I read in some AFTD blog that you can be a one-point and sense traumatic-death," Tiff said.

"Can *you*?" I asked her.

"I can sense the dead," her voice said, *duh.*

"All AFTDs can, the difference, is some are sensitive to the *cause* of death, not just its plane of existence," Gale said.

"Useful to cops, bad for crime," John pointed out.

"I bet violent crime is down," Bry said.

"We're seeing progress. As you know, AFTD is a rare ability, not all have the traumatic death aspect." Garcia shrugged, *them are the breaks.*

Gale looked at her pulse. "Almost one, let's go."

"Right," Garcia said.

We moved through the newly expanded tunnel, exiting through the freezer, breathing in the cool night air with a sky filled with stars tossed like diamonds on black velvet, nestled in the cloth of their sanctuary.

"I am glad to be alive," Jade said, her fierce eyes the color of the ocean at night.

I looked down at her. "I wouldn't let anything happen to you."

She smiled. "I know. It was scary and we survived it."

"Yeah, it was," Sophie said.

As we moved up to the parked cars, Gale said, "I'll take the girls home." A sense of dread spread through my gut. I didn't want Jade out of my sight. I wanted to see her safely inside her house with my own eyes.

I tried for casual. "I told her aunt I'd walk her home."

Jade gave me a sharp look, *what?*

"Take Tiff and Bry home," I suggested.

"... and me and the Jonester live by each other," John added. Nice move John.

"Okay," Gale said slowly, knowing something was up but not able to put her finger on it, the logic of my suggestions clear. "Weller kids, Jonesy, John... follow me,"

That left me, Jade and Sophie with Garcia.

Jonesy turned around and waved to Sophie. "See ya, Soph!"

She waved back, looking pleased that Jonesy had singled her out. Jonesy had the hots for Sophie. Onyx ran over to the cruiser, hopping in the front seat (traitor).

We got in the back, Jade and I touching hip to toe when I leaned forward, as far as the plexiglass would allow, and asked, "What about McGraw?"

Garcia was silent for a heartbeat, and I thought, can't take back the pause, pal.

"He's on the take."

"Corrupt?"

"Yes, he's the Graysheets eyes and ears, Caleb."

I leaned back again against Jade, thinking about being a partner with someone I couldn't trust at my back.

"What about the other officer? Wade, I think," Jade asked.

"Chuck's a good man."

That's a relief, three good cops anyway.

The night slid past, Sophie and Onyx's profiles in the front seat, Garcia's cruiser moving through Jade's neighborhood like a silent trespasser. As Brett's house came into view, the yard still littered with the gopher mounds, a look passed between Jade and I, remembering.

Garcia broke the silence, "If I work with McGraw I have a chance to eventually expose these hypocrites."

"What are they?" Jade asked.

"People bent on exploitation for warfare, controlling crime for gain. Instead of using these paranormals' gifts for the betterment of humankind, they're scheming up ways to control. It's always about control, about power."

We parked in front of Jade's place; Garcia kept the car idling. "I'll stay here with the dog," he winked.

Not half-bad for an adult.

The tall fence blocked our view of the façade of Jade's house, except for a portion of the porch and roof. We got out of Garcia's car, opening the gate, which I left ajar. We walked to the front porch, our hands entwined, the porch light casting a soft pool of pale color on the steps.

I grasped Jade's other hand and turned her to me pulling her close until she touched my body in a tight embrace, our bodies married together. Pressing my mouth on her lips, softly at first, my hands slid out of hers, moving to the small of her back. She wrapped hers around me. My free hand working up into the nape of her neck, the silky hair winding around my fingers as my mouth moved on hers.

The door wrenched open and Aunt Andrea stood there, anger making the planes of her face a brutal thing. As Jade and I jumped apart, her face flushed with high color, rosy under the glow of the light.

"Where the hell have you been?" Andrea said, anger twisting her words into a snarl.

Jade looked shocked and confused. "Ah... I pulsed you..."

"I wasn't going to get into it on pulse, but this boy," she jabbed a finger in my direction, "is bringing you home too late. It's one-twenty in the morning and you're fourteen years old!" she huffed.

What-the-hell? Where did all this venom come from? I unconsciously pulled Jade a little closer to me, her back against my chest.

A bulky figure moved up behind Andrea... Jade's dad.

Oh shit.

A look of terror came over Andrea's face. *That* was it, the drunk dad had made an appearance, and she was covering.

Jade's dad said in a low voice, "Get your ass in this house right now. You and me, we got some talkin' to do."

If he'd been shouting it would have been less threatening. But that soft voice promised bad-stuff-was-gonna-happen.

"Is there a problem here?" Garcia said, strolling up, Sophie peeking around from behind him, eyes like saucers in a pale face. Bet she knew old daddy dearest.

His hand hovered above the baton he wore on his utility belt, a whisper away from use. Jade's dad shoved Andrea aside, slamming her into the doorjamb.

"Jade!"she shouted in warning, clinging to the wood.

I heard the baton escape its sheath with a high whistle, at the same time that I threw myself backward, with Jade attached to my front. My arm was hooked around her waist, her dad's dinner plate sized hand, brushing the zipper of her hoodie as we flew, my body slamming into the grass behind us.

Every bit of air left my lungs in a whoosh, as I watched Jade's dad get past Garcia to come after us.

Slippery ass-monkey.

Garcia let him move past and landed a deliberate blow to the back of his knee. With a grunt, Jade's dad toppled like the tree he was, momentarily stunned.

He pushed him down to the ground, a knee planted in LeClerc's spine, the baton's tip piercing the tender flesh at the base of his skull.

Leaning down, Garcia said with soft menace, "We're taking a little ride, LeClerc. We're going to come to an understanding, you and I."

"No we're not, Pig!" he said, his words muffled by the press of the baton forcing his face into the ground. "She's my girl! She's gonna stop being with that boy! He's evil! A dead-lover! Satan worshiper!"

Right, that was me, a star in the basement.

"He's AFTD, in case you're too slow to understand," Garcia said, losing patience.

He got out his cuffs, slapping one side on a thick wrist. He was getting ready to secure the other when Jade's dad gave a last, great buck with his body, throwing off Garcia, launching himself at Jade.

I saw moonlight slide off the loose cuff as it dangled from his wrist swinging it down toward Jade. As I rolled her away from that descending hand with my body, his fist connected with her side and she screamed. I let her go, she lay flat on the grass, putting her hands above her face in a defensive position that broke something inside me to see.

Garcia wasn't going to get to us in time.

I rose up on all fours with him looming over us both. as he brought both fists up to mangle my face, I rolled back, placing my hands behind me and my feet wide, using one foot for balance, I slammed the other out just on his downward arc, barely missing the hands, hitting that defiant face square, his nose exploding with a satisfying crunch.

He staggered back. "My nose, he broke my fuckin' nose!" he spluttered, blood spraying out from behind his hands. If looks could kill I'd be dust.

Garcia jerked his hands behind his back, locking the cuffs, tightening them until LeClerc cried out, "Ow, that hurts!"

"Suck it up," Garcia said.

Without his hands covering the nose, it leaked. His frantic breathing caused a big bubble of snot to grow, pulsing with each breath.

Jade moaned, her hair fanning out behind her, grass stains on her pink hoodie. My eyes burned with the need to cry. But I was the guy here and my Jade was hurt.

"Where does it hurt?" I asked, gently exploring her side, she made a pain sound when I got to her lower ribs on the right side.

I asked with my face if I could look and she nodded.

I pulled up the lightweight shirt and saw a terrible welt, bright red, in the shape of the cuff, with a grape-colored bruise, blooming at the edges of the mark like an obscene flower.

Looking at her dad I said the first thing that entered my head, "You touch her again and I'll kill you."

He looked back at me for the space of seconds. "You'll try." and smiled with that nasty grin of his, the blood slowing to a trickle his swollen nose like a clown's.

It wasn't enough damage to satisfy me.

"Caleb," Garcia started, "... what did you say?"

Andrea and Sophie had their arms twined around each other as my eyes met Garcia's.

"He said he'd kill me, you dumb-ass! He's the one you should be arresting, the zombie-lover!" LeClerc shouted.

"I didn't hear that," Garcia said, trying for neutral and missing by a mile.

Garcia smiled and started hauling Jade's dad away, who shouted over his shoulder at Jade, "Keep your head down, girlie, get away from that loser."

"Look who's talking," Garcia said.

"Can I help you get up?" I asked.

She nodded and I braced my arm behind her back, lifting and holding at the same time. It wasn't an effort, she was so light.

Just then, Brett jogged up "What happened to Jade?"

I couldn't *believe* this night. There must have been a trouble-find-me-beacon flashing or something.

I opened my mouth to tell him to get screwed when Sophie smoothly interjected, "It's her dad, Brett."

"Yeah, I saw him in the cop car," a range of emotion swam across Brett's features. "What did he do to her?"

I didn't think he deserved an answer but he wasn't being an total dick. "He was pissed because she was with me."

"Yeah, he wants her with someone normal."

"Like you," I scoffed.

"Maybe," he admitted, giving me a look.

"Stop, both of you," Jade said, her face pinched.

"Sorry, Jade," Brett said.

"It's okay, don't start things with Caleb, please."

Brett and I stared at each other. I could taste that we were gonna have trouble in the future; like smelling rain right before it started to pour.

I made myself turn away from him to take Jade inside and saw Sophie out of my peripheral vision, walking over to Brett as they spoke softly.

Andrea led us into the family room, Jade walking stiffly over to the couch. Pivoting, we lowered her together as Andrea propped pillows behind her. I looked around briefly, seeing a smiling Jade in every corner, photos framing her childhood.

"Don't look at those, they're dumb," she said.

"Nah... you look cute," I said.

She gave me a dopey smile.

Garcia poked his head through the door. "I hate to do this to you..."

"It's okay," I interrupted. "I can walk home."

"I just can't have you in the car, as it is, he's fighting it."

I could hear Jade's dad, hammering his feet against the inside of the car door.

A prince of a guy.

I bent over Jade, giving her a kiss on her forehead. She grabbed a fistful of my shirt, jerking my mouth down on hers, kissing it softly. "There," she said. "*Now* you can go." She smiled through a wash of tears.

Garcia and I left Jade's house, walking back down the path that led to the front gate. He paused just inside the gate. "Did you mean what you said earlier?"

I could have pretended I didn't understand what he meant, a purposeful misunderstanding... but I didn't.

The silence rolled out, and he let it. "Yeah," I said finally.

Jade's dad was still slamming his feet against the inside of the car. "That gonna hold?" I asked.

"Yes," Garcia looked at me, taking my measure.

He reached out and squeezed my shoulder. "You're a good kid, Caleb. Don't worry so much about what you'll be, just keep doing the right thing, and you'll get where you're meant to go." With that, he turned, walking over to his cruiser, opening the front passenger side door.

Onyx flew out, bounding over to me, more than a little excited to be out of there. Stroking his head, I couldn't say I blamed him.

CHAPTER 33

I walked through my front door, Onyx at my heels, knowing he didn't need to go out and do his business. He'd peed on everything vertical the entire way home.

Mom spied me from her perch at the kitchen table and rushed over and gave me a bone-crushing hug. I stood there, finally giving her an awkward pat.

I saw Dad watching us, an expression I couldn't read.

"Garcia phoned," he told me. People didn't phone anymore but my parents still used the expression. "And I think it's time you came clean with us, son. He let us in on a plethora of disturbing occurrences."

Mom finally released me and we walked over to the couch, Onyx jumping up ahead of me. "Noooo... down, Onyx," Mom said.

Onyx jumped down on the floor, giving mom the big-eye.

I sat down, my eyes burning with tiredness, grainy and itchy feeling. The pulse-clock read two-ten.

My parents looked tired too. "I know it's late and it goes without saying that you won't be having quite as much 'leash' from your mom and I in the future."

Duh.

"We know there were extenuating circumstances...Garcia said something about Graysheets?" Mom asked.

I went through the whole story, starting with what was supposed to be a simple exploration of a ghost rumor, through the Graysheets showing up with Parker at their side.

Dad stopped pacing and interrupted with, "They thought they'd take you? Last time I looked, we were still living in America!"

Mom gave him the shush noise so I could continue, which I did. I thought I was tired when I began, but I was so tired at the end of my story my bones ached. I'd never wanted to sleep so bad in my life.

Mom rubbed her eyes and stood, arching her back, small popping sounds filling the silence. "Ahhhh..." she said. "Much better. Well, we can't solve all of this right now, in the middle of the night."

Dad had his eyes closed, chin resting in the fist of his hand which was balanced on a knee. "Dad?"

He opened his eyes, bloodshot lightning running through them. "Mom's right, but one thing that keeps nagging at me is this EMP phenomena, and..."

Mom and I both rolled our eyes. Unbelievable! I had nearly been kidnapped and Dad was dwelling on the electrical snafu.

Mom was struggling with her patience. "Okay, enlighten us, quickly...what is an EMP?"

"Electromagnetic Pulse," Dad said.

"Like *pulse,* pulse?" I asked, a spurt of energy chasing away cobwebs like a sudden breeze.

"No. Not like our pulse technology, but related. Have you asked yourself this, Caleb: what caused everything to stall? The helicopter, everyone's pulses, Garcia's police car? The Graysheets, or whoever they really are, they wouldn't have caused it. It stands to reason that they were well-thought out, planning this since when?"

Turning to Mom he asked, "How long has it been since our house was compromised?"

Mom thought about it. "A month at least."

"See!" Dad exclaimed, resuming his pacing. "That's what you need to think about, it's the one puzzle piece that doesn't fit. And with that, I am saying goodnight."

"Are we safe?" Mom asked, a frown on her face.

"For now. I think they'd be fools to attempt to reacquire him." Technically it was morning.

"Or maybe they think, we'll think that and *then* try to take him," Mom said, worried.

"Don't be anxious," he said to Mom, then turned to me. "Didn't Officer Gale say that her partner would be outside the house tonight?"

I nodded. "Wade."

"A reprieve for now; off to bed, that's an order."

My parents went into their bedroom, softly closing the door. Onyx and I climbed the steps to my room and as I opened the door

Onyx nudged it aside and jumped up on top of my bed, circling to find the perfect dog-spot. He finally settled at the foot, giving me just enough room to sink underneath the covers, which I did as I kicked off my clothes.

I was so tired that I was wide awake. It made no sense but that's the way it was; I'd tried to stay awake so long I had gone over the line. I pulled out my pulse and sent a message to Jade, my thumb swiping the pad:

Activated: *Just so you know, I love you...*CH

I powered it down, putting it on my windowsill, knowing that she was long asleep, that she would wake up to my words glowing on her pulse.

It'd be the first thing she saw.

I started to drift off just as Mom came into my room pulling up the covers until they were just under my chin. She hadn't tucked me in for years. I would have responded but was in that twilight of sleep, just as you're sinking under into unconsciousness but awake enough to be aware.

Her breath was warm on my face as she kissed my forehead, my thoughts ending as sleep pulled me under into dreamless oblivion.

CHAPTER 34

I woke up, feeling like I'd been in our washing machine on spin cycle... for a couple of hours. I opened one eye, trying to chase the blurry sleep out of it with a thorough rub. Ah! Seeing better, I squinted my eyes at the glowing numbers on my computer's monitor.

I leaned forward, one o'clock! I had a moment when I couldn't remember what day it was. Oh yeah, Saturday. I sat there for a second and then the whole night came rushing back in living color: the ghosts, Graysheets, Parker, escaping, Jade's dad and the cherry on top of the miserable cake, Brett.

I flung myself back down again, Onyx crawled up and gave my face a disgusting dog-lick. I absently petted his head, thinking.

I heard Mom downstairs in the kitchen and figured... pancakes.

Surprisingly, I wasn't that hungry. I powered up my pulse and messages came in:

Pulse-me, zombie-master.-MJ
We need a plan... like yesterday- John Terran.

Then, the message that was really cool:

I love you too... JLeC

I did the easy pulses first.

Jonesy, you moron, stop talking about stuff on the pulse! Let's get together at the hideaway at like three, we can talk there.-CH
Okay, don't get your shorts in a twist! I'll meet ya Have you talked to our-boy,Terran? MJ
No... wait-CH
Hey.-John Terran
*Would you fix your **Profanity-block!** name initials!*-MJ
Yeah, it royally gets on my nerves.-CH

Whatever irritates you guys, I'm all for that.-John Terran
sighs *K, listen...*CH
Listen? John Terran
You know what I mean, John! CH
Yeah... I do **laughs**-John Terran
Kind of a terrorist this mornin', huh? MJ
He got more sleep than me, that's for sure.-CH
Ewww...someone's grouchy, you get fed yet? MJ
No.-CH
K, what's the plan? John Terran
I told Jonesy we should meet at the hideaway at three.-CH
K-John Terran
Let's do it-MJ
See ya-CH

I pulsed Jade next as a huge rumble rolled through my stomach. Ouch, better make it fast, needed to fuel-up.

Hey- CH
Hi.-JLeC
How's your side? CH
It's okay, sore.-JLeC

My hate for Jade's dad bloomed anew.

So... is your aunt pissed at me or can we get together today with the Js? CH
No, it was an act. My dumb dad showed up and started hassling her about where I was now he's in jail... for now- JLeC

I wondered what they decided to get him for and asked her.

A lot. I overheard my aunt talking to Garcia on the phone today and he resisted arrest.-JLeC
Yeah he did **laughs**-CH
I gtg and eat something **sighs.**-JLeC
Me too... let's meet at the hideaway about three, K? CH
I'll be there... I can't wait to see you **smiles.**-JLeC
Same here **grins**-CH

I was still trying to play it a little cool with Jade, but it was getting harder by the week. More and more she was the center of my world, I orbited her.

****

I dismounted as my bike was slowing coming to a jog beside it, the Js already in view by the dump's gate.

They had their bikes too.

"You guys got your bikes too?" I said.

"Yeah, Jonesy said his was at the front of his house," John said.

"Maybe Wade," I said.

"The other cop?" Jonesy asked.

"Yeah, Gale's partner," John said.

"He watched our house last night," I said.

Jonesy whistled. "You must rank pretty high."

I shook my head. "Nah, you heard Garcia, he wants to bust the Graysheets bad. I think he's just being careful with me because they've targeted me. But we've got even more problems than the government psychos, listen."

I told them what happened after I got to Jade's house.

John said it best, "What an ass-wipe."

"He should be flogged," Jonesy said.

I liked that too.

Just then, Jade rode up on her bike, coming to a stop, she hit the kickstand. "We've all got our bikes," she said, looking around.

"Yeah, looks like a mystery cop got it handled."

"Garcia?" she asked.

"I don't think he wanted to risk being seen," I said.

John looked around. "Let's get these bikes hidden."

Good thinking.

Inside the hideout, we sat on the crates. I had the strangest, I-was-just-here feeling... 'cuz I was.

"I can't believe your parents let you go, aren't they worried?" Jade asked.

"My dad has a plan to relieve some of the pressure and expose them. Also," I shrugged, "I gave up the hideaway."

Jonesy face-palmed. "No! You told adults about here?"

John glared at me.

"I know, I know, so not-cool, but, they're not trying to interfere but look at it from their point of view."

The Js just looked at me, *what point of view?*

"I'm just gonna say it: adults don't think like us." Jonesy said.

That was true, but I couldn't let my parents think I was going to dangle myself out there like kidnap bait.

"If it makes ya feel any better, I didn't tell them about it, only that it was somewhere in the dump."

"It's kinda bad that the cops know about it too," John said.

"And Brett and Carson," Jade said.

"Yeah.... what-the-hell is with Brett?" Jonesy asked, crossing his arms. "He got a death-wish?"

Jade lowered her head. I put a hand under her chin. "This isn't your fault, you know."

She nodded, a lone tear sliding down her face, holding her side she spoke so quietly the three of us leaned forward, "It would be easier on you guys if I wasn't a part of this."

What?

John said, "Ah, Brett has nothing to do with you."

"Yeah!" Jonesy said. "He's a wet asshole without help from anyone."

Jade laughed and the sadness passed.

Jonesy nodded, warming up. "And he can join the needs-to-be-flogged group."

"Don't forget Carson," John reminded.

"Yeah, he's first on the list," Jonesy said.

Jade laughed again. "You guys!"

But we had made her happier, team players.

"Knock-knock!" A voice yelled from the freezer.

We jumped.

"What the hell...?" Jonesy said.

Jade put a hand on his dark forearm, her hand pale against it. "It's Tiff and Sophie."

"Oh, Soph! Great!"

We all looked at each other.

"I mean..." Jonesy paused awkwardly, Jonesy was never awkward, "I'm glad they're all okay."

Riiiiggghhht.

"Back here!" Jade said loudly.

Tiff and Sophie came first, with Bry bringing up the rear, ducking through that last spot.

Bry's face looked really bad.

Jonesy said, "Wow, those gnomes really tore you up!"

That made Bry smile. Tiff looked like she got scraped, but we knew the butt of a M-16 had done it, making the scrape harder to ignore.

"What about your parents?" John asked.

Tiff rolled her eyes. "They think he needs anger management help."

Jonesy barked out a laugh. "Are you kidding?"

"No. Remember, it's Bry's job to get the shit kicked out of him every time we go to a cemetery."

"Everyone has to do their part," John said cryptically.

"Right," I agreed.

Bry laughed. "You guys are okay."

I filled Bry, Tiff and Sophie in on the fun at Jade's house last night.

"Sounds like that guy needs to be flogged," Bry said.

Jonesy threw out his hands. "Great minds think alike."

"What?" Bry asked.

"Jonesy already thought of that. With a few other key people on the list," John said.

"I have a few more people," Bry said.

"Some teachers?" Tiff said.

We thought about that.

"Kids first, then we start working through the adults," I said.

"Nice, Hart," Bry said.

I did a mock-bow, laughing.

We finished up our mutual admiration and trooped down the tunnel, stepping out of the freezer, closing it up for the next meeting.

Our good mood dissipated like a candle blowing out, smiles fading on our faces as if they'd never been.

Brett and Carson stood there staring at the group. How long they'd been there was anyone's guess.

Bry looked around. "What? Did someone die?"

"Nah... but we have history with these two," Jonesy said in explanation.

"Okay, I'm feeling ya," Bry said, giving the two a hard look.

Brett asked, "Who's he?"

"My brother," Tiff said neutrally.

Carson and Brett gave Bry a good look, taking in his height and bulk.

"John?" I asked.

"I know," John responded.

"He your 'pet Null' now, Hart?" Carson laughed keeping an eye on Bry.

"We can exchange insults, Carson," John said. "But we're kinda busy so why don't you piss off instead?"

"That works," Bry said.

"I like it," Jonesy said.

Brett asked, "What happened to your face?"

"Who cares," Carson said, giving Brett a look.

I was tired of these two. "What do you want?"

"I've decided to call a truce," Carson said.

I couldn't have been more shocked if he pulled a pink elephant out of his ass. Who was he kidding?

The girls burst out laughing. It was *that* ridiculous sounding.

Carson glared at them and clenched his fists, Bry stepping forward.

Carson looked at him and licked his lips nervously.

Coward.

"Don't even think about it," Bry said, the battering of his face making him look more threatening, not less.

Brett elbowed Carson, who glared back. "I was just sayin'...that most of us will be at KPH next year..."

I shrugged.

"... and, I thought... we could just, avoid each other."

We were all silent at that. I couldn't believe that Carson would A) offer a solution, B) really not start shit.

It was Jonesy that was the voice for the group, "Let's just see how that works out, Hamilton."

"Okay, I can do that," I said slowly.

He looked out at the rest of the group, each one nodding.

Promising an uneasy truce would be hard with a proven enemy.

Brett looked relieved, Carson satisfied.

"See ya," Carson said, walking off with Brett, who cast a glance back at Jade.

I didn't like that.

Jonesy said real low, so they couldn't hear, "We close that gate from now on, I don't like them lurking around."

John laughed. "Lurking?"

"Yeah," I agreed.

Tiff said, "I trust him about as far as I can throw him."

"Me too," Bry said.

"You don't even know them," Jade said, puzzled.

"No, but I know guys like them."

"Carson's a pyro." Sophie said.

"Oh... great," Bry said. "Wait, why didn't he light somebody up? Those types *always* have to show off."

"I was tuned up," John said.

Bry looked a question at John. "*You're* the Null? That's right!" he smacked his forehead, then winced. "Last night, you guys were testing that out..."

John nodded.

"That works pretty well," Bry chuckled.

"We're all just pawns on his chessboard," John said. "He's made a move, trying to take us off-guard, then he'll strike when we're not expecting it."

"We'll have to be expecting it then," I said, my arm around Jade, who gave me a little squeeze back. "Ouch!"

"What?" I looked at her, she put her hand to her side.

"Let me see."

"We want to look," Jonesy said. Wounds fascinated him.

Jade blushed with all the attention but lifted up her shirt a little.

Somehow, it looked markendly worse in broad daylight. The beginning of the bruise from last night extended even further, a rainbow now of various shades.

"Definite flogging," Jonesy said.

"Yeah," John and I both said at the same time.

A reckoning.

All of us looked at each other grim faced. Jade lowered her shirt.

"He's in jail right now, he can't make bail and Andrea won't do it. She won't pay, I know it."

"That's the first piece of good news I've heard in the last 24 hours," Bry said.

"Let's get out of here. I need to regroup with my parents," I said.

Filling in everyone that arrived late, I mentioned my dad had a plan to take the heat off of me.

"That's good. I mean, they're just going to try for you again if there isn't anything done," Bry said.

"He's right, Caleb," Jade said.

Everyone nodded. "It's not just me," I said, looking at them all in turn. "It's any of us, all of us..."

"If Kyle can help with an idea, we can maybe have normal lives," John said, adding airquotes.

"Okay, pulse us," Bry said, indicating he and Tiff. "I want to know what's happening. And for the record, I don't trust that weasel, Carson."

"Don't," I said.

Bry raised his eyebrows.

Oh. "Yeah, I'll let ya know."

He nodded, the girls gave each other hugs, Jade getting handled more carefully.

"Hey Jade, maybe you should go to the doctor?" Sophie said.

"Can't. No health insurance."

What? "You don't have the chip?"

"No. Those were being done on a day I missed school, around the time when my mom died," she said softly.

Ouch. We let it drop but Jonesy said, "It's alright, if it's a busted rib, they can't do jack anyway."

He meant well and Jade got that.

We got on our bikes, Jade balancing and wincing.

"How come you rode?" I asked, noticing it hurt.

"Faster," she said, breathing through the pain. I balanced my right foot in the dirt, the bike seat riding right under my butt and put a hand on the back of Jade's head, showing her with my eyes I was sorry she was hurting.

"I'm sorry I couldn't stop him."

"It could have been worse, you deflected it."

"I guess," I said. She was "managing" my feelings.

"Caleb?" John asked.

Balancing on my toes I turned to him. "Yeah." My hand slid away from Jade.

"If Parker said your house was bugged and you guys talked about Garcia, don't the Graysheets know *all* now?" he asked.

I had a moment of panic so big that I couldn't breathe.

John and Jade saw my face. "It's okay, wouldn't something bad have happened by now if they knew?" Jade said.

My heart felt loaded up in my throat, stalled.

John shook my shoulder. "Hey, snap out of it."

Jonesy said, "Let's just ride to your house and ask your dad, he'll know."

I finally breathed out. Couldn't do anything about it right now. I needed to see if the Graysheets knew more, had nailed Garcia, what my dad's new scheme was.

I nodded.

"You okay now?" John asked.

Jonesy gave me a hard guy-clap on my back. "Caleb's okay, aren't ya?"

I looked at our group, the Js and Jade, yeah, I guess I was.

Whatever happened after I got home, I had them.

CHAPTER 35

I dumped my bike on the front lawn, glancing back at Jade once. She smiled and I rushed through the front door not bothering to close it.

The parents glanced up at me, startled. "What's the problem Caleb?" Dad asked, rising off the couch, looking behind me for possible pursuers.

Mom looked too, but it was only Jade and the Js coming through the front door. Mom gave me a puzzled look, with a dash of anxiety thrown in.

I put my index finger against my closed mouth, the universal sign for quiet.

Dad nodded and I pointed to the back deck. All of us moved out there.

"What's going on?"

"Remember I told you that the Graysheets bugged our house?"

"Yes."

"Well, we talked about everything last night, Garcia, everything. Then this morning I told you where the hideout was," I said in a rush.

"Oh. Okay, I'll explain. First, we can go back inside."

I shook my head no.

"It's okay Caleb, when I spoke with Garcia, he phoned me from a secure pulse, gave me directions on how to neutralize the bugs, and I answered yes or no. There's no way the Graysheets could have heard. Unless they're telepathic and could understand more than a yes or a no."

I let the breath I'd been holding out in a rush.

"How'd you deactivate the bugs?" John asked.

"Garcia figured it would be a pulse-based system interface. I used our security system, using the 'terminate all pulse sensors' feature."

"Doesn't that flat-line everything in your house; pulse, lights, everything?" Jade asked, Mom was nodding.

"Yes, our system has an automatic reset, if all pulse is deactivated, it automatically resets all *known* devices."

"Their stuff wasn't included in the start-up because..." I began.

"It didn't register," Mom finished.

"Nice," Jonesy said.

"Obvious, really," John said.

"They'll know when they can't hear us anymore," I said.

"It's temporary, putting the kibosh on their surveillance, which bring me to a new point," Dad said.

Here we go.

"I think we should go to that journalist that worked on those articles that John brought for you to read."

"Who?"

"Tim Anderson," John said quickly.

"Yes, that's the man," Dad said smiling at John.

"Why? What can he do for us?" I asked.

"He can make them hesitate," Mom said.

"You mean from taking me again?"

"Taking anyone, Caleb. It's bigger than just you. Everyone that is a five-point should not have to live under the threat of loss-of-liberty. I'm sorry, I misspoke, in your case, a six-point. Your safety is paramount. If we visit Anderson, he exposes them. Keeping the Graysheets planning their next strategy rather than executing."

"Let's lift their skirt and make them worry about their panties," Jonesy said.

Mom and Jade looked at him.

"What? That's like a perfect...."

"... analogy," John helped.

"Humph!" Mom commented.

Sometimes Jonesy really put his foot in it. Dad was making the I'm-not-going-to-smile face which gave his mouth a strange, crooked look.

"I've already contacted him and he'll meet with us at," Dad looked at the pulse-clock, "six."

I was starving. Even with Jade as a constant distraction, I needed to fill the hole. I looked at Mom.

"Those pancakes all gone?" she guessed.

"Mine are!" Jonesy said, sensing food was close.

"You didn't have pancakes," I said, suspicious.

Jonesy discounted my comment with a wave of his hand. "Doesn't matter, I haven't eaten in hours," he moaned dramatically, clutching his stomach.

Brother.

Mom grinned, she loved Jonesy's theatrics. "I have some leftover pizza?"

John asked, "Is there enough?"

"Always."

As we engulfed the pizza, Jade watched in a sort of numb horror as Jonesy ate four slices in ten minutes; we discussed who would visit Anderson. We decided that all of us going would give more credit to the story.

"The point is," Dad said, in between bites of cheesy pizza, "their presence may lend a degree of validity that would otherwise not be there. We'd go there and look like hysterical parents bent on some anti-government zealotry."

"But you're not hysterical," I said.

"I know that son, but Anderson doesn't," Dad said.

"Yeah, Caleb," Jonesy began, all his pizza crammed to one side of his mouth, hand on a glass filled with pop. "There's a ton of nut jobs out there, waiting to crack."

"You're on it today, Jonesy," John said.

"Every day, pal," Jonesy said.

Jade rolled her eyes and we all laughed.

****

Kent Station was in the valley and that's where the Seattle Post-Intelligencer's satellite office was located. Dad drove up, easily finding a parking spot, completely unheard of in our city of two hundred thousand. We tumbled out, the Js and Jade hanging around on the sidewalk while Dad put his thumb on the pulse-meter.

The Js tried to sprint ahead to the door. "Hang on, kids," Dad said, without looking up. Mom was still fumbling with her stuff, piling a hoodie, purse and her dedicated pulse-reader together.

"Mom, seriously? The DR?"

"It makes me frantic not having the option to read."

Like she was going to read when we were about to rat on the big, bad super-secret government dudes. Right.

We walked toward the building, all height and glass. It looked like a giant, sea-green jewel, spearing the sky above us. The huge sign on top read: Seattle Post-Intelligencer, and was illuminated with glowing, electric-blue letters.

We walked through the door, getting in line for the pulse-body scan. Terrorist threats were such a damn drag. All points of entry: police, fire, media were all protected by Pulse-scan.

The lady with the Pulse-wand stood at the ready, her bored face primed to do the next wand pass. "Come forward please, arms up, turn-around.... next."

I knew Jonesy was going to have trouble with the urge-to-laugh-at-inappropriate-times when he started to cover his mouth. This problem of his was terribly contagious. Thankfully, Jade and I were already through the line.

But John wasn't.

Out of the three of us, John being the most serious personality, had the worst trouble calming down once Jonesy began laughing.

John tried, he really did, but when Jonesy burst out laughing the instant the dour TSA worker said, "Next," John doubled over and couldn't stand up again, he laughed so hard his head turned tomato-red.

The TSA gal made it worse by saying, "young man, young man..." she sputtered. "Stand up!"

To which Jonesy interjected, "Anal-probe! Right here!" pointing over the top of John's back. Which caused John to roar with laughter, falling down on his bony ass.

The TSA agent pursed her lips in a thin line.

Dad stepped in and said, "I'm quite sorry about their behavior, it's been a trying day, they're a bit... giddy." He was trying to calm the storm.

The TSA gal looked down at John who was on the floor, tears streaming out of his eyes and made an exaggerated grunt, "Get off my floor, young man!"

Mom and Jade had mouths hanging agape, even my laid-back parents were somewhat embarrassed.

John got onto all fours and stood up, still making the funny mouth, trying not to burst out again, Mom was talking sternly to Jonesy, his back to us.

John finally stood up and said, "I'm really sorry about that, I don't know what my problem was."

"Arms up," humorless said. "Turn-around... next!" she nearly yelled.

John, suitably chagrined, walked over to our small group. Dad in the center of us said, "Come close fellas."

We all leaned in, Dad spoke to our group but his eyes were all for Jonesy, "I better not have any more of this behavior. Jonesy: control your bullshit."

Jonesy blanched, I don't think any of us had ever heard Dad swear. Truly, I hadn't thought he knew the words. A silence fell over our loose circle.

Dad straightened. "Come on, follow me." He strode off, Jonesy and John followed with their tails between their legs.

****

Tim Anderson just flat-out didn't believe us.

Dad tried to reason with him, but Anderson interrupted with a, "Dazzle me guys. Can something die and you raise it?" he asked me, eyes boring into mine.

A what? Did he mean, murder someone to bring back, here? In the tower-o-glass? I looked at Jade and she just shook her head, she didn't know either.

"Listen, Dr. Hart... I know you're the principal scientist with regard to the genome map, terrific. But, you expect me to put my, excuse me ladies, nut-sack on the line for some wild stories about a six-point AFTD, running amok with his friends, and some shadowy government co-op dispatched to 'acquire' him." He pointed at me, air-quoting, like it was alleged, not actual.

He was starting to piss me off.

Dad too, who began drumming his fingers on Anderson's desk.

"What do we gain from trumping up false stories?" Mom asked in a huff.

Good point.

"Who knows? I get whack-jobs all the time that come in here and spray their lies all over. I'm not inclined to believe things on hearsay. I'm a journalist guys."

Dad slapped his hand on the desk, rattling the glass pen holder, Anderson's eyes widened but he didn't comment (not easily intimidated). "We are not crazy *or* making things up."

Anderson leaned back in his chair.

"Jade, show Mr. Anderson what's going on."

I looked at Dad, what was this about?

Jade stood and came over to Anderson, a predatory smile played on her face that I didn't know she had.

"Dad..." I didn't know where this was going.

"It's okay, Caleb."

"What are you doing, girlie?" Anderson asked her.

Uh-oh, I knew her dad called her that.

Jade just smiled wider and touched his shoulder, he jumped like it'd hurt but I knew it hadn't.

"Seeing," she answered.

Emotions flew across her face as we watched her start to know Anderson.

He didn't let it continue though, picking her hand off his shirt like lint. "That's enough of that," he said, shaken.

"What's going on?" Dad asked.

"He wants an exclusive if he can have proof," she said and he nodded. "Otherwise, it's just a wild goose chase."

"Are you quoting him?" Mom asked.

"Yes... no. I mean, people think in images and I saw geese in his head and him chasing them...so, I know it was that," Jade said.

"It's an old expression," Anderson said quietly.

"He wants to go to the ghost cemetery," Jade said.

He glared at her.

"Well, you didn't believe us," I said.

"Let's do it. We go to the... honey, what's the name of that old place?"

"Kyle, I don't remember," Mom said.

"Anyway, we go there and Caleb raises a zombie, you see some of the evidence, and then you write something. Seems clear-cut."

"He will," Jade said.

"Must be a nice skill, young lady," Anderson said.

"It's Jade," adding, "not 'girlie'."

"Right. Okay... so, let's get going. The young la-*Jade*, has convinced me this may be authentic."

CHAPTER 36

The cemetery was exactly as I remembered it except instead of being silvered by moonlight, it had a hazy white quality. The evening sun laying low in the sky, slanting through trees and open slashes where the forest surrounding it broke.

Tim Anderson strode forward, squashing the tall blades of grass as he went, moving between the tombstones toward the caretaker's cottage. He arrived at the front steps, turning around to face us.

"Where-oh-where is the stealth chopper? The gun casings? The knives? The remnants of battle?"

Definitely this guy missed his calling and should have been on stage, not writing for the biggest paper in the state.

We all started scouring the graveyard and apart from a few tromped down places of flat pasture between the graves, there wasn't a mark anywhere.

No way they could have cleaned this place.

Jonesy opened his mouth and Dad held up a finger in warning. I guess Dad was up to *here* with Jonesy. "What about the tombstone that got whacked by the chopper blade? What about the chopper blade embedding itself into the ground?"

Right! We sprinted to the spot where we thought the chopper had landed and disintegrated the grave marker.

We stood in a circle around where the marker should have been but there was nothing. Well, not true, there was a hole that was deep, maybe almost a foot, long and rectangular, where a marker had been.

"They took the whole damn thing!" Jonesy yelled.

Dad and Mom were too shocked to get mad at Jonesy for being him again.

Anderson bent down, letting his fingers trail over dirt that hadn't been exposed to the outside for one hundred years. "You might have something here."

He walked the whole graveyard and every so often he would look at something closely until John yelled, "Look at this!"

We ran over there, the parents coming last.

A huge gouge had been punched into the dirt. On either side there was a a a swathe, crescent moon shaped, like a smile, with the center being a deep well.

Without looking up I said, "Jonesy, get a stick."

He came back with a long branch from an alder or something and I stuck it into the hole made by the helicopter blade. It went down until there was only six inches sticking out. Drawing it out, I put it beside my body.

Dad said, "Looks like about four feet."

"Looking like you guys might have been telling the truth," Anderson conceded.

*

Back at Anderson's office, where we passed through security unscathed by hysterics, we sat for a solid hour, telling our story. His voice-activated pulse-recorder loaded directly to his pulse-top.

On a couple of parts Anderson remarked or asked a question to clarify something. Finally, we were finished.

"Well, that's one helluva story there. A real humdinger."

"I can understand you coming to me, or someone like me. I will do my best, tonight," Anderson said.

"Tonight?" Dad asked.

"Yeah, my boss is going to be thrilled. But better than that, it offers a little protection for your kid there." Anderson became thoughtful. "I'm not a real introspective guy, but I'd say you've been given something special," he looked out at us all. "It's how you use it that will make the difference."

Standing up, he stuck his hand out. "Sorry I was so tough on you in the beginning. It's been a pleasure. You've got a good kid here, Dr. Hart."

"Kyle," Dad corrected. "I know we do." he smiled at me with what may have been pride.

"Those other two though..." he waggled his finger at the Js. "They may be trouble." He laughed, taking the sting out of it.

CHAPTER 37

The article came out and sensationalized the paranormal community. People believe what they want to believe; there were sides. Some thought that it was a greatly exaggerated story about a bunch of teens that got together to be wild in cemeteries. Others thought that the government was putting its nose where it didn't belong, endangering this new generation of kids.

Still others thought that the drug cocktail that gave human beings a key to power came with a price. Having survived the last few months I'd have to agree.

Summer rolled out like a great sea of time before us: an awesome girlfriend, Onyx (teen's best friend), the Js, ready to try anything.

Life was good.

But in the quiet dark of my room, questions pressed at me before sleep took hold. Where was Parker? What had they been planning for me? What *had* caused the electrical problem that ultimately saved us from possible capture and certain pain? Were we finished? That little (loud) voice in my head didn't think so.

A few days later, Jonesy asked me if we could go rouse some zombies. I told him no. For now, I was zombied out.

But maybe sometime, that would change... *sooner* rather than later.

The End

A Love Letter to My Readers:

As of March 31, 2011, it's been a year now since my first book, *Death Whispers*, was published. I'd like to take this opportunity to thank each and every one of you that has supported my writing. **Without my readers, I would not have an audience for my work.** Many of your emails, support via recommendation, encouragement and critical feedback/reviews have allowed my improvement as a writer and as a human being. Words are an inadequate thanks for the depth of my gratitude to you. Please know how much your support has meant, and will continue to mean in the future to come.

Thank you, from the bottom of my heart~

*

If you enjoyed this book, please support the author by posting your review on Amazon, Barnes & Noble and iBookstore.

Please also consider recommending or reviewing the book on your blog, Facebook, Twitter and Goodreads.

Connect with Me Online:

Twitter: http://twitter.com/#!/troseblodgett

Facebook: facebook.com/tamararose.blodgett

Smashwords:
http://www.smashwords.com/profile/view/tamararoseblodgett

goodreads:http://www.goodreads.com/tamara_rose_blodgett

Shelfari:http://www.shelfari.com/tamararose

Blog: http://tamararoseblodgett.blogspot.com/

Acknowledgments:

A few people have made this possible:

You, *my reader*, thank you!

My sons, without whom, I could never have made the dialogue realistic; and *especially Joshua*, whose faith was unshakable.

To my husband, *Danny*, who supports every scheme I come up with and ones I haven't yet. And puts up with a daydreaming wife without complaint (usually).

To Jen and Sirena, who put up with my intensity.

For the agent "C," that wanted to see this after the revisions, thank you. You gave me hope.

My editor, *Stephanie T. Lott*, for coming in here and making WHISPERS a cleaner copy.

And finally, my mother, *Camilla*, who nurtured the written and spoken word in a way that changed my life in this direction.

I miss you, Mom.

Books available now:

Death Whispers (Death Series, #1)
Death Speaks (#2)
Death Screams (#3)
Death Weeps (#4)
The Pearl Savage (Savage Series, #1)
The Savage Blood, (#2)
The Savage Vengeance (#3)
Blood Singers, (Blood Series, #1)

Books publishing in 2012:

Death Inception (A Death Prequel) July 13
tentative schedule as follows:
**Blood Song*, (Blood Series, #2) September
**The Savage Protector* (Savage Series, #4) November
Unrequited Death, (Death Series, #5) December 31

Future Titles:
2013

The Reflective, (Reflection Series, #1)
Blood Chosen, (#3)

Made in the USA
Lexington, KY
09 December 2012